THE ROYAL MARINE SPACE COMMANDOS

JON EVANS

JAMES EVANS

IMAGINARY BROTHER

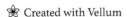

COMMANDO

THE ROYAL MARINE SPACE COMMANDOS
BOOK 1

PROLOGUE

His heart pounded as he dodged and weaved, showers of earth and brick exploding around him. Ducking behind a solar array, he collapsed to the ground, gasping for air. He wrenched the rebreather from his face. A shard of plastic had buried itself in the filters; the thing was useless.

Angus could breathe the air, but it would be decades before the atmosphere was balanced. Without the oxygen from his mask, he couldn't run for long. Or run far.

He turned his head, risking a glance around the panel. Nothing. But they were there, somewhere, getting closer with every second that he lay still. He scrabbled around, hugging the ground while he got on his front and faced himself east, away from the panel and his would-be killers. He felt like a sprinter trying to get into the blocks, and that's what he needed to be.

There was an algal atmosphere recycler ahead of him and a moisture collector twenty metres to the north of it. The recycler was closer, but while it looked substantial, it was mostly plastic tubing and sheets, filled with a pale green mixture of algae and water. It was superb for increasing the atmospheric oxygen level but made for flimsy cover.

The moisture collector was a collection of turbines, metal fan blades, concrete posts and solar cells. Not sturdy as such but still a damned sight more bullet resistant than the recycler.

He made his choice and dashed forward, determined to take cover before he had to go to ground and let his heart slow down. The solar panel exploded as bullets ripped through it, scattering shrapnel that destroyed the nearby panels and drove dust high into the air.

Jones dove to his belly behind the concrete base of the moisture farm as more rounds sheared through the turbine above him with metallic screeches. At least he was on his front for the next sprint, and the concrete behind him felt like a much better shield. He lay there, sucking down the thin air while his heart rate slowed, looking desperately for his next dash.

Then he spied it, a pallet sled, left out here instead of returned to its dock at the homestead. For once that forgetful bastard Eric had done something useful, if only by accident. Jones looked wildly around. His ears were ringing from the gunfire, but he couldn't hear his pursuers. Whoever they were, he had to move. They'd be here soon; there was no time to spare.

He crawled towards the sled, shuffling over the dusty ground as quickly as he could. The sled was low to the ground, powered by solar cells built into its flat surface and designed to haul equipment around the compound. Unlike his lungs, it didn't run on oxygen. It might not be fast, but it was convenient, all-terrain and available.

He heaved himself onto it, pulled the control stick from the side and pressed the button. It moved slowly at first and then began to pick up speed once its sensors confirmed the load was stable. These things could match the pace of a hab vehicle, if need be, but they'd slow to a crawl if there was a risk that their load might fall off.

The speed began to mount, and Jones clung to the cargo straps, keeping flat, cheek pressed to the sled's base. With his newfound speed, the main buildings of their hab were soon in sight. Eric must've been in the workshop, but Gillian was outside, tending to the greenhouses. Gillian looked up as Jones began to shout, jaw dropping when she saw him on his unusual transport.

No! Not towards me, he thought. *Run to the vehicles, we have to get out of here!*

He shouted, as loud as he could, "Run! Get out of here! They're coming!" but his friend couldn't hear or didn't understand.

He rammed the control down to the highest setting and the sled sped up again, hurtling across the open ground. She still couldn't hear his terrified warnings, so he got up on one knee and screamed.

The sled bounced over a bump, just a small one, but he was thrown clear, tumbling and spinning through the dust. His arms flailed uselessly until he came to a sudden stop against a mound of fertiliser. His chest heaved as he fought for breath and he winced at the sudden pain in his chest. *A broken rib, maybe two,* he thought as pain lanced through him.

A hundred metres to go, he staggered to his feet, running now in a low crouch with one arm wrapped around his chest. His eyes watered, his chest burned with the effort, his ribs stabbed at him. He waved his free arm and cried weakly, "Run, Gillian!"

She stopped, staring, eyes wide in confusion.

"Aliens, Gillian, for fuck's sake, run! Invasion," he croaked as she finally got close enough to hear.

She had known Angus Jones for years and he had always been solid, reliable and dull. Now he was half out of his mind, raving about an alien invasion? Across all the solar systems mankind had settled, they had never encountered intelligent alien life. Perhaps he was suffering from oxygen deprivation; he had dropped his rebreather. Was he dangerous?

These thoughts and more ran through her head at lightning speed as Jones drew near, staggering along in obvious pain. Then Angus's skull vanished in a spray of red mist and his body collapsed in the dust.

There was a loud crack, and her face and overalls were suddenly covered with a fine wet coating. She looked down at the blood and fragments of bone on her chest and began to scream, unable to understand what was happening.

A distant voice called out to her, asking her what was wrong. Eric never got an answer. As he came out of the workshop, wiping his hands on a cloth, he saw Gillian standing there, screaming her head off. Then her head was gone and Eric screamed too.

~

"Get the wormhole channel open, now!" Governor Denmead shouted as she crouched behind the concrete wall of the balcony, looking down the sight of her rifle and scanning for the enemy. The sound of fully automatic gunfire could be heard in the distance. That had to be the enemy. The sporadic single shots were the colonists, fighting for their lives with light rifles, mining lasers and sheer bloody-mindedness.

"Governor," her aide, Johnson, shouted from the office, "we're through!"

Denmead saw movement, a bulky figure aiming a large weapon around a habitat in the distance.

"Be right with you," she murmured. She squeezed the trigger slowly as she steadied her breath and aimed. There was a crack and the rifle bucked in her hand. It was a good shot: the enemy took the round in the neck rather than right between the eyes, but he fell back out of view all the same. These low calibre semi-automatic rifles were issued to all new colonies to keep any local wildlife at bay or deal with the rare instances of banditry or maybe even occasional unrest. They weren't intended for armoured opponents wielding good-quality military gear. For that, they needed the Royal Marines.

She scrambled back into the office and slid behind the desk with Johnson. It wasn't dignified, but then neither was finding out the hard way that an enemy sniper had found a perch with a view through the windows of City Hall.

"This is Governor Denmead. Who am I speaking to?"

"Sergeant Wainwright, Governor. Please verify your ID and explain the situation," the man on the screen said calmly.

"We're under attack," Denmead began as she put her palm on the scanner.

"ID authenticated, Governor. What kind of attack? Civilian, pirates, corporate?" the sergeant asked, cool as a cucumber.

"I don't fucking know," she yelled, her self-control slipping momentarily as staccato series of bangs made the desk judder. "They started attacking outlying areas of New Bristol several days ago, and we didn't hear immediately because they killed everyone at those sites. Now they're attacking Ashton, and we're losing a lot of people. They have armour and military grade weaponry. That's as close as we've got to identifying them," she said.

"Do you require assistance from 42 Commando, ma'am?" the sergeant asked.

She almost lost her rag at that point. "Yes, we require some fucking assistance! You need to activate the Marines immediately and get the fleet on its way!"

"How many enemy combatants are there, ma'am?" Wainwright asked.

Gunfire erupted from outside, and a few rounds bounced off the walls of the building. The enemy was getting closer.

"We don't know. We've killed a few but more keep coming. They're pushing us back all the time. Did you hear that gunfire?"

"Yes, ma'am."

"They're just outside my office. We need to move before this area is overrun," Denmead yelled over the noise outside.

"Very well, Ma'am. Get yourself somewhere safe. I've requested the activation of the Marine clones in New Bristol. Please re-establish contact with us as soon as you are secure. Your request for Naval deployment has been noted. If we can get more detail, it would help make your case, Governor. The Navy is only deployed if a major threat is confirmed. Good luck, Governor. 42 Commando HQ, signing off," Wainwright said before cutting the signal.

"Help make our case?" she groaned as her eyes met Johnson's. He looked panicked. She probably did too. At least they would soon have help from military-grade clones, the Royal Marine Space Commandos that were issued to every new colony. They would help the colonists of New Bristol fight back. She just wasn't sure it would be enough.

1

Atticus snapped awake, the first breath tasting like fresh mountain air in his new lungs. For a moment, all was calm and peaceful. Then a dull crump rattled the building and brought dust from the ceiling. Time to go to work.

As he rolled to his feet, he was already reviewing the briefing installed while the pod had been bringing him round. An attack, assailant unknown, on a New British Empire colony planet.

Atticus checked his clock chip; twenty-four minutes had elapsed between Governor Denmead's call for help and his company being injected via wormhole. It had taken a further six hours to decant their bodies. Almost a record turnaround. Whatever this was, it was being taken seriously.

He dressed quickly as around him the rest of the command team, all wearing standard RMSC combat clones, and A Troop of Company 971, 42 Commando, pushed themselves from their pods. Secure lockers disgorged combat gear, and within minutes his team was fully equipped, ready to face whatever was waiting.

"Sound off," called Atticus, issuing the command audibly and as text into his combat HUD. His command team and A Troop called in with practised efficiency, their names appearing on the ID strips on their uniforms and in their HUDs.

Atticus nodded, content, as more explosions shook the building.

"Nothing from B Troop," said Colour Sergeant Stephanie Jenkins, "could be a comms problem." That was optimistic, and Jenkins knew it. The comms kit was ultra-reliable, battle-tested over more worlds than she could count. A Troop knew it as well and fell silent as they processed the implications.

"Assume nothing," murmured Atticus, checking his weapons one last time before giving the order to move out.

Weapons raised, A Troop climbed the stairs and fanned out into the corridors above the emergency deployment bay. Their HUDs showed a map of the compound with blinking blue dots for civilians and red for invaders, the information drawn from sensors all over the colony.

Worryingly large parts of the map were shaded grey where sensors had failed or lost contact.

"Captain, at last," came a new voice, tense with worry but flooded with relief. Atticus turned to find a stern woman hurrying towards him with a hunting rifle slung over her shoulder. She glanced across the assembled Marines, their builds so similar it would be difficult to tell them apart, despite the differing faces. "I'm Governor Denmead. Please, this way."

"Captain Atticus, Governor," he replied, shaking her hand, "and this is Lieutenant Warden. Can you update us? There were no details in the briefing," he asked.

"Good to meet you, despite the circumstances," she replied as they followed her along a corridor that led out of the building, "and all I can really tell you is that we're under attack from an unknown force."

"Governor, we can't reach the second EDB on comms. Do you have any idea of its status?" asked Atticus.

Governor Denmead shook her head. "I'm sorry, no. We've lost parts of Ashton's sensor grid and there are system failures elsewhere.

We don't have an up-to-date picture of the intact buildings. We're just trying to survive."

"Understood. Warden," said Atticus, "get to the second EDB, find B Troop, rendezvous when you can. Take Wilson in case there's a tech problem with the pods themselves."

"It's off to your west, or at least, that's where we built it, Lieutenant," the governor said as they emerged from the building into the thin air of New Bristol.

"Thank you, Governor. Sir," said Lieutenant Warden, "Section 1 with me." He led them away at a swift trot, following the directions in his HUD for the location of the second marine deployment facility.

Atticus and the rest of A Troop followed Denmead through the compound towards the fighting. As they ran, she gave a quick description of all that had happened.

At the edge of the building, they paused. Beyond, across a short stretch of open ground, stood City Hall.

"So fast, Captain, it was so fast," said the governor as she shrugged her weapon from her shoulder.

"How many of them, ma'am?" asked Atticus as he stared across the city, searching for the enemy.

"Scores at least, Captain, possibly hundreds. Our dead..." she trailed off. The bodies were piling up; their numbers tracked in Atticus's HUD as their signals went offline, one after the other.

"How are the attackers armed?"

"Automatic rifles and sharp-shooters. Some sort of grenade launcher, I think. I haven't seen railguns or lasers. We've been fighting them as best as we can, pulling the children back and just trying to hold them off, but we have," she paused, holding up her rifle, "limited options."

Atticus nodded, "Right, get to your command post and try to pull your people back. We'll be laying down heavy fire, and I don't want them getting caught in it. Hughes, go with the governor and make sure the comms are working properly."

"Sir!" Hughes barked in acknowledgement as he turned and followed the governor.

There was a burst of gunfire from somewhere beyond City Hall. Outside, firing towards the Hall, according to their HUDs. Atticus signalled his troops forward, leading them out onto the open ground and quickly across.

"Campbell take Section 2, inside, sweep the building, head for the front. Section 3, with me, we'll flank them around the east of the building."

Atticus watched the Marines of Section 2 heading out, their brand new mil-tech clones in tip-top condition, equipment gleaming, uniforms as yet untainted by the muck of a new world.

Then he headed for the corner of the building and the dusty parkland beyond it. Section 3 followed him as Section 2 triggered the door controls and disappeared into the building. Atticus paused briefly as Section 3 flowed smoothly around the edge of the building, seeking the enemy. He watched their indicators, and those of Section 2, moving steadily across the map in his HUD.

Then he hefted his rifle and followed his troops, Sergeant Jenkins and Marine Butler at his side.

2

Atticus crouched behind a chest high concrete wall atop a squat building that housed what Governor Denmead assured him were dangerous, but not explosive, chemicals. Terraforming required sweeping, long-term changes to the atmosphere and soil of a planet. In the short term, what the colonists needed was massive hydroponic systems packed with the best nutrients chemistry could refine.

There were dozens of buildings like this across the city, all storing different resources that had been shipped in by unmanned supply craft before colonists arrived or else were being manufactured locally by the automated extraction plants the colonists had installed.

Powered armour and surveillance drones had changed the face of the battlefield but having a high vantage point from which to observe the enemy was still helpful. Atticus especially liked having two feet of brutally ugly concrete wall between him and the enemy. The building might be austerely functional, but the colonists had covered the roof with green matting, sunbeds and chairs. Not that there was much weather to enjoy, he supposed, but it was no worse than the average British seaside town.

He turned back to face Governor Denmead, wishing she hadn't

joined him but impressed that she was putting herself on the front line.

"What can you tell me, Governor? Anything about their weapons and equipment?"

"Some of them have powered armour but not all of them," she said.

Atticus took that news with aplomb. "You're certain?"

"Captain Atticus, I shot one in the face earlier today, and it barely fazed him. And I'm not the only one who's seen them in suits," she admonished him.

"Fair enough. It's unusual for brigands to have powered armour, but I'm sure we can take care of it," he replied.

"They have military clones as well," she went on as Atticus raised an eyebrow. Obtaining military-grade clones was not only utterly illegal for non-government bodies but also extremely difficult. The modifications built into such clones were strictly for combat use and even the Sol governments rarely deployed troops in such clones. Outside of a troop deployment ship, military-grade cloning bays were almost unheard of.

"What kind of modifications have you seen? Could they be fringe planet black market clones?" he said, suggesting these were inexpert hacks that the brigands might have jury-rigged onto civilian clones.

"Captain," said Denmead in a tone pitched to close the argument, "I've been around long enough to recognise a back-alley clone. This force has full-size wings for their scouts. Eight-foot-tall, heavy weapons grunts and reports of some kind of close combat trooper that was fully mutated with natural armour, bladed arms and fangs. They are definitely high-quality military clones," she insisted.

"Fangs?" asked Atticus sceptically.

Denmead shrugged. "That report might be a bit far-fetched," she admitted.

"Any idea where they're operating from?"

Denmead pulled a data slate from her jacket and projected an image on the concrete wall, a map of the central colonised areas of New Bristol.

"No, not yet," she said, tapping the slate and pinging a series of locations within thirty kilometres of Ashton, "I haven't had much time, but these are the places I think are most likely. I've made a lot of assumptions, of course, and I'm not a military expert. Everyone in the outlying settlements is dead or here with us in Ashton, in fact. They could be using any of the outlying sites."

"How long have they been here?"

"We don't know," Denmead said, flinching as a burst of fire echoed from a nearby street, "they attacked the most distant locations first. Atmospheric processors, automated mineral extractors, energy farms. Most elements of our terraforming infrastructure are distributed in small pockets in case of unexpected atmospheric conditions or accidents. Only larger sites that require regular attention have a team that live onsite; any others are visited on rotation. They'd probably been attacking us for days before anyone managed to survive long enough to raise the alarm."

"Do you have any working fab units capable of making small arms?"

"Yes, but nothing large scale," Denmead said.

"We'll take whatever you can produce. I'll authorise you to set them making military weapons," Atticus said. Through his HUD he sent a clearance code to the governor that would unlock the restricted military patterns held by the colony's fabricators, along with a priority list of items to manufacture.

"Thank you, Captain. Our weapons aren't much use against these clones or their powered armour."

"Can you show me where your teams are?"

Denmead tapped her slate again, and the projection on the wall showed a series of blue, green and red dots. Blue for citizens who had joined the improvised militia and green for non-combatants, who were mostly hiding in buildings back from the front line.

Great areas of red hatching showed ground already lost or where the enemy troops were known to be. She sent a data stream to Atticus and he reviewed it on his HUD. It was basic information, but the tactical overlay could absorb the feed and update the

Marines' maps once the drones started providing more accurate data.

With the data came the colonists' health statuses, streamed from their personal monitoring bracelets. It was less comprehensive than the information Atticus had on his Marines but just knowing where people were and whether they were injured or dead was invaluable.

"It's time to pull your people back, Governor. We'll take over and we don't want your people getting caught in the crossfire," Atticus.

"I understand. Where do you want our line? My people have children to protect."

"Here, here and there, are good." Atticus pointed at a few buildings that would give good sight lines around the colony and allow the militia to act as a rearguard for his teams.

"Very well, I'll issue the order to fall back and then I'll retreat to our administrative backup here," Denmead said, indicating a reserve building which also held a cluster of green dots. "It's nothing special but it's got reserve power and access to most systems in case of a major problem with city hall."

"Roger that, Governor. Best of British to you," Atticus said as she made her way back down from the roof.

3

"Coming up on EDB two in one hundred metres, sir," said Corporal Goodwin.

"A lot of smoke here. Something's wrong. Fan out, keep to cover. Goodwin, get a drone up," ordered Lieutenant Warden. It wasn't necessary to order his Marines to take cover, they all had more experience than he did, but it needed to be a habit. Someday, he would have brand new marines to look after and they would need his guidance.

Goodwin had already thrown a micro-drone, shaped like a giant dart, in as high an arc as she could. It unfurled and stabilised as its rotors activated. An icon appeared in Warden's heads-up display to indicate there was a recon drone actively broadcasting video.

<Section 1, advance by numbers> Warden ordered sub-vocally, the words appearing in text on each Marine's HUD to ensure commands were received, regardless of the volume or background noise.

"Got anything, Goodwin?" asked Sergeant Milton, not taking her eye from the sight of her carbine as she scanned the buildings ahead.

"Not yet, Sarge. Want me to have a shufty?" Goodwin asked.

"Get your bird out there, Goodwin. I want to know where that smoke is coming from before we get there," Warden said.

The tiny drone, not much larger than the hummingbird it imitated, darted forward scanning the combat zone ahead. Goodwin would be concentrating on the video feed, the infra-red and sonar information that the drone provided. Milton was tailing her close, much like a spotter looking after her sniper. If anything happened, Milton would have Goodwin down and in cover even if she was distracted by the wealth of data she was monitoring.

They'd made two advances, one group dashing to the next available cover while another covered them, then sprinted to safety themselves, before Goodwin received an update.

The icon blinked in Warden's view and Goodwin's message scrolled across his HUD.

<Bay B destroyed>

Warden swore under his breath. He ducked behind a concrete waste bin as the drone's feed expanded into his HUD.

The cloning bay, technically an RMSC Emergency Deployment Bay, was a squat concrete building with a staircase running up the outside and a high-bandwidth comms array on the roof. Or at least, it had been. Now, it was little more than rubble. The bay, effectively a bunker, had lost its north wall and its roof had collapsed.

Normally the bays were buried, hidden from hostile eyes beneath tons of soil or concrete, but build details were determined by the colonists and the local conditions. Colonies had considerable operating leeway and could make their own decisions about building deployments. It was part of the attraction of life on a frontier world.

In Ashton, the second bay had been built in the open. The bay that Atticus and A Troop had decanted into was underground in the basement of a solar plant control room, much better protected.

Goodwin sent the drone through the hole in the north wall, checking the damage. The message <Breaching charge> flashed across Warden's HUD. He didn't ask how she knew; Goodwin was a highly trained tech specialist and if she said it was a breaching charge, it was a breaching charge. *So,* he thought, *the wall had been an entry point to the bunker?*

They had targeted the cloning facility, presumably to destroy it and cripple the RMSC's response capability. That suggested a level of tactical thinking that was unusual in a bandit attack. Whoever the enemy was, they were far too aggressive, too well equipped and too skilled to be treated lightly.

He sent a direct query back to Goodwin, <Recent? Still here? >, then issued a command to hold position to the rest of the section. They all hunkered down, eyes scanning the surrounding buildings, searching for signs of the enemy.

<No more than an hour> she replied.

The enemy was likely still nearby.

The drone darted straight up, and Warden flinched at the sudden shift. Techs did this all the time, but he found it disorienting. *There's a reason I didn't go into an Intel Group,* he admitted to himself.

With a wide view of the area, Goodwin was able to switch to a search mode, focusing on movement, heat profiles, radiation, comms traffic and any other sign of the enemy's location.

A sea of data and strange imagery swam in front of Warden's eyes for a few seconds before the chaotic colours and dozens of icons went back to the live feed again. This time, a building to the east of the bay was highlighted, a tall, thin structure, five storeys high, with large panes of glass held in place by a web of foamcrete. Cheap, light-weight and easily constructed, it was unquestionably office space.

All heads in the section swivelled towards it, and the Marines began to reposition themselves without his having to give an order.

Goodwin and Milton caught up with him, using the building on the corner of the crossroads as cover until they could join Warden behind his waste bin on the pavement. "Numbers?" he asked quietly. The lance-corporal shook her head; she didn't know.

He pondered their options. This felt like a raiding group. They could hear gunfire in the distance, but these troops were here to target valuable assets. If they were a military force from another colonial government, they'd be highly trained specialists, just like his Marines. He was confident of his team's abilities, but nobody was immune to a sniper round, and they didn't have any heavy weaponry, let alone powered armour. It wasn't part of the emergency deployment package for a colony this size.

B Troop wasn't going to be joining them anytime soon. It would take days to grow more clones, even if they could hold the remaining bay. The civilian bay would be a poor alternative, producing less advanced bodies in smaller numbers.

If he charged in without more information, he could very well lose all his Marines. On the other hand, if they sent the drone in, they might reveal themselves to an otherwise oblivious enemy and lose the advantage of surprise.

What was the enemy's plan? The team that had taken down the bunker had been quick, discreet and efficient. Warden's Section was probably being watched, but they hadn't been engaged, so maybe the enemy had targets and orders to avoid conflict. If that were the case, they'd be going for something else of high value, probably the remaining cloning bay or a power facility. Every building contributed to the energy grid but taking out a sizeable generation plant would impact their production of clones and equipment.

Warden shook his head. The decision was easy.

"Goodwin, get me a view inside. I want numbers, locations and armament." He signalled everyone else to be ready to lay down heavy fire. It wouldn't be subtle, but if Goodwin could get locations, they could tear through that building even with their basic carbines.

The drone dived, swooping towards a balcony on the top floor. It settled on a narrow upper pane and began to cut through the glass with its laser. It was inside the building in seconds, flitting through the offices and confirming the floor was empty in under a minute. It did an abrupt flip that made Warden's stomach lurch and rolled to the atrium that plunged through the building.

Righting itself, it zipped into the offices on the fourth floor, angling for the corner that faced Warden's position. Six figures lit up ahead, and their locations popped on the HUDs of the Marines. Warden saw a glimpse of powered armour before one of the figures turned and raised a small hand weapon. There was a flash, and the feed went black. His HUD automatically went back to the default view; the drone's icon gained a red cross to show it was disabled.

"Son of a bitch!" Goodwin cried out. "Lieutenant, permission to engage?"

"Granted, Lance-Corporal," he said, turning to face the building in a crouch and bringing his carbine to bear. The icons on his HUD showed the last known location of each enemy.

Goodwin answered the destruction of her equipment with a two-pronged approach. First, the defunct drone detonated with an almighty noise and a light bright enough to blind. Secondly, she brought her carbine to bear and with a triple popping noise and a panning motion, expertly fired three grenades through windows on the fourth, third and second floors, one above the other.

The detonations were nigh on simultaneous, a staccato cacophony that could be felt as a bass rumble in their chest. It was accompanied by bursts of fire from the entire section. Goodwin had already thrown another drone and Warden could hear her cursing the enemy under her breath and vowing revenge.

It came quickly. As the clouds of dust billowed out and the drone's data reached their HUDs, the Marines could see the softly glowing outlines of four figures on the ground floor. Two more were outlined in blue, lying prone in the rubble.

As soon as the drone pinged the enemy powered armour units, Warden's section opened fire. Each marine fired bursts with expert precision into the dust cloud, guided by the drone's sensors. They were rewarded with the distinctive metallic pings of bullets striking powered armour.

"Grenades!" ordered Warden and a flurry of ordnance arced across the open space, detonating directly on or near the blue outlines as the drone skipped back to avoid the blasts.

The final grenade detonated at the roof of the building, still hanging precariously above the vacant space below it. It collapsed with a resounding crash, directly on top of the enemy position.

Warden glanced to his left and saw a smug grin on Milton's face. He nodded in approval and turned to Goodwin.

"Survivors?" he asked.

She jabbed at her drone interface a few times and shook her head. "Can't say for certain, sir, but no signs of life."

"Take a breather, folks. Let's see if any of those bastards get up," Warden cast over the comms.

"No movement, no energy signatures, sir," Goodwin announced a minute later.

"Let's move in then," Warden said as he ordered the advance via the section's HUDs.

They moved across the open ground, weapons trained on the pile of rubble that was all that remained of the corner of the building. The explosions had strewn debris all over the street, leaving everything within fifty metres of the shattered structure covered in dust and grime.

Goodwin's drone shot straight up, climbing to two hundred metres before it began to follow a spiral holding pattern, scanning a much broader area for signs of life, enemy or ally.

Warden pulled a pocket open on the neck of his jacket and slid an air filter up from it to cover his mouth and nose. It wasn't capable of protecting him from an active weapons attack, but it was ideal for sandstorms or billowing clouds of concrete dust and particulates. Most of the section followed suit; their HUDs already protected their eyes.

Something clanked against his boot, and he looked down at a prone armoured trooper lying in the dust. He stepped back and brought his weapon to bear. Milton moved up beside him and reached down to pull back a sheet of wall fibre, which covered the apparent corpse. No response.

"Do you recognise this armour pattern, Sergeant?"

"No, sir, never seen anything like it. It's thin. Delicate," she said as she knelt beside the corpse and rolled it over. The chest was buckled in, probably from the direct force of one of the grenades. Still, Warden would have expected it to have torn the trooper limb from limb if it had hit directly. Even powered armour wasn't invulnerable to a close-range detonation.

The head was crumpled too, not quite flat but damaged enough to give the owner a fatal headache. There were no markings on the suit that he recognised, in fact, no markings at all. It was a dull grey with a strangely shimmering surface.

Milton grabbed it by the joint at the neck and hauled the body upright. She turned to him with a puzzled look. "It's light. I mean, really light, sir. Russian-made, maybe? Or American?"

Warden nodded towards it. "Look at that." The suit had changed colour as she lifted it from the dust-covered rubble. "Some sort of chameleon coating."

"That's a new one on me. I'd keep it quiet if I'd developed that too. No wonder they got so far into the city without anyone noticing. I bet we wouldn't have even found them without the drone," Milton said.

"Ultra-light power armour designed for stealth by an unknown power," he mused, shaking his head. "No way bandits get hold of gear like this. Could be an actual covert action by a Sol government."

"I bloody well hope not, sir. Why would anyone even want this rock? It's not even halfway terraformed yet. It'll be, what, twenty or thirty years before this shit-hole starts to look habitable to normal people," she said.

"Maybe there are resources on New Bristol our teams didn't find. What's the alternative? That some underworld group managed to build an entirely new type of power armour? Maybe they attacked a top-secret lab that some government put on a remote asteroid base?" Warden scoffed.

"Yeah, well, I didn't say I had a better explanation, I just don't see any Sol government sending a strike force here. It's a huge risk for not very much reward. Well over a century since the last intra-Sol war and this would risk another." Milton shrugged.

Warden nodded thoughtfully and sent a comm request to Captain Atticus.

"Lieutenant?" came the terse response.

"Sir, Bravo Bay has been destroyed. We encountered an enemy

infiltration unit in some kind of light powered armour in a stealth configuration. They'd breached the bunker, set charges and looked to be heading towards Bay Alpha. We slotted them," Warden reported.

"One second," said Atticus, a burst of fire accompanying his response.

Warden turned to Goodwin.

"Get me a city-wide picture. The captain and Section 3 are bogged down in a firefight and we need to know where they are and what they're facing," he ordered while he waited for Atticus to come back to him.

"We're heavily engaged. Power armour here as well but nothing light about it. They have enhanced troops too," Atticus said as explosions went off in the background.

"They have military-grade clones?"

"Yes, and the powered armour to go with them. We have a serious problem here. We need a force multiplier, and that leaves only one option," Atticus said.

"Civilian clones?"

"Yes," Atticus said, patching in Governor Denmead. "Governor, our second bay has been destroyed. What shape are your bays in?"

"Shit. Let me check," Denmead replied. "No, we used most of our standby clones already and the facility has taken some damage. It's not able to accept downloads or start incubating new clones."

"Noted. Incubation would take a few days anyway. In that case, Warden, check what remains of Bay Bravo. If there are any military-grade weapons or material there, get them to Governor Denmead. Check the bodies, scavenge their weapons too, then double-time it to my position and get stuck in," Atticus ordered. "Signing off."

Warden took a deep breath and called his section, updating them face to face. Inefficient, maybe, but a better way of breaking the bad news. They took it surprisingly well, but they were Royal Marine Space Commandos and had the best part of a millennium of predecessors to live up to. Impossible odds were nothing to get all weepy over.

"Sir, you'd best take a look at this," said Milton.

"What's up?" He walked over to the sergeant, who was kneeling beside one of the power armoured corpses, and crouched beside her.

She leaned to one side so he could see what she was looking at. The helmet the soldier wore had been removed and his face was exposed. Or its face, rather. It wasn't human, not even vaguely. It wasn't just the eyes; the whole face was inhuman. Military clones sometimes had modified eyes, particularly snipers, but nothing like the black orbs that now stared, lifeless, at Milton.

Scales covered the face, the nose was flattened and shielded with a thick plate, rather like a lizard. The bone structure wasn't right either, too smooth, too ovoid, and the eyelids seemed reptilian. It was like looking at a humanoid dinosaur, something you'd see in a holo-show.

Warden looked at Milton, at her raised eyebrows and back down at the reptilian face.

"No," he said.

"Yes."

"No, absolutely not."

"Yes, Lieutenant."

"You want me to believe this is an alien, don't you?"

"No, I want it to be some kind of base layer balaclava they wear under their armour, but I already tried pulling it off. It's definitely got scales and it's definitely not human," said Milton.

"Well. Bollocks."

"Sounds about right. So, shall we get on with it, then?"

4

Warden's feet pounded the concrete as he ran towards Captain Atticus's current position. There'd been a heavy firefight up here and the colonists were hunkered down to the south. A HUD replay of their positions showed that Section 3 had pressed the enemy hard, forcing them back into an underground facility. He jumped over an enemy body and crouched behind the concrete base of a communications relay tower as he assessed the situation.

Around him, his section took a breather. They'd sprinted over and were now only a hundred metres from the captain's position. Regrouping in cover was the smart move.

The alien soldier wore a face-covering helmet and unpowered armour so light that it offered almost no protection, but it was the long, elegant, wings that made it notable. They stood out, as did the long-barrelled rifle nearby. A sniper's clone, with wings to help it to reach vantage points that would otherwise be inaccessible.

The replay showed the dots that represented Atticus and Section 3 descending into the underground hydroponic and storage facility to pursue the aliens. That was the way of the Commando; press the advantage, keep advancing, never give the enemy time to regroup.

They weren't about to worry about the presence of the first aliens humans had encountered. They knew their job, and they'd do that as efficiently as possible. Time to worry about aliens later; for now, they were just another enemy to defeat.

Goodwin's drone reported no enemy movement above ground. Reports were fuzzy from below ground where Atticus's team were, and Warden's HUD reported only a sixty-five per cent chance their location info was still correct. There should have been a network mesh in the facility, but either the colonists hadn't seen fit to install it or it had been damaged in the fighting. Either way, they would have to do this the old-fashioned way until they were underground and started to get reliable readouts from the Marines in Section 3. There was a gristly sound behind him and Warden turned to see Milton putting a blade into the neck of the sniper, just to be sure. Caution was sensible but there was no point wasting ammunition.

"Advance," he whispered, his voice carried clearly to each commando via their HUDs. They moved the last hundred metres, going from cover to cover, watching everything, scanning the skies. Where there was one winged alien sniper, there would doubtless be more, and the colonists had any number of relay towers, atmospheric processing units and even bio-engineered trees dotted around the city.

The entrance to the facility was still intact, though the greenhouse above it was nothing but a tangled mass of aluminium with a frosting of shattered glass. There was a goods elevator that all but screamed 'Obvious trap, die here'.

They took the wide concrete stairs, passing another alien corpse on the way. This one was in powered armour which had been pummelled with bullets; the entire section must have fired on it to do this much damage to powered armour with carbines. No need for Milton to draw her knife here.

The stairs led into a spacious garage for the electric carts used to ferry supplies around the colony. The elevator shaft was to their left, and Milton cautiously checked that it was empty as they advanced on the double doors in front of them. The garage was well lit but beyond the doors, the lighting seemed haphazard at best.

Warden tried the comms again but Atticus and his section were quiet, unanswering. Warden shook his head and pressed on.

Through the doorway was a large hydroponics hall, at least two storeys high and the size of a football field. It should have been flooded with light for the plants but even before they pushed the doors open, they could tell that the lighting was buggered.

There had been a gunfight. Smoke still hung in the air, and everywhere they saw the tell-tale signs of grenade damage. The planters were four-metre-high shelves full of crops in compost. Some of the rows were intact, but most were shot through or had been blown apart. The cover was poor, the earth in the planters barely sufficient to slow a bullet, and there was simply too much space between them to hide anything larger than a drone. The HUD showed more rooms directly opposite the double doors and to the north.

If the aliens had stopped in the hydroponics room and made a stand, the commandos would have been just as exposed as the enemy, so they'd have fallen back as quickly as possible to the next room. Warden checked his HUD. The plans were updating now, the accuracy percentage climbing rapidly as they came into range of the first members of Section 3.

They moved through the room at double time and found their first friendly casualty, a body so badly damaged even the HUD couldn't tell who it had been. The death would have been recorded by his colleagues' HUDs, so there was no point in stopping to confirm. Milton ordered the Marines bringing up the rear to strip the weapons and ammunition from the deceased, and they did so with grim efficiency as the rest of Section 2 advanced.

There were two sets of double doors, all peppered with dents and bullet holes. Atticus and his Marines had fired on the fleeing enemy, chasing them into this pit. They must have been here scant minutes earlier, leaving behind only shell casings as they hunted the enemy troopers.

The doors were spaced several metres apart, but both opened into the same chamber. Marines gathered on either side of each pair of doors, ready to rush in once they were opened.

It was a warehouse, filled with large shelving units all stacked with pallets of boxes. The aisles were wide enough for forklifts, and more goods elevators waited against the east and west walls. The HUD showed a maze of rooms behind the north wall. Office space, judging by the size and layout. The dots indicating the surviving members of Atticus's team were clustered in that area.

"Shit," muttered Warden, looking at his team and trying to not to get distracted by the shadows.

Warden hit the open button next to him, and the doors slid quickly back into the walls, his Marines flowing through the opening as he double-timed it down the aisle. Visibility in here was better, at least in the aisle itself, and the overhead lamps still filled the room with a sickly white glow. There was no sign of gunfire in the warehouse. The Marines spread out, small groups going down each aisle to properly clear the room, carbines pointing at all corners and up towards the ceiling, looking for hidden enemies.

"Captain? Are you reading me?" Warden asked as he hastened down the aisle.

A message flashed in his HUD.

<Pinned down. Resistance heavy, casualties rising, ammunition low. Have a flesh wound. Can't speak, would compromise position>

<Understood. Stay in cover. We've almost reached you> Warden sent back.

Seconds later, they approached the far side of the warehouse and could see into the office space. The offices and other rooms were constructed with stud walls to break up another large room, probably the same size as the warehouse and hydroponic farm rooms. There were two floors of rooms, but no indicators showed any of the marines upstairs.

They didn't need their HUDs to see that the walls provided no cover. There were bullet holes, scorch marks and shattered windows everywhere.

Warden was reasonably sure if he fired at one of the walls there was a good chance his round would make it all the way to the other side of the huge space. *Shit,* he thought, *that wasn't helpful.*

Not having cover was one thing. Having the semblance of cover was worse. You couldn't see the enemy, and it was tempting to stop behind something that seemed solid. Once you did that, your enemy could just shoot through whatever you had ducked behind. Better to have an open space that didn't impede movement than this mess.

He could already see a few corpses, though there was so much dust and debris that he wouldn't have been sure they were marines if his HUD hadn't identified them. A burst of gunfire came from the alien's direction, and sure enough, the bullets shattered glass and punched through walls as if they were tissue paper, impacting in the concrete of the wall separating the offices from the warehouse.

"Milton, we're going to have to rush through here. No one stop for casualties; we need to force them back," he ordered.

Quickly they issued orders to the section. Warden would head for the captain, who was about twenty-five metres away through a series of walls and offices. Milton would go left with a small team, hoping to flank the enemy and make it to the northwest corner of the concrete chamber before pressing them. The rest would fan out to provide covering fire, using combined readouts from infra-red sights and their HUDs to force the aliens to keep their heads down.

"Go," Warden said, simultaneously issuing the command via the HUD as well. The entire group rushed through the various doors and set about their tasks. As soon as Milton's team had veered left and Warden had started his crouched sprint towards Captain Atticus, the covering fire began. Wilson followed him; the tech specialist looked grimly determined, clearly peeved that the captain had been injured. The Marines fired as they moved, expertly suppressing the enemy with short bursts from their carbines.

Goodwin's drone made an almost certainly suicidal dash down the corridors and through shattered window holes, trying to get close enough to the enemy positions to reveal them on the HUD. If they could get a good enough update, the marines could target the aliens directly, and Atticus's team would be able to join in. They were scattered throughout the southern half of the space, probably all lying prone to avoid getting shot by the aliens' seemingly indiscriminate fire.

Warden would have given anything for a clear arc of fire. A few grenades might have made the difference but down here, in this mess, it would be an unacceptable risk.

With all the shredded walls and bundles of cabling dangling from semi-collapsed ceilings, he could imagine a grenade bouncing back towards his position and devastating his section. Instead, he fired a burst from his carbine in the general direction of the doors and made another sprint towards the captain.

There was an answering burst of fire from the aliens, and though it missed him, it was close enough for him to dive through an open door and land unceremoniously on the carpet, skidding to a stinging halt.

"Fucking carpet burns," he murmured in disbelief as he bounced, lucky not to crack a rib. The cloned body might only be a loaner, but he needed it to do his job and, clone or not, a broken rib still stung like hell.

Injury indifference, they called it. It was a risk all cloned soldiers faced: the semi-suicidal use of a new body that wasn't, technically, their own. The Canadian Coalition forces had reported the same problem as their British allies. New soldiers took unnecessary risks for the first year or two until they realised just how painful the higher injury rate was and that nobody was going to grow them a new body simply because they broke an arm.

Warden gritted his teeth and scrambled forward, keeping low to the floor as his section continued to lay down covering fire. It wasn't particularly dignified crawling around on the floor of a cheaply furnished office, but it was ultimately going to be quicker and a lot less dangerous to reach the captain this way.

Plus it was easy enough to devote some brainpower to monitoring the HUD updates. Half of Atticus's section was already marked as terminal casualties. Colour Sergeant Jenkins and Marine Butler were dead. Not good, especially when they were facing enemies with powered armour and they didn't yet have the weapons or kit to counter that properly. They needed numbers to make up the difference.

A short dash down an easterly corridor and a sharp turn into an office brought him to a filing cabinet, not two metres from Captain Atticus, who was slumped by a similar cabinet further along the same wall.

"Lieutenant," the captain acknowledged through gritted teeth that glistened with blood.

"Sir. Bit of a sticky wicket?" Warden asked cheerfully, forcing a grin.

"I've had better days. You?"

"We meet some charming gentlemen, dressed for a nice afternoon stroll through a war zone, but they seemed much more agreeable after we dropped a building on them. Turns out they're not from these parts and don't have passports or identification."

Atticus coughed in wry amusement, then cursed and spat blood.

"So we discovered. They still don't like it up 'em. We met their colleagues, tenacious buggers. I can't say I ever thought this is what a First Contact situation would be like."

"Doesn't really fit the tactical assessment briefing we got on First Contact. 'No chance aliens would be hostile' they said. Million to one against, the Professor said."

"How does the old saying go? Million to one chances crop up nine times out of ten?"

"One of my favourite books, sir. How are you feeling?"

"Well. I don't mind telling you, Tom, that I don't feel too clever. I'm reasonably sure I'm not getting out of here."

"Hmm. I was hoping it was just a flesh wound," Warden replied as another cacophony of gunfire was exchanged above their heads.

"Fair to say that my flesh is definitely wounded," hissed Atticus.

"What are your orders, sir?"

"Can't hang around here, you have work to do. I'm passing command authority to you. Unless we get a cloning facility active, I won't be back for a while. Has Wilson made it?"

"So far, sir."

"Good, keep him safe, you'll need him. I've been coming up with a plan while I lie here trying to hold my guts in. The balance of probability," he said, pausing as a wave of pain passed through him, "is that these aliens use cloning technology, just like we do. Mostly humanoid but the wings and some other differences look like augmentations to me. None of the xenobiology theory I've seen suggests a species would develop to space-era technology and have such a wide variety of forms. Have a look at this," Atticus said, sliding an object across the floor to Warden.

He picked it up. It was a heavy calibre pistol, probably made for a power armoured hand. Nothing out of the ordinary.

"Notice anything strange?" Atticus asked, and when Warden shook his head, he suggested, "Pop the magazine out a moment."

Warden thumbed the release and caught the half-full magazine as it ejected from the grip of the weapon. The rounds looked like a fairly standard caseless design, probably 15mm which was large but easily handled by the servo-motors in powered armour. It seemed entirely normal. He shrugged and pushed the magazine home. "Not sure I get it, sir?"

"Just like a normal personal weapon that we'd issue to powered armour troopers as a backup, yes?"

Warden nodded, then frowned. Atticus could practically see the light dawning on his subordinate's face. *There it is, comprehension,* he thought. *At least the lad isn't entirely stupid.*

"Wait. Why is an alien weapon so similar to our own?"

"Exactly. You got that magazine out like you'd been using that weapon for years. Because you have. Every service pistol you've used has been pretty much the same as that design. How the hell did an alien species independently come up with the design we use, eh?"

"Well, they couldn't, that's just... Well. It's improbable, to say the least. They must have copied our designs from somewhere. That explains why their powered armour looks the way it does. All their kit, it's just their version of equipment from Sol. Where the hell did they get the designs, though?"

A burst of fire cut through the office, punching the cabinets and filling the air with paper.

"I've been thinking about that too," said Atticus as the Marines returned fire. "I think it was an Ark ship. I think that these aliens found one, could have been any of the missing ships or even one of the fleets. They captured it or found the ship derelict. Perhaps it even landed on their home planet." Atticus shook his head, aware he was rambling. "They ended up with all sorts of advanced engineering information and they were similar enough to us to make use of it. Now, they know we're out here somewhere, and they've planned an invasion."

"An invasion?" It sounded thin to Warden, but he had to admit the firefight certainly leant strength to Atticus's argument.

"This might not be the only alien attack underway at the moment. Regardless, you now know that they're using weapons and armour not that dissimilar to our own. That makes me think they're also using our cloning technology. We're not fighting real aliens, just their clones. They might not even be humanoid on their home planet. Maybe they used our form because it's more practical for this work? For all we know, they're avian or water dwelling. It doesn't matter. What does matter is that they probably get around the galaxy the same way we do because they're using our technology against us. They go somewhere in a ship on auto-pilot, download into clones and then drop out of orbit to begin their attack," Atticus said.

"Makes sense. The Lost Arks had a lot of the same technology we use now, and cloning is still the best way to get around the galaxy. All they lacked was faster than light drives. What's your plan then, sir? Not to be too pushy but our cover might not last long, and you're looking paler by the minute," Warden said apologetically.

"They must have a base of operations somewhere," Atticus screwed his eyes closed as another wave of pain wracked his body. "Gather the troops, get some transport and attack. Check the outlying stations. Start with the first to fall. They probably chose one with plenty of power and buildings, far enough from here to be secure and near enough to launch attacks. I haven't seen vehicles, so I think they're operating largely on foot. Speak to the governor, find their base, then capture or destroy their cloning facility to prevent them reinforcing. Questions?" Atticus said.

"After we've dealt with their base, we have to track any remaining enemy and destroy them," Warden agreed.

"Yes, then prepare the locals for any follow-up that might come and get any intelligence back to HQ. Other colonies in this sector may be at risk," Atticus said. "Try not to destroy their cloning bay, you might need it, and maybe Wilson can use some of the components to repair the colonist's bays, anyway," he advised.

"Right. Time to get you out of here then, sir," Warden said.

"Hah!" Atticus responded, coughing up blood as he tried to laugh off the suggestion, "I don't think that's a worthwhile use of resources. This body is done for. My HUD has four of them left in this squad, but the drone feed shows another squad on its way."

He paused, fingers grasping weakly for Warden's arm.

"You have about four minutes to get out of here. I'm staying right here where, if I'm very careful not to move too much, the pain won't get any worse. Leave any explosives you can spare, and as soon as their mates turn up, I'll throw a little welcome party." He paused again, then gave a tiny nod. "Now, get cracking. Three minutes and counting. You have your orders."

Warden stared at the captain for a second, then nodded with grim determination. He unslung a pack from his waist and withdrew a block of explosive and a detonator. As he did so, he issued orders over his HUD and Atticus announced the transfer of command. The commandos began a tactical withdrawal back the way they'd come, stopping by their fallen comrades to assist the injured and grab useful kit from those beyond help.

Warden moved quickly to Atticus's side and opened his med kit, withdrawing a pair of dispensers and slamming them into the captain's thigh. His eyes snapped open, suddenly alert from the booster and additional painkiller. Not medically advisable, given his condition, but it would keep him conscious long enough for him to enact his plan.

Then Warden removed the captain's explosive pack and slapped it together with his own. He grabbed a couple of flares from the captain's webbing and mashed them in as well, adding a detonator and syncing it to the captain's HUD.

Atticus grabbed his wrist, brow beaded with sweat. "Take my carbine. I can't hold it anyway. Give these bastards hell, Warden, you hear? When I come back, I want your report to say they're all dead and the citizens are safe."

"Yes, Captain," was all Warden could say as he laid a comforting hand on his shoulder and squeezed it.

They fell back into the warehouse as quickly as possible. The next message from Atticus read <Ninety seconds> and they began to run as fast as they could, abandoning covering fire as they dashed through the warehouse and into the hydroponic farm.

<Fifteen seconds. Atticus signing off until the next time> as they burst onto the staircase.

There was a distant chatter of gunfire, far away under the earth, then an almighty explosion ripped through the underground building. The captain's indicator on their HUDs went dead as a choking cloud of hot dust billowed up the stairs and into the thin atmosphere. More than a dozen icons, the alien troops and their reinforcements, winked out of existence at the same time. The captain had not sold his final moments lightly.

Warden looked around the remaining Marines, some coughing and spitting dust from their mouths, some looking angry, some depressed.

"No time for a brew, we have work to do. Get the drones up; I want to know if there's any enemy movement in the city. And find the governor. The captain had a plan and we're going to carry it out." He paused and looked around at his troops.

"We're taking the fight to the enemy."

5

W arden entered the conference room and leant on the back of a chair, head hanging as his chest heaved and his heart pounded in his chest. Under normal conditions, it wasn't far to run, but New Bristol's atmosphere didn't really encourage vigorous exercise. The air was breathable but you really noticed the lack of oxygen when you exerted yourself.

They had moved quickly once Captain Atticus had made his sacrifice. His plan required the support of the colonists and, if his supposition was correct, the aliens could be downloading into new clone bodies even now.

"Lieutenant, you don't look like a man bringing good news," Governor Denmead said, leaving the question hanging.

Warden engaged the safety on his carbine, withdrew the magazine and cleared the chamber. Then he put the weapon on the table and did the same with Captain Atticus's carbine and pistol. A set of webbing packs followed. He opened one, withdrawing an ammunition packet. Then he sat down and began to reload the captain's magazines. Once settled into the familiar rhythm, he looked up at the governor.

"I'm not, Governor Denmead. Captain Atticus is dead. He gave his life buying time for the rest of us to escape the hydroponic farm. He took a dozen aliens with him but we'd already lost good Marines before I arrived with Section 2," Warden reported.

The governor cursed in a most impolite manner before summoning her self-control.

"I'm sorry to hear that, Lieutenant. The captain was a good officer and he was surely a brave man. The citizens of New Bristol owe him a debt. I wish I had time to say more but I need to know what your plan is."

"You don't seem bothered by the idea that the attackers are aliens, Governor."

She levelled him a cold look. "I had already wondered about that, Lieutenant, but I wasn't going to be the first to say it. We've always known there must be intelligent life elsewhere in the galaxy and Sol governments have been preparing for it for hundreds of years. Don't you think I've taken the First Contact training courses? I've been sitting in xenobiology lectures and first contact briefings since before you were born. Most are about peaceful results, but there were enough scenarios like this that I'm not entirely shocked. If you say they're aliens, they're aliens. What matters is, can we hold them off, can we survive?"

"Glad to hear it, Governor, and yes, I think we have a chance."

Warden stood, picked up the captain's carbine and the two magazines he'd loaded and walked over to the governor. He placed them on the table in front of her. "I think you should have these now. You may need them soon and it's a serious weapon. You remember how to use one?" he asked.

"Yes, Lieutenant Warden. Basic training was some time ago but we get annual refreshers along with the keys to the colony and the launch codes for the orbital nuclear strike weapons." She paused then shook her head. "Sorry, too soon for jokes. There are always risks on remote colonies in the outer rim, but I wasn't expecting this," said Governor Denmead. Then for emphasis, she checked the weapon was safe, reloaded it and made it safe again. "Frontier Governor isn't a role for the fainthearted."

"Good. Before he died, Captain Atticus gave me orders to attack the aliens' base of operations. This is one of their pistols," he said, producing the large calibre weapon designed for powered armour wearing alien troopers. Demonstrating the mechanism, he went on, "As you can see, this is a human design. Updated and modified, certainly, but far too similar to be a coincidence. Atticus believed that the aliens encountered one of the Lost Arks and their equipment is based on designs found within it. That means it may be compatible with ours and they're likely using our cloning technology as well. With me so far? I don't have time to discuss this overly much, I'm afraid."

Governor Denmead nodded. "I'm with you, Lieutenant. I'll let you know if I have any questions which can't wait."

"They will have captured a location within easy reach of the city. If you've seen no sign of them using vehicles, then their base has to be within practical marching distance. A day of walking, maybe a little more, but no further than that. It must have good power supplies or a good range of buildings and be defensible. Anything else wouldn't have enough strategic value to be worth using. I need to know the likely candidates. After that, I need to know what vehicles you have that we can use to get there," Warden said.

Denmead put the carbine down and picked up her data slate. A wall screen flicked on, and a satellite imagery map of New Bristol appeared. She caught his look of surprise and answered the very question that was on his mind, "No, Lieutenant, our satellites are gone. This is last year's data. The topography and locations are correct, of course, but for all we know, the outposts depicted here," she zoomed the map out, "have been completely destroyed."

That was disappointing but not particularly surprising. An alien ship in orbit could easily have destroyed or disabled the colony's satellites. Surveillance by low-atmosphere drone was now their only option. Warden issued an order through his HUD, and the tech specialists shared their data with the governor's systems. The map of New Bristol began to update, showing the destroyed hydroponic farm and cloning bay.

"These are the largest outposts that might match your description," Denmead said as three locations on the map pinged. "All of these have some sturdy buildings, they're within a reasonable distance for troops to march on the city and they have decent energy supplies."

"May I?" Warden asked, holding his hand out for the slate. The governor nodded and passed it to him.

He worked the controls, viewing each site from various angles, examining the relief map. "I think we can rule these ones out, they're all on flat terrain. Cavendish Station has the right mix of buildings but it's overlooked by this outcrop here and far too easily attacked. I'd bet against Weston Farm as well; the ravine would make it difficult to get here quickly and efficiently."

"So that just leaves...North Solar Farm," Denmead said.

"What can you tell me about it?" Warden asked.

"Nothing interesting. There's a solar power plant there, obviously," she said pointing to an array of panels on the western side of the display. "There are some laboratory greenhouses there for testing plants that might survive outside a hydroponic farm. Then there's some accommodation and a storage bunker."

"Looks promising. What's this area here?" Warden asked.

"Land cleared for a new expansion. A concrete base prepped for new buildings."

"Must be a pretty big expansion, that has to be a hundred metres across. This is our best site. Landing a dropship there wouldn't be any problem at all; it's ideal. They know they've got a stable landing site, power, ready-made barracks and even a bunker. It couldn't be better for them if they'd sent you the specification themselves," Warden said.

"We have some rovers you can use to get out there. They're civilian vehicles, but they have good range and will cope with the terrain."

"Right, we need to get moving. We're going to leave you the spare weapons we recovered from our casualties. Have you managed to produce any of your own?" Warden asked.

"Not quite. The fabrication plants are still working on the materiel that Captain Atticus authorised. If you want to leave now, none of the weapons will be ready, but we should have plenty of ammunition. Do you want to wait?"

"No, we can't. We must press the advantage now. We'll restock at the armoury, release everything we don't need to you and then get stuck in. We captured a few enemy weapons and we'll test those en route, see if any will be of use. Beyond that, we're limited to the light, small arms the emergency bay armouries are equipped with. Grenades and a few sniper rifles are the heaviest we've got." Warden shrugged. "We'll make do."

"I wish I could help, Lieutenant, but we haven't the population or economy to justify rapid fabricators at this stage of the colony's development. They burn too much energy to be supported at the moment. If you came back in a few years," she said apologetically, letting the sentence die.

Warden grinned. "Governor, we're Commandos. Improvising our tactics and weapons is a regimental tradition."

6

The rovers made easy work of the rocky terrain between New Bristol and the unimaginatively named North Solar Farm. Not that that was surprising; their design had been refined and put to the test on dozens of colony worlds.

Most Sol governments used something similar and even the early Mars explorers would have recognised the basic design. Six large wheels, suitable for all terrain, computer controlled and with high-travel suspension.

Getting in quickly was a pain, though; the vehicles were not ideal for military purposes. You had to wait for the vehicle to settle on its hydraulic suspension or use one of the sets of steps that appeared only when the vehicle couldn't lower itself because of obstructions under the chassis. Leaping down meant taking a chance on a two-metre drop.

With no weapon mounts, the Marines would have to dismount to engage the enemy, so they planned to get as close as they could without bringing the vehicles into view, then yomp across the remaining distance under cover of their snipers and light support weapons.

Warden sat with Sergeant Milton at a navigation and mapping station going over all the data the colonists had gathered about the ground between the city and North Solar Farm. They were looking for somewhere that they could test the alien weapons in relative safety, far enough from both the city and their destination that the enemy would not know what they were doing.

"There," said Sergeant Milton, pointing at a shallow canyon in the top right of the screen. "It's deep enough to contain any firing and the gradient leading into it should be manageable by the rover."

"It's a little further out of the way than I'd hoped," Warden replied, "but I suppose it's better to be discreet than get into an unexpected firefight."

"There's a cliff face over there, but there's nothing to shield it from either side and no cover for the teams staying with the vehicles. There are rocks by the canyon mouth that we can use as fire positions in case the aliens do find us."

Warden nodded. "Agreed." He used a stylus at the station to enter a change of route on the nav computer and sent it to the driver, a colonist who had volunteered to get them to North Solar Farm. She called back to him to confirm she'd received the updated route, "Why there, though, Captain?"

"It's Lieutenant Warden, actually. We captured some weapons and we want to test them, make sure we can use them before we have to rely on them. The emergency bays don't carry the heavy weapons we'd want for a task like this and we don't have time to wait for the fabricators to produce them. The canyon is a good place to test them away from enemy sight lines and without getting too far away from our attack vector. Can you get us there safely?" he asked.

"Not a problem for the rover, Lieutenant. It can handle the trip easily, even with this load. I'll pass the details to the other rovers," she replied before hailing the drivers in the two trailing vehicles.

Warden turned to Milton. "So, what's your bet on the contents of our haul?"

"I'd eat my socks if we don't have a few railguns there. Two of them are very similar with drum magazines and big shells, but I think one is a grenade launcher and the other is some sort of heavy shotgun. The shells are big, though, so it's either massive explosions or a ridiculous load of pellets," she replied, rocking her hand side to side to indicate the uncertainty about those weapons.

"Railguns would be useful against vehicles or infantry in powered armour. I want the base intact, if possible, but I'm guessing we'll have to flush them out of the buildings once we've taken care of their perimeter personnel," Warden said.

"Yes, sir. The shotgun might be useful for room clearance, but you can't be letting off railguns in a civilian habitat. The rounds will go straight through the walls, and if there are pressurised canisters in the building or one of the team is out of position... It's a recipe for disaster. A grenade launcher would be even worse. Flashbangs only inside, I think," Milton answered.

"We do have a couple of rifles and some personal weapons that might be useful if we've got enough ammunition," mused Warden.

"Possibly. Our carbines are great in close quarters, but if we can use the rifles, we should. I think it's safe to assume they'll have more troops in power armour defending this site, if it really is their forward operating base. The carbines are next to useless against armour – far too risky to rely on them for that – and if we don't want to use our grenade launchers or the alien's heavy weapons inside, armour is going to be a real problem," Milton said.

"If there's evidence of significant armour, we have to do everything we can to overwhelm it before we step inside the buildings. You saw how little damage those armoured scouts took, even after we'd dropped a building on them. Their armour is tougher and lighter than ours. If they have heavier suits for assault troops, we're screwed if we get too close to them."

"Lieutenant? We've reached the canyon," the driver called back over her shoulder.

"Thanks. We'll go on foot from here, shouldn't be more than half an hour," Warden said, turning to the squad. "Masks on, everyone.

This far from the habitats, I don't want our performance suffering from the thin atmosphere." The commandos duly attached their breathing gear, checking function and the levels of gas from their HUDs. The gear they had was nothing like a space suit or powered armour but it was more than enough to handle the local environment. It was comforting to know that equipment or air supply failure, even out here, wasn't going to cause them to suffocate in the air of New Bristol. But it would dramatically slow them down.

The driver hit the seal on the cockpit and a thin door slid across, separating the passenger and cargo area from the front of the vehicle. It was a simple way to reduce the amount of atmosphere lost when loading and unloading the vehicle.

Moments later the Marines were on the ground, walking down the shallow incline to the canyon floor. Twenty metres in they found a suitable spot, a bend in the canyon that gave them a good backstop for the weapons to discharge against and sufficient range to keep them safe from ricochets or explosives.

It actually took longer to set up, safety check the weapons and establish a testing protocol than it did to run the tests. They'd recovered a fair amount of ammunition for all the items they had brought along but Warden didn't want to waste too much all the same.

They quickly established that the function of each weapon was nearly identical to their own heavier armaments. The railguns were clearly sniping weapons, with near silent operation and very high target penetration, similar to their own weapons, though they couldn't be exact in a test against a rock wall.

Fired within or at the buildings of the solar farm, the railgun's rounds would punch through the walls and anything that might be on the other side. Warden gave instructions to use these only sparingly, as Milton had suggested. There was a reason nobody had ever produced a railgun capable of burst fire.

The grenade launcher and shotgun were more easily tested. They had anti-armour high explosive grenades as well as fragmentation models, differentiated by colours, just as their own were, although the markings and design were quite different. The shotgun was entirely dull, though it would be useful for clearing rooms of lightly armoured hostiles.

The pistols were high calibre but perfectly usable as backup weapons. All had integral silencers, suggesting that they were intended for stealthy takedowns during the opening stages of an attack. The commandos rarely used pistols because it wasn't necessary to have so much weaponry on a typical deployment but they had their uses.

The alien rifles were full-length assault rifles, not the smaller bullpup carbines the Marines had taken from the armoury. The rounds were a heavier calibre, making them preferable to the carbines, even in close quarters, and they were much more likely to penetrate powered armour than the weapons the Marines carried.

All in all, Warden was pleased. He would have preferred weapons they were familiar with but despite the outward appearances of all of these, the functional designs were similar enough that the Marines weren't going to have any problems changing magazines or firing the weapons. It seemed strange that the first aliens they had encountered were sufficiently similar to humans to be able to use their weapons but he wasn't going to look a gift horse in the mouth and now wasn't the time for serious introspection.

They were back in the rovers within half an hour. Warden and Milton distributed the railguns to the snipers. Each section had at least one Marine who had been through the extensive training required to qualify as a sniper. Lance Corporal Bailey was the senior sniper in A Troop and would lead the team of three snipers, along with their spotters, and the tech specialists who would be using drones to sweep the area.

They gave the grenade launcher and shotgun to the spotters. Without clear targets, their main role was to protect the snipers.

There were only a few assault rifles, so they went to the close quarter specialists, while Milton handed out the alien pistols to as many people as possible. Anyone left with only standard-issue carbines was given more grenades for the underslung launchers. If they encountered powered armour, a grenade would be their best option. Either that or they'd flag the enemy in their HUD and hope the railguns could shoot it through a wall.

Warden looked around the vehicle, checking his team. The Marines looked confident, comfortable. They were as ready as they would ever be.

"Move out," he ordered.

7

As soon as they were underway, Warden reviewed the layout of the solar plant and the settlers' plans of the base with Milton, looking for ways to incorporate the alien weapons into their plan. Together they selected overwatch positions for the snipers, agreed on an approach route and found a rock formation close to the base for the drivers to park behind. Then they polished their plan of attack and issued it to the commandos via their HUDs.

The Marines sat in silence while they reviewed their assigned positions and the lines of attack. The HUDs showed their expected flow through the buildings to clear them, so by the time they reached the vehicles parked, they were ready to do the job.

They piled out of the vehicles without a word, snipers and their support teams breaking away to find positions on a formation of basalt columns. Warden blinked in surprise and spared a glance for Milton, who stood open-mouthed.

"Perfect for snipers," he muttered, watching as the teams climbed the natural terraces and disappeared. The column tops were flat and lacked concealing vegetation but that hardly mattered in this case; the attack would be swift and brutal, and if the snipers were under fire, you couldn't ask for better cover than the hard rock.

While the snipers found their spots, the tech specialists launched their drones, sending them zipping over the columns of rock and down the other side. The drones hugged the ground, skimming low to avoid detection. No bigger than a hummingbird, their bird-like movements would be totally out of place on New Bristol. The indigenous lifeforms generally kept well away from the colonists, and it looked like the local bird equivalents weren't keen on the Marines either. The drones' movements would stand out like a sore thumb to any alien sentries, but it was a risk they had to take.

Warden and Milton split the remaining Marines into two teams while they waited for updated maps to be built from the information returned by the drones. They were watching the video feeds from the drones as some flitted clockwise and some counter-clockwise around the solar plant, scanning everything.

"There," said Warden, zooming in, "that looks like a dropship to me. A large one."

"Seems too big, doesn't it?" said Milton sceptically. "If that was full of troops when it landed, where are they? This camp should be swarming."

"One platoon at the city, a few patrols at other sites." Warden frowned. "There could be two or three platoons here if that thing came down full."

"Unless they carry something else. Vehicles, perhaps? They could have their own colony equipment in there. Do they want to kill us or capture New Bristol and colonise it?"

Warden shrugged. "There's little value in New Bristol, it won't be terraformed for decades, and they don't seem so dissimilar from us that they'd want to call this rock home. Would you come to another solar system and fight a war only to colonise a planet you still had to terraform?"

"No, I wouldn't, but our own history has a lot of similar examples. Maybe aliens are just as stupid as humans?"

"Fair point," conceded Warden with a shrug. "Can't really argue with that. Either way, we can't charge in there unless we know more about their numbers. Agreed?"

"Yes, sir. I have no interest in finding out the hard way that they have three platoons of power armoured troopers just waiting to welcome us."

Warden nodded and briefed the tech specialists, sending new instructions via the HUD. In moments, a dozen more drones were in the air and heading into the camp.

"Now we'll see," murmured Warden as the camp's plan unfolded in his HUD.

He turned his attention back to the drone feeds, but there wasn't anything new. The updated layout showed only superficial changes, like new tool sheds and shifted storage containers, but nothing that presented a challenge for their plan of attack. The only remaining question was the number of enemy troops.

"Milton, get the grenade launchers up on the ridge in case they twig to the drones," he said, advancing on the ridge himself as the sergeant set about reorganising the teams.

Warden climbed the stepped columns, making his way up towards the highest point. He picked a spot a couple of metres down from the peak and hoped he would avoid the sight line of any sentries. Being silhouetted on a ridge was a classic mistake that had been thoroughly drilled out of him in commando training. You could only take so many paintball bruises from the sniping instructors before you got the point about keeping your head down.

The data from the drones and the various displays and map overlays he could access from his HUD were good, he knew, but there was nothing quite like a Mark 1 eyeball to make a location seem real. He glanced to either side. The snipers waited a little below his position, scanning back and forth, looking for targets.

He took a deep breath and raised his head just far enough above the rock to see the alien spaceship. As he'd seen from the drones, it was large and odd-looking to boot. There were similarities to human ships but it was smoother and less blocky than the Royal Navy's ships, more elegant, somehow.

Dropships didn't need to be attractive beasts and the Navy's certainly weren't, but this one had a somewhat pleasing aesthetic, even if the metal was a strange swirling mix of blues and greens.

But the camouflage hadn't been achieved with mere paint; it was built into the metal of the hull. There was little point camouflaging a dropship designed for rapid entry; it was hardly a subtle affair. Warden shook his head. Alien paint schemes were a puzzle for a quieter day.

There were no sentries around the base and that surprised him. It would be incredibly lax of the enemy commander to have no patrols or sentries guarding their perimeter. Perhaps they were using drones or dumb sensors? Maybe they had launched an attack elsewhere?

"Anyone got an update for me? Come on, people, give me something," he said, clenching his fist, trying to keep the frustration from his voice. He needed to know what was going on here, where the enemy were and how many of them were running around. If they didn't get something soon, they'd have to push on regardless. The captain had given him a job to do and the colonists expected results. He gave the solar plant one last look and then began to descend the steps of rock.

"Grenade launchers are in place, sir," said Milton. "We're three hundred metres from the first building we can use as cover. Do you want to move in now or wait to confirm numbers?"

"We'll give the techs two more minutes, then we move. We'll just have to risk it."

Milton nodded and they moved to their respective teams, walking them towards the side of the rock formation. The drones had advanced well into the plant by the time Milton's and Warden's teams reached the last of the rocks. Any further and they would be in the open terrain between the rocks and the first buildings.

<Anyone else?> Warden asked across the HUD.

Cooke, the tech specialist for Section 1 responded, sending his report to Warden and Milton only.

<Negative, sir. We've flagged the buildings the drones have cleared but we can't get into the central structure, so we expect the enemy are in there if they're here at all. No sentries or automated

defences. The dropship is cold; engines haven't been fired recently, the ship is at atmospheric temperature, and there are no signs of active scanning. We have drones at all the breaching points. We're ready to go. If there's no immediate contact when you breach, we can send the drones in so they can scout the interior. The structure is like a bunker, and it's blocking our scans, but the interior walls probably aren't any more solid than they were in Ashton. There's some accommodation in there for a few people and storage space, so plenty of room to put their barracks and armour in there>

<Understood> replied Warden. He switched to the public channel. <Overwatch, we're moving out in thirty seconds. Any enemy contact, fire at will> he ordered.

He glanced at the time on his HUD, counting down, "Three, two, one. Go!" he called as he broke into a run. Even wearing breathers, the thin air took its toll; without them, the three hundred metre dash would have been a real lung-buster. Warden's heart pounded in his chest as he broke free of the safety offered by the basalt.

Section 2 followed behind him, eyes on the base, everyone looking for the first sign of trouble. The ground was flat and hard, no dips to dive into or boulders to shelter behind. They were horribly exposed to enemy fire.

<All clear, Lieutenant, no sign> sent Bailey when Warden reached the halfway point.

<Noted> he responded <Don't let up the pace>

They skidded to a halt behind the first building, not much more than a low concrete ridge topped with thin metal walls and a roof. It wasn't the best cover but it was long enough that both teams could shelter behind it while they caught their breath. Warden took a moment to check the drone feeds. Still no sign of enemy movement.

It was beginning to irritate him. Where were the bastards? He would almost rather see sentries and some defensive positions, if only to confirm that they were in the right place. He checked the bio-readouts for his team; heart rates were almost settled, so he moved up from his crouch and made another run.

The teams split up now, filtering through the buildings in smaller groups, double-checking the drones' information as they went, bursting through doors and checking for concealed sentries.

They quickly made their way to the main building, coordinating their approach so that they hit both entrances at the same time. The building was squat and ugly, another bunker with a single storey above ground and more space below.

Marine X drew his standard-issue pistol and fitted a suppressor as Harrington reached for the door handle. Locked. Harrington made space for Fletcher, who pressed a mechanical pick against the handle. The machine buzzed briefly then the lock clicked open, and Fletcher stepped back. Warden shouldered his weapon and checked the grenade launcher. The silenced pistol would make short work of an unarmoured alien but wouldn't dent power armour.

The door came open at Harrington's touch to reveal a small room with a concrete staircase descending into the basement on the left and another set of doors opposite. To the right were benches and coats as well as breathing gear. Still no guards.

Warden wanted to check on Milton at the other end of the building, but she didn't need his help and wouldn't thank him for distracting her. Milton's target, the main entrance, had a door for workers and a large roller shutter for forklift access. No carbine fire, so no serious contact yet. Warden nodded to himself and signalled his team to move in.

Marine X, or Ten, as he was known to the Marines, slipped into the room. Four other Marines followed, silenced pistols at the ready, to clear the way as quietly as possible.

The plans suggested the lower floor was mostly storage, but Warden wasn't going to leave any part of the base unchecked, no matter how unlikely the enemy's presence. The colonists' inventory listed a workshop and dozens of containers full of solar panel spare parts and other equipment. That didn't mean the aliens hadn't barracked more soldiers down here or filled the place with weapons.

Marine X, Harrington and Fletcher headed down the staircase to the lower level as per the plan, so Warden ordered the bulk of the section forward. Lee and Campbell took the lead with their suppressed pistols at the ready. They were backed by colleagues carrying the more robust alien weapons. Two more quietly opened the doors and the lead Marines crept forward.

Like the offices at the hydroponics hall, the floor space was divided by thin partition walls, some of which had windows into corridors. There was an office area to their right, every wall of which was glazed along the upper half. No aliens to be seen, nothing to be heard.

Warden sent two Marines to check the offices. Lee and Campbell advanced down a corridor to the left and Warden hunkered down in the front room to watch the feed from their HUDs. They came to a windowed door and Lee risked a quick glance inside. A canteen.

Though Lee had only looked through the window for a fraction of a second, they replayed the video via the HUD. Three aliens were inside, two with wings eating at a table, the third at a coffee machine, waiting for it to dispense. It had scaly skin, completely different from the winged snipers'. None of them wore armour. Campbell sent a query to Warden.

The reply was a simple confirmation: <Execute>

Lee and Campbell opened the door and strode into the room bold as brass. Nothing flashy, nothing dramatic, not like in a movie. These soldiers weren't expecting an attack; they hadn't even posted guards.

The winged snipers barely had time to react before Lee's rounds punched into their skulls, one looking up in surprise over the slumping shoulder of his colleague before his head rocked back, shattered. The coffee-drinker slumped to the ground with two bullets in the spine and one in the back of the head. Warden nodded, grimly pleased. Textbook and swift.

He updated the kills on the HUD and sent a message to Milton. Her response showed her team on the north side of the bunker. They had found a barracks but no aliens and no sign that they had yet been detected.

Warden could imagine her contempt for their enemy's lax attitude. Not that anyone wanted a fair fight, but Milton would surely also be experiencing the strange mix of embarrassment and pity that

Warden felt. Then he shook his head. Bollocks to that; these bastards had invaded New Bristol and killed colonists and Marines alike. They deserved no sympathy.

Warden ordered Milton to hold as long as possible while his section made their way through this floor towards her and Marine X cleared the basement. Milton acknowledged while Warden checked in with Marine X, who merely confirmed they had found nothing of interest. They were heading towards the north wall where there was a staircase that would bring them out on the other side of the barracks area.

Warden updated the HUD and issued new orders. Section 1 would advance slowly and check each room, Marine X would come up from the basement, and together they would clear the barracks area after rendezvousing with Milton's section.

The bunker had multiple rooms, some small and private, some larger bunks. They were probably only used when the colonists were moving across New Bristol from site to site or doing a maintenance run. There hadn't been many people stationed here day to day as solar plants didn't need much care and attention.

Terraformers liked to build plenty of capacity into their infrastructure. When the terraforming was done, population growth would consume any surplus and if the weather or atmospheric conditions changed, it was always good to have a backup. Bunker-like storm shelters were also popular, as was excess capacity in everything from food production to sleeping quarters to energy plants.

Warden was ready to declare the area clear, already heading back to join his section, when a door opened and a huge alien stepped into the corridor. Eight feet tall, heavily muscled and with scales for skin, the thing had to duck its head to avoid the ceiling. It stood frozen for a moment, caught between Warden and the Marines, nobody able to shoot in the narrow corridor.

Then it roared and took a step towards the Marines. Warden charged, pistol discarded and knife out, reaching for the alien's head with one hand while the other swept round to chop out the beast's throat.

But the alien was fast, much faster than Warden would have believed possible. It whipped around and batted the knife away with one huge fist, then hurled the other at Warden's head. The lieutenant ducked, narrowly avoiding the blow, but the beast was canny and cool, and a heavy cross caught him across the jaw, knocking him back and messing with his vision. Before he could move, another blow caught him and sent him sprawling, sliding along the corridor on his back.

As he lay there, dazed and half-senseless, he heard a long series of sharp pops. Then the alien slumped back against the wall and slid to the floor.

The Marines hurried forward and Campbell helped Warden to his feet.

"You okay, sir? Ya took a couple of good shots to the bonce, there."

Warden shook his head, blinking as his vision cleared, then spat blood on the floor. Campbell pressed Warden's knife and pistol into his hands.

"Mebbe next time ya let us shoot the buggers first, eh, sir? Save the fisticuffs for when we get home."

The lieutenant nodded, rubbing his jaw.

Then the HUD lit up with a message from Milton.

<Contact>

8

Milton swore. Profusely. They had been approaching the barracks, as quiet as mice and as good as gold when it had all gone to shit. A squad of alien troopers had spewed from the room like a bad choice at a buffet. These ones wore body armour and they all carried the powerful rifles that seemed to be their main weapon. They might not all have shoes or trousers on, but that didn't mean they weren't a serious threat.

The Marines had been forced back, abandoning the forward positions in favour of not being cut to ribbons. Milton hunkered down behind a storage locker, hoping it didn't contain anything sensitive to high-velocity impacts. *Mustn't grumble,* she thought. The locker door was nice and flat, so at least her back was comfortable.

The corridor she was supposed to have taken, the one that was only inches past her left shoulder, was currently a horizontal hailstorm of death. That was a bit of a problem. She had to admit that they were in a spot of bother. Milton looked to her left, where Justine Barber was crouching on the other side of the corridor.

Barber let out a huge sigh as if to express just how bored she was at having to wait her turn. She put her rifle in her lap, drew a pistol, passed it into her left hand and twisted at the waist. The suppressor was attached and she poked the barrel around the corner and pulled the trigger, randomly returning fire until the magazine was empty. Barber looked up at Sergeant Milton and shrugged.

It was worth a try, Milton supposed. It was certainly better than sticking your head out. They were at a T-junction, and the wall opposite the corridor was thoroughly peppered with bullet holes. On the plus side, if the aliens kept up that rate of fire, they would have to run out of ammunition soon. Surely?

Milton switched her gaze to her HUD, checked the status of her team and noted that, although the aliens had surprised them, only a few had picked up flesh wounds. It wasn't her best day as a Commando but it could have been a whole lot more painful.

<What's the situation?> sent Warden, the text flowing into Milton's HUD.

<Bit of a pickle, sir. They pushed hard and we only got a couple before we had to fall back. The aliens have the better positions and an apparently unlimited supply of ammunition. Any chance you can lend a hand?> Milton replied via the HUD, flagging the problematic control points she needed to clear on the map.

<Let me check with my secretary; I'm not sure what's on today's calendar. Can I call you back after lunch?>

<I'd prefer it if you could make it a little earlier>

<Smoke me a kipper then and we'll see you for breakfast>

"The Lieutenant is on the way," said Milton to Barber and Mitchell, shouting to be heard over the din, "he wants smoked kippers for breakfast so let's stop buggering about, shall we?" Milton pulled a smoke grenade from her pouch. Barber copied her as Mitchell readied his rifle, standing up and turning to face the corridor.

Milton and Barber threw their grenades and a second later smoke began to pour into the corridor. Mitchell leaned around the corner, fired a couple of bursts into the smoke, then ducked back. *That should give the buggers something to think about while Warden brings his group to bear.*

Milton messaged the rest of her team, telling them to keep their heads down until backup arrived. Sporadic bursts of fire cracked nearby, but the aliens hadn't returned fire down the smoke-filled corridor yet. Maybe they were waiting for the smoke to clear.

Milton turned around to her right and inspected lockers on the wall. Access was by key card, so she tried the one she'd taken off the enemy. None of the locks responded so they were probably meant for specific personnel or roles like engineering crew. Her pistol didn't have any problems opening the lock, though. These weren't safes, after all.

Inside she found boxes of spare parts. Barber looked at her quizzically and fired a short burst down the corridor while Milton rooted around in the boxes. She found what she was looking for and crouched by the corner again, facing the corridor.

The object Milton lobbed sailed into the smoke and bounced across the floor. There was a break in the firing around them and they could hear it rolling down the corridor. They heard footsteps and a few thuds. Someone had hit the deck. Barber grinned at her and Milton winked. She waited a couple of seconds then threw another.

There was more frantic scrabbling from the far end of the corridor so she bounced the third off a wall, high up, hoping it would find an open doorway. More shouting and a burst of fire. She lobbed one more, but they were wise to the game, now, and instead of dodging away they simply fired back, shooting indiscriminately down the corridor.

The arrival of the fifth fake grenade must have caught them by surprise when it exploded in their midst. It certainly sounded like someone was in pain.

"Nice one, Sarge," Mitchell said with a grin and Barber gave a thumbs up. At least one enemy trooper was down, groaning at the end of the corridor. Milton lobbed a few more of her fake grenades then another smoke grenade. Then she hefted her rifle, listening for the sound of enemy movement.

At the other end of the barracks, Warden pulled the trigger and stitched a neat line across the exposed back of an alien trooper. He switched targets but the next one was already down, so he marked the point as safe on the HUD and saw that two more were already cleared.

<Milton, how are you doing?> he sent.

<We're all good, sir. Quieter here, now. They seem to have other things on their minds>

Warden checked the HUD, examining the positions of his troops and the enemy. The Marines now had the aliens boxed in on two sides now, but the barracks could hold, what, another dozen troops or so? They could press forward and find out the hard way, but that wasn't his only option.

<Are you in position?> he asked. The only response was an affirmative ping, the silent method used by commandos waiting stealthily to attack.

<Milton, it's time to invite our guests to the buffet. Let's make sure they get the message, in three, two, one>

Noise erupted around the barracks, as both Milton's team and Warden's directed fire at the points controlled by the aliens. Bursts of fire hammered the doors and hurtled down the corridors. No sane alien would poke its head out while that cacophony was going on.

Harrington and Fletcher advanced from the lower level, their guns trained on two targets. Marine X was between them, his attention on a third alien. All three of the enemy were shooting, their attention entirely on the hail of bullets that was suppressing them. Big mistake.

Marine X closed with his target, his hand clamping around the forehead and the blade of his knife sinking smoothly between the vertebrae in its neck. He wrenched the knife from side to side, completely severing the spinal column, then withdrew it.

On either side of him, there were soft coughs as Harrington and Fletcher discharged their responsibilities, their suppressed weapons inaudible over the exchanges of gunfire between the aliens and the Marines.

None of the aliens noticed until it was too late for them to react. The weapons of Marine X, Harrington and Fletcher dealt with five more enemy troopers before the aliens finally realised they were surrounded. Warden watched through his HUD and as soon as the aliens began to turn he ordered a full assault.

They all rushed forward, converging under cover of fire and overwhelming the remaining half-dozen aliens in seconds. A few additional shots were put into still thrashing bodies to make sure, and then there was deathly quiet. Warden stood breathing heavily for a few moments as he surveyed the scene and nodded in satisfaction.

"Commandos, log your kills, we need numbers," he ordered, and a steady flow of data began to come in via his HUD. Twenty-eight, in total, since entering the base.

Warden switched channels. <Overwatch, any activity> he sent <or any movement from the dropship?>

<No, sir. All quiet on the southern front. No sensor sweeps from the ship, engines are not powering up. The techs have got their main drones up, and there's nothing at the nearest outposts either> came the response from Wilson.

Warden acknowledged the updates and walked over to the barracks, issuing orders as he went.

<Overwatch, maintain alert and keep an eye on that dropship. Anyone with alien hardware, get yourselves into cover as close to the dropship as possible. We need to breach it as soon as we can, and I don't want any surprises coming out of it>

Warden surveyed the carnage in the barracks room. Maybe the aliens were nocturnal? They might come from a planet with a hostile daylight environment or predators. Or a variety of planets, perhaps. He'd spotted at least four types of aliens so far.

"Check the lockers, search the bodies. We're looking for their dropship pilots so we can find their access cards or whatever they use," he barked to the commandos standing around in the barracks.

Milton issued the same order to those near the individual bedrooms: look for a pilot or officers, bring everything you find back to the barracks room for sorting.

"Marine X – did you find an armoury downstairs by any chance? I don't see anything but personal weapons up here," Warden asked.

Ten grinned broadly. "Yes, sir. Want me to show you?"

He nodded and followed the Marine down the nearby staircase, signalling a few nearby commandos to join them.

"You might want to get someone to count the dead down here, sir," Ten said as they descended the staircase.

"What? I didn't hear anything. How many was it and why didn't you say before now?"

"I kept it quiet, as ordered, sir. That's what you pay me for," replied the unrepentant Marine.

"Point of fact, Marine X," said Warden pointedly, "you're still serving at Her Majesty's pleasure for that incident on Arcturus 4, so you're not being paid at all. You have to complete another four deployments before you earn a salary again."

Marine X shrugged as if it wasn't a big deal. "True," he conceded. "And I didn't log the kills, too busy. Sorry, sir," he added, not looking even slightly sorry.

"Use your bloody HUD next time," snapped Warden, "that's what it's for and you might have needed more backup," he said, trying to get the Marine to understand. Marine X might be serving a penal sentence for his earlier breaches of military conduct but he was still a valuable commando.

Aside from discipline issues, Marine X was probably the most skilled and dangerous commando in Captain Atticus's command, maybe even the battalion. But that didn't explain why he had been deployed to the front line instead of serving out his sentence somewhere safe and boring. Warden shook his head. Marine X was an enigma for another day.

Besides, in this situation, Warden couldn't afford to lose any Marines early, certainly not before they had an active cloning bay again. He doubted his point would make it into Ten's brain, though. The man was incorrigible. Warden had heard that the only person who had been killed more times in action was Captain Atticus himself.

"Sorry, sir. Harrington and Fletcher can count them, though. They went past the ones I found when they joined me on the staircase, so they know where all the bodies are," said Ten cheerfully.

"They weren't with you? They were your backup!" Warden snapped again, now thoroughly pissed off.

"I told them to hang back and cover me. No point risking them if I ran across any problems."

Warden sighed. There were good reasons why Ten was an administrative and disciplinary nightmare but you couldn't argue with his demonstrable and obvious bravery. The man would much rather die himself than let a fellow Marine take a fatality.

Warden made a note in his HUD to review the Marine's progress through this ground floor later. In most cases, commanders didn't have the time or need to review individual troopers' feeds. Penal Marine X's videos, however, were always educational and Warden wasn't afraid to admit that he could learn from them and improve his future performance.

"Here it is, sir," said Ten, pointing to a large storage cage. There were two dead aliens outside it. One was in fairly normal body armour and had been carrying what Warden was fairly sure was one of the combat shotguns they had tested earlier. Its head lolled at an obscene angle, a huge gash across its throat. Any more and it would have been decapitated.

The other was more of a surprise. It was wearing power armour. Warden looked at it, then glanced at Marine X, who wore a beatific expression that seemed to say, 'Who, sir? Me, sir? I ain't done nuffin.' He could almost hear it in Ten's south London accent. Clearly, he should have called for backup to deal with this target as he wasn't carrying anything that should have been used to engage a trooper in powered armour except grenades.

"Why didn't you request backup or use a grenade?" Warden asked incredulously. If he hadn't seen the psychologists reports, he would have thought the man insane.

Ten shrugged again. "Looked like this was their armoury, sir. Didn't think you'd want me to destroy any of their weapons, what with us not having anything that's much use."

Warden looked at the corpse again. He wasn't even going to ask how Marine X had managed it; he'd just watch the HUD feed later.

Milton isn't going to believe this, he thought.

Ten dragged the smaller alien away from the storage cage door so that it could open fully. It hung ajar, a broken lock dangling from the bolt. Warden went inside and looked around. The space was large, about the size of a standard shipping container.

There were several large crates secured with electronic locks and the shelves had been neatly stacked with small arms. He nodded thoughtfully; there was probably enough in here to equip all the remaining men and women of the commando with the aliens' superior weapons.

He inspected the lock on one of the crates then turned back to Ten who was kneeling by the heavily armoured alien, rifling through its pouches. He found something and held it up with a triumphant grin, standing and walking to the doorway to toss it to Warden.

A key card, alien in appearance but entirely the same concept they used on their restricted munitions. If you broke open a crate of RMSC grenade launchers, explosive charges would destroy the contents and put you at considerable risk. It wouldn't surprise him if the aliens took similar measures and, if their technology had developed based on that found on a Lost Ark ship, it might be identical.

Warden wasn't a historian, so he had no idea if self-destruct protocols were in use during the period of the Lost Ark missions. They didn't even know which ship these aliens had encountered; it could have been one of the first lost or the most recent.

He motioned for Marine X to stand back, just in case there were any additional security measures and using the card went wrong, then he waved the key card in front of the dull, red lock on the case. It went green, and there was a series of pops and clicks as the locks opened. Gingerly, he lifted the lid, as if gentleness itself might stop it exploding.

The crate contained three of the huge combat shotguns.

"What do you think, Marine X – useful for boarding their dropship?"

"Works for me, but I wouldn't use them around any engineering equipment or the bridge."

"Worried something might explode?"

"No, I just assumed you wanted the dropship intact so we could get to the ship in orbit and deal with it, sir."

Warden stared at him for a moment. *Shit,* he thought. He hadn't thought that far ahead. The aliens must have a ship in orbit and he had no idea what its capabilities were or what sort of threat it posed. The aliens' weapons and armour were recognisable but significantly different to models from Sol and its colonies. The dropship itself looked substantially different and what did that say about the rest of their fleet?

What would their orbital ship be like? Did it have orbital bombardment capacity or was it a troop carrier? Was it a scout ship or a battleship, or maybe a capital ship? It could even be based on an Ark ship; the earliest models had hangar bays for launching smaller craft like this dropship. Some orbital ships could land planetside but most used shuttles and dropships to deploy personnel and equipment, whether military or civilian.

"Shit," muttered Warden. They couldn't leave the damned thing up there; it could launch a second invasion or, worse, simply bombard the planet from orbit. Marine X was right; they had to take the dropship intact and get into orbit as soon as possible.

"Yes, well, if we can work out how to pilot it, you're right," Warden said.

"Probably got an autopilot for returning to the ship, unless we're deeply unlucky."

Warden nodded, setting the question to one side. "Right, help me open up the rest of these crates. We need to know what's worth taking up and what we should leave here."

"Right ho, sir."

They set about counting the weapons and classifying them, entering them into the HUD to create an updated list of all weapons and munitions available to the local RMSC. The Marines' weapons all reported ammunition usage so that commanders could monitor their units' combat readiness. A warning would pop up in a Marine's

HUD when they hit key stages, such as a 50% ammunition depletion or exhaustion of all anti-aircraft rockets.

The alien weapons wouldn't feed data back to the Marines but, long ago, some bright young HUD interface designer had decided the commandos might need to avail themselves of captured weapons to continue fighting. As a result, the facility to manually record data had been in the HUD since before Warden joined up.

They'd gained some more grenade launchers, a couple of rocket launchers that he guessed were for anti-aircraft use and some more sniper rifles, both standard and railgun. They wouldn't take the latter because railguns could easily open a ship to vacuum if you found the right spot; grenades and rocket launchers were similarly problematic.

Fortunately, they also found plenty of combat rifles, which would be far more effective than the Marines' standard carbines, especially if they encountered heavy resistance from powered armour.

"Need a really big knife?" Warden said, holding up an enormous alien combat knife as he turned to show it to Marine X.

Ten grinned and produced an identical knife with a flourish that made it materialize in his fist as if plucked from this air. "Already found 'em, sir."

"Ohhh-kay," Warden replied, "you don't think they're a bit much, maybe?"

"Yeah, bigger than you really need, but flip the thumb switch and give it a go," said Ten with a glint in his eye.

Thumb switch? Warden looked down at the knife and saw a depression under the hilt, cunningly concealed by the metal of the cross guard so you couldn't accidentally activate it. He held the knife up and pushed his thumb into the button. Immediately the knife began to hum and gently vibrate, shimmering faintly in the dim light of the cage.

"Hmmm. Well, that's a new one on me. Worked out what it does yet?" Warden asked.

Ten nodded and pointed at the side of the cage to Warden's left. There was a neat circular hole as if someone had cut through the wire of the cage and one of the metal supports with an arc welder.

Warden stepped over and put the edge of the knife against the wire; it parted as easily as you'd slice a tomato. The knife barely slowed as he dragged it through the solid steel frame of the cage.

"It only stays on as long as you keep your thumb in the hole," explained Ten. "A dead man's handle in case you drop it on your leg while it's still buzzing. It's bloody useless if you're trying to creep up on a sentry, but with one of these you could make short work of him, even if he was in power armour."

At that comment, Warden looked back at the box he'd pulled the knife from. There were three empty slots, so it looked like Ten hadn't got his knife in time to use it on the sentries outside. And he had taken two, for some reason. Warden sighed, but if anyone was going to find a use for two huge knives that could cut through power armour, it would be Marine X. Warden decided to leave him to it as long as he didn't catch him playing around with it in the company mess.

"Find anything else we might want for the boarding party?" Warden asked.

"Yeah. Have a butcher's at these," said Ten, pointing to a medium-sized crate he'd opened.

It was full of large pistols with long, thick barrels. Warden picked one up and ejected the magazine. Unloaded, as you would hope. They checked the shelves and found the bullets that fit the weapon.

The grip seemed to fit his hand reasonably well, and he aimed it, squeezing the trigger until it discharged a round. The flak armoured alien corpse bucked with the impact. The gun was remarkably quiet, which meant it had a high-quality suppression system as well as subsonic ammunition.

"Nice," he said, passing the weapon to Ten who promptly fired a couple more shots into each alien.

"Yeah, not much cop against the power armour, but they're better than our pistols all the same," Ten shrugged, "and if you're hoping to take the orbital ship against superior numbers, these would help to start things quietly."

"Okay, let's get everything upstairs and get this assault underway. I don't want to hang about here longer than necessary," Warden ordered. He told Milton to send down some more bodies so they could get their haul up top quickly. The goods elevators were still working so it didn't take long to move the weapons and begin distributing them to the eager Marines.

"New plan," Warden said to Milton before outlining his concerns about a ship in orbit. The sergeant listened impassively then nodded.

"Makes sense," she admitted, although it was clear she didn't really like the plan. "How do you want to do it?"

"Dropship first," said Warden as they watched the alien weapons being distributed.

There was still no sign of life in the enemy dropship; it was entirely possible that there weren't any personnel aboard to guard it, but they wouldn't be taking any risks. Milton had found two aliens whose lockers had held what appeared to be flight suits. They had key cards and their personal weapons were pistols. The fact they had been assigned individual bedrooms and appeared to be officers strongly supported the conclusion that they were the dropship's flight crew.

They were ready. Warden gave the signal and the team loped across the open ground to the dropship.

He leaned against the outer hull, near what looked like the main door. It had been agreed that Marine X would lead the breaching party, a small group of Marines who had all taken the specialist courses in stealth operations. Marine X had served long enough that he had done most of the courses available at one time or another, but the younger recruits were always more specialised.

Warden glanced once more at Milton and the other NCOs. No sign of doubt in their eyes.

"Breach!" he ordered.

9

Ten had strapped one of the alien knives to his chest for easy access. It was ungainly but the ability to penetrate armour was a significant advantage over his standard-issue Fairbairn-Sykes commando dagger. He also carried two of the alien pistols and a number of flashbang grenades. He took a deep breath and nodded at Fletcher, who swiped the pilot's access card over the lock. It went green, and the doors at the top of the ramp slipped noiselessly into the walls.

There was no ambush waiting for them, just a typical loading bay. A small all-terrain vehicle sat on the floor with a few lockers and storage cages but there were no enemy personnel or automated defences to be seen.

Ten climbed the ramp, a pistol in each hand, checking the bay properly before signalling his team. He made his way to the personnel door and looked around. Some ships had maps at important junctions to help visitors, but he hadn't really expected them on an invading dropship. *Pity*, he thought, *would have been handy.*

Their goal was to neutralise the crew as quickly as possible. They might not know the internal layout of the dropship but they knew where the entrances, engines and cockpit were. The ramp had come down facing the nose of the ship, and the cockpit was somewhere above and behind them as a result. There were two more ramps on the port and starboard side of the ship, further back towards the engines.

As the pilots were dead, the cockpit was probably empty but two Marines were tasked to clear it anyway while the rest headed for the central area of the ship. They planned to dominate each junction and clear every space they passed, looking for crew quarters, engineering section and the mess hall – the most likely places to find the crew.

Ten didn't really know why ships had engineering sections. It seemed redundant since aside from pilots, weapons crew and medics, almost everyone on a ship of any size was an engineer, mechanic or technician of some sort. They were the majority of the crew, so they were everywhere.

Still, as soon as a ship got large enough, there was always a section that was referred to as 'engineering' and that usually held only an array of displays and chairs, much like every other position on the ship. Only the very largest ships could support an actual engineering bay for producing spare parts and repairing portable systems. Smaller ships simply carried a few spares for emergency replacements.

Yet since the crews who maintained the ships tended to hold affection for them, it was likely that the aliens had left some personnel on the ship rather than taking everyone to the solar plant.

The ramp access room's only personnel exit faced away from the cockpit. There was also a goods lift that went up to the next deck. Ten elected to take the lift, on his own, and start clearing the next deck. As soon as they had cleared the front of the ship, Warden would move the rest of the force into position and storm the ship, should a firefight ensue.

Ten got into the lift, located the control and signalled the rest of his team to proceed. As they flowed silently into the next room, Ten pressed the button and the lift smoothly ascended one deck. He found himself in a large room similar to the ramp room but with displays on each wall and a series of desks and chairs before each display. There was a command chair in the middle, but all the seats were empty.

"Like the bloody *Mary Celeste*," muttered Ten as he looked around.

This was a tactical room for directing ground forces rather than ship-to-ship combat. Each display showed a different view of New Bristol. Some were showing feeds from orbit, so either the aliens had more ships or they had left satellites in geostationary orbit. Ten pinged that information to Warden. The Marines might not be able to scan objects in orbit at the moment, but this was exactly the sort of information that would keep Warden off his back while he got on with the real work.

None of the displays showed the ship's interior and Ten was no technical specialist. He could pilot a drone, in a pinch, but the specialists who knew him would never have offered him their kit. *Probably worried I'd break their toys*, he thought. Playing with the controls seemed like an easy way to disclose his presence on the dropship to the crew or the ships in orbit, so instead he concentrated on his core skillset – sneaking around and killing things.

The TacRoom had three exits: port, starboard and toward the engines. He went through the nearest exit on the port side. He was fine with port and starboard; it was planetside and orbit that got confusing. Planetside could be the top of the ship or the bottom, depending on the ship's orientation; it changed if the ship moved.

For now, though, up and down were fine, and there weren't any Naval crew around to give him grief about his sense of direction in space. They always seemed to know which way the planets were, though he was buggered if he could work out how. He'd been in the brig more than once after explaining to some gobby rating or other how little he cared about the matter.

Ten opened the door and checked to his right. Nothing but an empty wall, as he had expected. The front of the dropship was sloped, so this upper deck ended further back on the ship than the lower one which held the cockpit. The left was clear and he padded down it, focussing on the slightest sound that might give away an enemy presence. Past the TacRoom was a door on the left. No window.

Ten eased the handle down and stepped into the room. It was pitch black, but a dim light came on the moment the door opened more than a crack. At first, he started, thinking there might be someone in there, but it was a small, empty cabin. Clearly a space for an officer with an automatic light.

The corridor ran along the inside of the hull so there were no rooms on the port side. He had two more doors to check before he reached the end of this section. More empty cabins. At the corner, he thought he heard a noise. Crouched, he tried to relax, ready to spring into action.

He gave it thirty seconds but nothing came around the corner, so he raised his weapon and leant out to peer into the next corridor. Nothing. The short length of corridor was an empty T-junction, leading aft and across to the cabins on the starboard side of this deck. There was no sign of anyone to aft when he rounded that corner either.

Ten was in the zone, aware of everything around him and moving like a buttered cat, alert to any noise and ready for action. He checked the cabins, still searching for crew members. The first was empty and he was moving faster now, taking more risks. If the rooms were empty, noise hardly mattered; if they were occupied, even the quietest opening of the door would give him away. The second cabin was also empty.

The last door opened before he could reach it. An alien stuck its head out and looked aft.

Mistake, thought Ten with a wicked grin. *I'm behind you.*

He fired two rounds into the back of the alien's skull, and it crumpled to the ground. Dirty overalls and a data slate marked it as an engineer and something about the form seemed feminine. Ten gritted his teeth. He preferred not to kill women, but this was an invasion force and, male or female, they had come looking for him.

Still, he wasn't likely to tell anyone at a family get-together about this not-so-glorious moment. Someone always wanted to know why he didn't simply knock out the bad guys and arrest them as if he were some kind of intergalactic policeman. Perhaps he should use some kind of multi-purpose sonic device to incapacitate them before delivering a stern lecture about modern ethical standards.

He headed aft, following the short corridor between two food storage rooms. He took a guess at the next space and was proved right, a mess hall. Nothing large, nothing fancy. You kept things simple if you didn't want crockery flying around when the ship manoeuvred near a planet. Or, of course, when your dropship went through re-entry.

His musings were abruptly interrupted by the two aliens in coveralls who were waiting for him. They looked up as he entered, bearing expressions that went quickly from puzzled, to surprised, to terrified as they realised he wasn't the colleague who'd just gone to its room, he wasn't their species, and he was aiming a weapon at them. The gun spat six times, and he had loaded a new magazine before they finished slumping to the table they'd been eating at.

Where there's a mess, there's a galley, and, sure enough, there was a hatch in the opposite wall. Ten checked it, but there was no sign of a cook. He passed through the only door out of the mess and checked the galley. Empty. On a ship this size, the crew probably just heated their own meals and the troops weren't on it long enough to care.

There were toilet facilities next door and then another goods lift with a ladder next to it. Ten liked ladders; they were silent, they never failed, and they were easy to use in zero-g. Ten sent an update to the rest of his team then took the lift, since the crew wouldn't be surprised when it moved.

Most of the ship was empty, just the engine compartment left to clear. The team had killed two more of the engineering crew and managed to do it silently.

Ten reached the lower deck as the rest of the team came around the corner. They flowed through the two doors, half a team to each, without stopping to greet him. Ten following along behind.

The first room was somewhat unexpected. Large and almost the width of the ship, there were exits to the boarding ramps on either side. More surprising were the pods that lined the fore and aft walls. None of them had expected that.

They also hadn't really expected four power-armoured enemy troopers. The first Marine through each door was riddled with bullets the moment they reached the centre of the room. The rest dived for cover.

Bringing up the rear on the starboard side, Ten saw the hitherto successful mission collapse into pandemonium. The first Marine from his group was pummelled to the ground by shots that struck between his shoulder blades, punched through his chest and ruined the decking below. He was dead before he knew what hit him.

Ten knew, though. The room was almost double height and above the doors was a balcony. The enemy were up there, and they had battle rifles. While his team dived for cover and desperately searched for the source of the shots, Ten dashed to his left and up the steep metal staircase to the balcony, yanking two grenades from his webbing as he went.

Halfway up the stairs, he lobbed the grenades onto the balcony then crouched and waited, eyes closed. The grenades detonated with a deafening crack and what would have been a blinding flash if he hadn't been prepared for it.

He dashed up the remaining steps, spinning as he did and twitching the trigger of his pistol. His ears were ringing, and his shots were wild, but he emptied the magazine, steadying his aim as he moved. Press the enemy hard, when they least expect it. Soldiers don't expect to meet an enemy who simply charges them head on, bringing the fight right to them.

So that's what Ten did.

The first alien, shocked by the flashbangs and the shots ringing from its armour, hunched back as if it were seriously threatened. Maybe it was hurt. More likely it was only disoriented, stunned by the grenades and surprised by the pistol rounds striking its armour.

Ten dropped his pistol, drew both knives and thumbed the mechanisms. They purred to life and he slashed them at the alien's chest, left then right. The blades skittered across the armour, screeching and jumping as the alien tried to stumble clear of its attacker. Closer now, inside the alien's reach, Ten struck again. A blade bit home, driving through a weak point in the armpit, and the monster roared in pain. Ten twisted the handle, hands suddenly wet with blood.

The other knife slammed into the alien's hip joint, an instinctive strike that would have been fatal to a human. Ten pushed hard, both knives twisting as he drove the alien back. It fell, screaming behind its mask, and Ten let it go, the blades still in place. He caught the alien's rifle as it fell and spun it round, shouldering it smoothly as he dropped to one knee. The aliens were recovering, the effects of the grenades already fading, but they were slow, far too slow.

Ten's grin was manic as the rifle bucked against his shoulder. He gritted his teeth, muscles straining to keep the muzzle climb under control. He forced the gun down, fighting for control, envious of the aliens in their servo-assisted powered-armour. And then the second alien's faceplate collapsed and the head disappeared, blown away by the relentless attack.

But it had taken too long. The two aliens on the other side of the bay turned towards him and all he could do was move. He grabbed the collar of the alien who was busy dying from knife wounds and dragged it upright. Crouched behind the power armour as bullets began to slam into the back of the suit, Ten snatched something from the alien's belt with a feral grin.

A second later, the alien grenade exploded, and he was punched backwards, the power armour collapsing on top of him. He ripped the shattered HUD from his eyes, rolled the alien off him and grabbed the rifle. Lying on his back, he fired bursts into the heads of the remaining aliens as they tried to regain their feet.

The rifle clicked, magazine exhausted, and suddenly the only sound was a sort of wordless scream. Ten drew breath and realised it was him screaming. The aliens were gone, their shattered bodies sprawled across the walkways, and he was alone in a room full of corpses.

For a moment he lay there, breathing heavily, the rifle's smoking barrel resting on his boots. Then he kicked himself to his feet and grabbed a knife. Powered armour didn't always need a living host and Ten didn't fancy being killed by some keyboard jockey with a fetish for remote murder. The blade made short work of the suits' controls, sparks flying as he jammed it home.

Then he slumped down on the nearest armour corpse as the adrenaline drained away. What he really wanted now was a good cuppa. Small chance of that here. He found a bottle of water on the floor, but it wasn't really the same.

10

W arden's eyes narrowed as he surveyed the carnage, a sure sign that he wanted to swear. Five Marines dead, three wounded so severely that they'd be little use for days or even weeks, several others carrying minor injuries. They had captured the solar farm and the ship, it was true, but the cost had been high.

His HUD flashed a clear signal. The overwatch team hadn't seen any more movement and were heading over in the rovers. He acknowledged it with a glance, confirming their update was read and understood.

Warden turned his attention to the damage that Marine X had caused with grenades and heavy gunfire. No hull ruptures, it seemed, but one end of the balcony had been destroyed, and twisted metal blocked the port door. Other than that, the damage appeared to be cosmetic and there was no reason to think the ship wasn't spaceworthy. He sent Patel to the other side to see if the blocked door still worked.

Then he turned to the elephant in the room, namely the pods that had surprised the boarding party. He walked over to one and peered through the glass cover. Inside, a winged alien floated in a thick, translucent gel. There were sixteen pods in total, all occupied.

Two held enormous hulking brutes like the one they had killed in the base.

He turned to Milton. "They're clones. The bloody aliens are using our own bloody cloning tech against us. They must have captured military files on the Ark ship; these are definitely mil-tech clones."

"Yes, sir. Not the same as ours, though. Look at all the scales and the strange eyes. Our geneticists don't do things like that; they keep even the mil-tech clones as close to human as possible. Wings notwithstanding, of course," said Milton.

Warden closes his eyes for a moment, taking deep breaths and contemplating their next steps. Then he snapped back, alert and confident.

"Right, I want the casualties off the ship, and the rovers stowed somewhere safe. If we make it back, we'll land here and drive back to Ashton. Make sure the drivers have weapons, plenty of munitions and that they stay out of sight until we return. Get the techs working on the ship. If they can't get it flying, everything else we do here is a waste of time."

"Roger that," Milton replied.

"Marine X, get your arse down here," he bellowed. "Sergeant Milton, take a team through the ship again and make sure every single compartment is double checked. I don't want to be surprised by these things," he said, pointing at a pod that contained an alien clone that appeared to be the pilot or officer class.

"Then a weapons check. Reload magazines, search the ship for anything we can add to our armoury," he said, turning to Ten who had dropped down from the balcony.

"Prep for low-pressure boarding. Take half a squad and ransack the stores. Find any breathing apparatus or environment suits and bring them here," he turned again as Ten peeled off, "someone get this ramp down, and the rest of you, bring the arsenal aboard." He paused to look at his team then he clapped his hands. "Hop to it, people."

He paced around the room, looking at the controls and checking the systems. It was pretty familiar stuff but it seemed strange, outdated even.

Tech from an ancient Ark, he thought, centuries old.

He flipped up a cover and pressed the button it concealed. Warning beeps sounded, and lights appeared on the floors of the loading bays. Launch chairs rose from the floor space on both sides of the cloning bay. There were enough for more troops than would be deployed in one round of cloning. It made it easy to retrieve any planetside troops, even if more than one round of clones had been decanted during a mission.

Warden looked around as everyone got on with their assigned tasks. He assumed the dropship would navigate itself to the alien vessel and land in an enclosed bay. Low-pressure boardings were dangerous but he hoped it wouldn't be necessary.

Even if they didn't need to breach the outer hull of the ship, there was still a question over the alien's air. Just because they could breathe the air on New Bristol didn't mean the Marines would be able to breathe on the ship. Any difference in the gas mixture could cause problems, so he wanted to be sure that everyone had a reliable air supply for their breathing masks.

And he needed an option of last resort. That the aliens had clones altered everything. Every soldier they'd killed on New Bristol would be backed up, probably to the vessel in orbit. How long till they were decanted into new bodies and dropped back to the surface? Even if they didn't have cloning bays as part of the vessel, they might have more dropships. How many, he wondered, and how fast would they move?

He scratched his head and sighed as he walked into the cockpit. If his tech specialists couldn't get this thing in the air, they would need a new plan, fast.

Richardson looked up as he entered the cockpit. "Good news, sir. The ship's systems are intact. The aliens have things arranged just like we do in our own ships. Good job they stole our technology, I suppose. It looks like they haven't really changed everything. I reckon if we pulled the panels off, some of the circuits would be exactly as they were when they were designed."

"Great. Can you pilot it without knowing their language?"

"Don't need to, sir. Just need to identify the auto-pilot. The drop-ship will get us back to their ship on its own. I think we can work out the necessary basics in maybe ten more minutes? Just don't ask us to get into a dogfight, not that I imagine this crate has any weaponry to speak of. If they haven't changed basic cockpit layout, they probably won't have changed that either."

"Is there any way to tell how many dropships they have on their ship?" asked Warden hopefully.

"Not really, sir. If we spoke their language we could probably bring up an inventory, but that's about it," Richardson said apologetically.

"It'll be at least three," murmured Barlow. He cautiously pressed a button, then quickly pressed it again when the lighting panel above his head went out.

Warden and Richardson looked at him. He didn't seem to notice their stares. Warden coughed. "Would you care to explain, Corporal?"

Barlow looked up. "Hmm? Oh well, it's elementary really. This ship is the Something in Alien Three. So there must be at least two more dropships aboard the vessel unless they have really odd naming schemes."

"How do you know it's three?" asked Warden.

"It's written on the side of the ship. Also, on this panel here," Barlow said, pointing to a plaque with a series of symbols on the overhead bank of panels in front of the pilot's chairs.

"Yes, okay," said Warden slowly, as he contemplated the squiggles and dots which could have been an ancient Earth language for all the good it did him, "but how do you know that says that this is ship number three?"

"This bit," said Barlow pointing, "is the same as the bit on the third pod from the left on the fore and aft side of the clone bay. So my conclusion is it's their glyph for 'three'. Look, it's here on this button too," he said pointing to a button on the console, "so these buttons are probably two and four."

Warden looked as directed. Barlow had a gift for noticing these things and Warden couldn't fault his logic.

"I see. So at the very least they have two more dropships, which means at least thirty-two clones available to them, plus whatever crew or active troops are left on the mothership. If they have four dropships for a nice even number, they have forty-eight clones, ready to be deployed," said Warden. He slumped a little in his chair, thinking.

"How long would it take to decant an alien clone?"

Both techs shrugged. "No idea, sir. Probably about the same as ours, although they don't have to inject brain patterns via wormhole here. Corporal Wilson might know more."

"Right," said Warden, standing up decisively, "get this thing ready to fly as quickly as possible. If there's even a slim chance we can dock with the ship in orbit and complete the assault before they decant more clones, we need to take it. Every minute we waste here could make our task up there much more difficult."

"Yes, sir. One working dropship, coming right up."

11

Warden gritted his teeth as the acceleration of the dropship pushed him into the seat. The flight had started easily, like an ordinary aeroplane, but the ship had climbed quickly before standing on its tail to point straight up. And then the main engines had fired, rocketing the vessel towards escape velocity.

It took only twenty seconds or so to leave behind the atmosphere of the planet and reach the edge of space, but the g-force was extraordinary and, to Warden, it felt like it went on for hours.

Then it was over and, just like that, they were free of the planet's grip and on their way to orbit. The transition from the daylight of the atmosphere to the night-time environment of planetary orbit was stark and sudden, like turning off a light.

Warden had clipped his HUD to his belt for the launch. Richardson's jury-rigged countdown played through the ship's speakers so the Marines would know when main acceleration was coming and when they'd get the relief of it ending. Ten minutes was a good rule of thumb for this type of flight.

It was a desperate mission. Even at full strength, the risks would have been high. With A Troop depleted, no Command team and large parts of Section 3 currently dead, the attack was truly a forlorn hope. What they really needed was time. And B Troop, thought Warden, denied action by the destruction of the second cloning bay, to say nothing of C Troop, who were safely at home enjoying the luck of the draw.

Warden grinned grimly. C Troop would be doing more than the normal amount of cleanup and physical training at the moment. They'd 'won' the deployment lottery and been left back at base, but they would be working just as hard as A Troop, albeit with less risk of a gruesome death under an alien sky.

The pre-launch briefing had been short and the questions few. Now they flew in silence, HUDs off, weapons locked down, everyone focusing on what was to come.

Why were HUDs off for launch? Warden couldn't remember, but maybe it was something to do with safety. Black eyes, maybe? He shook his head; it didn't matter, the standing order was to launch with HUDs stowed.

In free fall, though, HUDs were safe, and Warden slipped his back on. The command panel he would have had on an RMSC drop-ship was absent, so he patched through to the pilot's view.

There was a moment of disorientation as he tried to work out what he was seeing. Then the grey, almost featureless, slab of the ship in front of them slid open to expose a docking bay.

"It's big," muttered Warden, surprised despite his long-nurtured cynicism, "very big." Around him, he could see that the Marines were similarly awed, all watching the pilot's feed.

"How does it look?" Warden asked.

"Coming on nice, sir," said Richardson. "Thrusters firing, nothing to do up here but watch. Very dull."

"Good, let's hope it stays that way."

In the last five decades, there had never been a need to breach an enemy ship, certainly not while under fire. The Marines were trained for it, of course, but they didn't have the kit. Their only option was to dock and if the alien ship took action against them, their assault would be over before it had properly started.

Warden looked around at the Marines of A Troop.

"Thirty seconds," said Richardson. "Matching velocities."

The thrusters fired again, more violently this time as the ship moved in towards its hanger.

"Weapons ready," ordered Warden as they passed into the shadow of the great ship and the thrusters fired again, slowing them still further. There was a ripple of movement amongst the Marines as they checked their weapons and kit one last time.

Then the view changed as they passed into the hanger. A clang reverberated through the hull, and everyone jumped.

"Docking complete," reported Richardson, "outer door closed, atmosphere coming in." And gravity, which returned with a welcome thump when the ship stopped moving, pushing everyone firmly into their seats.

Warden sent a command via the HUD for everyone to don their breathers until they could check the atmosphere against human tolerances. Pre-launch, he and Milton had made sure everyone understood to keep their breathers on until they were out of the hangar, as that would be the most easily vented compartment should any of the crew realise what was going on.

"Almost there," said Richardson, voice tense. "Ten seconds till doors open."

The commandos unstrapped and stood, checking weapons and lining up on the exit ramps.

"Doors open in three, two, one," said Richardson, punching the door control.

The Marines pounded down the ramps and sprinted for the exits, gathering in teams around each doorway. With the access cards retrieved from the dropship troops, they opened three doors simulta-neously. Marine X and Warden's best-trained stealth troops slipped through the doors and moved into the giant ship to begin clearing the area.

Micro-drones followed, tracking each team so the rest of the Marines could follow closely behind without giving away their pres-ence. Richardson stayed in the dropship, locking herself in and prepping for launch in case they had to evacuate early, although nobody really expected that to be a survivable experience.

Warden looked around before he left the room, found a storage locker that Richardson could see from the cockpit and dumped a bag in it. He saw Richardson hold up a small object in her hand and nod at him through the cockpit window. Warden nodded to her. If it all went to hell, Richardson had orders to launch the dropship and press the detonator before returning planetside.

Warden went through the door, following Marine X's team and waiting for something to give them away and sound the alarm.

12

Marine X had killed two aliens so far, taking them down before they knew he was there. Now he moved, unseen and silent, checking for movement as his team tidied up behind him and checked the rooms he'd skipped.

At the end of the corridor, his way was blocked by a bulkhead door. A quick glance through the porthole revealed an engineering bay. No sign of movement.

He opened the door and stepped inside. The room was long and closed off at the other end; this was the only entrance he could see. There was nobody around. He paced down the room slowly. He was on the port side of the vessel and heavy equipment was stacked against the exterior bulkhead. Guns, he decided; these were gun emplacements, and this was the servicing bay.

The huge room was open, but there were bulkheads between each gun that could be sealed if there was a breach. Damaged cannons could be easily accessed for repair or isolation and containment. There wasn't likely to be anyone in here, so he picked up his pace and jogged to the other end of the bay. Better to move quickly than risk getting sealed behind bulkheads and exposed to vacuum.

But the room was clear and he walked back down the bay,

reloading his weapon and updating the map for the rest of the troop as he went.

So far, the ship was symmetrical, which was hardly surprising. Most starships' layouts were designed to be easily understood, even in pitch blackness. Areas were repeated and identical apart from markings to show where you were in the ship. The weapons bay had glyphs near the doors and on each cannon, and though he couldn't read them, he knew they would tell the crew exactly where they were on the ship. He marked the room clear, glanced to the right where his team were catching up, then moved to the next door.

There was a thick transparent panel in the upper half of the door, and he tilted his head forward to glance through it. A barracks room with rows of sleeping compartments against the walls and in the middle of the room, four high, stretching from floor to ceiling.

Each bay was sealed with an opaque shutter. If the artificial gravity failed, which wasn't unlikely in an emergency, waking up to find that you were falling towards the middle of the room was not helpful. Better to be safely sealed in your sleeping pod. But that meant he couldn't see whether the compartments were occupied.

He paused for a few seconds, peering along the corridor between the pods, but no enemy personnel were visible.

Ten motioned for his team to join him and opened the door, sliding inside to check the first compartment. The translucent panel opened at his touch and revealed an empty bed. He checked two more compartments, both empty, before his team arrived and began clearing the other side of the room.

The fourth compartment was occupied, and Ten swiftly folded the pillow towards the head, jammed the barrel of his pistol into it and fired. There was a wet crunching sound, but the foam further muffled the noise of his already suppressed pistol. In a chamber like this, even a quiet weapon was loud enough to wake the enemy.

He heard a couple of dull shots behind him as the team dealt with more of the enemy. Another compartment, another swift execution, but their luck wouldn't hold much longer.

In the next compartment, the occupant was already moving as Ten reached for the pillow. He cursed under his breath as the intended victim turned its head towards him and the eyes flicked open, widening in panic.

Ten fired but the alien was already moving. It shifted quickly, trying to sit up and twist out of the sleeping chamber. The shot went wide, thudding into the mattress. Then the alien slapped its left arm towards him, knocking the gun from Ten's hand. The alien began to shout, loudly. Ten yanked the arm, pulling the alien close then wrapping his right arm around its neck. He tightened the hold and fell back on the floor with the alien on top of him as it kicked and struggled.

He wrapped his legs around the alien's waist to control it and scrabbled for a knife, stabbing it into the alien's torso while trying to keep it quiet. It took too long, far too long. The alien kicked, struggled and gurgled as it died, but Ten could already hear other compartments opening around the room.

"Don't let them raise the alarm!" he called out as he flung the corpse away and rolled to his feet.

Ten snatched up his pistol and hurried to the open compartments, firing on instinct and without caution, trying to kill as many of the enemy as he could. He could hear the faint coughs of pistol fire around him from the rest of the team and, for a few glorious seconds, he thought they might recover the situation and stop it from becoming an absolute shit show.

Then someone found a rifle and he wasn't friendly.

Automatic weapons fire screamed through the barracks, rounds ricocheting from the sleeping compartments.

"Fuck!" shouted one of the Marines, Ten couldn't tell who, as they all sought cover.

Ten holstered his pistol and sheathed his knife, unslinging the alien rifle he carried across his back. His team were doing the same as they knelt or lay behind cover. Fortunately, the sleeping chambers were pretty solid, designed to protect an occupant from decompression, and they made good cover.

<Lieutenant, we're in the barracks, and it's gone hot. No alarm yet but it won't be long> he sent via his HUD.

<Understood> replied Warden. He sent a message to the entire team.

<Heads up! Switch to primary weapons, press hard and fast, expect resistance. Let's not give these bastards time to work out what's going on or where we are>

The map showed that they had swept about an eighth of the ship so far, including two dropship bays.

<Let's clear the barracks, secure the next bays, then find the bridge. No quarter to be given> ordered Warden.

Ten grinned, reached into a pouch, pulled out a grenade and threw it to the far end of the room.

"Flashbang," he shouted for the benefit of his team, then, "grenade," as he threw the second object. It wasn't exactly sporting to disorient the enemy and then throw a fragmentation grenade but the time for fair play was long gone.

He rolled over and up into a crouch behind the compartment that was his shelter, clapping his hands over his ears and squeezing his eyes shut. The HUDs lenses would block most of the flash and he had time and cover to his advantage.

After the second explosion, Ten hefted his weapon and advanced, quickly but quietly. He knew from experience that ear-splitting sounds could still be heard by the victims of a flashbang. Well, by humans, at any rate; he had no idea how the aliens might react. Fast and quiet, then. No shouting or screaming war cries, which was about the stupidest thing you could do in a situation like this.

Instead, he moved up the room like a panther searching for prey, rapidly but smoothly and on the balls of his feet. One round to the head or a couple to the chest of any alien he thought might still be able to move, then immediately on to the next. His HUD showed the bulk of A Troop already at the door of this barracks or the one on the other side of the ship. His job wasn't to be one hundred per cent sure about each enemy but to kill, injure or incapacitate so the Marines following could tidy up behind him.

There was a burst of fire from somewhere ahead but it wasn't aimed at him, and he sprinted around the side of a row of sleeping bays to find one determined alien, in its underwear, desperately trying to reload its rifle.

Ten coughed politely and, as it turned towards him, put a quick burst into its face.

"Sorry, old chum, good effort, though." A quick death was the best he could do.

There was a moment of sudden silence after the appalling noise of the grenades. No enemy movement, no shouts or shots. Ten looked around to double check then grabbed the alien's weapon, slamming a new magazine into it before reloading his other weapons.

<Lieutenant> sent Ten.

<Marine X. How's it going?>

<We're secure for the moment, but I'd be amazed if we didn't have a tough fight ahead> replied Ten. Then he turned to speak to his team. "There's a spare rifle here if anyone needs one."

Warden checked his HUD; the second barracks was secure. Two Marines were down, though – Maxwell and McDonald. Just twenty-five commandos left to finish the mission.

Will it be enough? he wondered.

13

"Barlow, Cooke, Goodwin! Get the drones out, full offensive mode. I want to know what's ahead and I want to know now," Warden called out. Milton had her half of the Troop lined up in the barracks opposite, ready to storm the next area of the ship. There were only two exits from each barracks, the ones they had entered by at port and starboard and one facing the front of the ship. Warden had sent Goodwin back out into the corridor, to the crossroads that ran between the two barracks, along with Lance Corporal Jean Bailey and her spotter, Marine Adam Parker.

The micro-drones went first, the smallest the tech-specialists had with them. Warden cursed their lack of equipment; a more established colony would have had far more toys for them to play with.

It was the specialist pico-drones he really missed, the ones normally used for exploring and mapping enemy buildings or vessels. They were tiny, fast and hard to detect, far smaller than the micro-drones which were a multi-purpose compromise.

In the sterile environment of a ship, especially one as densely fitted-out as this one appeared to be, the micro-drone wasn't nearly as discreet as he'd have liked. But it was still better than sticking your head around a corner and finding an enemy with a shotgun waiting for you.

The drones quickly added the next corridors, which were empty, to the floor plan. They couldn't get through bulkheads or locked doors but they were perfect for scouting open areas. Barlow sent an update identifying two doors at port and starboard as matches to the ones in the other docking bays.

It looked like they had found their objective. Between the remains of A Troop and those all-important dropship bays, there was a series of smaller rooms, possibly officer's quarters judging by the number of doors and size.

"Marines X, Fletcher and Harrington. Clear those rooms, quick as you can please. Techs, I want combat drones guarding those launch bay doors. Once we breach, attack the storerooms and armoury between the bays. Milton, once the cabins are clear, take the rest of your team through that dropship bay as fast as possible. Everyone else, keep your breathers handy in case of a hull breach," Warden ordered.

Ten was done with the first cabin before Warden had finished his orders and they swept from port to starboard along the corridor. Resistance was light, only a few rounds were discharged, and no firefight broke out. It was over in less than two minutes and Warden ordered an immediate assault on the bays.

The commandos surged forward, rushing for their assigned doors, the techs and sniper teams bringing up the rear. Warden's team stormed into the port dropship bay. Aside from markings and the dropship being clean of mud and dust, it was identical to the starboard bay. No enemies were visible, so they jogged across the hangar.

<Contact> Milton sent. Warden took cover and checked her viewpoint. They were taking fire from the other side of the hangar.

"Marine X, get that door open now, we need to flank them, Milton's team is under heavy fire in the other dropship bay."

Ten nodded grimly and sprinted to the door across the bay in the direction of the bow.

Warden issued orders rapidly, sending half his group through the door with Ten and the other half east into the armoury and workshop area that linked the two dropship bays. He sent the techs and the sniper teams toward the storage rooms. If the layout was symmetrical, when they reached the middle of the three storerooms, they could go north into the armoury and workshop area.

If the enemy were in there as well as the starboard dropship hangar, they would be caught between Warden's team on their port side, the techs and sniper teams coming from the aft and Marine X's group from the bow. They'd flip the enemy ambush on its head and turn the hunters into the hunted.

He checked Milton's view again. It was bad. Not everyone had found cover and casualties were mounting.

Warden sprinted starboard, cursing the doors that responded only slowly to his key card.

Too slow, too slow, he thought.

<We're on our way, Milton. Keep your heads down> he sent.

<It's a bit unfriendly in here, sir. Hope you can lighten the mood soon> she replied.

He reached the middle room, bursting in behind the techs as they reached the bow door.

"Go, go, go!" he yelled as he crossed the room, pressing his card against the lock. His HUD was alive with contact markers.

Ten and his team were in a firefight in the corridor.

Milton was still pinned down. The munition and repair equipment storage areas were well-defended.

Someone went down as Warden reached the last storeroom door. Behind it, the remnants of Milton's team were pinned in the hanger.

Warden crouched as it opened, bringing his carbine to his shoulder and wishing he had grabbed one of the more substantial alien weapons. No time for regrets, though. He leaned just far enough to his right to sight the weapon towards the wall opposite Milton, where the enemy was taking cover. They were on the balcony at the same height as him and on the floor below, all well sheltered from the Marines' fire. Lots of metal storage crates were clamped to the floor and the railings had safety panels to fill the gaps.

With a trio of whumpfs that sounded a lot like a fast-moving drift of snow falling off a roof, Warden launched a series of grenades at the balcony. He gave a count of one and then sighted roughly where the enemy was on the ground floor and pulled the trigger, keeping it depressed and controlling the muzzle climb as best he could while he emptied the magazine.

He ducked back into cover as he smoothly swapped the magazine, cycling through the views of his team, trying to get a better sight line of the area he'd hit. Nothing clear.

"Get me a drone in the hangar for fuck's sake! I don't care if it gets hit, we're losing people," he ordered. "We need visibility."

He leaned around the doorway again and emptied another magazine. He sprayed indiscriminately into the cloud of smoke and dust from the grenades, then took cover again. He wasn't likely to inflict any damage, but it should keep the enemy's heads down.

Finally, a drone made it into the hangar, hugging the ceiling as it scanned the huge bay. Ghostly red imagery overlaid his own view and now Warden knew where the enemy were. There was movement in the cloud, so at least one enemy was still active. He reloaded his carbine with grenades and a fresh magazine, slung it across his back and pulled out his pistol, suppressor already attached.

He threw two more grenades and sent a silent message to Milton's team.

<Flashbangs>

Then he ran through the doorway and along the balcony, directly at the aliens and into the smoke. He skidded to his knees as the first infra-red blob loomed out of the smoke before him. The greyness shifted and the kneeling alien seemed to coalesce out of the fog. It turned towards him, a look of horror on its face, as Warden's suppressor touched its forehead.

The weapon bucked and the alien fell back. Warden was already rising, rebreather on, moving into the smoke. It was risky, but the drone would have painted him a friendly blue and they didn't have the numbers to be cautious.

He took the next alien with three hurried rounds to the chest, not even stopping as he rounded the corner of the balcony and began to move down it. Another blob appeared, coughing in the swirling smoke, and Warden lifted his weapon. He heard the tell-tale pings of rounds bouncing off powered armour as the towering figure became visible. His heart pounded. It was one of the enormous brutes he had tackled planetside, only this time in full power armour.

Warden glanced despondently at his pistol. The alien hadn't seen him yet, but the smoke was clearing. He holstered his weapon and began to reach for another, staying as still as possible in the hope it wouldn't spot him.

Then the head snapped towards him, the helmet expressionless. Warden could almost see the alien's face, hear its grunt of surprise. He imagined the alien was looking at him and mouthing the equivalent of "What the fuck?"

Warden grinned lopsidedly and threw his weapons to the floor at the feet of the gigantic trooper. It looked down for a moment then looked back up as Warden waved and bravely ran away. He took three steps, unslinging his carbine as he ran towards the corner, then dove for cover through an open door.

The explosion of the grenades he'd gifted the alien was deafening. His ears rang and the air was acrid with smoke. He checked his HUD and realised where he was. Lifting his head from the deck, he saw two alien troopers gaping at him. He was in the armoury. Behind the enemy. Not the ideal place to take cover.

Their weapons came around and he had nowhere to go. His teams were behind cover but the space between them and Warden was wide open. He rolled and alien rounds chattered from the barrels. He kept rolling, waiting for the impact. Then he hit a wall and fumbled at his carbine, scrabbling to point it at the enemy.

He blinked. Both alien troopers were dead.

Ten stood over them, one foot on the crushed neck of an alien. Something dripped in his left hand and in his right was the large, glowing alien knife.

"I fucking love this knife, Lieutenant," said Ten with obvious glee.

Warden looked at the body and back at the head Ten gripped by its hair. He'd taken it clean off with the knife. Then he casually tossed it out through the door, towards the spot in the hangar where the aliens had been. There were several bursts of fire.

"For fuck's sake! Was that Ten? Would you tell him to stop doing that, Lieutenant, it's not bloody funny anymore," Milton shouted into her radio.

Warden sucked in a lungful of air and rolled onto his back laughing, "Sorry, Sergeant, not this time."

14

"What's the casualty list, Milton?"

"We lost Barber, Mitchell and Lee, sir, and Corporal Campbell is mortally injured. Some further injuries but nothing serious. All told, we have twenty-one personnel," she replied.

Warden clenched his fist, the nails digging into his palm. The odds were not in their favour. They still had a substantial portion of the ship to clear and no way of knowing how many enemy combatants were still active. There could be half a dozen ship crew or thirty power-armoured troopers waiting for them.

"Wilson, what's our drone situation?" he asked, turning to the corporal who was the most senior of their tech specialists.

"We lost a few in that engagement, sir. We have a handful of micro-drones but only two functioning combat drones. Not that they're much use on board this ship," he said apologetically.

"We need visibility, Wilson. I want any drones you have out there mapping the rest of the ship and gathering intel. If the combat drones can take any action, do so. We don't need to worry about discretion now," said Warden.

"Can do, sir, but it won't leave us any spares. When we're planet-side, we won't have surveillance until we can fabricate more drones.

And the colonists lost their satellite network, as well as a lot of their communications grid. Do you want us to go ahead, bearing that in mind?"

Warden considered for a moment, then nodded. "We don't have a choice, Corporal. If we don't complete our mission here, we won't be getting planetside anyway. Even if we retreated, they have three more dropships, and we'd be facing overwhelming odds within twenty-four hours if they deployed just the clones they already have. I'd rather have this ship crippled and be blind planetside than face those odds. Be careful with the combat drones but don't hesitate to sacrifice them if you can take out an armoured trooper or we get another firefight like this one, okay?"

"Yes, sir. Thank you, sir," Wilson nodded and turned to his colleagues. They set up out of the way and launched all their drones, the tiny hummingbirds zipping off to map the next area of corridors. The two combat drones, much larger but with only light arms, launched last. They hovered, advancing more cautiously, following the plans left by their smaller brethren.

Warden surveyed the rest of his team, only twenty strong with Richardson in the dropship. He frowned.

"Moyes, is that a railgun on your back?"

"Yes, sir," the young Marine replied.

"Didn't I specifically order that we weren't to use railguns due to the risk of venting atmosphere?"

"I haven't used it, sir," she replied.

"I meant that we should leave them behind. Why did you bring it?"

"I thought if we had it, we could use it, sir. My sniping instructors always told me to be prepared."

"That's good advice, Moyes, but please tell me you understand why I don't want to expose us all to vacuum when we don't even have environment suits?"

She nodded. "Yes, sir, I just wanted to be able to vent the atmosphere if you needed me to. Like, if we shot some rounds through their bridge, the crew might find it hard to control the ship.

They don't seem to be well prepared for a boarding action. Maybe they won't have their breathers at hand?"

Warden blinked. He turned to look at Milton who was having obvious difficulty stifling the impulse to laugh. He turned back to Moyes then called Lance Corporal Bailey and Marine Findlay over.

"Moyes, tell Bailey and Findlay what you just suggested."

She looked a little shy about the prospect of suggesting her idea to the older Marines and Warden realised just how young she was. It was easy to lose track of such things when operating in clones, but his HUD confirmed Moyes was only twenty-two. She'd been in the Royal Marine Cadet program while pursuing her degree in fine art, of all things.

Moyes could easily have gone straight into the officer training course but instead had chosen the rapid acceleration track which would take her through the non-commissioned ranks before giving her the opportunity to attend officer training and be commissioned. It was an unusual route, but it spoke to a deep level of commitment and forethought.

Moyes cleared her throat and said, "Well, I thought that if we used the alien's railgun against the ship's bridge, we could vent their atmosphere into space. Even if they do have environment suits in there, it would be a bit inconvenient for them."

"Assessment, Bailey?" Warden asked.

"I can't think of a reason we shouldn't, sir. If we can reach the corridor outside the bridge, we would have to shoot through one wall and out the other side. That would give us decent penetration, and if we can shoot from a doorway we can retreat quickly, seal the door behind us, and we'll be secure. If they have power armour in there, though, you can bet they'll follow us."

"I can rig tripwires with our spare grenades," Ten suggested.

"That might work," said Bailey, nodding.

Warden walked over to the techs. "Report."

"We have a good visualisation of this section, sir," Wilson said, looking up. He pointed to a data slate and highlighted several rooms. "This is a cloning bay and, look, the monitors show clones being activated as we speak. No way of knowing how long that will take. This is a cafeteria," he said, pointing at a new spot, "and what looks like a recreation room, currently unoccupied. This is a medical bay, there's a couple of staff in it, presumably medics. We can't see inside the next three rooms so we'll need to open those bulkhead doors to get drones in but we have the general corridor layout, and there aren't any nasty surprises in the areas we can see. We have strong emissions from the other side of the bulkheads, so it's reasonable to assume we're not far from their communications and bridge areas, assuming they've got similar ship layouts and functionality to our own, which has been true so far."

"Marine X, get those rooms cleared, pronto. Everyone else, ready to move out. I want to breach those doors and then get the drones in immediately."

They moved out, going about their tasks efficiently. The techs gathered their gear and went mobile, ready to support if necessary and preparing their drones for the breach of the bulkhead doors. Warden pulled the snipers' spotters from that duty and assigned them to the breaching team. At this range, the snipers' only role was to use the railgun and they only had one, so the other two would look after Moyes.

<Cleared> came across the HUD from Marine X.

<Move> Warden broadcast. The commandos dashed forward, in position in under thirty seconds.

Marines stepped forward to each of the three sealed doors, spinning the wheel locks and pulling them wide open. The micro-drones zipped through, visually clearing the corridors beyond in seconds. Warden checked the feeds and issued the next order to move.

Ten led the way through the starboard door and stormed into a communications room, glowing knife in one hand and pistol in the other. The aliens inside weren't in a position to fight back; they barely freed their sidearms before Ten finished them.

Warden closed the feed from Ten and moved as the team cleared two staterooms on the port side of the ship. One large room between the communications room and the staterooms remained. He closed on it at the same time as Ten, and they burst through the door together.

It wasn't surprising to find a war room with a large illuminated data table showing a map of the solar system and images of New Bristol. There were displays on all the walls. The surprise came from the two alien troopers in powered-armour who were waiting inside.

Warden admitted to himself later that the shock had thrown off his response time. Not so for Penal Marine X. Ten threw himself forward at the nearest enemy, his pistol firing as he closed the gap.

Warden targeted the second figure and emptied his magazine. He knew the alien rifle was powerful, but he wasn't taking any chances with powered armour. It wouldn't be a waste of ammo if he took down this trooper.

Ten dropped his pistol and switched the knife to his right hand. He batted the alien trooper's weapon aside and closed into a close grapple. His left arm wrapped around the alien's right and the knife came down hard, punching in and out through the weaker points in the alien's armour. Under the armpit, the neck, the join between thigh and waist.

Warden's alien staggered back, knocked off its feet by the rounds striking its helmet and chest. The lieutenant sprang forward, pulling the twin to Ten's knife from its sheath and thumbing the mechanism as he landed on top of the trooper. He snarled as he raised the knife to finish his opponent and then let his hand drop. The front of the helmet was gone, smashed to pieces, and the face behind it was shattered. The rifle, it seemed, had been more than a match for the armour.

Warden got to his feet and sheathed the knife. He rammed a fresh magazine into the rifle and looked around.

"Charges, sir?"

"You think the next room is the bridge?"

"Only two doors and they're close together. Looks like one room to me, Lieutenant."

"Go ahead then. Let's finish this."

<Move up, Moyes> Warden ordered.

Warden pointed his rifle at the doors while Ten set the charges. The other teams took up positions in the doorways and corridors that had sight lines to the room they'd decided must be the bridge.

"How long, Marine X?" he asked.

"Want it good and efficient or quick and unreliable?"

"I'm an officer, Marine X. I want it done quickly and I want it done well."

"Bloody typical," Ten muttered, though hardly sotto voce.

"Do you want another thirty days on your sentence, Marine X?" Warden asked.

"Oh, yes please, sir? Can I? I do so love coming to shitholes and looking after moisture farmers and asteroid miners. Another couple of minutes should do it, if you want my best work."

"Cut the comedy routine, Ten. Just get it done."

"It'll never be enough, I tell you! As if I have anything else in my life."

Warden rolled his eyes and checked the HUD readouts again. He glanced down at Ten's work; he was almost done.

A metallic whir from his left drew his attention. The wheel lock on the bulkhead door was turning. Warden's eyes tracked down to the cluster of grenades and the jury-rigged mechanism Ten had attached to them and the door. It was already armed. His head snapped back to Ten, oblivious and muttering under his breath.

As the wheel creaked ominously, Warden shot out, stooping as he moved, his arms tucking under Ten's armpits and lifting him as he headed for the doorway. "What the..." was all that Ten managed to splutter before the grenades behind them detonated.

The blast slammed into Warden's back and punched him sideways into the room with Ten under him. He slammed into the door frame on his way through, hearing at least one rib break. *Bollocks,* he thought, *I don't have time for this.* Worse, he'd ended up lying on top of a prone Ten in an entirely unflattering position.

Automatic weapons fire erupted behind him as Warden staggered to his feet. Ten stood up too and glared at Moyes, who'd been dragged back out of the way by Bailey and was staring at him in shock.

"Not a word," he growled.

Warden clutched his side and gritted his teeth. Ten looked him up and down and swore. Then he pulled an auto-injector from a belt pouch and slammed it into Warden's thigh before the lieutenant could protest.

"Shut up, Lieutenant. I heard the rib break and you need to stay functional. Unless you want to stay behind when we blow this rust bucket," Ten said.

The drug flooded through Warden and the pain in his chest faded into the background.

"What does it look like?" he asked.

Ten grabbed a rifle and risked sticking his head out to check the corridor. His reward was a sustained burst of fully automatic weapon fire. The rounds were ricocheting around the whole corridor as Ten jerked back into the room.

"Bloody hellfire! It's one of those big bastards in heavy power armour. He's only got a massive Gatling gun on each arm."

<Lieutenant, we have people down> sent Milton, <we're pulling back; nothing is getting through that thing's armour>

<Understood, Milton, the grenades didn't faze it. The armour must be heavier than we've seen before>

Warden turned to Moyes. "Marine, want to show us what you can do with that?"

She gulped. "I don't have a clear shot, sir."

She was right; it would be suicide to stick her head into that corridor and try to aim at that thing.

Bailey solved it. She threw something into the corridor and pulled Warden further into the room, leaving nothing but the wall of the room between Moyes and the gargantuan alien.

"The reflection, Moyes, check it, fire and adjust. The rifle is semi-automatic. Don't think, just shoot."

Moyes looked through the doorway; the object was a display Bailey had grabbed off a desk. The surface wasn't mirrored, but it was reflective enough to give a distorted view of the corridor. She squinted to pick out details, matching them to the layout she had in her HUD, then she brought the rifle to bear.

The railgun spat and the sabot tore through the wall.

"To the left, Moyes," Ten called out.

She adjusted the angle and fired again.

"That's it!" Ten shouted gleefully. "Pile on."

Moyes fired again, adjusted a fraction to the left and fired a fourth time.

"Nice, throw it to me, Moyes," Ten shouted. She tossed the railgun to him, and he shouldered it, leaned out into the corridor and fired again. "Done," he said, handing the rifle back to her, "nicely done, newbie. You're empty, reload."

"How many magazines do you have?" asked Warden.

"Five, sir," Moyes replied.

Well, that really was prepared.

"How do you feel about filling that bridge room with as many as you can get out?" suggested Warden. Moyes nodded.

<Milton. Breathers on and pull everyone back through the bulkheads, we'll take it from here. Let me know when you're clear> Warden sent through the UD. He turned to Ten and Bailey.

"Covering fire for the retreat. Breathers on." He slipped his mask up and over his nose and mouth and flipped it on.

Ten and Bailey let loose a few bursts down the corridor before Milton confirmed everyone else was back through the bulkhead and it was sealed.

"Let rip, Moyes," said Warden.

Moyes moved to the doorway and fired five rounds, ejecting the magazine and emptying the next into the bridge room as well. At least one must have penetrated the outer hull as an awful whistling began to suck the atmosphere from the ship.

<That's it, everyone out> Warden ordered and they retreated as fast as they could. They slammed the door behind them and spun the wheel but already the oxygen level was well down. They still needed their breathers.

"Richardson, can we get any more of the dropships down? How much time would it take if we can?"

"Sir, we might be able to. We'd need a tech to operate them, though. A few minutes for each dropship, maybe."

"Great. Get going, folks, I want those dropships on the surface and under our control. Milton, I want overwatch on the dropship bays. Let's make this an orderly retreat and deal with any crew we've missed before they have a chance to hit back." They'd lost Fletcher and Parker when the monster on the bridge had attacked and he didn't want to lose anyone else on the retreat.

Warden got back to the dropship bay more or less intact. He could feel a dull ache from his ribs though and his back ached. If he pushed it, he would be out of action himself.

This had not been a good day, but at least it was almost over. *Nothing much left to do now but clean up*, he thought.

Then the flashing red lights and a klaxon started.

"What the hell is that? Anyone got an idea what's going on? Come on, people – is the bridge crew still alive?"

It was a long, agonising minute before Richardson responded.

"Err. Yeah, we have a bit of a problem, sir. We may not have as much time as we thought."

"Spit it out, Richardson."

"We're falling out of orbit. Either someone scuttled the ship or we damaged something important a bit prematurely, sir. Maybe six minutes before it's going to get a bit dicey launching these dropships. As soon as we hit the upper atmosphere, it'll get really bumpy and very hot very quickly."

"Acknowledged. Has anyone got another dropship ready yet? We're in this bay and I don't see a tech inside the cockpit." Six minutes wasn't long to get to the next bay.

"We've got two more going, sir. Can you get to the port bay? It's closer than the stern one?" Goodwin responded.

"Roger that," Warden responded, turning to his snipers and Marine X. "Get moving and keep your eyes peeled. If the ship was scuttled, we might not be alone."

They moved out, darting across the dropship bay and towards the storerooms, moving fast. Warden ignored the tightness in his chest, gritting his teeth at the grinding sensation.

<Four minutes, Lieutenant. You need to get a shift on> sent Milton.

<Don't worry about us> he responded as they passed through the second storeroom, <just make sure all the dropships are ready to go>

A chatter of fire from behind made him turn his head.

"Moyes, get the lieutenant out of here, now! I'll hold these bastards!" Ten shouted over his shoulder.

Moyes dropped the railgun and inserted herself under Warden's arm. They started to jog as fast as Warden could manage with her supporting him.

"Lieutenant, you're bleeding. There's blood all over my hand," she panted.

"Don't worry about it," he replied through gritted teeth as they reached the dropship hangar, "it's not my body anyway." Probably explained why a broken rib was giving him so much trouble though, and why he was suddenly feeling cold. He'd probably caught some shrapnel when the giant alien had triggered Ten's booby trap.

Then they were at the ramp of the dropship, pushing past Milton who was crouched at the base firing bursts across the bay. Warden tried to turn but Moyes insisted and bundled him up the ramp. She and Goodwin forced him into a chair and strapped him in.

"Get that stupid bastard Marine X back here on the double," he slurred. Something was making his forearm hurt; he looked down to see a needle sticking out of it and frowned. *Where had that come from?* he wondered.

He heard shouting in the background, gunfire; then the world swam in front of his eyes for a moment or two.

Warden felt his stomach lurch, the distinctive sensation of a dropship entering the atmosphere.

"Back with us, Lieutenant?" said Ten, grinning from the seat opposite. Warden blinked. He must have blacked out for a few minutes. He looked down to see a blood pack attached to his chest and a tube leading to the needle in his arm. Well, that was a bit worrying. Judging by how alert he felt, they'd given him a combat stimulant as well.

"What happened? Milton?"

She was sitting next to Ten.

"We got two of the dropships ready, but you came under attack as you retreated. You've been bleeding for a while now. We've slapped a bandage on it, but you'll need some attention once we hit the ground. The aliens backed off when most of you got to the ship and we laid down enough fire for Ten to reach us. We dropped the moment the ramp was sealed. Richardson hit the detonator as soon as we were clear. It blew a hole in the hangar and caused a fair bit of damage. I don't think they'll be able to pull the ship out of its decaying orbit but we're monitoring it."

"Good work, everyone. Good work," Warden said, tilting his head back as the world shook and went dark around him.

EPILOGUE

"Captain? Can you hear me, Captain Atticus?" asked Wilson, leaning over the open pod.

Atticus raised his eyelids, blinking against the harsh light of the EDB. His new eyes stung and he felt strange. It was always strange waking up in a new body. Even though the blank clones came in very few varieties, a new one always seemed unfamiliar. The muscles hadn't been used for ages. Neither had the brain, for that matter.

He reached up to feel his face, a habit that he'd had for years. The facial features were always the last part of the clone that the tank grew after the imprint was designated to a particular blank. Essentially, the face was finished last and often took a few extra hours to settle in. The old joke was that if you played with your face before it had settled, it would set in a strange shape.

The earliest blanks, when the cloning technology had first been deployed, had been left complete but the result was that an entire deployment of troops would look exactly the same, which caused an astonishing number of problems. Instead, a close approximation of the person's real face was built in the final stages of clone deployment. It added hours to the process but it was better in the long run.

Wilson gripped his wrist before he could reach his face. His fingers felt odd on his skin.

"Wait, sir. We have to tell you something."

Atticus croaked, "What?" His voice sounded strange.

The cloning specialist looked a bit uncomfortable.

"We haven't been able to get our cloning bays working yet, sir. We had to improvise to get you redeployed."

"What is it?" Atticus demanded, trying to get the hang of his vocal chords.

"Barlow, whatever it is can wait. I need to talk to the captain. Just hold your horses and I'll get to you in a minute," Warden said. He moved into Atticus's eye line, supporting himself awkwardly on a crutch. "Don't panic, Captain, but what Wilson is dancing around is that we had to redeploy you in an enemy clone. You're in a military body, sir, just not a human one."

Atticus pulled his wrist from Wilson's grip and raised his hand. It was humanoid. Opposable thumb and four fingers, albeit unusually long and delicate. The palms were soft but the back of the hand was covered in scales.

"Oh. Shit. I'm an alien," Atticus sighed. "You really had to put me in an enemy clone? Are things that desperate?"

"I don't know, sir," said Warden, "but we're still growing new clones in the remaining bay and repairing the civilian one. I thought we should at least try this, though, because we captured three alien dropships since you went down. We have dozens of their clones and a working bay in each of the dropships, so a trial seemed like a good idea, and I didn't think you'd be happy if I used anyone else. I'm concerned they might have more troops deployed across the planet already. We have no way of knowing how many dropships landed or when," Warden explained. "We destroyed the ship they had in orbit, but that doesn't mean we're done with them."

"So we're trapped planetside and the aliens could have a battalion of soldiers somewhere on New Bristol?" Atticus asked.

"No, sir, that's what I've been –" Barlow started from the corner of the room but Warden cut him off, "Marine, I will get to you in a minute."

Atticus put an arm on Warden's shoulder and pulled himself upright.

"No, let him speak, Warden. He looks like he might burst. What's so urgent, Barlow?"

"They're not aliens, Captain," the tech specialist said.

There was a chorus of disagreement around the room and Atticus waved his scaled hand for silence.

"How do you come to that conclusion, Barlow?" looking at his hand as if to emphasise the evidence to the contrary.

"I thought something seemed odd, so I've been examining the bodies and equipment. I sampled the DNA of a few of the clones and ran it through the colony's sequencer. It's human, or at least, mostly human."

"You mean these are human military clones? But they have a different language, different character sets to any Sol culture. They even have new technology like that chameleon coating. Are you saying they're from Sol? A black op perhaps from another government or a corporation?" Warden asked.

"Not sure where they came from, sir, but the bodies are human. Brains too. I don't think these are aliens in human clones. I think you'd have to clone an alien brain format to be able to imprint an alien mind on a blank," he said, turning to Wilson for support.

"That makes a lot of sense, sir," said Wilson, "I was surprised when we were able to deploy you to that blank. I thought they must have created an interface to edit their pattern so it would fit a human brain. We can't imprint a human on a gorilla brain; the structure isn't similar enough. If we meet an actual alien species, they'd need to adjust the brain of the blanks they were using at a minimum or else they'd never be able to imprint to them. The rest could stay human but they couldn't get away with it without changing that."

"Can you be more specific about who these people are, Barlow?" Atticus asked.

"Only if we contact Sol, sir. They might have records of the Lost

Arks and we could compare the DNA we have here with the blanks that went out with the arks that went missing in this region. The earliest ark ships didn't even carry blanks; they pre-dated cloning, so we can rule those out. We could rule out more recent ones if we knew when some parts of the DNA of our basic and military blanks were first used," Barlow confirmed. "I'd need to contact HQ and send them a lot of data, though."

"Noted. Draft a report and I'll speak to HQ, explain the situation. Do we still have wormhole communications?" Atticus said, turning to Warden.

"No, sir," said the Lieutenant, shaking his head, "they went down at some point while we were dealing with the alien, I mean, enemy base. I'm expecting it back up in a few hours, though. We prioritised it so we could get updates and in case we needed more deployments."

"Okay. Get to it then, Barlow, we still need something to send when we have communications back up."

"How are you feeling, sir?" Warden asked.

"I seem to have picked up a bit of a skin complaint," said Atticus, staring at the back of his hand, "but I'm definitely better than last time we spoke. I need to get up to date. What's our current strength?"

Warden gave a rapid account of everything that had happened since Atticus had died.

"So we're down to twenty, including you, Captain."

Atticus frowned.

"That could be better, but it could be a lot worse, Lieutenant. I'm sure our people sold themselves dearly."

"They did, sir. We captured three of the four enemy dropships as well as a good number of their clones, including some heavily modified for combat. We also have a lot of their armour, weapons and munitions. It's good gear, some of it is better than ours."

"Well done, Lieutenant. Give me a moment to put something on and then I need to see the governor."

"She's waiting outside for you, sir. I told her we were going to try to deploy you into an enemy clone."

Atticus nodded and began to get dressed. He slipped some underwear on without daring to look at what these people might use; he would worry about that later. At least this body wasn't permanent. As long they could still back up their imprints, he'd be able to get home and leave this body for fertiliser.

He'd worn plenty of military clones in the past, but this one was different. The vision was particularly sharp and his hearing was excellent. He rapped a knuckle against the scales on the back of his arm. Tough but flexible. Nice, but he still wanted to get out of this body as soon as he could. He sighed and opened the door, stepping into the room beyond.

"Governor Denmead. How is New Bristol holding up?" he said, wondering if his scales were showing the blushing sensation he could feel creeping up his neck.

"Captain Atticus, glad to see you back on your feet," said the governor, barely glancing at his new body, "or on someone's feet, at least. We're doing as well as can be expected, given the week we've had. Let's go outside, and you can see for yourself." She hadn't batted an eyelid when confronted with his strange new body. A governor of the old school; not easily fazed.

An elevator took them to the roof. The building stood only four storeys above the ground but Ashton was a new colony city and lacked the horrific concrete canyons common to the metropolises of Earth or Mars.

"You can see the damage," Denmead said, pointing at a number of locations across the city that had collapsed or were still smoking. "We've lost a lot of people too, and even if we had a cloning bay, it would take months to grow enough blanks to deploy everyone."

"Warden tells me the enemy had four dropships but only one at their planetside base. There could be more of them out there. If I were them, I'd have landed across the planet and set up more than one base, then gathered intelligence about the colony. I'm not sure their grasp of strategy is that good, though. They strike me as a touch brash. Satellites down, I assume? Drones up?"

Warden shook his head. "We don't have long-range scouting drones, sir. We're repairing the fabricators and the production facilities and arming the citizens with whatever we can scrape together."

Atticus thought about this for a moment as he stared across the smoking city. Then he nodded.

"We need to reassess our priorities; arming civilians won't help if we have hundreds of enemy troops out there. Let's get inside and take a hard look at the numbers," Atticus said.

They took a final look across the city and then turned to leave the roof. There was a beep from a communicator in Governor Denmead's jacket pocket. She took it out and flipped it open. "Yes, Johnson. What is it?"

"Governor, we need you in the command centre urgently."

"We were just on our way. What's wrong, Johnson? Don't be coy, spit it out, man!" she said, a hint of impatience in her tone.

"A beacon, ma'am, on the edge of the system. Ships are dropping out of hyperspace," he said, his voice betraying a definite hint of panic. Denmead made a mental note to speak to him about the importance of remaining calm for the citizens of New Bristol.

"It's just the fleet, Johnson. We requested support when we called in the Marines," she said, turning to Atticus and rolling her eyes apologetically. Atticus frowned, the expression amplified by his inhuman face, and glanced at Warden, who was looking distinctly worried. *What's wrong with them?* Denmead wondered.

"But there are no transponder signals, Governor," said Johnson, now sounding truly scared. "It's not our fleet. I think it's them, ma'am. I think it's the aliens."

Denmead took a couple of seconds to digest this.

"We're on our way, Johnson."

She turned to Atticus and Warden and gave them a brittle smile.

"Well, it could be worse. It could be raining."

GUERRILLA

THE ROYAL MARINE SPACE COMMANDOS
BOOK 2

PROLOGUE

The rain was coming down hard across the valley, so hard the scout could no longer see the hills. He squatted behind a shattered wall and tried to shelter from the weather. The three other surviving members of his platoon were squashed together under what was left of the first floor of the building, all trying to stay out of the storm.

He tried the communicator again, tapping at the hardened controls and hoping to get some sort of response from his comrades. They had to be out there, somewhere, but they'd lost touch a few hours before. Then the storm had blown in and shut everything down. He fiddled with the communicator, switching to the orbital channel to try to reach the ship's crew, but they weren't answering either.

He swore and stuffed the communicator back in his pocket. Then he ran through the rest of his kit. Uniform, soaked and torn but mostly usable. Rifle and sidearm, both in good working order. His communicator was probably working, although it was impossible to be sure since nobody was bloody answering. But that was about the end of the good news.

They were out of food and water – ha, ha – but that wasn't going to be a problem for a day or two. They had run out of drones, but they didn't have enough energy to run them anyway. Worse, their low energy reserves meant they would soon have to ditch their armour if they couldn't scrounge something from the wreckage of this damned city.

Most worrying was the ammunition, of which they had almost none. The colonists had put up a hell of a fight, for a bunch of civilians, and his platoon had been hard-pressed. Half his team were dead, their corpses spread across the last few blocks of the city as they had fought to extricate themselves from the trap they'd fallen into.

He swore again then jumped like a frightened child when his communicator beeped. He snatched it out and opened the link.

"Platoon Six here," he said, speaking more loudly than he would have liked in order to make himself heard above the din of the storm.

"This is, *Varpulis*. What is your status, Six?"

"Situation dire," he reported, relieved to have someone to give him orders. "We lack supplies, we're low on ammunition and we have injured comrades. Immediate extraction requested."

"Understood, Lieutenant. Extraction not immediately possible, timing unknown due to the uncertainty of operational parameters. Remain on this channel. Retreat to safety and do not engage the enemy."

"Acknowledged," he said, hopes of an early rescue dashed. "Six out."

He swore again, although it didn't make him feel any better.

Then he saw figures emerging from a building. The shorter, long-haired one led the way, one of the local females. There was a figure walking behind her and two more bringing up the rear; one was carrying weapons. He couldn't believe it – the figure in the middle was a prisoner, they'd captured one of his fellow officers. How? There had been no reports of anyone going missing; then again, the fighting had been chaotic, the withdrawal even more so.

The tattered remnants of his command joined him to peer over the wall. Two hundred metres away, the small group moved quickly across the open ground, heading for another of the large buildings. In seconds they would be too far away, and their captured comrade would be beyond help. Intolerable! Damn his orders; he had to act.

He signalled the attack, pulled out his rifle, and all four troopers opened fire, blasting away at the enemy to give their comrade a chance to escape.

The lead figure went down in the first seconds, struck by at least one round, hair flailing as she fell. The other two were luckier and dived away into cover. They returned fire almost immediately, and one of his comrades was hit in the face, his helmet smashed apart, bits of skull and brain matter spattering the ground.

An ominous click from his rifle told him that he was out of ammunition, but the captured comrade was free, racing towards them in giant, ungainly leaps. They must have drugged him; surely no comrade officer would move so inelegantly, and so slowly, towards freedom?

Then he ducked as rounds slammed into the wall and whistled close to his helmet. When he looked again, their captured comrade had almost reached their position. One more leap and he cleared the wall, landing behind them in the remains of the building. Platoon Six might have lost a man, but they had rescued a fellow officer, and that was a fair exchange, worth the risk. The comrade officer had been captured and would have useful intelligence. The enemy was foolish to allow him to escape so easily.

He tossed aside his useless rifle and turned to signal the retreat. It was only then that he saw that his freed comrade was armed with a pistol and was blasting rounds into the two troopers who were still shooting at the enemy.

The lieutenant shouted in alarm and dived forward. He grappled with the turncoat, batting aside the pistol and groping for the man's throat or eyes, all the time shouting at him, screaming questions, burning to understand why they had been betrayed. Why had he lost more men? Good men, his comrades, his friends.

The traitorous scum punched and kicked, but the young platoon leader had momentum on his side and bore his opponent to the ground. They wrestled furiously for a moment as the rain hammered down around them, then he found himself astride the rebel officer. Fuelled by his righteous fury, he attacked with all the ferocity he could bring to bear. He was no longer concerned with escape or survival; he just needed to punish this traitor, to beat the life from him with his bare fists.

Having gained the upper hand, he lashed out, pummelling his enemy with blow after blow, screaming in wordless fury, blinded by rage and rainwater. All his opponent could do was feebly try to fend off his blows with one hand.

Through the red mist, he saw that the bastard was frantically reaching for something, even as his fists smashed again and again into his face.

He looked down and, in the fraction of a second left to him, he saw what it was. A pistol, lying in a puddle died red with blood that had oozed from one of his men. Then he collapsed back against the wall, his own personal universe snuffed out.

Atticus rolled to one side, coughing and spitting blood from his mouth. He ran his tongue over his teeth but, by some miracle, none were broken. This clone was tough. He was amazed he could still see straight after the pounding he'd taken. He kicked his legs free from the tangle of the last enemy and got to his knees. There was a pair of binoculars attached to the webbing of the corpse, and he unclipped them, moving to the wall to get a look at Warden and Governor Denmead.

A burst of fire greeted him the moment he popped his head up, stitching along the wall just below his head. He ducked immediately. Bugger. He couldn't blame them; he did look exactly like the enemy.

"Warden, the enemy patrol is down. What's your status?" he asked, wondering why the hell he hadn't just used his HUD in the first place. "Also, I'm going to stand up, so please don't shoot at me anymore."

"Ahh. Sorry, Captain."

"Not a problem, Lieutenant, just update me."

"The hospital director was hit in the head; he never stood a chance. Johnson has a couple of minor flesh wounds, but he's operational."

"What about Governor Denmead?" Atticus asked.

There was a pause before Warden replied. "She was hit in the shoulder, sir. I'm doing my best until the medics arrive. It's bad."

Atticus swore at that news. "Understood. I'm on my way."

1

There was a bright light in her eyes that didn't get any dimmer even when she squeezed them shut. Strange. Her head was pounding as well, and there was an uncomfortable feeling around her shoulder. Her chest felt tight, and her alarm was beeping incessantly and to a strange rhythm. She tried to reach out and slap it away, but somehow she just didn't have the energy.

And why was someone singing in the next room? What the hell had she drunk last night? Not more of that miserable attempt at producing gin that the self-professed 'best biologist on the planet' had cobbled together from potatoes and engine grease.

At least the beeping had stopped. No. Not stopped, changed to a single dull tone. Why couldn't she find the alarm clock? Was she on the wrong side of the bed or simply in the wrong bed entirely. Oh no, had she got so drunk she'd gone home with a biologist? That would be hard to live down; it was bad enough most of them were less than a third of her age, but a biologist? If her friends found out, she'd never hear the end of it. More sleep, that was the trick. Just fall back and ignore the alarm, maybe the headache would go away.

The voices in the other room got louder.

"Fuck! No, we're losing her. She's flatlining."

"Stay calm. Give me 10cc of adrenaline and another bag of plasma, please."

Denmead dozed for a few minutes and when she awoke the alarm was back on. It must have a second round in case you slept through the first. Bloody alarm clocks, it was like they were designed just to disrupt your sleep, she thought, giggling inanely. She coughed and felt something pressing down around her mouth; she tried to reach for it, but her left arm wouldn't budge. She must have slept on it, and it had gone dead. Right arm then.

"No," said one of the voices from the other room. "Leave that on, Governor. No, leave it on. Nurse, help me out here!"

A hand closed around hers and gently but firmly held it back from her face.

"It's all right. You're in the hospital. We're trying to help you. Can you hear me?"

How could she not? This strange man was screaming at the top of his lungs. It didn't seem much like a hospital voice. She tried to respond.

"I'm not sure what that was, you're slurring a bit because of the anaesthetic. My guess is you want to know what happened. Squeeze my hand if you can," the male voice said, and she did her best to grip his hand firmly.

"Good. You had a bit of an accident. Well, usually we get accidents. This is the first time I've had to say this, Governor, but you've been shot. No, don't worry, you're going to be okay. No need for a new body, it's just a flesh wound. You've lost a lot of blood, though, so you will probably feel a bit grotty for a while. Lie back, and we'll have you back on your feet in no time," the nurse said.

A hand waved slowly in front of her eyes, and she tried to focus. It was blurry but getting clearer. "That's better; you're starting to come round from the knock out drops. You'll be right as rain soon, you'll see. I'm going to give you a shot to help you come around properly, okay?"

She tried to nod, but the sharp pain in her neck took her breath away. She wished she had the energy to wince, but instead, she just passed out again.

The next time she came round, her head was pounding a little less, the light wasn't so bright, and she didn't have a mask strapped to her face. Her left arm still wasn't responding but, by grasping something with her right hand, she managed to sit up. She had barely swung her legs over the side of the bed before the panicking nurse appeared, shouting for the doctor.

"Governor, you stop that right now! You've been shot. You're in no condition to get out of bed," the doctor suggested. Well, ordered – Denmead supposed that was how the doctor would see it. She was buggered if some quack was going to give her orders.

"Is the wound sealed? Do I have enough blood to be going on with?"

"Yes, but you need bed rest to recover, complete immobility."

"I see. And will bed rest help me deal with an orbital strike or a few rounds from a rifle or a grenade?" she asked in her best icy tone.

"You are my patient, and I am not going to discharge you until I'm satisfied that you are fit for duty and won't collapse in a heap. Other people can deal with the business of the colony for a while. You need to focus on your recovery," the doctor tried.

"No, they can't. I don't have time to argue, Doctor. I'm getting up, I'm getting dressed, and I'm going to work. You can help me get dressed. You can give me something for my headache and stims to keep me alert. What you may not do, young lady, is tell me to sit idly by like some lazy hipster drinking flat whites while my colony burns. Now, are you going to help me, or would you prefer to be charged with treason?"

The doctor stared at her, eyes narrowing. Then she bit back whatever retort she'd been considering and started giving orders to the nurse.

They got her dressed, or at least decent. Her jacket and shirt were ruined. The bullet hole might have been sewn up, but the clothes had been drenched in blood, and whatever had survived the attack had been cut to ribbons by the medical team.

"The bullet went through your upper arm, into your chest, and exited under the collarbone. Your arm must have been on the backswing. You were centimetres away from death."

"Well, a hospital T-shirt will do just fine for now. How long have I been out?"

"About an hour and a half since you were shot, Governor."

"As little as that? Excellent work. Now, find me whatever painkillers you recommend and whatever stimulant you think will strike the right balance between utility and safety, and help me get over to my headquarters. There will be a lot more people in here with far worse injuries than me if we don't get this right, Doctor."

"I must advise against this course of action most strongly," said the doctor, holding up her hand when Denmead opened her mouth to speak. "I will do as you ask, but I want you back here in two hours, no more. We need to check your wounds, change your bandages and push more fluids into you. You're to drink frequently while you are up, and if you lose consciousness or do anything to further risk your health, I'll sedate you for a week to let your body recover. Is that clear?"

Denmead looked at the doctor for a moment then gave a curt nod, ignoring the sharp pains that shot down her neck.

"Nurse Gailey will accompany you, just in case." Gailey nodded, although the look on his face was no more encouraging than the doctor's.

A few minutes later, dosed with painkillers and with more in her pocket, she was on her way, Gailey following along behind, muttering all the while. Denmead found that she didn't have the strength to object.

2

_____

"Right, let's have a little order here, people," said Atticus, rapping his long fingers on the table to call the meeting to order. His gaze was drawn to his hand and he flexed the odd, spindly fingers. They looked thin and fragile, but he'd discovered they were deceptively strong with an unyielding grip.

Being deployed in an unfamiliar clone type was strange. The proportions of his body felt wrong, somehow, as if he were wearing someone else's clothes, which he supposed he was, in a way.

Looking up at the rest of the people sitting around the conference table, he saw telltale signs of nervousness and not just because of the dire situation that New Bristol faced. Some were fidgeting. Some studied data slates in a manner too intense to be convincing. Others were paying attention but their eyes flickered about, unable to settle on him. A few snuck glances at him, or rather, at what he was wearing.

The colonists were worried by his use of an alien clone body as well, and from what Warden had told him, the unusual dental arrangements of his new skull made him sound menacingly inhuman.

"Where is the governor?" asked Smith, the aptly-named Chief

Manufacturing Engineer. "She should be chairing this meeting. It's not good to break protocol, especially in situations like this," lectured Smith, working himself up to give Atticus a proper tongue-lashing. "Just because things are bad, there's no reason to jettison our long-standing Colony World procedures. They've endured for a reason, you know!" he said, wagging his finger.

Atticus hissed at him, and the man stopped talking and started blinking instead, then he lowered his finger and sat back in his chair. Intimidating hissing, it seemed, was something this body did well. It would probably make an excellent pianist as well, mused Atticus, trying to keep the smirk from his face.

"We're all familiar with the protocols, Smith," said Grimes, his strong Yorkshire accent carried over from his youth and thriving, hundreds of light years from home, "and we need to give Captain Atticus a chance to speak."

"Thank you, Mr Grimes," said Atticus, somewhat relieved that the taciturn head of civil engineering was taking part in the discussion.

"Don't thank me yet, son, I haven't done anything for you, and we're still deep in the shit," said Grimes, demonstrating an admirable, if gruff, honesty that Atticus hadn't expected from members of this council.

"Our agenda is short," said Atticus in an attempt to move things along, "as is our time. The enemy fleet is only days away, there may be troops still on the ground that we don't know about and we don't know when we will be reinforced. That means we need to evacuate the city, move our vital equipment to safe, easily defended positions and conscript every person who can be spared into a militia. The goal will be simply to survive long enough for the fleet to arrive and effect a rescue."

"Evacuate?" said Smith. "Are you mad? This is our home, we can't just abandon it to the enemy!" Atticus opened his mouth to explain but it seemed Smith wasn't the only councillor unhappy with his suggestions.

"I must agree with my colleague," said Liz Sharp, deputy chief medical officer and the most senior doctor in the colony while her superior was in the queue for a new clone body. "We have injured people in the hospital and more equipment than we can feasibly move. Evacuation isn't an option."

"And even if it were," interjected Smith, leaning forward and wagging his finger again to emphasise his points, "even if it were, we have nowhere to go. So no, we'll have to stay in the city, it's as simple as that." The captain was beginning to find the finger-wagging irritating and he briefly considered grabbing the offending digit and giving it a sharp twist.

Atticus looked around the group and saw the heads nodding in agreement. This was going to be more difficult than he had hoped. He sighed, a peculiarly aggressive sound in his borrowed body, and placed his hands flat on the table.

"Ladies, gentlemen. We have to be realistic about what is militarily possible and strategically achievable. We'll be fighting a guerrilla war, striking hard and moving quickly to confuse the enemy and disrupt their plans. My force isn't large enough to defend the city, so if we stay, everyone will die." He paused to emphasise the point then continued just as the councillors realised they could speak. "If we evacuate, some at least will have the chance of avoiding body death, and we should have an opportunity to recover everyone else." He paused again to look around the room, assessing the continuing unease at abandoning the city.

"So let's just look at how we'll manage the evacuation," he said, moving on as Sharp raised her hand to speak.

"How many people are left in the city?" he asked, trying to keep the discussion moving. "And what options do we have to move them?"

And now everyone spoke at once. Smith wanted to talk about the practicalities of moving large numbers of people, Sharp was witheringly critical of any suggestion that the hospital would have to move or even change, and Grimes's deep voice growled out his scepticism about the difficulties of repositioning civil facilities and heavy equipment. Atticus could feel his patience being buried in a stream of administrative objections.

Then the door opened and, to Atticus's considerable relief, Governor Denmead walked into the council chamber. She looked awful, her face pale and her arm heavily strapped. The room fell silent as she walked slowly to her chair and waited pointedly until Smith pulled it out for her so that she could sit. Then she looked around at the councillors and senior personnel that ran Ashton.

"We begin the evacuation of the city today. Captain Atticus and I have already reviewed the situation and agreed on a plan that maximises our chances of survival. This plan will now be put into operation." She paused to take a deep breath and give her words time to sink in. "You are all, individually, welcome to stay here if you choose, but your assistance in the execution of this plan is required and expected. Is that clear?"

"But the patients in the hospital –" Sharp began.

"Will be evacuated along with everyone else. You have a contingency plan for this sort of thing, I believe, Doctor?"

"Well, yes, it's standard protocol for all colonies in the event of a disaster, but we never expected to actually need it," the hospital administrator whined.

"No, I dare say you didn't. Nonetheless, we are facing just such a disaster, and this is not the first time a British colony has had to evacuate a hospital during an emergency. The protocols for doing so are well established, so please activate your plan."

"What about the fabrication plants?" asked Smith as Sharp, defeated, began tapping instructions into her tablet. "We can't just unplug the manufactories and simply plonk them down somewhere else, and we'll need all the production capacity we can get. How are we going to manage that?"

"The Redcliffe cave system was earmarked for precisely this sort of eventuality," said Denmead, "as you all know from the extensive planning meetings of last year." Extensive, detailed and very, very long. "Work began on the caves in the middle of last year and, incomplete though they are, we will be moving there immediately."

Smith blinked and shared a look with Grimes.

"The fabricator plants aren't ready, Governor," said Grimes, "it'll take months just to finish the foundations and prepare the ground, not to mention the time needed to actually move and install the larger manufactory units."

"You have five days," said Atticus, "and the smaller fabs need to be up and running by this evening."

"What?" said Smith. "That's outrageous! Governor, I must protest. We must have time to do the work properly."

"Well, we don't have time. Either we get the fabs installed and working or we're finished. You're quite right; we need all the manufacturing capacity we can get, both for the colonists and to supply Captain Atticus." Denmead stared coldly at Smith and spared a little glare for Grimes as well, who looked like he might object. "This is war, gentlemen, and we can't hamper our chances by constraining our supply of vital materiel."

"The cloning bays also need to be relocated," said Atticus, piling on the pressure, "because we're going to make heavy use of them. We need them running constantly, so they need to be continuously supplied with raw materials and power."

Grimes sat back in his chair, scrolling through something on his tablet and muttering under his breath. Smith just shook his head, still not able to grasp the scale of the undertaking.

"I've triggered the hospital's contingency plan," said Sharp, looking up from her data slate. "We have around a hundred patients in the wards plus beds and equipment for another hundred. The first people can be moved within thirty minutes, and the building can be clear by the end of the day."

"Good, thank you, Doctor," said Denmead, satisfied that something, finally, was beginning to happen.

"We'll need transport, of course, and somewhere to set up shop." She paused as Denmead raised an eyebrow. "It's thirty kilometres to the caves, Governor, and we don't keep enough ATVs to move everyone and everything that distance in the time allowed. You'll need to find us some lifters."

"Leave that to me," said Atticus. "I have a squad out scavenging for working or repairable vehicles. You're their top priority."

"And what about the conditions at the caves, Mr Grimes?" asked Governor Denmead. "How are we for power, water, space, etc.?"

"Let me pull up the latest report," muttered Grimes, flicking at his tablet. "Okay, there are two small fusion generators in the deepest part of the system, so power should be fine. They're up and running, providing emergency power to the city. We'll divert the cables, no problem.

"Water is more complicated, but we have a filtration system and some tanks in place. They were intended for hydroponics, of course, but they produce potable water. We'll need to run hoses and channel additional pipes and tanks into the network to cope with the load. Water will be in short supply for a few weeks at least. There won't be enough for bathing, but we won't die of thirst."

"Good, thank you," Denmead said.

"Floor space is more difficult. Levelling the caverns takes a very great deal of work and it wasn't a high priority task, so we've been doing it only when we needed to. There's a rudimentary road network so that you can drive to and into the caves but, beyond that, it's been fairly ad hoc. Same with the walkways. Some of the caverns have raised paths, some have paths ground into the floor, but most don't have anything, at all, yet."

"Some of our patients need sterile environments, Mr Grimes. Can that be managed?" Sharp asked.

Grunes nodded. "There are some prefabricated building units that can be assembled in the caves and they would be at least as sterile as your hospital. Probably better, as they're completely new."

"Our hospital is completely clean, Mr Grimes," said Sharp testily.

"I'm sorry, I didn't mean to imply anything, Doctor," Grimes said, "but newer buildings should be easy to control and cleanse."

Denmead waved her hands. "Ladies and gentlemen, we don't have time for these sorts of arguments. Dr Sharp, I'm sure the hospital is normally clean, and we'll do whatever we can to provide you with as many sterile rooms as possible, but resources are limited. Mr Grimes, I'll need you to work with Dr Sharp to establish how many prefabricated units are needed. Dr Sharp, I need you to pare everything to the bone and take only the minimum facilities necessary to support your patients."

Dr Sharp opened her mouth, clearly about to protest, but Denmead held up her hand. "No. I'm sorry, Doctor. I understand you must have objections, but we don't have the luxury of providing the standard of care you're used to. You are not setting up a civilian hospital facility, you are going to be running a military field hospital. I need you to cope with the bare minimum you can. If we can spare resources later then you'll have them, but right now we're facing a harsh choice. Either we supply Captain Atticus, his Marines and our own militia, or New Bristol will become an occupied world."

Grimes spoke up. "We can get you enough pre-fabricated units, Doctor, I just need to discuss numbers with you. The rest of the beds might have to be in open cavern space with improvised flooring that won't all be on the same level. It'll be well lit, and the temperature in the caves is pretty constant. Unfortunately, the fabricators can't operate without being level so the majority of the existing foamcrete floor spaces will have to be used for manufacturing space."

"We'll cope," said Sharp, standing up, "but I need to go. There is much to oversee, especially with Flint offline for the foreseeable future." She looked to the governor for permission to leave, and Denmead nodded. Sharp was already talking into her comm before she had left the room.

The governor turned to Smith, the manager of the production facilities. "Mr Smith?"

"Hmm, what?" said Smith, looking up from his data slate. "Oh, yes, sorry. Well, er, tricky," he said, sucking air through his teeth. "We can relocate the smaller fabs easily enough – they'll fit on the standard transport sleds. The larger fabs will need the heavy transport lifters because they're too big to be moved that distance with a sled over rough ground. We can get them out of the buildings and then they need to be airlifted."

Smith sighed heavily. "The problem is, the lifters are designed for efficiency not speed, so they aren't quick, and we need them for anything heavy or bulky. That means we don't have lots of spare transport capacity to move the cloning pods and the supporting equipment to the cave. Would it be possible to use the dropships that the lieutenant captured?"

Atticus nodded and made a note. "Yes, for the next few days until the fleet is close enough to pick up their movement. I'll ask Colour Sergeant Jenkins to be your liaison on that as soon as she's been decanted into her new clone. She'll get you a window that will minimise the risk of dropships being detected as you move your materials. The same restrictions will apply to the transport lifters; they have a smaller signature but could still be picked up by enemy scanning and, obviously, we don't want to reveal the location of our base. Once the window closes, we'll have to mothball any air or spacecraft but that's a discussion for another time. You should move the heaviest gear as early as possible."

"So really it's just a question of time, space and materials. Relocating everything in five days is going to be very challenging, especially as half my people are either dead or missing," said Smith, frowning at his tablet again.

"I know your teams were badly hit, Phil," said Governor Denmead sympathetically, "but anything you can do would help. Drones, arms and ammunition are the immediate priorities. We have to know what's going on and we need tools to defend ourselves. After that, larger items like, oh, tanks, or something."

"Armour and larger-calibre specialist weapons are likely to be more useful than tanks," said Atticus. "I'll have Lieutenant Warden bring you a list of our needs, if that would help?"

"It would, thank you, Captain. And I've got a few ideas about how we might provide you with drones and other light equipment. Let me look into that, and I'll get back to you."

"Is there anything else you need, Mr Smith?" Denmead asked.

"Only everything we haven't got," he said, "but it wouldn't be a challenge if there weren't a few tricky bits."

"Good. Let me know if anything comes up. Carry on."

"By the way, I've been meaning to ask, do we have a name for the cave site, Governor?" Smith said. "I think it would help during discussions."

"Does anyone which to suggest something?" Denmead asked.

"How about Fort Widley?" Atticus offered. "It's a Palmerston fort overlooking Pompey, and it's famously concealed within the hill so an army approaching from the north wouldn't know it was there until they were caught out."

"Fort Widley it is." Denmead turned to Sandra Walker, her Director of Communications. "Let's release a colony-wide communication announcing the evacuation to the newly named Fort Widley. Advise everyone to be on standby to receive their assignments and that every uninjured colonist above the age of thirteen will be given a role." Walker nodded and began typing up a statement for immediate release. It would go directly to the comms system of each colonist and interrupt anything non-critical they might be looking at.

Denmead stood up with some effort and faced her audience. It was a fairly even split between the councillors of Ashton, who formed the local government, and the staff from her own office, which oversaw the colony on behalf of the British government.

"Ladies and gentlemen, I know that the situation is dire, but we can deal with it. I am only following one guideline during this invasion: utter commitment to the protection of New Bristol and the colony we have worked so hard to build. That's it. One guiding principle to bring us all together and in our darkest hour, bind us so that we are of one will, one purpose. I expect each of you to do your duty, whether civilian or military. If my expectation is too high, if you aren't committed, I will take your resignation now and show you to the window myself," she said, pointing towards the end of the conference room which overlooked New Ashton and offered an impressive view of the city.

"Governor, we're on the fifth floor, I think you mean you'd show people to the door," said Councillor Stoat with a laugh that didn't seem to catch on. After a moment he looked around the table, but nobody caught his eye.

Denmead let it hang for just a second longer.

"I meant what I said, Councillor Stoat. I will have total commitment from you all to the defence of this colony and if anyone doesn't intend to give me that, I expect them to take the honourable way out and retire their body for spare parts or redeployment. We don't have the food or resources to support anyone who won't contribute and I'm not sending adults to Fort Widley to hide with the small children and the wounded."

The room was completely silent. Stoat, pale-faced, opened his mouth as if to reply then thought better of it and just nodded instead. Governor Denmead faced the full table, expression grim and features ashen from the loss of blood and the nagging pain of her injuries.

"I will take your silence as confirmation that I have your full commitment, ladies and gentlemen. Now, we must move on to other business. I would like to keep these meetings as short and decisive as possible, folks. Better to meet again later if need be. Please remember we are at war and we don't have time for extensive back and forth debates; we need to keep the decision-making process as efficient as possible. I will step in and make final decisions when required, though I'd rather the council, the captain and my team work together. I will point out that as the ranking officer on New Bristol, all military decisions rest with Captain Atticus and his team."

The councillors all mutely nodded.

"Mr Smith and Mr Grimes, unless you have anything immediate, I believe you will be needed elsewhere."

Smith nodded and turned to Grimes. "Shall we?" The two men left, heads together and deep in conversation.

"Captain Atticus, do you have anything further to add? I was intending to move on to the civilian issues for now. If you don't have anything to we need to address right now, I suggest you and I reconvene later, and we'll bring the full group together for an update in the early evening."

Atticus stood up. "Thank you, Governor. I only want to say that you have my full support and that my Marines will do everything possible to defeat this invasion." With that, he turned and left, off to deal with the next problem and thoroughly relieved that the governor was back in play.

"And that leaves the rest of us," said Governor Denmead, as she eased herself back into her chair, "to work out how to move several thousand people to the newly named Fort Widley in the caves at Redcliffe. We need to divide up the long list of tasks that are necessary for our survival, and identify the people to lead each team." She paused to look again at her councillors and staff. They seemed to be suitably attentive. "Good, let's get cracking."

Maybe, just maybe, this would be the first meeting of the colonial government and city council that would not consist of interminable disputes and endless discussions with no sign of action.

If not, there was always the window.

3

———————

"Give me an update, Barlow. What's the status of the wormhole comms?" barked Atticus. The tech was rummaging around in the back of a server cabinet.

"We just got back up while you were in your meeting, sir," Barlow called out from behind the cabinet. "I'm trying to get the redundant system up and running as well, so we have a bit more resilience."

"Have you got a response from the Puzzle Palace yet? We need to know when the fleet will arrive or if they've even sent anything," Atticus said, walking past the control console so he could at least see Barlow's face.

"Yes, sir," Barlow said as he continued to connect fibres and slot in new parts. "The good news is that HQ requested naval support based on the governor's initial report and the admiralty has sent their closest patrol group. The bad news is that it will take just over seven days more for them to arrive, and it's not a full squadron."

"What's the makeup of the patrol group?"

"One Nelson class frigate, an Albion support ship and a Cook survey ship, sir. Under the command of Vice Admiral Staines."

"That's better than expected. I'll need a full briefing on their manpower, armaments and capabilities as soon as possible. Now, we need to find out about our enemy. Send the DNA profiles that Wilson extracted from the clones. Tell them we need to know everything they can tell us about that line of blanks. We need to know which of the Lost Arks these people came from."

Barlow looked up and saw the expression on the captain's face, he put down the component and his screwdriver and moved quickly to the command console. He began to tap away at the keyboard, locating the data block that Wilson had prepared and constructing a message to HQ. "Maximum priority, sir?" he asked, rhetorically he supposed, but in the RMSC he needed the order.

"Correct. I'm going to prepare a follow-up message for General Bonneville as well. I think we're going to need some bigger ships."

4

Warden and Milton walked over to the dropship landing pad, although that was a grandiose name for it. Until recently, it had been a collection of tennis courts but half an hour with a las-cutter to remove the fencing and nets had put paid to that. Now the area played host to the three captured dropships.

"I hope he's got some good news for us," Milton said.

"Such as?"

"He found a weapon system on the dropships or a cupboard with some more blank clones in it."

Warden chuckled. Either of those would be a big help.

"That wouldn't hurt. I don't think we're going to have that kind of luck today though, do you?"

"No, but a girl can dream, right?"

"Whatever you say, Sergeant," Warden said as he swiped his card to open the ramp into the cloning bay.

They found Corporal Wilson tinkering with the controls of the cloning pods and dictating notes to a tablet. He looked up as they approached.

"Do we have permission to proceed, sir?" he asked Warden.

"Yes, we have the go-ahead. We are to redeploy our losses from A

Troop first. The governor is sending us some medics to help with orientation. After that, we'll deploy B Troop and then with any remaining clones will go to C Troop. The captain is recalling them from training now."

"Right you are, sir. We've got a few specialist clones types here. Any particular assignments you want me to make?"

"We need to give these clone types designations so we can match them to equivalent specialities. What do we have so far?"

"Okay, well, the flyers are obviously snipers," replied Barlow. "They've got clever adaptations in their legs, hips and backs to allow them to lie prone without discomfort. All our snipers have the appropriate qualifications and, as we didn't lose any from A Troop, I've assigned the snipers from Troops B and C to these blanks. Here's the list I've made of the clones we have available. There are six flyers, six of the officer types like the one we put Captain Atticus in, then there are thirty of what seems to be the default trooper clone and six of the big bastards that look like ogres."

"Ogres, eh? That's a good name for them. Seems fitting to me, Lieutenant," said Milton.

"Fine, ogres they are. Anyone got a good idea for the flyers?"

"Batmen?" suggested Barlow, but he couldn't keep the nerdy smirk from his face.

"Doesn't sound quite right," said Warden, shaking his head. "What about Valkyries? Vultures? Harpies?"

Barlow and Milton both confirmed, "Harpies."

"And these standard ones?"

"That one's easy – they're lizardmen. Scales all over them."

"All, over them?" Milton enquired, one eyebrow raised.

Barlow coughed.

Warden joined in, "Very, umm, diligent of you Barlow, not sure why we needed to know that but, thank you, I suppose?"

Barlow sighed. "I don't suppose there's any chance I won't be hearing about this in the mess later?"

Warden slapped him on the back. "Don't worry, Barlow, Marine X is bound to do something that will take the attention from you. Now, what are we calling the ones that they use for pilots?"

"Ruperts," Barlow responded with malicious glee.

"Well, we don't have time to be dainty, I suppose, even if we do have time to inspect the contents of the clones' underpants," Warden responded.

"Now, now, boys," said Milton, suppressing a grin, "shall we decide who is going to get which body type and start the deployments? We do have an alien fleet bearing down on us, after all." She took the data slate from Barlow and flicked through the list of Marines and clones.

"First up is the company command. Who wants to pick a body type for Colour Sergeant Jenkins, hmm?" she asked sweetly, pausing to see if Warden would speak up. "No? Very brave. Shall I pick one, then?"

Both men nodded enthusiastically and with obvious relief and Sergeant Milton sighed. Grown men and Royal Marines, both battle-hardened and experienced, and for some reason Stephanie Jenkins, who couldn't be nicer if she tried, terrified them. Milton honestly didn't know why the colour sergeant invoked such visceral reactions in the troops; she wasn't intimidated at all.

Tutting to herself, she flagged the profile for deployment to a clone labelled 'Ogre' and noted alongside the order 'As agreed by Lt. Warden'.

"Right," she said, hiding her grin, "let's work through this list."

5

Atticus sat in the empty conference suite and skimmed the information in the comms update that Barlow had forwarded to him. The gist of it was that they were getting some support from HQ but too little and, in Atticus's opinion, too late. Not good.

The captain sat back, slate on the table, and considered his options. There really was only one, now that the wormhole comm system was working again. He picked up his slate and queued a call for General Bonneville, marking it 'urgent'. The general was a busy man, so this might take a while, and Atticus settled back for a long wait.

Six seconds later the call was answered, and Atticus was surprised to see the general's face appear on the screen.

"Atticus?" he said uncertainly, leaning forward to peer into the camera. "Is that you?"

"Yes, sir, I'm wearing an enemy clone."

The general did not look convinced even though Atticus had used his personal cypher, so they danced the identification two-step, an age-old protocol to verify personality integrity in an age when downloads were everyday and facial recognition was no longer sufficient.

Eventually, the general was satisfied, and Atticus was able to discuss the situation on New Bristol.

"It's bad, sir. We're hard-pressed and short of pretty much every-thing," said Atticus, slightly despondent. "About the only things we have in sufficient quantities are tea and gin."

Bonneville frowned and Atticus could feel his disapproval across the light years.

"Keep it together, Edward, this whole business rests on your shoulders."

"Yes, sir, sorry. It's been a long day."

"Never mind that. The researchers are making progress and should have more information for you soon. They're preparing a package of information and will send it once they complete their analysis."

There was a pause as Bonneville glared at something off-screen. Atticus couldn't shake the feeling that the general was preparing to impart bad news.

"The review of the DNA sequences you sent is not yet conclusive but the preliminary results suggest that it might indeed have origi-nated on one of the lost Ark ships."

"Any idea which one?"

"Not yet, but it wasn't one of ours. The boffins are certain of that, or as close to certain as they ever admit to being. Something to do with the marker sequences that were added to the DNA of travellers on the Ark ships. Frankly, I don't understand more than one word in six, but I'll send it to you. Maybe it'll make sense when you read it."

Atticus didn't think it likely, but that was a problem for another day.

"Anyway," said Bonneville, "we've asked around and shared the marker sequences with the usual suspects. Nobody has admitted ownership yet, but it's only a matter of time. How do things look at your end?"

"Sticky, if I'm honest. I wasn't joking about the tea. We're pressing every able-bodied person into service, but really our only hope is the fleet. If they arrive in time, we should avoid complete body death and stand a decent chance of making it through with the backups intact. If not..." He didn't finish the sentence; there was no need.

"Quite," said Bonneville, his face grim, "keep me informed when you can, Captain Atticus, but otherwise just get on with the job. I'll let you know if anything changes on this end."

"Will do, thank you, sir. Goodbye."

6

The cavern was, well, cavernous. Wilson took a moment to look around and marvel at the enormous space. He'd been told by a rather excited geologist that it was a solutional cave of unusual size and formation, whatever the hell that meant. All Corporal Wilson cared about was that this part of the cave system was deep enough underground that it would be hard to assault from orbit. That, and the fact that the composition of the rocks would render their base near-impossible to detect.

To the horror of the geologists, the decision had been made to bring in the heaviest equipment available and grind smooth the floor of several of the larger, more useful chambers. Wilson could see the quandary. The cave was both impressive and strangely beautiful, but as important as it was geologically, beauty today was a secondary concern.

He turned to his colleagues. "Enough gawking, folks. They took plenty of records of this place before we even got here, so you can review those at your leisure when New Bristol is safe. Right now, it's time for us to crack on and make sure that happens." The other tech specialists of A troop nodded and started moving.

Wilson turned to Eileen Robinson, one of the colony's top civil engineers. Her normal role was to design efficient terraforming solutions and deploy the equipment that would give New Bristol the atmosphere and environment it needed to support a much larger population. Today, her talents were being put to more urgent use, namely smoothing out the floor, filling in the cracks and creating enough space for the machinery of day-to-day life to be installed and set up.

"What do you think? Can we get it all done?" asked Wilson.

She smiled at him, but her lips were a little too tightly pressed and her frown a little too prominent for the expression to come across as particularly confident. She sniffed then said, more confidently than Wilson had expected, "Absolutely. I don't see any reason why not."

And their needs were great. As well as utilities – power, plumbing, sewerage – they needed communications stations, housing, canteens and several big flat spaces for cloning bays. And they needed it all done and ready to be used before the enemy fleet pounded Ashton back into the barren rocks from which it had grown. A challenge for even the best-equipped team.

Perhaps the biggest headache was working out what they had to do first in this mammoth project. Fortunately for Wilson, that wasn't his job. He and the other Marine tech specialists had added their work items to the list of outstanding jobs, but they weren't being asked to organise the project. The colonists of New Bristol were heavily biased towards science, engineering, project management, hydroponics, manufacturing and similar skills. You had to be useful if you wanted to join a frontier colony, so everyone had multiple skillsets. Except for the children, of course, but there really wasn't much use for children out here.

"Great. I was a little worried we might not have time for a hot wet," he said, laughing. Then he saw her face. "We do, right?" he asked, not a little worried.

"There's always time for tea, Corporal Wilson. We don't have to be barbaric just because the colony isn't very old. I think tea was the second plant the hydroponics folks started cultivating in earnest."

"Really? What was the first? I'm betting potatoes. Biologists love growing potatoes. I think it's the challenge."

"Juniper, or so I'm told."

Wilson grinned and nodded appreciatively.

"Good call. Who needs cabbage and mash anyway?"

"Agreed. Shall we look at the locations we've suggested for your cloning bays?" she asked. Wilson nodded, and they walked around the cave, Robinson looking at her data tablet to confirm the areas that were marked for the new bays to be constructed.

Two hundred colonists had been assigned to the task of preparing the ground and the platforms for the new bays then extracting the necessary pods and equipment from the dropships. As soon as the current batch of clones had been deployed, the teams would pull the first dropship cloning bay apart and reconstruct it in the caves. They would run a battery of tests on the first of the stolen enemy bays to confirm it was operating correctly; then the techs would start growing new clones.

If the first bay worked, the teams would dismantle the bays in the other two ships and re-install them elsewhere in the caverns. If there were problems, the backup plan was to use the bays where they were but bury the dropships under improvised shelters covered in rock to protect them from discovery. That would mean losing the dropships' flight capabilities, though, and Captain Atticus wasn't keen on having to fall back to that plan, not keen at all. Wilson had learned a long time ago that when the captain wasn't keen on something, it was a really good idea to find an alternative solution.

"What about weapons production?" asked Wilson.

"We're trying to gather all the facilities from the outlying sites and anything that hasn't already been destroyed in the city. Look, here are the numbers we've identified, and the units we can confirm were already destroyed. These tables here," she said, flicking at her data slate and zooming out to show the whole picture, "show the production queue we have and the dependencies."

Wilson whistled, the list was huge, and almost every item was depending on several other things. The number of lines connecting the various components was so great that it was difficult to see where the first piece of work sat within the whole.

"The timescale looks wrong," Wilson said, peering at a copy of the chart on his own slate. "It says it'll take six more days to get phase one done and that doesn't leave us enough time for the things we need in phase two."

"It does look bad at the moment," conceded Robinson. "I've asked the governor to provide more people to help with production but we're running out of bodies. We need to find more creative ways to increase productivity or we'll have problems."

"We're going to have to cut back on something then," said Wilson glumly. "There must be something we can do without."

"Be my guest. We should get all the senior people to check the list and see if there's anything they can do without, but I haven't found much in the way of improvements, yet. We need more people to get things done, or we need to cut tasks from the list, or we need to increase our manufacturing capabilities. Or some kind of genius idea. I don't see any option but to prioritise everything we need, pare back the quantities as far as possible and make do with what we can produce in the short term."

Wilson flicked around the list and chart on his slate and sat down on a flattened stalactite. Or stalagmite. Had to be one or the other, he thought. He scrolled up and down the list, looking for items he thought they could do without.

Guns would be a sticking point, he knew. They'd inventoried every weapon in the colony, including the captured alien gear, and they knew how many colonists needed guns. They were already only aiming to produce enough weapons for the colonists who were being conscripted for the defence of New Bristol. They could cut back further, but that would leave no room for losses or damage.

The surveillance drones were another issue. Captain Atticus and Lieutenant Warden were convinced they had to have a large number of drones to replace the satellite and sensor grid networks. They didn't have time to re-build the sensor grid and launching satellites wasn't going to go unnoticed, so drones were their only option for gathering the information required to organise an effective defence. The large military surveillance drones weren't simple to produce, and they competed directly with weapons and munitions for manufacturing time.

If they cut the number of drones, they'd be able to produce more guns. Maybe he should ask Captain Atticus if he'd rather have fewer armed conscripts or a smaller area under surveillance by drone. Wilson sighed and slipped the slate back into his jacket pocket. Then a thought occurred to him.

"We need more drones, but they're eating into our production time and stretching our timelines for other equipment. Do you know how many drones the colony has?"

"Yes, of course. Look, here. These are our monitoring, weather and delivery drones. There aren't that many, I'm afraid, and their capabilities are a lot more specialised than yours. You can probably repurpose some of them, though, and link them into your network."

"Yeah, but what about the civilian drones? There are no numbers here."

"Civilian drones? All our drones are civilian, Corporal."

"No, I don't mean that kind of civilian, I mean the drones the citizens own for their own use."

"It can't be that many, surely. Are there really that many grown men that want to play with drones?"

"I'll take that in the spirit it was intended, Mrs Robinson. But I wasn't thinking of the adults. You've got kids here as well, right?"

7

Atticus stared at the holo-table, amazed that the thing had survived the firefight that had engulfed the city. It was an absolute boon. It was showing the terrain around Ashton, and the colony's geologists and engineers had marked several sites that could be used to conceal the dropships. Atticus had been trying all morning to decide the best way to distribute them. His eyes were beginning to glaze over with the mind-numbing tedium.

The problem was to balance utility and security. Keeping the dropships close to Fort Widley maximised their value by ensuring they would be available if they needed to evacuate civilians or run med-evac from hot zones.

But any launch might be noticed by the enemy, and a launch close to Fort Widley might draw attention to their base. Did they dare use the dropships except in an emergency?

Atticus twiddled the stylus between his fingers, thinking. He was vacillating, stuck with an awkward decision that could easily go either way, and he needed to break the deadlock.

"Get a second opinion," he muttered to himself, drafting a message to request assistance from Lieutenant Warden and Governor Denmead.

Then he went back to his pondering. His feeling was that the dropships should be far enough from Widley to allow launches to take place without revealing the location of their base. That would leave just two proposals and a limited set of options for locations.

Governor Denmead arrived just before Lieutenant Warden, and Atticus went straight to work, laying out the risks and rewards of the two options. He answered their questions quickly then called a vote. Each of them scrawled a letter on their data slate.

"And I vote option B," said Atticus, turning his slate around to show his choice.

"Unanimous," said Denmead once she and Warden had flipped around their own slates. "Well, that was easy."

"So you say," grunted Atticus, guiltily aware that he'd spent half the morning on a question that they had just settled in under fifteen minutes.

"To summarise," he said, repeating himself to be sure that everyone agreed and understood, "the pods will be stripped from the dropships, installed in Fort Widley and the dropships positioned well away from both Ashton and the caves. The locations are reasonably accessible, but the dropships will be concealed, to some degree, by the surrounding terrain. Two will be in canyons over here," he said, pointing at a spot on the holo-table, "and the third will be below a rock arch near some cliffs over there. We'll add anti-scan camo-netting to make life a little more complicated for the enemy."

He paused to look at Denmead and Warden.

"Any questions?"

"Are the dropships armed?" asked Governor Denmead.

"Not with anything worth mentioning," answered Warden, "and before you ask, it's not likely we can build and mount anything that would make them useful as gunships for assaulting ground troops." He paused but spoke again as he saw a new question in Denmead's face. "And don't even think of suggesting ship to ship engagements," he said, watching her face as the question died.

"Is there anything else we should take out along with the pods?" she asked next.

"Weapons, armour and munitions are already taken care of," said Warden.

"We aren't going to spend any significant time in them," said Atticus thoughtfully, "so there are probably some creature comforts that could be dumped. We need the beds in case we have to use them for medical evacuation. Let's have a couple of Marines go through the dropships again with your team, Governor, just in case there's anything we won't need, and you can use in Fort Widley."

Warden nodded, making notes on his slate.

"Good, thanks. We lost a lot of equipment to building collapses, and I don't want to spend manufacturing resources on anything that you don't need for the fight. We're scavenging what we can from the city and moving it to the caves or to other places we can use as temporary stores," said Governor Denmead.

"Fine. Warden, get it done. Unless anyone has anything else on this subject, I suggest we get a move on and strip the dropships as quickly as possible. The sooner it's done, and they're away from the caves, the better."

And the easier I'll sleep, thought Atticus as he followed the other two out of the room and flicked off the light switch.

8

"Right," said Governor Denmead, rubbing her tired eyes, "so that's the last of the task assignments unless anyone can think of anything else to add to the list?" She paused, but nobody else had the strength to make suggestions.

"Good, which means that there's only one topic left to cover, namely how we will form our militia. The civilians will have to help with the defence," she said, speaking over the angry voices of her councillors. "They will help because there's no other way. Captain Atticus will explain how the militia will function and how we will integrate his force to make our very limited resources stretch as far as possible. Captain?"

Atticus nodded and prepared to launch into the details of the plan that he and Denmead had concocted. He'd lost count of how many times they had reconvened that day, but at least he had only had to attend some of the meetings.

Denmead, on the other hand, had been in every significant meeting and he'd seen the updates flashing across his HUD all day. Items would get added to the main list to be actioned, assigned to someone and sometimes, completed. Then as each new meeting started, a flurry of additional items would be added to the list.

They had covered food, water, energy, the hospital and the fabs and transport. Then there'd been meetings to update on earlier meetings and add further actions. Attendees changed as necessary, and Denmead was enforcing strict discipline on time-wasting; it seemed her earlier comments had been taken to heart. Now, finally, most of the tasks they had identified had been categorised, prioritised and pushed to their assignees and, Atticus hoped, things were starting to happen.

"As the governor says, I've joined you to discuss what I hope is the final topic of the day, namely the formation of a militia. I don't have the numbers to mount a solid defence, let alone a counterattack, and we now know that the fleet isn't carrying significant numbers of clones, so it'll be weeks at least before reinforcements arrive to allow us to fight back and drive the enemy from the city."

"Anyone not already assigned a task or a team," said the Governor, stepping in smoothly with the next part of the explanation, "will be issued weapons and given as much training as we can manage. They'll divide into troops and provide what support they can to the captain's Marines. Only citizens whose roles are essential to our survival will be excluded from the militia."

"B Troop of my company are deploying as we speak. After this meeting is done, I'll be going to brief Lieutenant Hayes, who leads the troop. She will be taking the lead with the militia and training the recruits. You've already been through the list of available citizens, and the good news is that we have enough to deploy a battalion," said Atticus.

He moved to stand beside a large display on the wall and sent a diagram of the battalion structure to the display.

"As you can see from this diagram, the lieutenant becomes a battalion commander, quite a promotion at her age. Each group of civilian militia will be led by a Marine, and the overall companies will be led by NCOs. The militia will be instructed on the absolute basics – shooting, keeping to cover, working as a team. Then they'll be deployed in defence of the colony," Atticus said.

"But we've got only a few days before the enemy arrive!" Councillor Stoat blurted out. "You propose to give them less than a week's training and then hurl them into battle against those... those... things?"

Atticus shook his head. "Most of them have either already been involved in the fighting, or they've been here during the defence of Ashton. They're used to being in a war zone, albeit not at the level we're now facing. I'm also not planning to hurl them into battle as you put it. The militia will be used primarily for defensive purposes so that our professional forces, the Marines, can focus elsewhere."

He brought up an image of the city with locations marked for the defensive positions he'd planned with Warden and Colour Jenkins.

"I won't go into much detail, but these are the locations we'll be using as our defensive positions. The militia, along with B Troop, will be responsible for holding Ashton as long as we can. A Troop will be launching attacks on the enemy in an attempt to disrupt their operations."

He paused, looking around to see if anyone would ask questions.

"Regarding the training period," he said when it was clear that the councillors were too shocked to ask anything at all, "it won't be a full week of combat drilling. None of the militia recruits were in essential roles, and they don't have other duties, but we need a lot of manpower to get Fort Widley up and running. They will be our labour force and will spend some of each day doing those tasks under the guidance of their section leaders. We'll give them as much training as we can, and that's the best we can do," said Atticus.

"The NCOs are used to looking after new recruits and remember, Marines will be distributed amongst the militia to lead by example. They'll provide instruction on the basics and then position them, wherever possible, in defensive positions with clear and straightforward instructions on how long to stand and when to retreat. That should maximise their effectiveness and minimise the number of body deaths."

Atticus paused to allow all this to sink in. The councillors looked somewhat shocked and not a little scared but, strangely, they seemed to have accepted the general strategy with remarkably few complaints.

"If there are no objections," said Denmead, "we'll wrap up there. Captain Atticus will make the arrangements with his people, but you will need to speak to your constituents and make sure they get their assignments. And you must field all the complaints. The captain and his Marines can't be dealing with anyone who doesn't like the cards they've been dealt, they're far too busy. If you have anyone who has finished their assigned duties and is no longer needed, they'll be moved to the militia. We will have casualties to replace." She stood up before anyone could ask questions and, with a slight grimace at the pain, left the room.

Atticus answered a few minor questions about practical matters of organisation, and then the meeting broke up, and they all went about their work. He sat there a few minutes longer, working through his own checklist, then went to find volunteers amongst B Troop.

He grinned. They were going to love this.

9

Atticus looked at the limited tactical overview they'd been able to pull together and tried to factor in everything they knew about the enemy, which wasn't enough for his tastes. He shook his head.

"It's not going to be enough," he said quietly so that only Denmead could hear him. He'd found that they worked well as a team. She was an effective administrator and a gifted politician and had proved her worth a dozen times over in the last few days. "There's just too much that can go wrong and we don't have the forces."

It was a discussion they'd had several times and repetition wasn't making things any better. Denmead gave him a stern look and checked the scanners again.

"A day out," she said, pointing at the map of the solar system showing the enemy fleet's rough position in relation to New Bristol and the other planets, "a day out and there's nothing we can do but watch."

That wasn't quite right, of course, but they had already done everything they could think of doing and now it was just a case of seeing how the plan went.

They sat for several minutes watching as the map updated slowly before them. It was depressingly mesmerising.

Then the comms tech, Barlow came in and Atticus could tell from his face that the news was unlikely to be good.

"Message from HQ, sir," said Barlow. "There was an update on our own fleet – nothing interesting there – and an encrypted package marked for your eyes only. I've forwarded it to your tablet, sir."

"Thank you, Barlow," said Atticus, turning his attention to his tablet as Barlow nodded and left. There was indeed a package of encrypted information in his inbox, just arrived. Atticus tapped into it, entered his private key and waited while the tablet re-confirmed his identity. Then he began to wade through the information that HQ had deemed useful for him to have.

"They've matched the markers in the DNA samples we sent to the clones supplied to a Lost Ark ship that went missing a couple of hundred years ago," he said finally, summarising the information for Denmead. "It seems that it was a privately funded club of malcontents who weren't happy with the worldwide legal restrictions agreed by Sol governments. The core members of the group were ethnically Russian but had members from every continent and country still capable of supporting life in the years before they launched. A multi-cultural melting-pot of people seeking the freedom to experiment with genetic manipulation, body-hacking and cloning in an attempt to achieve functional biological immortality."

He skimmed the rest of the information as Denmead nodded and thought about that.

"The ship was the *Koschei*, named after, if you can believe it, an ancient Slavic or Russian archetypal antagonist, Koschei the Deathless or Koschei the Immortal. Appropriate, given the crew's philosophy and intentions." Atticus read on then snorted. "Very thorough. They've even sent us an image of a painting from 1927, for all the good it'll do us." He turned the tablet around to show Denmead a picture of an ancient king cuddling a maiden.

"Gruesome," murmured Denmead, frowning at the image. Then she paused at a brief spasm of pain in her shoulder. "So what we're facing is some kind of ancient rebel group?"

Atticus shrugged. "If I recall my history, at the time a lot of groups sent out Arks. The control of the national governments was more fragile and international relations hadn't recovered. Lots of private groups and companies funded their own Ark ships because the governments weren't sending enough. Earth was a cesspool back then, and everyone wanted off it."

"Skip forward a couple of hundred years and these people have gone out, far beyond the frontier of colonised space. Where the hell did they go?"

Atticus looked at her and frowned. He steepled his fingers and then pressed his hands to his face, holding his head in his long-fingered hands for a moment. The gesture was utterly human, in an utterly alien-seeming body. But it wasn't alien. Not really, she thought. It was human, just not in a way she recognised.

"More importantly," he suggested as he leaned back and looked up again, "why did they come back?"

That stopped her train of thought. Why had they come back? Where had they been? Where and why? "I don't have an answer for that. They've come here and attacked without warning, as if we were the hostile party."

The attack on New Bristol was really just another in a long string of human encounters where explorers from one country had discovered or claimed a land that was already settled. Natives and invaders had probably looked at each other, wondering about their strange appearance, and often the encounters had ended in hideous violence even if they had started peacefully.

"Yes, they're aggressive but... why? There's nothing in this report that suggests this group was anything but a slightly crackpot bunch of people who wanted to modify their bodies and live as they pleased. They weren't violent or disruptive. They didn't have any strong political ideology, and they weren't suggesting anyone else should do what they wanted to. They just wanted to go out and explore, as so many of our ancestors have done, and adapt their bodies according to their own rules. From this, they seem more like scientists than soldiers or revolutionaries," Atticus said.

Denmead looked through some of the information, then suggested they both get through the entire report. They read in silence for some time, Atticus making copious notes.

It was a while before Denmead spoke again.

"You're right. Almost none had any military or police service. They were mostly scientists and engineers of one form or another. Computing, biology, bionics, cryogenics, high energy physics, electronics, clean energy. They probably had the best-educated crew and passengers for centuries. But does it matter at this stage?"

"Yes. Yes, it does, Governor. I'm a military man; I need to know about my enemy to defeat him. They've been out there somewhere, possibly for a century or more. They had the people and capability to improve their engines en route. We have no idea how far they've been, but we do know their ship was unusually large and sophisticated for the time. They weren't dreamers, they were realists and they assembled a large group of like-minded, talented and smart people. Their goal was to establish a colony, that much is clear, and for a long time they even sent back updates." He paused for a moment to think about that.

"Not all of the Arks communicated; some were highly isolationist. These people weren't. They wanted to remain in touch but, eventually, the updates stopped and they joined the ranks of the Lost Arks. It was assumed they had encountered something terminal, but I've been looking at the population projections. They were headed past New Bristol on the route they broadcast back to Sol. If they founded a colony out there, they would have had at least a hundred years to build it, maybe more."

Denmead asked which section it was, and he told her. She skipped back to population figures and looked at the charts for a few minutes, muttering to herself as she read.

"Bugger. Bugger me," she said, "bloody buggering hell. Buuugger." Finally, she looked up at him in, her eyes wide and a frown creasing her forehead. "Bugger it. Atticus, these buggers are going to bugger us up completely if these figures are right! Do you have any idea how much more production capacity they would have available, compared to us, if this estimate is even halfway right? They could bugger us up and down the street all week and twice on Sundays. Their economy could bugger the entire sector without so much as a please or thank you."

"That was among my many concerns. But think about that for a moment. They've been out there and even a pessimistic calculation that they only settled on a colony world seventy-five years ago and came back in this direction at a leisurely pace could still mean their economy is huge. We've already seen they've made improvements in a wide range of technologies, as you might expect from a society entirely composed of people with that sort of background," Atticus said.

He projected a map of the local sectors of space on the conference table they were sat at. New Bristol was far away from the nearest colonies. It wasn't the only colony that existed outside the main bubble of human space, but it was the furthest out in the region. A blinking icon sprang up further away from Sol.

"What if this is where they went? Just for the sake of argument. It's one of the possible colony worlds the boys back at the Puzzle Palace have identified. We know there are exo-planets, so it'll get probed one day and colonists will follow eventually. If their voyage ended here," said Atticus, pointing at the gently strobing icon, "and they set up shop on a Goldilocks planet, they could have had more than a century to build their colony, their world.

"How big would their population be by now? It might be enormous, by young colony standards. If they went the route their interests suggest, they could have a truly vast number of people. These other systems," he pointed at a string of other stars between New Bristol and the icon, "could also hold colonies and they'd have known that before they left their new paradise. Any suitable exo-planets were already known before they launched," he paused and seemed to be struggling for words.

"Yes? If all that is true, then so what?" she asked, not sure where Atticus was going with this line of reasoning.

"If all that is true, then they already have a functioning colony, a functioning civilisation, even, of their own."

"Agreed. What of it, Captain?"

"With all due respect, Governor, what the fucking hell would they want with New Bristol?"

She took a deep breath and held it for a moment, exhaling slowly before answering.

"You're quite right, Captain. I have no idea what they want. New Bristol is the very definition of a fixer-upper. In fact, if you review our colonist files, at least the adult ones who chose to come here, you'd see that most of them, myself included, came here for precisely that reason. We wanted to challenge ourselves in a universe gone bland with the ease of modern convenience. Some people want to create art, raise families, grow organic vegetables or conduct scientific research. Some become Marines. Some become pirates."

She sat back in her chair.

"We wanted to be explorers, I suppose. We wanted to turn a dead world into a bountiful paradise. We can do that now, you know? Terraforming isn't a pipe dream anymore, we have the technology. New Bristol is in a race to create a fully functioning ecology capable of supporting human life. The planet has everything we need to start an Earth-like world, we just have to add a few asteroids and a great deal of elbow grease. There are far easier targets, with not much more defence in place, that they could have attacked."

"I know, and worse than that, why bother to attack at all? There are plenty of systems out there they could have colonised if population growth or expansion was there issue. So, bearing that in mind, why did they go all that way to get away from Sol, to obtain freedom, then come back? It doesn't make any sense," he said, trailing off.

"What's your 'or else'?" she asked quietly. He looked at her, his eyes haunted by some vision he'd seen of the future. "I can tell you have one. They wouldn't have come back unless...?"

He sighed and closed his eyes, not really wanting to give voice to his deeper fears.

"Unless they had no choice. Unless they had no choice but to leave their world and come here. Unless something so bad has happened, they can't stay there anymore and New Bristol is the first world on their flight path that is safe."

"And what sort of threat could that be?" prompted Denmead when Atticus ground to a halt.

"I have no idea, but if I'm right, they aren't going to stop coming. They won't give up just because we fight off this attack. They want a new colony world and they've picked New Bristol. They'll get it too, unless we find a way to stop them." He paused again. "And I'm not sure that's possible," he added quietly.

Denmead digested that for a while as they sat in silence. Finally, she looked up at him.

"Right, so they have more advanced clones?"

"Yes."

"They have more of them?"

"Undoubtedly."

"They have more advanced ships?"

"Probably."

"They have more advanced weapons?"

"Some, certainly."

"They have a huge population and economy?"

"Almost definitely."

"And they have a really good reason for abandoning their planet and taking ours?"

"I think so."

"Okay, but aside from that, what have they got going for them?" Denmead asked.

Atticus smiled.

"I'm serious, Captain. Fuck these – what was it? These crew of the Koschei the Deathless?"

Atticus nodded.

"Fuck these Deathless bastards then," Denmead continued. "Lets you and I put on our adult trousers and work out how to send these rude buggers back the way they came with a bloody nose, all right?"

"Deathless. That's a good name for them, that'll stick."

"Good, that's a start then. They're the Deathless, and they're bastards. All those in favour, say aye."

Atticus said, "Aye," and Denmead followed suit.

"See, Captain? That's one problem solved. They might have a lot going for them, but they're just a series of small problems we have to solve, one after the other. Now, what else have we got going for us? Aside from an immobile philtrum?" Denmead asked.

Atticus looked at his notes then back up at the governor.

"We know they started out human and they're basically still human. We know that most of their founders were Russian."

"Which means?" Denmead asked.

"Which means we have a way to crack the code of their technology. It's based on models from Sol, we even have the technical specifications and original data. It means we have a chance of deciphering their glyphs, translating their language and accessing their systems. They aren't using Cyrillic, but they may still be writing in something that's recognisably Russian, or a combination of Russian and some other languages. Maybe that'll be enough to give us access to their computers. Which would mean we can use their captured gear properly."

"That sounds useful, particularly with all those weapons and armour you've captured. Let's solve that problem first then," she said.

Atticus summoned Barlow and gave him a brief outline of the information from the private package.

"I want you to have a look at some of the texts we think we've understood and try to match them to equivalent Russian words. If we can do that and work out the alphabet, we should be able to translate their UIs and, finally, get complete control of their computers."

"Yes, sir, makes sense. We've got images from the dropships and other bits of short text from weapons and armour, so it shouldn't be a problem." He paused, suddenly aware that he'd inadvertently made a promise to a senior officer without having appropriately managed expectations. A rookie error. He coughed. "That is, I'll get started right away and let you know when we make progress, sir."

Barlow hurried out before his runaway mouth could get him into any more problems.

10

"Priscilla, isn't it?" asked Wilson. "Are you the leader around here?"

The teenager gave a sullen shrug.

Bloody hell, even out here with all that the new world has to offer, they still find something to be grumpy about, thought Wilson.

"Mrs Robinson said so anyway. She said you've been looking after the other kids, getting them to help out, and keep the younger ones from getting upset."

Another noncommittal grunt was the only response.

"But maybe she's got it backwards. Yeah, sorry to bother you. I guess you can't help with something like this anyway. Probably more the sort of thing boys are into," he said, putting his hands on his knees then standing up with a sigh.

He called over to Elaine Robinson. "Hey Elaine, she's not interested. Can you get me the school records? I need to find out which of your lads know their way around a racing drone."

Priscilla's head tilted up and she shot a sideways glance at him, which he pretended not to notice.

"Give me a second, Mark."

"Sure, sure." Wilson scuffed his shoe against the dirt of the cave, and whistled softly.

"What do you want with racing drones, Mister?"

"Doesn't much matter, does it? If you'd rather be looking after the little kids, that's fine. We each have our strengths."

Priscilla snorted. "You think you're going to find some boy who knows all about racing drones?"

"I heard the competition is pretty serious on New Bristol. Racing drones are the in thing for the kids on this rock. I'd heard you were a leader, so I thought you might be able to help organise things. But what I really need is pilots, you see? I'm sure Elaine, Mrs Robinson to you, can help me find the right lads," Wilson said cheerfully.

"Yeah," said Priscilla contemptuously. "I suppose you *could* get the boys to fly drones."

"Absolutely. And you can look after the six-year-olds when they're crying because the aliens are coming."

The teenager ignored that and went on. "As long as you don't need them to get the drones anywhere quickly and you don't mind them crashing half of them." Priscilla shrugged. "You'll be fine with slow drones that crash a lot, right?"

Wilson frowned. "Actually, that wouldn't be much use. Not for what we need. That would be the exact opposite of great, in fact. It sounds like my idea won't fly in that case. No pun intended."

"What do you need them for anyway?" Priscilla asked hesitantly.

Wilson shrugged. "Defending the colony. Pity, I thought it was a good idea, but if the drones are just going to crash because the pilots are rubbish, I guess I was wrong." He began to walk away.

Priscilla stood up. "What if they didn't crash?"

He turned to look back over his shoulder. "Well, in that case, my idea would be a bloody stroke of genius, wouldn't it?"

Priscilla gave him a long look, staring up at him with her head on one side.

"My team can pilot the drones," she said eventually. "What do you need them to do?"

"Your team? I'm sorry, what team is that?"

"All right, cut the shit. I'm the captain of the Blues. We're the best drone racing team in Ashton, and in our team we don't have any boys," she said, spitting on the floor as if boys weren't even worth mentioning in this conversation, "because we only take the best pilots."

"Oh? You're the best drone pilots in Ashton, are you? Well, slap my thigh with a wet kipper. What an astounding piece of luck that I should just happen to ask you first."

She poked her tongue out at him. Then withdrew it, blushing and stuck up her finger instead in a particularly vulgar gesture.

"Priscilla Smith!" snapped Mrs Robinson as she walked over. "You apologise to Corporal Wilson this instant, young lady."

Priscilla blushed even more furiously and gritted her teeth. Then she turned to him all sweetness and light. "I'm sorry, Corporal Wilson, that I saw so easily through your blatant reverse psychology. Sexist reverse psychology, at that."

Mrs Robinson put her hands on her hips and rounded on Wilson, fixing him with a stony glare. He coughed and smiled weakly. "Mea culpa. It was a cheap trick. Fortunately, despite seeing through it, young Ms Smith here fell for it hook, line and sinker and has volunteered to help."

"I've done no such thing!"

He shrugged. "Boys team it is, then!" He grinned at her and she rolled her eyes.

"What do you want us to do?"

"Top secret, I'm afraid. Unless you're on the team, I can't tell you anything more," Wilson said apologetically. "You have to join the team to get clearance for the rest."

"Fine. I'll join your team. I'm in charge, though, and the Blues are my officers," Priscilla said defiantly. "Take it or leave it."

"I'll take it. Okay, so here's what we need to do," he said, grinning. He projected a low-res 3D holographic image of New Bristol from his data slate. "This shows the real-time locations of our personnel. That big spot by the hills is Fort Widley. The Deathless knocked out the satellites around New Bristol, so we don't have surveillance data. You know there's another invasion fleet coming, right?" he asked.

Priscilla nodded. "Yeah, we haven't told the little kids, but all the older kids know."

Older, he thought, *she turned fifteen during the invasion, according to her file. They're growing up fast on this colony.*

"Good. We don't have enough military drones to cover the whole area, and that's where you would come in. We need pilots who can fly and program drones to get us data about which areas are clear, where the enemy are landing and what their numbers are. Think you can do that?"

"The Ashton Blues can handle anything."

"Good to hear. You build your own drones? Can you program them to fly automated patterns?"

"Of course," she said with forthright sarcasm. "How else do you think we get them? The shopping mall?"

"Haha, very funny. What about flying this?" he said, handing her a micro-drone.

Her eyes went wide as she took the tiny device. It was the size of a small hummingbird. He passed her a control slate, and she quickly synced it to her HUD, flipping down the lenses over her eyes and launching the drone. It rocketed towards the ceiling of the cave, then rolled onto its back before weaving through the stalactites at breakneck speed. Then she cut the engine mid-flight, and it dropped like a stone. She restarted the engine moments before it hit the ground, flipped the tiny drone the right way up and looped it back across the cave to land gently in her palm.

"Probably not. Seems a bit tricky," she said nonchalantly.

He nodded. "Can you do it without showing off? Can you do it when it's boring? More boring than you can imagine? Can you set it down on a wall and wait hours to see if anything happens? This is serious, Priscilla. It's not make-work to keep you busy," Wilson said softly.

She looked at him hard, her eyes boring into him, sizing him up. Then she nodded. "Yeah, I can do that. The Blues can do that."

"Okay. Good. You're hired. We'll give you some drone plans to build, and you can organise as many kids as you can to build them and fly them. We can't help you with building them, you'll have to do it all on your own, but we'll tell you where we need them flown and show you what you have to look for. Deal?" he asked, standing up and offering his hand.

"Deal," she replied, a huge grin on her face as she stood up and shook it. Wilson handed her a military data slate with her name embossed along the top.

"That's yours now. It's coded to you and it's got all the plans you need to build surveillance drones, which, young lady, we will be taking back when we leave, lest you get any ideas about spying on teachers or your parents," he said with a wink.

She grinned again. "No problem. I'll get the Blues right on it," she said confidently.

He smiled back. "Oh yeah, just one more thing, Priscilla. You have to recruit the boys as well."

Her smile vanished and she opened her mouth to protest, but he had already vanished out of the cave mouth. Mrs Robinson had made herself scarce at some point as well.

Boys? Yuck. Why did she have to work with those smelly dopes?

11

"Jennifer, how are the new drones coming?" Priscilla asked.

"Not bad, Captain," the mousy girl replied. There was something in the twelve-year-old's voice that made Priscilla stop her rounds.

"What is it, Jenn?"

"Nothing, it's okay," Jennifer replied.

"Jenn, what's up? You can tell me. Something not going well? Someone giving you trouble?"

The younger girl sighed and looked at her askance through her long curly fringe. "It's the boys from Team Rocket. They're behind on their quota. They're taking breaks all the time, playing games when they should be working. I try to get them to work but they just call me names and tell me to go away. We're not going to have enough of the larger drones at this rate. I'm sorry."

Priscilla could tell she was close to tears and she reached out to pat her on the shoulder. "It's okay, Jenn. I'll take care of it. We'll get them to do their share and catch up, you'll see."

After seeing Jennifer, she checked in on the rest of her Ashton Blues: Sue, Pip, Debbie, Alison and Annabel. They'd grown up together on New Bristol, arriving with the first wave of colonists on a new world. Drone racing had been a way to make friends and have some fun despite the differences in their ages.

The Ashton Blues were formed and they'd fought their way to the top of the league. Terry and Team Rocket were a pain in the neck. Jealous and disruptive, they always had a ready excuse for their losses in competition when really they didn't work as hard as the Blues.

But she was still surprised that they'd be lazy while their home was being invaded. The other boys were doing fine, but Team Rocket were older than most. They'd been tasked with assembling the larger, more complicated drones because they were supposed to be more mature. Priscilla had wanted to have some of the girls she knew to be the best engineers do it, but Mrs Robinson persuaded her to let Team Rocket have a go.

She looked across the cave to the assembly benches they were supposed to be working at. Empty, at eleven in the morning. There was no way Priscilla was going to let this stand. Team Rocket had picked the wrong war to skive in.

∼

"Luke, I need a word."

"Later, I'm in the middle of a game," said the lanky teen without turning away from his vid screen.

"It's urgent, Luke. I need to speak with you in private."

"Ohhh, she wants a word in private, Luke," leered one of his henchmen.

"Sod off, Prissy, you little snotrag," Luke snarled, puffing himself up and showing off in response to the round of sniggering from his team.

Priscilla took a deep breath before she replied, trying to calm herself before she spoke, just as her mother had asked. Then she spotted the remote control for the screen, and a second later she had his attention.

He launched himself upright and span to face her, his face

turning purple. "What'd you do that for, you little bitch? I was getting a high score!"

"Doesn't seem very likely, but whatever you reckon, Luke." She pointed outside. "I need a word. Now!"

Luke was a couple of years older but she wasn't going to let him think she was scared of him. She didn't have time for bullies today. She kept her finger pointed and her eyes on him, staring him down until he shook his head.

"For pity's sake, bloody women and their nagging, eh, lads?" He got a round of politely supportive chuckling as he slouched reluctantly from the room.

Priscilla followed him into the small cafeteria space that had been set up for the drone teams by Mrs Robinson to give them a sense of independence.

"Luke, your team is behind on the quota. What's the problem? We aren't going to have enough drones at this rate," she asked, in the most reasonable tone she could manage while imagining pouring a hot pot of tea down the front of his baggy shorts.

"We're here working every day. Check the logs, you'll see," he protested.

"I did. It was the first thing I did when I found out. You and your team are here every day, but you spend almost as much time in the break room, playing games and drinking coffee, as you spend making drones. You do know we're at war, right?"

"This isn't a real war," he sneered, "and we're not soldiers."

"We might not be soldiers, but people are dying in this war, Luke. Our parents and our parents' friends are out there right now, training to fight back the next invasion. The Deathless are only a few days away, and the Marines need our drones to tell them what's going on. What part of this escapes you? Don't you understand how important this work is?"

"They don't need us. They're just trying to keep us out from underfoot. You really bought their bullshit, didn't you? If they needed us, really needed us, we'd be out there training with the militia. But they don't, this is just more space pirates, desperate outcasts trying to make a name for themselves. I could be a soldier if they really needed them, I'm old enough and I'd be great at it," Luke said.

"You couldn't be a soldier! They have to show up every morning and fight. You can't even assemble drones for a full day, you can't pilot them well enough to be a tech specialist, and you don't have the balls to hold a rifle!" she shouted back, finally losing her rag.

"I could be a soldier! I could be in the militia! You don't know what you're talking about, you're just a little girl!" he shouted before stomping off in a huff.

"You sign up, Luke, I'll sign the transfer papers!" she roared at him. *What an idiot*, she thought as she walked out. Then she grinned maliciously as an idea struck her.

～

Corporal Mark Wilson squinted down the barrel he'd removed from the drone, frowned and slid a cleaning rod down it again. "Hi, Priscilla. What can I do for you?" he asked as he checked the barrel again. Satisfied that it was clean, he clipped it back into its receiver on the drone he was working on.

"I wondered if I could ask you something."

"Yup. Fire away; I could do this in my sleep."

"Who's the toughest, scariest Marine on New Bristol? Is it Captain Atticus? He seems quite stern."

Wilson raised his eyebrows. Not the question he had expected. "Well, he's a bit gruff, but he's not nearly as grim as you might think."

"Colour Sergeant Jenkins then?"

"Colour Jenkins? Nah. She just shouts a lot, it's part of the job. Why do you ask?"

Priscilla blushed as he turned to face her and she gave him a guilty look. "Just trying to settle an argument."

"Gambling, Captain Smith? I'm shocked. Shocked, I say. Well, if you're looking for the toughest commando, it's not any of the officers or NCOs. You want Marine X."

"Who?" asked Priscilla, a frown of confusion on her face. "Does X stand for Xavier or something embarrassing?"

Wilson smiled. "No, Marine X is the designation given to him at his last court martial. He's a Penal Marine, and part of his punishment was to lose his name until he's served his sentence. So he's Marine X until he's done his time. We mostly call him Ten."

Priscilla was a little taken aback by that. She hadn't heard of Penal Marines before. A few of the kids were military buffs who knew all sorts of things about the Marines and their weapons, but she hadn't known much about them until the invasion started. Engineering was her thing. Engineering and drones.

"What did he do?"

Wilson shrugged. "Originally? No idea. Something pretty bloody serious, though. You don't get in that much trouble for failing to clean your boots properly. He must have pissed someone off, but I've never heard him discuss it. Ten is all business when we're deployed and he keeps to himself when we aren't." He leant forward, looking around to check they weren't overheard. "Rumour says it's all top secret, not part of the public record. I couldn't even tell you how long he's been a Penal Marine, but since before I joined up."

"If he did something that bad, why isn't he in prison?"

Wilson shook his head and put down the drone.

"Look, Penal Marines are really rare. You have to have done something really serious but not so bad that they want to boot you out of the service or send you to prison forever. You need to be really good at the job and it's not even an option unless a senior officer recommends it, so someone must have thought he deserved another chance."

He paused, looking around again.

"Why is Ten here? Because he's really, really good at the job. He runs training courses when he's not deployed. He's been doing this job so long, he knows how to do almost everything. I've never seen him pick up a weapon and not be able to use it as well as anyone else."

"That doesn't make him scary," Priscilla pointed out, "that just makes him competent."

"The scary bit," said Wilson, looking her in the eyes and now completely serious, "is that he always does what needs doing. He sees a problem, fixes on a solution then just gets it done."

Priscilla frowned, her scepticism visible.

"Trust me," said Wilson emphatically, "that's enough to make him the scariest Marine here. Probably the scariest man alive. And whatever you do..." he said, lowering his voice to a whisper and scanning the room again.

"What?" whispered Priscilla, her curiosity almost palpable.

"Don't play him at cards. You don't want any part of that."

Priscilla gulped. "Why? Does he get angry when he loses?"

"Angry? Oh no, he just cheats a lot and he's really good at it. You'll lose your proverbial shirt."

She found him in Fort Widley's new armoury, unpacking weapons fresh from the manufactories and inspecting them for flaws. He didn't stop what he was doing until she coughed loudly.

He stared at her for a moment before finally sighing and asking. "Is there something you need? And if the answer is 'a rifle' or anything else that goes bang, you might as well not ask."

"No, not that. I was wondering if you could help me with a problem I'm having with one of the boys, Mr Ten."

Marine X frowned a little and nodded thoughtfully. "It's just Ten, no Mister, and the answer is, probably. What do you need, a good chat up line? I mean, presumably you've done sex education at your age so I don't have to explain that stuff? Just remember he's as scared as you are and don't let him talk you into anything you don't want to do." He turned back to his crate of weapons.

She almost ran from the room at that point, but she steeled herself and coughed again.

"Still here? You know, I'm probably not the best person to ask about this sort of stuff. I'm a lot older than I look, and quite out of touch. Try Sergeant Milton," he offered.

"No, I mean, that's not the sort of problem I'm having."

"Ah. Well, that's awkward. Perhaps you should explain what sort of problem it is before I give you any more completely unwanted advice that will make us both uncomfortable, eh?"

"Yeah, not that your advice wasn't good," she said quickly. "I'll remember boys are scared of me for a while, I'm sure."

Ten waved at a crate and Priscilla sat down. "I'm in charge of producing drones for Corporal Wilson and it's going well. The problem I'm having is that there's a group of boys who are supposed to be helping and they spend all their time playing games. I tried to get their team leader to take it seriously, but he just said it's not a real war and he didn't have to do what I said," Priscilla explained, the words tumbling from her with barely a pause for breath.

"Right, gotcha. You need to enforce some military discipline then? I'm not sure why you came to me. You do know I'm a Penal Marine, right? I'm literally the last person anyone asks for advice on discipline," Ten said.

"No, Luke says he could be a soldier but he isn't one so he doesn't have to take orders. I don't want military discipline, I want to terrify him into doing the right thing."

Ten cocked his head then shrugged. "Fair enough. That I can help you with." He walked across the room and unlocked one of the cages, withdrawing a short black baton. He presented it to her, handle first. "Stun baton. Just press your thumb on the button and prod him in the gut with that, about here," he said, tapping just below his solar plexus. "He'll drop like a, well, like an arsehole who's just been electrocuted. One or two of those, and they'll all fall into line. I'd do his favourite henchman as well, if I were you, for good measure. Don't let the second bully in charge take over."

Priscilla frowned at the weapon for a moment before carefully placing it back on the workbench.

"No? I'm still not giving you a rifle. I don't like bullies, but even I probably can't get away with that."

"I had another idea. Something less direct than, er, a stun baton," said Priscilla with her most devious grin.

"Oh, do tell," said Marine X, now genuinely interested.

Ten strode through the kitchen area into the break room, clipboard in hand, his green beret worn neatly atop his head. Priscilla followed behind and stood slightly to one side.

Luke and the boys barely spared him a glance, playing it cool despite the sudden appearance of an adult in their kingdom.

"Are these the lads you recommended to me, Miss Smith?"

"Yes. Luke was very keen indeed and I'm happy to relinquish him from my team if you need him," Priscilla answered. At this point a couple of heads turned.

"And the rest?"

"Oh yes, where Luke goes, they follow. They're a team of drone racers you see, the closest of friends. Like the Pals Battalions of World War I. A group of young men, all friends and colleagues, signing up to go to war together. It's all very exciting," Priscilla said eagerly.

"Nothing exciting about war, young lady. War is horrible, dirty, violent, painful and above all, terrifying. These lads are brave to volunteer, especially for frontline duty at their age," Ten said gravely.

Luke turned his head at that, looking half puzzled and half angry.

Much like a warthog, Priscilla thought. She smiled sweetly at him, in complete contrast to her current feelings toward him. He didn't seem to take it well.

"What are you talking about?" he asked.

"Your request to join the militia and serve as a frontline soldier," Ten said.

"Get lost. I'm not joining the militia," Luke snorted. He went back to the game he'd been playing, unpausing it as he picked up the controller and advancing the character on the view screen towards the enemy. In the middle of an actual war, here was this snotty little shit playing war games on a vid screen.

Ten nodded slowly. He could see now why Priscilla didn't like this little prick. Two minutes in and Ten already wanted to slap him.

"You can turn that off now, lads," said Ten quietly. "You're in the militia now. The time for playing is over, you'll have a real gun to shoot now, though if you shoot it as badly as that, you'll probably spend your time digging latrines."

One of the more precious followers of Luke laughed. "We don't need latrines now, you idiot, we have plenty of toilets."

Ten's eyes narrowed, and his stance underwent a subtle change. The atmosphere shifted a little, and Priscilla glanced around to see that the other teams had followed them into the room and were standing quietly at the back, watching everything.

"New recruits still dig latrines, lad. Never know when you might need to know how to dig a latrine, and I'm betting you've never dug so much as a flowerbed in your life. First time for everything. Then you fill it in and dig another one for practice. Or you can learn to shoot properly, unlike your pals playing that game, and maybe get trusted with a rifle. Either way, the time for games is over." Ten paused to glance around the group. "Turn it off and lets be having you," he said.

"I'm not joining your stupid militia," sneered Luke. "They're not joining it either, so why don't you just fuck off like a good little soldier and do something useful."

Quick as a flash, Ten had a Deathless hand cannon in his palm and three high-calibre rounds shattered the vid screen. The noise was tremendous and Priscilla flinched at his side. She hadn't known he would do that, but maybe this was what Corporal Wilson had meant. One of the boys literally screamed and Priscilla fought back the urge to snigger.

"I am not a soldier, you miserable little shit," Ten roared in his best impersonation of a sergeant major, a role he'd never held himself, "I am a Royal Marine Space Commando! We are not soldiers. We are Marines, and you will remember that, if I have to beat it into your thick skull with your right arm while there's still blood dripping from it after I rip it from its socket, which I will in short order if you do not stand to attention right now!" He ended his tirade almost screaming, and the boys jumped to their feet, looking utterly bewildered by the gunfire and his shouting.

That's better, thought Ten, *finally a decent reaction.*

He pointed to the wall. "Line up over there. Tallest to shortest. Hop to it! Faster, faster, faster! Backs straight, eyes front." The boys stumbled about, make a complete bodge job of it, as he'd expected. Eventually, they got themselves in height order, a task they seemed to find extremely confusing and difficult.

Ten rounded on the first lad. "What's your name? What? I can't hear you!" he roared in the face off the little shit that had been giving Priscilla grief. He was quite enjoying this.

"L-L-Luke, sir," the boy stammered.

"Don't you call me, sir! I work for a living! You think you can be a soldier in the militia, do you?"

"No, sir. I mean, no."

"No? No?" he roared up close to the boy. "What do you mean, no? I have it here on this paperwork that you insisted to your duly appointed captain that you were militia material and that they'd be lucky to have you. Are you saying the captain lied? Well, boy, are you?"

Luke looked to his left for support, but none of the other boys caught his eye, they stood there shaking and staring determinedly straight ahead, trying not to wince at the shouting or draw attention to themselves.

"No, I just... I was exaggerating. I don't want to be in the militia," Luke managed to squeak out.

"You don't? Well, I am most perplexed by this turn of events," said Ten, lowering his voice back to a more normal level. "I was told you and all your mates had decided that making and piloting drones was beneath you and that you would far rather serve in the militia to defend your fine colony. I'm therefore extremely surprised to hear you say that you don't want to be a soldier after all!" said Ten, shaking his head and assuming an exaggerated look of befuddlement.

"What about you, lad?" he said to the next boy in the row, the cheeky one who thought latrine digging was beneath him. "Surely a big strong lad like you would rather be out there, taking the fight to the enemy, face to face, than just flying little cameras about?" he said, gripping the kid by his bicep and squeezing it as if he were a big man.

The kid shook with terror and Priscilla saw his trousers darken as he wet himself. Ten didn't seem to notice.

"No? Not a rifleman, then? You'd rather be making and piloting drones, would you?" The boy nodded emphatically. "Fair enough."

Ten walked down the line. "How about you, militia rifleman, or drone pilot?" he asked.

"Drone pilot," was the only verbal response he extracted from the rest of Luke's crew. Most of them just nodded or shook their head to indicate their preferred option. Finally, he returned to Luke.

"Well, Luke. It seems you may have exaggerated your team's fervour for becoming militiamen. You sure you don't want to be a soldier? You could handle yourself, couldn't you? You're the biggest here, right? Go on, son. You just have to get up close and personal, get right up to that Deathless bastard that wants to shoot your mum and dad, then stick one of these in his guts," he said quietly, producing a glowing Deathless combat knife as if from nowhere and waving it in front of Luke's panicked face. The lad shied away and shook his head fractionally. Ten disappeared the knife.

"Alright then. What we seem to have here, is a failure on your part to communicate with your appointed officer, Captain Priscilla Smith, who has been appointed by your government to lead this team. It seems none of you want to join the militia proper, after all. Am I right?"

The line of boys nodded pathetically, and he went on.

"My paperwork here says you're all sixteen or above. That means, under Commonwealth law, you can put in a decent day's work or volunteering. Captain Smith's figures tell me you'll need to do double shifts until the invasion force arrives to get your share of the work done. Doesn't sound too much for a group of lads who've been slacking off, getting plenty of rest and who haven't had to go to school or anything, right? Any of you got a problem with a good day's work?" he asked.

It seemed none of them did after all.

"That's settled then. You'll fulfil your quota, and you won't have to join the militia or dig me a bunch of latrines. I'll come back each day and see how you're doing, and I won't ever find you shirking off or turning up late, will I?" he asked to another round of semi-audible confirmation.

Ten looked around the group, nodding grimly in the sudden silence. Then he seemed to notice the audience at the back of the room, which had grown to include a host of adults and most of the drone pilots.

"Back to work," he said loudly, clapping his hands, and the spell was broken. The audience disappeared and Luke's team followed, heading quickly for the workrooms.

Ten turned to Priscilla and shook her hand.

"I expect you'll be caught up soon enough." She nodded, quiet and pale. "Wilson picked well with you, you'll be fine. But if you have any trouble, you give me a shout."

Then he sauntered from the room, chasing the last of the stragglers back to their work stations and ignoring the Mrs Robinson's glares.

———————

12

"Can you say that again, Captain?" said Idol into his HUD comms, furiously waving his hand at the militia troops nearest him to shut up so he could hear properly.

"We have reports that the enemy has been sighted west of you. Can you confirm?" Captain Atticus repeated.

"No, sir. We have no enemy in sight yet."

"Roger that, Captain Idol. You have some time to prepare for their arrival. Make sure your company keep their heads down and their eyes peeled, and watch your flanks. Remember, they use snipers so if you sit around with your head on display, that'll be your first sign that they've arrived," advised Atticus. "We have Marine patrols out hunting them, so don't shoot the wrong teams and don't advance from your position without orders. Confirm."

"Confirmed, Captain. We'll hold here, and I'll remind everyone not to get shot or shoot your people," Idol said, grinning at his command team sergeant, Charles Adams. This was certainly different from their day jobs as botanists working on atmospheric regulation.

Sergeant Adams used his HUD to send instructions to the company to stay out of sight because the aliens were on the way. The three lieutenants under Captain Idol acknowledged the message.

Then Adams turned and rolled his eyes at Idol, reaching up to tap his fingers on the top of his helmet.

Idol looked to his right and realised he had shifted his legs to a more comfortable position. Most of his head and neck were now above the line of the shattered window. He dropped to his bottom and felt the warmth of a profuse blush rise up his neck as he mouthed "Fuck" at the smirking Adams.

They were on the first floor of a building that had once been Ashton's main brewery. Not that it looked much like a brewery at the moment. Most of the equipment had been removed and shredded, ready to be fed into the fabricators and turned into weapons and equipment. Despite the spirited arguments of a number of people, Governor Denmead had concluded that beer wasn't a priority.

To be fair, the lack of beer was more than balanced by a ready supply of gin, as the governor had been quick to point out. The early fears that the entire colony's stock of spirits had been destroyed in a collapsed building during the initial invasion had proven unfounded. A volunteer rescue team, working in hazardous conditions, had been able to pull multiple crates from the cellars despite the wanton destruction inflicted as the combatants had fought their way across New Ashton.

"We need to watch out for this," said Idol, waving vaguely at the windowsill. "If I'm in charge and can't get it right, we have to assume some of the others will forget as well. I'll visit C platoon, you talk to B, and on the way we'll check in with the rest of A platoon, right? Make sure people are watching the drone feeds and everyone actually does have their heads down."

"Yeah, probably sensible. B platoon is mostly geologists," said Adams with mock horror.

"What, the rock people? I didn't realise we'd been lumbered with them!" Idol exclaimed, feigning protest. The rivalry between the botany teams and the geologists had evolved from simple professional competition into a friendly variety of sports matches and quiz nights, during which they mostly failed to demonstrate sufficient skills to overwhelm the 'enemy'.

"Yeah, I doubt they understood the orders, they're always so dense," said Adams as he moved off in an uncomfortable looking crouching run.

Bloody hell, thought Idol, *do we all look like that? It seems natural when the Marines do it, but we must look a right bunch of prats.*

He shuffled away self-consciously. Keeping his head down and his dignity intact seemed like an impossible balance as he crawled below the blown out windows.

Better than getting your head blown off though, you vain old sod. Lots better than that.

13

They had a few minutes' warning, no more. The techs had set up sirens at key points around the city, but it was mostly deserted with only a few teams still working to clear supplies and equipment.

Everyone froze, just for a moment, as the sirens wailed and personal communicators pinged increasingly desperate warnings of imminent doom. Then things started to move as tasks and machinery were abandoned and the teams rushed to clear the impact sites.

"Kinetic bombardment," said Atticus in a matter-of-fact tone as he reviewed the stream of updates coming in from the ground-based monitors they'd been able to set up over the last few days, "at least, I hope it's kinetic."

They had discussed contingency plans for other forms of attack – nuclear, biological, chemical, high-explosive and the old favourite, boots on the ground – but kinetic bombardment from orbit was always the most likely option, now that the Deathless knew they were opposed.

"Simple, cheap, effective and with little lasting environmental impact," Warden had said as he summarised the advantages of dropping high-velocity asteroids on the city, "and there's bugger all we can do to defend against it."

And now it looked like Warden had been right. The monitors had found several fast-moving missiles heading towards Ashton but there were bound to be others, possibly hundreds of others, that wouldn't be spotted until they struck the ground.

Atticus and Denmead made their way to the designated lifters, chasing the last of the salvage teams from Government House as they went. The people were surprisingly calm given what was happening but the atmosphere was one of tense excitement. After days of fevered work under horrible pressure, the time of preparations was now over and, soon, the real fighting would begin.

"Is that everyone?" yelled, Atticus, standing up in the lifter to get a better view. "Come on!" he yelled at a pair of stragglers who were moving slowly under the weight of an archive crate.

"Leave it," screamed Denmead, the delay now starting to disturb her. The pair struggled a little further then one tripped, pitching over onto the road and dropping the crate.

"Shit," said Atticus, springing down from the lifter and sprinting across the open ground. This Deathless body had a few advantages over the standard human combat clones and speed was one of them. He covered a hundred metres in a few seconds, shouting at the two salvagers to forget about the archive drives that had fallen from the crate.

"Just move," he yelled. He gave one a shove then grabbed the half-full crate, hefting it easily. The two men sprinted away and Atticus loped easily along behind them, crate tucked under one arm.

"Hurry," shouted Denmead, one eye on the sky as the time ticked down.

The two men scrambled into the lifter and Atticus tossed the crate in behind them before leaping up onto the flatbed.

"Go, go, go," yelled Denmead and the driver needed no further encouragement. She punched the controls and the lifter pulled away, slowly at first but accelerating all the time.

"Fifteen seconds," said Atticus, shouting to be heard across the sound of the rushing wind. "Five seconds, everybody down." He ducked down as low as he could and closed his eyes, pulling one of the salvage men and Governor Denmead down as well.

Then there was a flash of light so bright it was clear even through closed eyelids. The earth rumbled beneath the lifter and then the noise arrived, a great, long, rolling boom that seemed to go on forever. The lifter shook and rocked as the blast wave passed over them and then it was gone.

Atticus looked back at Government House but could see only dust. Then it started to rain stones. They pinged off the body of the lifter and bounced from the bodies of the humans that sheltered within it. A rock the size of a fist caught Atticus on the shoulder and knocked him down. For a moment it looked like they were going to be buried alive under a shower of rock but then they were clear, and the way ahead was open. The lifter shot forward, heading down a road that would take them past the cloning facility.

Too late, Articus realised the danger and shouted at the driver to turn off the road. Even as she looked back to see what was going on, Atticus's HUD lit up with a warning of incoming projectiles. The captain had only enough time to register the warning before the missile landed, striking directly at the cloning facility just as the lifter was passing by.

This time the flash and the shock wave arrived at the same time. The lifter swerved wildly across the street as the blast struck, engines screaming as they tried to hold the driver's course. Then it struck a low wall and bounced into the ruined forecourt of a school.

The engines failed, dumping the lifter on the ground as the noise finally passed. It skidded across the courtyard, spun around in a slow circle, and blasted through the remains of the school's front door to end up wedged against a staircase.

14
––––––––

"Umm, we're done with quadrant P7, Captain," said Luke.

Priscilla looked up and smiled cheerfully. Luke still looked a little nervous around her, which was an improvement on the sullen grunts she'd received in the days after Ten's first visit.

"Thanks, Luke. Anything we need to tell the Marines about?"

He shook his head. "Nothing, everything was clear. There's no sign of recent activity but the drop pods are still there and the whole area's a mess, just like they said," he grimaced, as if he'd tasted something unpleasant. "Don't let any of the younger ones see the footage. There are still bodies. I flagged it restricted."

"Are you okay? Was it bad?" she asked sympathetically. She'd forgotten that quadrant held the site of one of the fights between the Deathless and the militia. It had been a bad one, judging by the gossip.

"Yeah, it was pretty gross. After we had a bit of a look, we pulled all the drones back and stayed away from anything that looked messy. It was like watching a programme on surgery while you're eating," he said, shivering. "I think the younger ones might have nightmares."

"Thanks," said Priscilla, "but look after your team. If anyone seems upset, we'll ask Mrs Robinson if one of the doctors can chat with them. They're not going to tell their mums they're having night-mares, are they?"

He chuckled, the first time he'd done that in her presence for a long time. "Yeah, I can't see Billy telling his mum he saw a dead body and now he's scared. So what's our next area? P8?"

"I was thinking maybe we should launch a long-range probe out to here, she said, highlighting S13. P8-11 are mostly barren and flat. But the area in and around S13 has hills and ravines and maybe caves, so it's more likely the Deathless might hole up there. What do you think?" she asked.

"Sure. You want us to set up an operating area out there?"

"Yup. I thought with all those hills you could get the long-range drones out there by the end of the day and probably find a nice roost, then we could send more first thing tomorrow morning? It's almost your lunch break so you could take that early if you want and then spend the afternoon sorting it out?"

Luke nodded. "I'll tell the team to knock off early and we'll start after lunch. I'm sure they'll find that area more interesting. Thanks, boss."

He turned and left, apparently completely happy. Priscilla smiled and put her attention back into piloting her drone. Having guided it to a new area, she flicked the drone back to autopilot and returned her attention to the huge vidscreen mounted on the wall of the room. 'Cave' would be a more accurate description, but it was hard not to think of it as a room, even if the walls weren't smooth and the ceiling was crusted with stalactites.

There were thirty desks, arranged in three long rows facing the largest wall. Each desk had a curved vidscreen to give the pilot a wide angle view from their drone's cameras, but the ones on the wall were for what Corporal Wilson called 'a strategic overview of ground oper-ations and reconnaissance data with real-time mapping and target acquisition overlays'. Priscilla and the pilots called it 'the Grid'.

The Grid displayed various depictions of New Bristol on different screens around the cave. One screen showed a large chunk of the planet, with the 'fog of war' as the pilots who played a lot of games called it, obscuring the parts of the planet they'd not flown drones over yet. Another showed a relief map, with buildings and roads highlighted. Another displayed power grids and there was one that showed a split-screen view of all the areas they were operating in. Still more screens were available to display any particularly interesting drone footage.

All the pilots wore their HUDs of course, although they'd been issued upgraded versions that had some limited options to interface with the Marines. They couldn't look at Lieutenant Warden's view from his HUD but they could send him a message if they needed to, or provide him with updated information from the drones.

The back wall of the cave was where the drone assembly benches had been set up. Above them were more vidscreens displaying the less vital information from the Grid system. Turning around wasn't ideal, but there were so many different views it was still easier than turning off the main map display to look at an updated tactical map showing where the Marines or militia were.

They had constructed a range of different drones for the Marines to use and for them to carry out their surveillance tasks. Each had a specific purpose and their own strengths and weaknesses.

A few miniature airship drones were floating at extremely high altitude on autopilot to provide low-resolution imagery over a few thousand square kilometres of New Bristol. They had been simple to make, didn't require much piloting time and were quite unobtrusive. They were mostly watching for large-scale disturbances on the ground, raising alerts to allow the pilots to investigate with other drones if necessary. Corporal Wilson said a column of vehicles would kick up enough dust that the algorithm monitoring the images would spot it and, if it did, they should contact the duty officer immediately.

The techs had placed big red buttons under plastic covers around the cave. They were linked to an alarm that would summon help if the teams spotted anything important. One of the boys, Jacob, who wasn't part of Luke's crew of reprobates and thus hadn't been present at Ten's now infamous bollocking, had flipped open a cover and hit the button to see what would happen.

Both Corporal Wilson and Ten had arrived at speed, ready for action. They had been distinctly unimpressed to discover they'd been tricked, and had set a punishment duty to remind everyone that this wasn't a game. Jacob had spent the rest of the day digging an emergency latrine trench, much to the rest of the team's amusement. By late afternoon, Ten had decided the trench wasn't really needed, so Jacob spent the next couple of hours filling it back in again, lest someone fall in. Nobody played with the alarms after that.

And now that the teams had been flying drones for most of the week, they had a lot of data to display on their overview screens. The high-altitude airships were roaming far and wide, updating the pre-war maps of the area around Ashton and identifying areas that needed closer inspection.

The teams had been using the data from the airships to set sweep and monitor paths for the long-range drones, which were now flying regular patterns, watching anything of value. The information the drones gathered was collated with everything the Marines had seen with their HUDs to produce maps that were at least as good as those the colonists had used before their geostationary satellites were destroyed during the first invasion.

But it was the Marines' specialist drones that were the most fun to build and fly. They were completely different to the normal racing drones and were designed for endurance, stealth or out and out mayhem. To general groans of dismay, the pilots had been told early on that they would only be building, not flying, the large combat drones that the Marine tech specialists used in firefights to surveil and attack the enemy.

Corporal Wilson had said that after the invasion was done, they might disarm some of the drones and let the pilots try flying them. Some of the boys and girls had pleaded with him, but he'd said that he was under orders and suggested that, if they thought that was unfair, they could talk to Governor Denmead. That had dampened interest fairly quickly.

That left two main types of drones for Priscilla's team of about thirty kids to build, pilot and maintain. The first were similar to the combat drones: long-range, fast, laden with cameras and sensors, about the size of a breakfast tray and completely unarmed.

At first, they'd flown them around the local area. Then they'd thoroughly investigated New Ashton, the area around Fort Widley and then all the major settlements, farms, solar plants, storage depots, manufactories, mining operations and atmospheric processors that surrounded the city for miles around.

Then the Grid had marked new areas for them to explore at mid-altitude, setting the teams an area to cover in each shift. That had taken them into the wilderness beyond the city, pushing out in long, probing sweeps. Interesting at first, the pilots had quickly automated these flights to avoid the awful boredom of watching kilometres of empty desert, and now one pilot could manage several drones.

Priscilla had settled everyone into a routine of regular shifts. The bio-bracelets worn by all the kids on New Bristol monitored sleep patterns and general health, so the medical team had been able to confirm who rose early risers and Priscilla had tailored the shift plans accordingly.

The adults had been interested at first but now they mostly left them to it, although there was always someone near at hand in case anything interesting happened. The caverns weren't so spacious that the citizens of New Bristol had room to spare, but the pilot's rooms were comparatively spacious even though they were so deep in the system that it took twenty minutes to walk to the outside. Mrs Robinson came by every day to make sure they had cleaned up after themselves.

Priscilla's favourite models to fly were the micro-drones. Just like the long-range drones, they were powered by high-efficiency solar cells. Their size – barely the length of her finger – meant they didn't do well in high winds, although you could let the wind carry them if that was convenient and you liked the challenge of landing them somewhere safe.

Piloting the micro-drones in normal weather was a joy, though, and Priscilla relished the opportunity to investigate a new cave or one of the colony's outlying facilities for signs of Deathless activities. That was their major function: get in close, observe and report.

Beyond about thirty metres, the tiny drones were near invisible unless silhouetted against just the right material or given away by a glint of sunlight. In the evening, they would find somewhere to land each of the micro-drones, high up away from passers-by and sheltered from the wind and prying eyes. New Bristol was replete with cliffs, ravines and rocky escarpments filled with nooks and crannies that made ideal drone roosts. They parked the long-range drones too, resting the batteries and allowing them to recharge in the evening sun.

Some of the larger, long-range drones were used as motherships for the micro-drones. To scout a new area, they would launch a long-range drone carrying dozens of micro-drones. At top speed, the mothership could be two hundred kilometres away in an hour, at which point it would release its micro-drones and find somewhere safe to hide until it was needed again.

So that was the rhythm of the teams' days. They would fly larger drones in the patterns laid out on the Grid, deposit micro-drones at safe locations, and then use the micro-drones to explore anything they thought was suspicious. They had started with all the buildings, of course, but now they were out there, exploring the far reaches of New Bristol.

The last duty in their portfolio, other than to raise the alarm if they encountered any of the Deathless that still roamed the planet, was to leave surveillance sensors at certain sites, starting with the buildings. These were tiny packages that were static and could be carried by certain models of the micro-drones. They were left atop buildings, in the mouths of caves, at either end of ravines large enough to conceal troop carriers and anywhere else that looked like it might be of interest to the enemy. How many you could deposit in an hour was a matter of pride amongst the pilots, as was demonstrating that they'd found the smartest hiding places.

Whenever a surveillance sensor was approached, the location would ping on the Grid's vidscreens and a real-time video would be displayed. Often they saw grinning Marines or members of the militia waving at them, but mostly, if the pilot had done their job well, the system just logged someone moving past the unseen drone, unaware of its existence.

Early on, someone had rigged an extra vidscreen as a scoreboard, and now it showed the number of unobserved interactions logged against each pilot's drones. Luke had taken an early lead with Priscilla getting no higher than sixth place, but Debbie had blown past them all and was now so far ahead that nobody was even trying to catch up.

The pilots had evolved a solid daily routine. If it hadn't been for the clock on the wall counting down to the expected arrival of more Deathless invaders, the work of monitoring the area around Ashton would have become boring. Soon, Priscilla knew, the mission would change from observing the landscape to following the invasion forces and reporting on their movements. Keeping the HUD maps of the Marines and militia up to date would help keep everyone safe, including the relatives who were out there fighting to defend New Bristol. Priscilla pushed that thought from her mind, focussing on the job at hand whenever she found herself worrying about the future.

"We think we should train the pilots to run close reconnaissance operations," Priscilla had announced one day after the morning briefing with Corporal Wilson. "We might want to stay close to the Deathless and watch what they're doing. If we've practised before they arrive...?"

So Wilson and Ten had worked out a training regime that consisted of setting the pilots to follow the Marines and militia around. That was really fun, and every time a drone was spotted, the pilot lost points.

"If you're spotted," Corporal Wilson had said, "your drone is toast, so stay close but be careful not to get too close, or you'll run out of drones." And that had given Priscilla another problem to worry about, one whose solution had come from an unexpected direction.

They hit their production quota earlier than expected, and Luke had sought her out in the break room to ask meekly if they should have more drones, just in case any were destroyed. It was the end of a long day and everyone was tired, but Priscilla called the team together for a meeting and they discussed their options in a surprisingly calm manner.

At the end of the meeting, Priscilla had asked for a show of hands and the teams had unanimously voted to keep building drones in the evenings and while they weren't actively monitoring the drones that were flying on autopilot. That way they'd never run out. If anything, they'd worked harder and faster. They now had plenty of raw material to supply the fabricators, and building the micro-drones only required them to clip together a few parts.

Then Jenny had suggested they could try building some of their own designs.

"Like the racing drones?" Priscilla had asked.

"I thought maybe something more useful?" said Jenny, grinning. "What about a large drone that could bring a wounded person back to the base for treatment? Or one that could deliver ammunition?"

That had got everyone excited, and Priscilla had agreed that the teams could work on their own drones during their downtime if they focussed on the Marines' combat drones and the long-range drones during their shifts. Priscilla particularly liked the idea of the stretcher drone, which a whole team were now working on, and by now they could put together a micro-drone in between taking bites of a sandwich. With luck, they would finish some of their creations before the Deathless arrived.

Priscilla turned her attention away from the assembly benches and back to the Grid, where her list of repeating tasks was waiting to be checked off. Nothing out of the ordinary, as usual. Good, but boring. She leaned back in her chair and smiled, things were going really well.

Then an alarm sounded and she almost jumped out of her skin. But it wasn't the alarm that summoned Corporal Wilson or the duty liaison officer. It was the team's internal alarm, one that said someone had found something of interest.

"What have you got, Jenny?" she called as she hurried over to her desk.

"Nothing good, boss, nothing good."

≈

"What do you think?"

"Is this the best imagery we've got?" Priscilla asked again, knowing the answer.

"Yes," Jenny replied, "it was only because I was pushing out Debbie's new airship drone that I saw it. It's twice the size of the others, a fair bit faster and it's got extra cameras. You still get the big overview, but you also get a view of space at night, an infrared view and a camera with a halfway decent zoom."

"Okay, okay, I get it, it's a fancy new drone. But what is it you've found, Jenny?" She pointed at what could only be described as a large, slightly shiny hill.

"I'm getting to that. I was looking for somewhere we hadn't got an airship so we could test it out, and that's when I saw this," said Jenny, flicking a moving image to her screen as the drone moved into its stationary position.

"No, I missed it. Play it again."

Jenny replayed the footage and waved a cursor over it. "Look here, three, two, one and flash!" She was quite animated, gesturing at the screen with excitement. "It's a glint of something shiny. So that's when I tried the new camera with the zoom. I had the drone do a few passes so we could shoot it from different angles, and look!"

She smiled up at Priscilla and rolled her eyes in exasperation when she realised her captain still didn't get it. Jenny sighed. "Okay, try this, it's easier to see it when it's sped up."

Priscilla watched the indicated spot as the camera moved back and forth. It wasn't detailed, but it was easier to see the shadows and the line of what looked like a large, circular wall. It was pretty big, and if it was a hill, then it had a very regular shape. If she squinted and applied some imagination, Priscilla could almost persuade herself that there were buildings within a perimeter wall and objects that could be made of metal glinted in the sunlight.

"So what do you think, boss?"

"I think you're on to something, and if that's not something to do with the Deathless, I think you're going to have some excited geologists in here asking for your footage," said Priscilla. Then she went into action.

"Jenny, get that airship in the best position you can. Then we have to get some long-range drones out there to take a closer look. We need the hi-res imagery to work out exactly what we're looking at."

She went along the desks, retasking anyone she could spare to gathering micro-drones on to the nearest of the long-range motherships. Then she went to Luke and updated his team with their new mission while they bolted down their lunch.

"Forget S13 for now. I want the same drone package, but get it over to F15 instead. Jenny's found something, and it might be important. It's a new area so even if it's a false alarm, we can run the same flight paths, right?" Luke nodded and hustled his team out of the break room, lunch unfinished.

This could be it, their first real taste of success. Everything up to now had been a rush of building drones, working out how to update the Grid and getting organised. Now they had something real to investigate, and the whole team was laser-focused on the task at hand. If Jenny had found something built by the Deathless, their contribution was going to get real, really quickly.

"What's the ETA, Debbie?" Priscilla called out, her concentration firmly on piloting her drone. They were making their final approaches, hugging the earth as close as possible to avoid detection. Nap-of-the-earth was the official terminology, apparently. For Priscilla, it was just fun, or it would have been with her racing drone. Given the importance of what they were doing, this was just nerve-wracking.

"You're about six minutes out, boss. Jenny is just under nineteen and Luke's team is at thirty-five, they'll be dropping to low-altitude in just over fifteen minutes," said Debbie, taking the role of flight controller.

"Roger that," Priscilla mumbled through gritted teeth as she flicked her drone around a rock formation. She had to fight the urge to lean with it, so engrossed was she in the screen before her.

It was tricky work. The drones' top speed meant there wasn't much room for error but, unlike the airship drones, the long-range models weren't capable of extreme altitude. If they wanted to be discreet, and Priscilla assumed that Corporal Wilson would want them to be, then they couldn't come within the sightline of the target.

The other pilots were doing their best to be unobtrusive. Thankfully, the extremely low-level contouring races the league sometimes held had taught them all the correct etiquette. Nobody wanted to win because their coughing had distracted an opponent and they'd crashed their drone. The drones were a labour of love and watching a crash would make even the meanest of competitors wince in sympathy.

So the cave was quiet, with everyone on tenterhooks as they waited for the transport drones to arrive and the next phase of the operation to begin. Once parked, they would release a swarm of micro-drones and then they'd begin the slow, careful work of scanning the structure without being detected.

It seemed like no time at all before Priscilla was parking her drone on a ledge high up on a rocky outcrop. The first micro-drones fanned out, their pilots taking over, and Priscilla felt the tension wash out of her arms as she relaxed. That was a race-winning performance but over a much longer distance than any of the league events. Debbie leaned in and whispered, "Well done, boss, that was some amazing flying. You were six per cent under the initial estimate."

As predicted, Jenny and Luke's drones were down in under half an hour. The first tentative micro-drones had reached a point where they could finally get a picture of the target. Priscilla had ordered everyone to take it slow and make sure no drone advanced without good cover and a cleared approach. The pilots worked as a team, meticulously checking for Deathless sentries and watching for spy posts or enemy drones. Nobody wanted one of their drones to be spotted by some patrol who might report back to the Deathless.

At night, Priscilla had been reading ancient books on warfare, and if there was one thing she clearly understood, it was the value of surprising the enemy. As far as the Deathless knew, New Bristol had no satellite surveillance, no ships in orbit, and therefore no way to find them or monitor their every move. Priscilla didn't want to shatter that belief by exposing a drone.

Once they were close enough, she ordered a halt and a quick huddle with the team leaders. Then they picked a single drone and eased it forwards into a position where it could get the first clear footage of the strange, shiny hill. Minimal footprint before they did anything further was the order of the day.

Then the footage hit the main display and there was an audible reaction from the watching pilots.

"A Deathless base," muttered Priscilla, hardly able to believe what she was seeing. Huge and horrifying, the base was a hive of activity.

"You were right, Jenny, you've found the enemy. Everyone else, excellent piloting, hold your positions until further orders. Jenny, would you do the honours please?" said Priscilla, her voice firm and clear above the rising hubbub. They all hushed as Jenny flipped open the plastic cover on her desk and turned to look at Priscilla, who gave her a nod. Jenny hit the button with the palm of her hand and the klaxon went off.

Moments later the pounding of booted feet announced the arrival of Marine X and Corporal Wilson, who rushed into the room almost at the same time.

"What's up?" asked Wilson.

But Marine X was just staring at the screen.

"They've found me something to kill, Corporal, that's what's up," said Ten with a broad grin. "It must be my birthday."

15

The bombardment had been swift, heavy and brutal. In the aftermath, drone surveys and the feeds from the remaining ground monitors showed a wrecked city of craters and shattered structures. Almost all the government and important infrastructure buildings had been destroyed or severely damaged, but the strikes had been carefully targeted to leave civilian buildings untouched.

"Lucky we didn't land in a target building," muttered Atticus, as he and Denmead reviewed the damage. The blast wave had carried them into the foyer of Ashton High School and they had gathered in the main hall with the other survivors of the crash.

Atticus put down his tablet and looked at their kit. They had gathered everything from the lifter and their salvage now sat on a pair of folding tables.

"This lot won't keep us alive very long," said Atticus looking at their meagre collection, "we need to find B Troop and get these people to the caves."

Denmead nodded. The crash had aggravated her shoulder wound but she wasn't going to let it slow her down. She hefted her rifle, one of only two they had.

"It's a pity there aren't any flying mammals on this planet," she said to Atticus as she collected her gear. He frowned, unable to see the relevance. "I've always wanted to issue a 'To the bat cave' order, but without bats..." She shrugged then grimaced a little at the pain.

"I wouldn't have pegged you as a fan of the winged vigilante," said Atticus, grinning.

"Only the classics," said Denmead, "and I prefer the darker material." A rumble shook the walls and dropped dust from the ceiling. Atticus reviewed his HUD.

"That'll be B Troop getting started," he said with no small degree of satisfaction, "so let's make like the three shepherds..."

"...and get the flock out of here? I see you're one for the classics as well."

~

Outside, the city had become a dark, dust-strewn hell-scape. The sun had gone, hidden from view by the vast quantities of muck thrown into the atmosphere by the bombardment. Beneath the darkened skies, the city had taken on a menacing orange hue and visibility was no more than twenty metres.

"Stay close," said Atticus as he led the governor and four colonists into the open. "We'll head for B Troop's position and try to link up with them."

They walked through the dark and eerily quiet city, weaving around buildings damaged by the fighting, making their way towards the positions that B Troop had taken up. Occasional bursts of gunfire could be heard in the distance as they walked but they saw nothing until they rounded a corner and Atticus halted the party, waving at them to take cover.

"A four-man drop pod, by the size of it, but no sign of the enemy," he said to Denmead. "They may have moved away, or they could be in the building. No way to know."

"So what do we do?"

Atticus was silent for a moment, checking his HUD again for any information that might help. "Nothing on the monitors but that doesn't mean much, given the dust. We'll circle around, try to avoid exposing ourselves." He paused as Denmead touched his arm and nodded at the street.

Four Deathless troopers in thin, mobile clone bodies and armed with light armour and weapons were walking down the street. They were in pairs, moving slowly and cautiously, checking doorways and alleys, but they hadn't spotted the humans yet.

"Back," hissed Atticus, "get inside." He ushered the group back into the building they were crouching behind. "Stay down, make no noise." He squatted down with them, well below the windows, and called up the monitor and drone coverage in his HUD. "Nothing," he muttered, "this bloody dust is covering everything."

They could hear the Deathless in the street chattering quietly and walking with care. As the second pair passed by and disappeared into the dust cloud, Atticus risked a look out of the window. It was clear, as far as he could tell, but the air was so clogged with muck that nothing was certain.

"Out the back," he muttered, leading the party through the building to the back door. It lay ajar, unmoving in the dead air but somehow foreboding and ominous. Atticus crouched down, raised his rifle and gently pushed the door.

It swung open to show a narrow, deserted alley whose every surface was covered in fine orange muck.

"Let's go," said Atticus, motioning for the party to head out into the alley. There was a bang at the other end of the building, and Atticus's head whipped round. "Shit. It looks like they spotted our footprints. Go, quickly, turn right at the end and head that way for a couple of kilometres. I'll catch you up."

The party moved off but Denmead hung back.

"What are you going to do?" she said, one hand resting on Atticus's arm.

"Something nasty. Go, I'll be right behind you." She looked very doubtful, but he slipped her grasp and pushed her away. "Go!" Then he took a grenade from his pack, wedged it into the door and pulled the pin. He stepped back carefully and almost stood on Denmead.

"Why are you still here? Go!" She backed off, following the rest of the party, and Atticus hurried after her, no longer caring about making a noise.

Thirty-seven seconds later, by the clock in Atticus's HUD, there was a muffled bang from behind them. They had caught up with the rest of the group, who were struggling to move quickly in the choking dust, and Atticus urged them on.

"Dampened cloths," said Atticus, tearing long strips from the sleeves of his shirt, "but don't stop." He wrapped the cloth around his head to cover his mouth and nose and kept moving, driving the others before him.

<Enemy soldiers all over the place> sent Warden, his message popping into Atticus's HUD, <sporadic engagements, looks like light scouts, mostly>

<Noted> sent Atticus, <they're clearing the city. We are twenty minutes from B Troop's position>

<Acknowledged. Hayes has sent Corporal Hamilton to rendezvous with you. Do you have injured?>

<Nothing serious. I'm with the governor> sent Atticus.

"We're almost there," said Atticus to Denmead. "Keep your eyes..." He paused as shapes moved in the dust ahead. "Cover," he yelled, pushing Denmead into a doorway and diving forward into the shadow of a low wall. The rest of the party scattered into the building as the shadows ahead paused, stopped, then spread out.

<Contact> sent Atticus as he fired on the first shadow. It disappeared, but he couldn't tell if it was injured, dead or merely irritated. The other shadows dispersed, at least five of them, before Atticus could fire again.

"Inside," he yelled, but it looked like only Denmead was left on the street. He hustled her through the doorway as the enemy returned fire. The concrete prefab structure was tough but there were a lot of enemy troopers out there. Sooner or later, they'd come looking.

Atticus hurried down the corridor, pausing on to fire a few rounds back towards the front door as he followed Denmead.

A noise caught his attention and he paused, aiming at the door. Then something peered cautiously around the door and Atticus fired a quick burst then dragged Denmead into a room. More gunfire and bullets ripped down the corridor.

"Not ideal," said Atticus, looking around. The room was big, but the only door was the one they'd come through. "Up the stairs," he whispered, backing away from the door. Denmead padded up the stairs and peered out at the top.

"All clear," she whispered.

"Then run," said Atticus as he reached the top of the stairs and threw a grenade into the room below so that it bounced off the wall and ricocheted back towards the corridor.

They ran, and the boom of the exploding grenade chased them away from the stairs and towards a door that opened onto a balcony.

Denmead just had time to see bodies in the street before gunfire erupted and drove her back inside.

"Not that way," she said, "maybe down there?" They charged through another doorway into a long room lined with desks. At the far end, they burst out onto a small patio.

"Huh, ground level," said Atticus in a surprised voice. They ran down a slope and across the street into a park where small, scrubby trees had been planted, a triumph of gardener's hope over biologist's experience.

"Hold on," said Denmead, leaning on her knees and breathing heavily, "this shoulder isn't helping things."

Atticus knelt, rifle aimed across the patio as Denmead recovered her breath. They waited a couple of minutes but there was no sign of the Deathless. Atticus couldn't tell if that meant they were dead, distracted, lost or laying a new ambush.

"We go slow from here," said Atticus, "slow and quiet. It's not far now."

~

Thirty minutes later they had travelled only half a kilometre towards B Troop's position. The area swarmed with Deathless scouts and light troops, their abandoned drop pods littering the streets.

Atticus and Denmead pressed on, hoping to find a friendly face, but her injury slowed them both. They paused to rest in an abandoned hydroponics facility before venturing out again. The air here was clearer, now, and the visibility was better, but that meant they could be seen from further away.

"B Troop should be the other side of these buildings," said Atticus finally, looking down the long slope to a large warehouse and chemical plant. It was undamaged, as far as he could tell, probably because the Deathless wanted it for their own purposes.

"Drop pods," murmured Denmead, pointing across the slope. Atticus followed her gaze and saw a cluster of pods, four at least. He hefted his rifle and moved slowly forward.

<On the north side of the chemical plant> he sent, hoping that his people were close by.

<Southside, sir> came the welcome answer, <enemies in the plant, numbers unknown> That was far less welcome but not unexpected.

"Stay close," said Atticus as they made their way across the street. Ahead, the dust had been kicked up by something. Deathless troopers, he assumed.

They skulked through the first warehouse, chemical tanks and packaging materials on either side.

"Over there," said Denmead, pointing at a door that swung in the breeze. Atticus nodded and followed his rifle towards the door.

There was a burst of gunfire, Deathless by the sound, then return fire from either Marines or militia. A serious firefight, close by.

Atticus edged forward and peered around the doorway. The enemy troopers were no more than twenty metres away, six of them, all lying in a shallow ditch and shooting at something across the street.

He signalled Denmead to stay back then waited until the Deathless were firing before shooting the first in the back. He managed to shoot the next two before the rest finally realised what was going on.

Atticus grinned and shot the fourth Deathless trooper as it turned to look his way, confused to see one of their own clones. Then he hurled himself back as someone across the way, mistaking Atticus for a Deathless soldier, opened up on his position.

Rounds punched easily through the thin walls of the warehouse and stitched a jagged line across the tanks beyond.

<I'm in the warehouse> sent Atticus as he lay on his back with rounds flying above, <focus on the two in the trench>

Denmead was beside him, face down, hands over her head. After a moment, the shooting stopped. There was a brief pause then a final burst and everything went quiet.

"You'd better take a look," said Atticus. "I don't think they're prepared for me."

Denmead looked up from the floor, face pale, and nodded. She grabbed her rifle and edged cautiously to the door and peered out.

"This is Governor Denmead," she called out. "I'm with Captain Atticus."

There was a moment's silence then a pair of Marines appeared, jogging across the open area.

"Corporal Hamilton, ma'am," said one of the Marines politely, then they hurried her across the street with Atticus following along behind. He paused at the Deathless corpses, considered taking one of their weapons then decided against it. His people were already mistaking him for the enemy; it wouldn't be healthy to improve his disguise.

"What's the situation, Lieutenant Hayes?" asked Atticus as soon as they were clear of the enemy.

"Drop pods across the city, sir, a great deal of damage from the bombardment and now they seem to be mopping up, checking for stragglers." Her eyes flicked up and down, sizing him up in his new body. It was taking everyone time to get used to it. Funny, if he'd been in one of the more exotic clones the British forces used, she'd have taken it in her stride, he thought.

"Have they taken prisoners?"

Hayes sniffed, clearly unhappy, and said in a firmly disapproving tone, "I don't think they're observing any niceties, sir. Doesn't seem to be in their nature."

"Right, let's clear this plant and give them something other than civilians to worry about."

~

The snipers were working in teams of four, focussing their attention on the longer avenues where the Deathless soldiers seemed to have problems staying out of sight.

"Two coming from the right, three hundred metres," said the spotter, binoculars trained on the remains of an office building.

"Got 'em," said Pete, fingers fiddling with the sights of the captured railgun, "just about there..." He pressed the firing stud, and the gun thrummed, dispatching its projectile at Mach 6. Before he'd even seen it hit, he was activating the loading cycle to prepare another round.

"Lower body, just above the hip," said Phil, the spotter. "Its mate is moving, heading for the wall." He paused, watching. "Yup, gone to ground, marking the point." Phil planted a virtual flag, and the indicator flashed up in Pete's HUD. "See it?"

"Hold on, yup. Behind the wall, eh? Let's give this a go." The gun thrummed again, and a huge hole appeared in the wall.

"Looked like a blood spray," said Phil, playing the video back in slow motion, "yup, definite blood, solid hit. No movement, so I'll log that as a kill."

"Time to move," said Pete. "Wanna try the next building over?"

"Sure," said Phil, packing his binoculars and grabbing his rifle, "we're good on ammo, good on time and the dust is subsiding."

"Happy days."

"Snipers report multiple contacts, sir," said Lieutenant Hayes, "and Marine X is requesting permission to engage."

"X is with A Troop, Lieutenant, let Warden handle him."

"He was supposed to be, sir, but he turned up on one of our vehicles. It seems he mistook our transport for A Troop's assigned position."

"Really," said Atticus, eyebrow raised to indicate his profound scepticism. "Just make sure he gets back to Warden before he's needed."

"Sir," said Hayes, turning away.

Marine X slammed a new magazine into his rifle and peered through the sights along the narrow alley. Nothing was moving at the moment but he was sure they were still following him.

"Perfect spot for a surprise," he muttered, grinning to himself as he set a trap with a grenade and a length of thin, transparent line, "that ought to slow the buggers down." He grabbed his rifle and retreated down the alley, scanning carefully for 'surprises' left by the other side.

As he reached the end, there was a shout behind him, and he ducked away just as a burst of fire rattled, tearing holes in the buildings across the street.

"Three, two, o–" A grenade exploded, interrupting his countdown. He glanced cautiously back down the alley and wondered for a moment if it might be worth checking the bodies for supplies. Then a shape moved in the smoke, and he ducked back out of sight.

"Guess not," he muttered. "Better keep moving forward."

He checked the street again – still empty – then crossed into an office building and climbed up to the first floor where he'd get a good view of the mouth of the alley and any Deathless troopers daft enough still to be following. He found himself a nice comfortable spot, well back from the front of the building but with a good view, and settled down to wait.

But not for a long, as it happened. No more than a minute after setting up shop, a Deathless trooper stepped out of the alleyway, rifle up, looking around. A second followed, then a third, fanning out into the street. Ten waited, just in case more followed, then he opened up using short, controlled bursts.

The first two went down quickly but the third made it to cover and returned fire, spraying the front of the office with bullets.

"Nice try," said Ten, moving across the room to improve his angle. He switched the rifle to single shot and put a round into the wall where he thought the Deathless trooper was sheltering. Another round to the same spot and a hole opened up. The Deathless stumbled up, looking for better cover, and Ten shot it in the side then again in the neck as it tried to recover its balance. Once more, in the chest, and the thing went down for good.

Ten breathed out slowly and backed away towards the exit.

"Time to rejoin the crew," he muttered, heading down the stairs. He loved working alone, especially in situations like this, but you could have too much of a good thing. Anyway, it was getting close to teatime, and he had the tea. There'd be hell to pay if he wasn't back by the time the crew were ready to brew a hot wet.

16

"I don't have any good news," said Atticus, calling the meeting to order, "our situation is grim and getting worse." He looked around the table at the tired, filthy faces of the other attendees. Grimes had warned that water might not be freely available and he had been right. Laundry and bathing had all but stopped.

"Are we not winning?" said Smith, frowning.

"We're surviving, Mr Smith, but I wouldn't like to claim more than that. My troops are fighting hard, as are the civilian militia, but our rate of attrition is too high, and, as expected, we're giving ground instead of taking it. Sooner or later, we'll suffer a collapse, and they'll break through our lines."

"Or they will work out where we are and bombard Fort Widley from orbit," said Denmead, voicing the fear that had stalked the colony since the evacuation of Ashton. They had all seen the video, seen the missiles falling and the city disintegrating. There was no defence against an attack like that and everyone knew it.

"The Deathless are out there, searching for this base, and when they find us, it'll come down either to a fight in the caves, which is not something any of us want, or an orbital bombardment. So we're not going to wait for that to happen."

Silence greeted this information, as if everyone were waiting for Atticus to finish sticking his head in the trap before they sprang.

"Instead we'll be taking the fight to the Deathless," he went on, ignoring the disbelieving looks and the somewhat defeatist cries of despair and raising his voice to speak over the dissenters. "That means finding their base of operations, developing a suitable plan and then hitting them as hard as possible."

"To what end?" whined Smith, clearly unhappy with the idea. "Do you hope to destroy them?"

"Yes," said Atticus simply, "the nearby forces, at least. But we also need materiel and supplies. The Deathless are well-equipped and comprehensively supplied. We've made some progress deciphering their glyphs, maybe enough to allow us to operate their equipment, so we want to test our theories and see if we can make use of their kit."

It was an impressive achievement. Barlow had been ecstatic when they had first translated the word 'stop', found above a big red button. The councillors looked less impressed.

Governor Denmead took over, "Now, I'm sure some had already heard the rumours, and I'm able to confirm that some of them, at least, are true."

There was a murmur of surprise at that announcement. They had all heard the rumours, of course, but the ingrained suspicion of 'false narratives' and the lingering hangover from the impacts of media manipulation in earlier centuries had made everyone wary. Nothing was taken at face value, especially good news received against the odds.

"I'm pleased to say that we have had good results from the reconnaissance drones that the children have been building with their domestic fabs. Just a few hours ago, their pilots reported that they'd found the enemy base Captain Atticus has said we need to target, and it seems that they're correct. There is a regrettable downside to this news, I'm afraid," Denmead said, holding the tension for a few seconds.

Then she turned to address one person at the table. "Councilman

Smith, it was your daughter, Priscilla, who made the decision to investigate what could have just been a smudge on the map. Wisely she ordered her pilots to investigate fully and they gathered comprehensive intelligence. I know she's only thirteen and it was against your strong objection that she was allowed to participate. I'm sorry to say, any future attempt you make to give her a curfew or get her to tidy your room may be met with a response that she saved the colony. I'm sure you have the sympathy of all those parents who've had teenagers, and we'll happily make a counsellor available to you after all this blows over." Denmead shrugged apologetically. Those gathered laughed as Smith hung his head in his hands and the tension eased somewhat.

Presently though, the doubtful whispering started up again.

"I know, I know," said Denmead, holding up her hands, "this is the first piece of good news we've had in a long time, and nobody really believes it. Well, let me tell you now that, as far as we can tell, we've found the base the Deathless are using and, we think, a vulnerability we can exploit."

"Is it a tiny exhaust port, Governor?" said some nameless wit at the far end of the room. Denmead ignored him.

"It's a fair question," said Grimes in his thick accent, "what can you tell us?"

Denmead sent the aerial view of the base to a large display screen, and Grimes whistled quietly. A large, circular fortification surrounded the buildings. Slightly off centre sat an enormous ship, its hull broken up by weapon turrets and, by each cargo bay presumably, even cranes for moving heavy gear.

"It's big," admitted Denmead, "far bigger than the other ships we've seen. It looks like they landed a command and fabrication vessel on the surface and they've been busy ever since building out from there. The ship is now surrounded by buildings and a defensive wall which we suspect is foamcrete, although there don't seem to be all that many Deathless on the ground yet."

"Worse, this level of production activity suggests a long-term strategic plan," said Atticus, looking around the room. "Colonisation was always the most likely explanation for their presence; now it looks like the only possible explanation. They're building for future needs, not for the troops they've already deployed,"

"So, what?" said Smith, "We go in, guns blazing, and hope to do enough damage to scare them off? Is that your plan?"

"No," said Atticus, "our key advantage remains that they underestimate or at least fear us. Their attacks have tickled our defences, destroyed some landmarks and killed a lot of clones, but they haven't seriously damaged us. They've been probing, testing maybe, to keep us busy and find out what we're made of and learn how we would respond. They're overconfident."

"Now they know that we're here for the long-term and that we're prepared to fight, so they're bound to change their tactics, sooner or later. They'll learn better habits soon enough. As long as they keep probing, we know they're not ready for an all-out assault. Soon, though, the phoney war will end, and the real fighting will begin."

"Real fighting?" said Idol, one of the civilians whose leadership and tenacity had quickly earned the respect of Bristolians and Marines alike. He raised an eyebrow and scratched at the scabs of a long cut on his arm. "You think we've maybe just been playing so far?"

"So far," said Atticus, leaning forward to take advantage of the disquieting appearance of his Deathless clone body, "since they found we weren't just going to roll over, we've seen only small numbers of Deathless. As I said, they're probing, searching for us, nibbling away at us while they dig in and prepare for the final assault.

"When they're ready, they'll come in great force, very fast, and they won't stop. Everything we've seen so far is just a prelude. They'll try to overwhelm us, drive us from our positions and kill us all until there's nothing left."

"You make it sound like we've no way of winning," said Idol, still smarting from Atticus's comments, "so what was the point of fighting at all?"

"The point," said the governor firmly, looking at each of the councillors to make sure that they all understood her words, "was to hold out long enough for the fleet to arrive."

"And to get us to this day, where we finally have the information we need to strike back," said Atticus before Idol could object to the hopelessness of the situation. "And now, that's exactly what we're going to do. Lieutenant Warden, whom you all now know, will take all the Marines from A Troop who can be spared, including those now working in Deathless clones, and attack the enemy in an attempt to destroy their principal operating base and set back their plans."

"Lieutenant Hayes and B Troop will remain here in Ashton with the militia to defend the city and keep the enemy focussed on us," Denmead finished.

The silence around the table said it all. Nobody believed it was feasible.

"You're sceptical and I understand. That's why Lieutenant Warden is here to explain the plan. We want your input and support, so it's important that you all understand what we're going to be doing."

Warden stood up and sent a projection from the old satellite network to the display screen, an entirely different site to the enemy base but one with which all the colonists were familiar.

"This is the first stage of my plan," said Warden, aiming a laser pointer at the image.

"After all you've just told us," interrupted Idol, carefully fitting his words together like shells being loaded into a magazine, "how can you possibly hope to win?"

"We're Royal Marines Space Commandos, Mr Idol," said Warden, "it's what we do."

17

"Grenade!"

Idol pulled the pin and threw the grenade through the hole in the wall that had once held a window.

Would the rounds spattering through the opening and against the far wall hit the grenade in flight and throw it back in his face? He didn't know, but the thought flashed across his mind as his arm cartwheeled around.

There was an explosion that could have been across the other side of the street, in the area he thought the Deathless had taken cover. For twenty minutes, bursts of fire had been going through every window in the brewery just enough to keep them pinned down. It felt hopeless. His HUD screamed at him that a number of people already had gunshot wounds, some minor and some probably fatal.

Adams leaned out and fired a burst across the street, then slammed back against the foamcrete, turning his face away from the window as a cacophony of bullets answered him. When the shooting abated, he turned his head to his left and shouted to Idol. "Yeah, that didn't do much of anything. If we keep this up much longer, we'll be out of ammo and grenades."

Idol nodded in agreement and called Lieutenant Hayes via the

HUD. "We've been pinned down here for twenty minutes or so. We're running low on ammunition and taking casualties. Are there any Marine patrols coming that could outflank the Deathless here?"

"Negative, all my teams have their own firefights," said Hayes, gunfire audible over the HUD. "Including me."

"What should we do then, Lieutenant? Hold out here?"

"One moment," she replied. There was another burst of gunfire. "Sorry, some rude bugger interrupted me. I'm just checking our tactical data."

There was an interminable pause while she reviewed the recent updates that flowed continuously from skirmishes all across Ashton. Around him, Idol's team exchanged fire with the Deathless in a pointless stalemate exercise.

"Right, sorry about that, I've been too bogged down to keep up to date. We don't have anyone to send to help you out. Your position is good, but if you're running low on ammunition, evacuate any walking wounded immediately. Then manage an orderly retreat to your fallback. I've checked, it's still clear. Remember, use bounding overwatch for the retreat. Understood?" Hayes asked.

Idol's mind went blank. He hissed to attract Adams's attention then mouthed "Bounding overwatch," raising his hands to beg help.

"One team moves, another gives covering fire, then they flip," said Adams. "Attacking or retreating. Why are we whispering?"

Idol nodded as memory came hurtling back. Less than a week of training wasn't anywhere near long enough to master all the new jargon.

"Yes, Lieutenant," he said with a confidence he didn't feel. "Understood, we'll have teams covering each other as they move."

"Good luck, Captain. You're holding out well. We'll make it through this. Hayes out." The Marine Lieutenant, much younger than him, he guessed, sounded supremely confident. But here was Idol, glad still to have all his limbs and thanking his lucky stars that he'd been to the toilet before the shooting started.

He crawled away from the window and motioned for Adams to do the same. They headed back into the room, away from the windows, and hid behind a cluster of thick piping and foamcrete supports that hadn't been removed when the brewery was stripped of useful materials.

They had left their rations and supplies here, safely away from the windows and the firefight.

"You got the idea, yes?" Idol asked as he stuff a ration bar that tasted of cardboard into his mouth. He washed it down with water then began replenishing his ammunition. The water was unnaturally sweet, stuffed with sugar and electrolytes to replenish energy.

Adams nodded, gulping from his canteen. "Yeah. We evacuate the wounded, then run away from these bastards and hope we don't have to keep doing that until they've overrun our entire colony."

Idol looked up at his friend in surprise. Adams was a quiet man, usually, contemplative and compassionate. Now he was seething with anger. Idol hadn't seen him this pissed off since the infamous plant transcription incident, and that had happened long before the invasion. Clearly, Adams was not impressed with the lieutenant's orders.

"You don't like the plan?" Idol asked.

"No, I don't, Roger. It's bollocks. Yeah, we can run away with our tail between our legs, but we've done enough of that already. These bastards come here and they want to take our planet from us, they kill our friends and kids even. Kids have been killed, Roger, and now we're just supposed to back off and let the Marines fight our battles for us?" said Adams, his teeth gritted and his face turning a nasty shade of puce. He spoke quietly and emphatically, despite his anger, so the nearest militia wouldn't hear.

"Well, we have orders to retreat, Charles. We can't just disobey."

"No, no," said Adams, shaking his head. "You asked a lieutenant for advice, she gave you some. But you're a captain and you're in charge of our militia company. The decision is yours. You outrank her. If you say we attack, that's what we'll do. It's not the Marines' city, it's not up to them to defend New Bristol. It's our home, it's up to us."

"It's their job, Charles. They're Marines, it's what they're paid for! I may be a captain, but she's a professional, Charles. We're strictly amateurs."

"Fuck that. I'll do what you say, but don't hand that decision to her. It's yours to make," insisted Roger.

"What are you suggesting, Sergeant Adams? That we forget about our casualties and what, just hold out here until we run out of ammunition? What then?" Idol asked.

"No. We evacuate the casualties and send the walking wounded to escort them to safety. Then the rest of us attack. We give them everything we've got and overrun them," Sergeant Adams said.

"We overrun them? Do you even know how?"

"Yeah, I do. How many of them are there? We've got about eighty people still fresh. What have they got?" the sergeant asked.

"I've no idea. I only see one or two at a time. Can't say I fancy doing a headcount, do you?" Idol said with as much sarcasm as he could muster, which was quite a lot even on a bad day.

Adams smiled then called someone on his HUD. "Captain Smith, this is Sergeant Adams of G Company."

"Yes, Sergeant, what can I do for you?" Priscilla asked.

"We're in a bit of a stalemate here, we're taking casualties and running short of supplies. We need to make a move, and that means either retreating like beaten dogs or attacking. Problem is, we don't know the enemy numbers or disposition, and if we stick our heads up to look, we'll lose them," he explained. Idol listened but didn't interrupt.

"One second, let me check something," Priscilla replied. They waited for a tense minute. "Okay, we have your position on the Grid. We have assets nearby. Can you hold out for a few minutes while we get you some updates? If you want discretion, that is. We could just pop some micro-drones in and get you a rough headcount, if that's all you want, but if we rush the job, they'll probably be spotted."

Adams looked at Idol, who put his finger to his lips to indicate silence.

"We can hold out for ten minutes if it gives us the element of surprise."

"Roger that. Standby for updates," the drone queen confirmed.

Sergeant Adams took another swig of water. "What do you think?" he asked.

Idol looked at the HUD data as it currently stood. Then he nodded and issued orders for the wounded to be evacuated. He took another swig of water before responding. "Okay. If we get the enemy numbers and disposition, we'll know if your plan will work. But if we don't outnumber them two to one, we retreat."

"Aye aye, Captain," Sergeant Adams replied with a wink that he probably meant to be masculine but came across as a bit suggestive instead.

"I'm pretty sure that's sailors, Charles, not soldiers," said Idol with a sigh.

~

"I have updates for you, Captain Idol, Sergeant Adams," said Priscilla after patching them both in to a HUD conversation.

"Go ahead, Captain Smith," Idol replied. Priscilla fought to keep her blushing under control. Her teammates on the Ashton Blues had called her captain for a few years but it was weird when adults did it. She'd been given the honorary rank in the militia when Governor Denmead had thanked her and the team for their work discovering the enemy base.

"You'll see updates on your HUD now. We've placed micro-drones behind all the enemy positions near you. You're clear to the east and west. We count twenty-four Deathless troops, six in power armour. There's live video feed of all of them," said Priscilla, walking them through the feeds and maps.

The Marines didn't need the guidance about HUD tactical updates because they used them habitually. The drone pilots flagged anything of interest and let the Marine officers and NCOs deal with it. This was the first time the militia had made a specific request, though, and they were as new to this as she was.

"Have you seen any railguns?" asked Sergeant Adams. "We don't seem to have been shot at by any."

"No, these troops are flagged as light infantry. They don't seem to have any heavier weapons, just rifles," said Priscilla. "If you're going to attack, Captain, can you hold off for just a few minutes more?"

Idol frowned and looked at Adams, who shrugged.

"We can," he responded, "but why?"

"It will give us time to get you some more support. Go to the coordinates I've marked on your HUD. It's the south side of the brewery where the first-floor wall is blown out. You'll have help in two minutes," said Priscilla.

"We're on our way," said Idol.

Priscilla's chosen rendezvous had previously been a windowless storage room, but now the south wall and part of the floor had gone. The other end was a safe flat space for a brew, but it looked like someone had taken a giant bite out of the floor and the militia were staying well away, even though the lack of windows meant the area was safe from enemy fire. Nobody wanted to fall three floors through a hole in the floor.

That left a nice big space that ran the whole length of the brewery. The contents of the room had been stripped out a week earlier and taken for reprocessing into raw materials for the fabricators. Most of the offices and buildings in New Ashton had been similarly cleared as part of the colony's struggle to survive.

Idol and Adams got to the other room just as a large drone almost three metres long hoved into view. It manoeuvred delicately through the gaping hole in the wall, hovered for a moment in the middle of what remained of the floor, then settled briefly amongst the dust and rubble. There were a few brief clicks, then the drone lifted off and backed out the way it had come. In moments, it was gone, disappearing across the shattered city and leaving behind four large crates.

Each of the crates was covered with messages in marker pen, like "Kill them all!" and "Drink me!" and "Just say no to aliens!" as well as smiley faces and messages of good luck.

Adams grinned as he opened the first box and pulled out some of the contents – chocolate bars, boxes of fruit drink and packets of snacks – it looked like the drone pilots had raided a set of vending machines in the kids' break room. The militia had ration packs, but nothing you'd choose to eat given a choice.

The second crate contained an assortment of unfamiliar drones and the last two, on opposite corners of the drone for weight distribution, held ammunition.

Idol called Priscilla back. "Where did you get all this from?"

"We requisitioned it from the armoury, of course," replied Priscilla.

Idol smelt something fishy. "And by 'requisitioned' you mean what, exactly?"

Priscilla paused before replying. "This was our first chance to test the resupply drone, but I realise now we forgot to send the consignment note from the quartermaster. I'm happy to retrieve the supplies if you want the paperwork sorted before you accept the delivery, Captain. I'm afraid it might take a while, though, 'cos the quartermaster is on a lunch break."

Adams waved his hands urgently at Idol and shook his head vigorously, indicating that he didn't care how the cheeky little buggers had got hold of the stuff, he just wanted the grenades. Or perhaps it was the individual fruit drinks.

"Err, no, that's fine, the paperwork can wait," Idol replied as a series of loud bangs sounded from the front of the building.

"I'm sure we can sort that out when this war's over," Priscilla promised.

Idol chose to ignore that. "What are the drones for?"

"Just some new models we need to test. If you could lay them out on the floor, we'll take it from there. If you decide to proceed with an attack, please let me know so we can make sure to give you the best updates and support possible."

"Roger that. We will be proceeding, once we've distributed these very welcome supplies. Thank you, Captain Smith. Thank you very much indeed," said Idol.

~

While Adams distributed the junk food, the ammunition and, more worryingly, the grenades it seemed the kids had purloined without too much trouble, Idol dealt with the drones.

He unpacked each carefully and laid them on the floor near the edge of room. There were six in total, four were long and looked for all the world like flying flutes. The other two were... sparkly? They were brightly coloured, had boxes of what looked like glitter attached to them, and lots of unidentifiable electronics, all of which were painted in psychedelic fluorescent colour schemes.

"What the hell is all that about?" he muttered to himself, before deciding that it really didn't matter. Priscilla had given him the tools he needed to turn a huge risk, with luck, into a minor victory and perhaps win this skirmish. He wasn't going to quibble about the odd drones they'd included.

<Drones ready> he sent, then he went to find Adams.

They gathered in the empty room and projected their battle plan on the floor space the boxes had previously occupied. It was a simple layout of the street across which they'd been duelling with the Death-less for the better part of an hour. Except now they had precise loca-tions for all the Deathless troopers. Idol patched in the NCOs and the company's two surviving Lieutenants via their HUDs and went over the strategy Adams had suggested.

B and C platoons were holed up in buildings adjacent to the brewery, one on the west side, the other on the east. Idol had taken direct command of A platoon, who were in the brewery itself and had lost their lieutenant earlier in the day.

The idea was for the two wings to cross the street and outflank the Deathless position. They'd be cut to ribbons if they were spotted, so A platoon had been tasked with providing a distraction. Half the platoon had worked their way up to the flat roof of the building and were now huddled along the southern edge, awaiting the go order. The rest had taken up new positions at as many of the unused windows as possible.

<Everyone in position?> he sent to his officers and NCOs. There was a brief flurry of positive replies, then Idol realised he had no more excuses. For a moment, he considered cancelling the whole idea and pulling his troops back. But then he looked at Adams, who nodded grimly, and Idol allowed the last of his doubts to be submerged in the sergeant's confidence.

"Priscilla, we are going in thirty seconds," he said, receiving a terse acknowledgement.

<Stand ready, attack on my order> he sent to the whole company.

He and Adams jogged down to the ground floor and took up positions either side of a goods door.

"Good view of the street," muttered Idol.

"Nice firing lines as well," said Adams.

Taking a deep breath, he broadcast voice to A Platoon. "Fire in three, two, one."

Bursts of fire erupted throughout the building and then seconds later, a series of explosions was heard from across the street. Lobbing grenades from the top of the roof seemed to help, and it was much harder for the enemy to return any kind of fire, let alone throw one back.

<Go, go, go> he sent through the HUDs of platoons B and C, watching the vid feed from one of Priscilla's drones as it flew high over the street. His troops sprinted quietly across the street, running from one piece of cover to another as they made their way toward the wings of the building the Deathless were hiding in.

Idol sprayed a burst of fire across the street using the data on the overhead map to confirm a Deathless soldier was in the right spot. He ducked back into cover again and Adams took his turn, firing a quick burst then throwing a pair of grenades.

Then a strange sound filled the street, a loud screaming noise, something like a cross between a whistle and a whine.

"What the fuck is that?" shouted Adams.

Half a second later, the noise peaked and a thin silver shaped streaked in front of the Deathless position, so fast Idol barely saw it. It was followed by three more in quick succession. The noise was horrendous. It was the drones.

Idol watched, mouth open. He could see the Deathless reaction from the feeds on the micro-drones. They'd been hunkering down, sheltering from the militia's heavy fire, but now they were looking frantically around for some new weapon or source of danger.

Then he heard the deafening noise of a teen pop song. No, two different songs, both equally irritating but completely different. The sparkly drones arrived carrying speakers and weaponised pop music. They floated down out of the sky to target two separate clusters of Deathless soldiers, their presence announced not just by sound but by puffs of glitter that filled each room with colourful, sparkling chaff.

Their innocuous sparkly cargo deposited, the drones shot out of windows and disappeared before the Deathless could respond, other than to desperately cough and splutter and try to waft glitter away from their faces.

"They're on the roof, sir," one of the grenadiers reported. "They've parked the drones on the roof above the Deathless position. Permission to shoot them, sir?"

"The Deathless? By all means, fire away."

"No, sir, the drones. That music is horrendous," the militia soldier complained.

"Yeah, well. Imagine what it sounds like to the enemy. Permission denied," Idol responded.

He checked the status of his flanking platoons. They'd all made it. Not even an injury. Right now, they were completing their stealthy advances, getting into position before springing their attack.

Idol turned back to the feeds from the micro-drones and saw one of the Deathless Ruperts shouting at a soldier in power armour and gesturing towards the roof. The soldier nodded and bounded up the stairs.

"Grenadiers, move to the north side switch to rifles. A power armoured soldier is heading to the roof. As soon as it gets in the clear, give it everything you've got. Don't stop shooting until it stops moving," Idol ordered.

He could hear the dart-like flute drones coming in for another pass, their noise level increasing smoothly as they accelerated toward the Deathless position.

"Nice work on those new drones, Priscilla. They seem to be quite the distraction."

"Thank you, Captain. I shall pass that along. ETA twenty seconds."

"Roger that," Idol confirmed.

He flipped to the view from inside the enemy position. The drone pilots had done amazing work. Idol could see the enemy officer getting agitated, waiting for the awful noise above to stop. He actually felt a twinge of sympathy for the poor bastards. That music was bad enough to make anyone take risks to silence it.

He glanced at Adams and felt a new sense of pity. The sergeant had two small children, and if tastes didn't change soon, he'd have a house that sounded just like this one day soon enough. That was one advantage of the single life — total control over your music and vid shows.

The flute drones arrived as he finished that thought, but this time they didn't just pass the Deathless position. The first screamed through an open ground floor window, and Idol saw the Rupert's face register shock before the thing hit him full in the chest and knocked him to the floor.

Another drone passed all the Deathless to shatter against a wall. There was panic in the room. The drones were incredibly light, but a strike to the face at high speed would be most unpleasant, and Idol could hear the other two flute drones circling around for another pass.

Then there was a tremendous sound of fire from the roof above him. He flicked his view up to that of one of his grenadiers and watched as the hapless Deathless soldier was pummelled with rifle fire from six different locations. It staggered back and dropped to one knee but it collapsed before it could reach cover. As ordered, his team were relentless. They rained fire down on the helmet until it was shattered. One down.

And then it all kicked off. The Deathless Rupert was getting to his feet, so Adams threw a grenade at the wall in front of their position to give them something to think about. It was just as it exploded that the real trap was sprung. Bursts of fire erupted all around the Deathless position as B and C platoons swung in to complete their encircling moves.

Idol fired another burst from his doorway, the bullets spattering against the foamcrete edge of the window near the Deathless Rupert. It was strange, seeing the enemy react on a small window of his HUD while he shot at them. Idol changed magazines and looked at Adams who was doing the same.

"Ready?" Adams asked.

"For what?" shouted Idol, too late. The crazy bastard ran out into the street, rifle barking as he sprinted toward the enemy position.

"Fuck!" shouted Idol as, against all sense, he felt his legs following, like they had a mind of their own. Before he knew what was happening, he was running for dear life, hunched over and following his soon to be ex-friend into the danger zone.

Adams ran straight for the room where the Rupert hid, right in the middle of the enemy position. It was suicide; the room was heavily defended. There were three more power armoured troopers in there, plus several other Deathless. And the flanking platoons hadn't finished with their rooms, so there was no support available.

Nevertheless, Adams charged and Idol followed. Sergeant Adams emptied his magazine through the window as he neared it, then dove to the floor just under it. Idol saw a fully armoured figure stick his head out to look into the street, staring directly at him.

Idol pulled the trigger of his rifle, firing from the hip as he ran and miraculously, the Deathless ducked back, despite his armour. He threw himself down beside Adams. Fuck! They were completely exposed.

He scrabbled frantically to remove his empty magazine before the troopers stepped out and ended them. Beside him, Adams reached for his webbing and pulled the pin on two grenades, reaching up with his hand over his head and almost casually dropping them over the windowsill. He didn't even throw them, just sort of rolled them off his hand.

A wicked double explosion followed, and dust billowed out of the room to smother them. Idol finished swapping in his new magazine and looked at Adams, who seemed weirdly calm. Idol's heart was pounding in his chest. Perhaps Adams liked this a little too much?

The sergeant threw another grenade through the window to the left of the door, and they waited for half a second for the detonation before bursting into the room. They had practised this only a few times with the Marines during training, but they all remembered the lessons.

Grenade, explosion, heartbeat, enter the room. The heartbeat allowed time to think and decide, to 'check that the bloody thing has actually exploded,' as Marine X had gruffly put it. "I've seen people follow their grenades into a room too quickly, and none of them came out with all their limbs," he had said. "I don't want any of you making the same mistake."

And then to illustrate his point, as if his description hadn't been graphic enough, he had mounted a simple demonstration with half a dozen melons and a grenade in a mid-sized room of an abandoned building. The resulting pulp-splattered walls had chillingly clarified the risks and focused everyone's attention.

A platoon team swept the room, checking for survivors and firing precautionary bursts into the faces of the power armoured troopers. That had been another piece of Marine X's never-ending advice. The occupant of even the most hideously mangled power armour could still bring a weapon to bear, but a few rounds to the helmet deterred even the most ardent of foes.

"Make sure they really have shuffled off their mortal coil," was how Marine X had expressed it.

Idol's team cleared the room, narrowly avoiding a nasty accident when a second team came through from the other direction. He lowered his rifle and took a deep breath before immediately regretting it and coughing up a lungful of dust and other airborne rubbish. Several people shouted 'Clear', perhaps a little belatedly, but the sudden silence was welcome.

His HUD reported twelve fresh injuries but no immediate deaths. *That was good, wasn't it?* He wasn't sure.

Quickly he gathered his officers and NCOs, issuing orders to evacuate the wounded and strip the Deathless of any arms and munitions found, operational or otherwise. They called for a vehicle to pick up the armour. Grenades and automatic weapons fire might have pummeled it, but it was still extremely valuable equipment. Each suit they could pass to the Marines, whether serviceable or simply as spares, gave them an exponential advantage in the fight against the Deathless.

"What now, Captain? Are we holding this position?" Adams asked.

"Hold here? No, Sergeant," Idol said, looking around at his command team, suddenly thirsty for more action. "No, we are not. We're going to look for more of these bastards. We're taking the fight to the enemy!"

W arden threw open the door and jumped down from the rover as it pulled up a short distance from the quarry. He hit the ground running and made his way to a row of boulders near the lip of the quarry. Milton joined him a heartbeat later, crouching next to him. They got themselves settled then inched forward until they could see past the rocks and into the quarry itself.

"You were right," said Warden, "smoke and activity."

Milton nodded, as if it had never been in doubt. She had called it from the vehicle, half a mile out, even though it could have been anything at that point. Up close, from their new vantage point, the wispy columns of smoke were unmistakable.

They hit the deck and crawled slowly forward until they could look right over the cliff's edge and into the quarry. Warden was not at all surprised to see that the smoke wasn't from a fire that had been burning for days but was instead the result of recent activity. The Deathless were on site and they were busy, working the quarry as hard as they could.

"Quarry or opencast mine, would you say?" asked Warden, trying to judge the size of the pit.

"Probably a mine, but it reminds me of abseiling in the quarries in south Wales," said Milton.

"Damned big, though. Easily ten times the size of that place in the Brecons, I think," said Warden, struggling to make sense of the scale. "A rich source of metal and minerals," continued Warden, as if quoting a lecture, "and it looks like they've been hitting it hard."

Which was not a surprise; terraforming a planet took vast amounts of infrastructure and this mine was one of the best sources of raw materials.

Warden activated the zoom on his HUD, carefully scanning back and forth and noting everything that the Deathless were doing. Milton was doing the same, counting heads and noting the placement of the small number of sentries and watchpoints. Their HUDs worked together, mapping the mine and logging enemy movements, compiling a complete picture of what they faced.

"Why do you think they're here?" Milton whispered.

"Without wishing to sound sarcastic, I'd say they're mining. I presume their needs are the same as the colonists'. They need vast quantities of raw materials to feed their manufacturing plants," Warden replied. "Think how much that base must have needed for construction alone. Either they dropped everything they needed from orbit or, more likely, they came here to find most of their raw materials."

"Shit. I wonder how many loads they've taken? Who knows what they could have built after they finished the base," said Milton as they watched a small truck manoeuvre near the cliff face.

Warden nodded then flagged something with his HUD.

"There she is, that's the vehicle we need."

"She?"

"All right, he. I don't know what the correct word is; ships are female but what is a fucking enormous dumper truck?"

"It's big, ugly and looks like it's full of useless shit to me, Lieutenant."

She turned to look at him and whispered, "He," at the same time he did. Milton grinned.

"Looks about half full to me. What did they say? It would take a six hundred and fifty ton load?" Warden mused.

"I don't think I could tell if that's two hundred and fifty or three hundred and fifty tons, really."

"Either way, we want that truck."

"I suppose we'd best work out how to do that then, sir."

"Indeed. Let's get back to the rovers and work out a plan. We should get the snipers moving, though, just in case the Deathless decide to patrol the area."

"Roger that," Milton said as they shuffled away from the edge, careful not to dislodge anything that might fall into the mine and reveal their presence.

Once they were clear, they moved in a crouching run for a short distance then stood up. Milton sent orders to the snipers as they moved. They were about halfway to the rovers when they met the sniper teams coming the other way.

"I've marked possible positions," said Milton, sending the information directly to the Marines' HUDs, "but use your initiative. There's plenty of high ground. We're about a hundred metres higher on this side of the quarry, so you shouldn't struggle to find decent perches."

The rest of the troop disembarked and Warden slid open the side hatch where the techs had rigged monitors for use as a command vehicle. The data their HUDs had gathered was now displayed on a large flexi-screen as a top-down view of the quarry. There were around sixty Deathless who were obviously armed and at least another thirty others of indeterminate status. Those thirty were mostly operating the mining machinery and didn't appear to be wearing armour or carrying guns but that didn't mean they weren't dangerous.

"We haven't seen any civilians yet but it's a quarry, there could be loads of them. Standard rules of engagement – kill the soldiers unless they surrender, secure the civilians unless they become dangerous," said Warden firmly. They hadn't yet seen any non-military Deathless and he didn't want to escalate this war by killing civilians, but they weren't going to take any chances.

"The snipers are deploying now and the HUD maps will update as they scope the area. They'll be flagging hotspots for you," said Milton.

"Sir, do you want to wait for nightfall?" asked Lance Corporal Price.

Warden shook his head. "Negative. If we had the luxury of time or someone watching our backs from orbit, then maybe, but this is one we're going to have to do the hard way. Fast, loud and efficient. I want these bastards to feel your maximum controlled aggression, understood?"

"Yes, sir," Price replied.

"Good. Once the sniper teams are in place, we'll move. We have the advantage of elevation, but we can't just sit up here taking pot shots all afternoon. As soon as they take cover our position will become vulnerable, so we'll be performing a forward abseil down the cliff, under cover of sniper fire and heavy weapons from the lip of the mine. Once on the ground, the sections will sweep forward and press the enemy from each flank."

As he spoke, the map showed the expected movement for each section. He could hear the disquiet and understood it. It was a high-risk strategy, but they had no choice. Capturing the truck was crucial to their plan and they couldn't stop just because they had found the enemy here ahead of them.

"Sir, wouldn't it be better to send teams around to the entrance and have them attack from there? I mean, the death dive is a great way to test your bottle in training, but it hasn't been used in combat since, well, I don't know when," said Price, shifting nervously.

"World War II, in case you're wondering. We're all qualified and we don't practice it for shits and giggles. It's not as if you have to take these bodies home to your respectable other halves, but please don't fuck it up. I don't want to land in a puddle of guts when I hit the ground and I'm sure nobody else does either," said Warden, aiming for a lightness that he didn't quite hit.

The gallows humour drew a round of chuckles anyway and Lance Corporal Long punched Price on the arm. "Don't be a pussy, mate. Should be a right laugh."

Price shrugged and sighed. "Oh well, as long as you're doing it too, sir, who am I to complain?"

"Remember, we're here for the dumper truck. You can't miss it; it's bright yellow, shaped like a kids toy and about the size of a decent pub. Do not, I repeat, do not, puncture the tyres. I do not want to have to learn how to change a tyre that weighs over eight tons, all right?"

"That means you, Price," said Milton. "If you shit your pants, I don't want a negligent discharge puncturing a tyre. Or my back."

"Just tuck your trouser legs into our boots, Price. You can empty them later," quipped Long.

"You can shut it too, Long. But thanks for volunteering to be first down," Milton snapped, rounding on him before turning to the rest, "and that's enough silly buggers from you lot. We've got a job to do, Marines. If you've got a note from your dear old Mum, you can stay up here where it's safe. Otherwise, stop fucking about and get ready to move."

Warden paused for a moment then cleared his throat.

"Yes. What Sergeant Milton said. Get the gear out and into position. If you need an incentive, apparently there's a good chance you'll get to see Price shit his pants or Long get shot, if he doesn't smack straight into the rock."

He turned back to the map on the screen as A Troop got to work. They'd need to kick some serious arse if they were going to clear the mine and capture the truck.

"Bailey. Got anything for me yet?"

"Yes, sir, all three sniper teams are in place. We've got strong vantage points and clear views of the target area," said Bailey, the snipers' team leader. "There's lots of cover down there, sir. Might be tricky."

"Understood. Anything else?"

"Yeah, there's a large equipment shed and the workers are taking whatever they're mining in there. They've brought a couple of sleds out with crates on them," Bailey said.

"Crates? They're processing the ore?"

"No, sir, I don't think so. The crates have stamps I don't recognise, but they don't look like any of the mining gear around here. In fact, they look like the crates Ten found in the solar plant. My guess is they're making munitions right here in the quarry."

Warden beckoned Milton over. If the Deathless were processing ore and turning it into any kind of weapons or equipment, they must have a manufactory. An advanced one at that, if it was capable of turning rock and raw ore into finished goods. Capturing the manufactory might give them a serious boost to their production capability and hurt the Deathless at the same time.

"What do you think?" he asked Milton as they reviewed the map. Milton nodded, and together they adjusted the plan of attack to take the shed and its likely contents into account.

Minutes later they were ready to go. The tech specialists would stay up top, deploying drones to spot enemy troops who managed to take cover and using their carbines to suppress any that tried to return fire. That left six Marines from each section to abseil down the mine's cliff face and get stuck in.

The forward abseil was a high-speed descent, usually practised for use in a retreat or a night assault where speed was paramount. Today, though, they'd be doing it in broad daylight and there wouldn't be any covering fire until the Deathless spotted them. The enemy sentries didn't seem to be very alert and the fact they didn't have lookouts on the rim of the mine suggested a certain arrogance that Warden was keen to exploit.

That said, nobody was going to miss eighteen Marines abseiling down a cliff. They would need every second they could get. Once the enemy troops brought weapons to bear, everything would get a whole lot dicier.

Warden started the countdown in everyone's HUDs and took up his own position on the rope. He would be first down, going as quickly as possible before acting as the belayer for the Marines that followed on his rope. They would drop, falling under gravity, and he would pull them up short, one after the other, just before they became a messy splash on the rock. His descent would be ridiculously fast; theirs would be even faster.

Ideally, they'd have had a rope for each Marine and all eighteen would have gone at the same time and been on the ground in a few seconds. As it was, this exercise would take at least six times as long but there was no other way, they had to go over the long drop. Over seventy metres but under a hundred, which was good, because if it had been any higher, this plan wouldn't have worked at all.

The number 3 flashed green in their HUDs and a tone sounded, audible only to the Marines. Warden pushed up from his crouch, dashing forward and lobbing the coiled rope away from the cliff even as he went over the edge. Then he was over, running down the almost vertical cliff face, going as fast as he dared and applying only enough tension to slow his descent to the point of non-fatality. Adrenaline coursed through his system. The rope hissed, the belay device whirred and his boots crunched as he plunged towards the rock floor of the mine.

A mere handful of metres from the ground he brought his dive to a brutally hard stop, the harness punching into his body as he flipped upright, knees bending to absorb the last of the energy. It was a rough landing but he wasn't injured.

Warden scanned his surroundings as he unclipped from the rope, checking that he hadn't landed amongst a group of enemy soldiers. He hadn't heard the telltale scream of a railgun round and it looked like he was clear. He grabbed the rope, taking control of the next Marine down and bringing her to a much smoother and easier stop than he'd had.

One, two, three, four Marines down before anything bad happened. He was looking up, so technically he'd seen the muzzle flashes before he'd heard the guns but there was no time to worry about that. Either he was about to get shot in the back or he wasn't, and his focus was on the two Marines still coming down his rope.

Then his HUD started to flash with contact signals. The counts of active and injured enemies started to change and by the time his sixth Marine hit the floor, both numbers were moving quickly in the right direction.

The Marines who were already on the deck weren't wasting any time now that things had turned hot and they pressed the attack, as per training and orders.

Warden turned and brought his weapon to bear, caning half a magazine toward an unlucky cluster of Deathless, then turning slightly to empty the rest at one of the ogres. He needn't have bothered; its head vanished as one of the snipers shot it with a railgun. The round went through its armoured head, into the rocky floor of the mine and sent rock chips flying in all directions, scything down two more nearby Deathless.

Fuck. There was a good chance his team would pick up injuries if they got too close to a high angled shot like that. *Tough*, he thought, *no time to worry about that now*. There were thousands of colonists counting on A Troop to complete this mission. Bagging the manufactory would make everyone's lives easier.

Somewhere out there in the chaos, Marine X was wreaking bloody havoc on the enemy. He'd check the HUD footage later to find out exactly what had gone on.

A drone spotted two Deathless that had taken cover in what appeared to be a makeshift latrine shed. Warden tossed a grenade in after them as he sprinted past and away – the detonation was going to get messy and he had no intention of spending the next few hours covered in guts or shit.

His charge took him between two boulders and into the midst of a squad of Deathless, all staring at him, agog, as he sprinted between them. Warden dived into a roll and when he came up he had managed to turn to face back the way he'd come. The Deathless were scrabbling for sidearms, rifles and blades, horrified by his sudden appearance in their ranks. Warden put a three-round burst into each of them then swapped in another magazine.

There was a wet splatter behind him, and something nasty landed on the other side of the boulders he'd just passed, evidence of his toilet grenade doing its work. He really hoped there weren't any valuable weapons in that area because they couldn't afford to leave materiel behind and retrieving them would not be a fun job.

It seemed that they had caught the enemy unawares. Most of the Marines had made it to the floor of the mine, ready to attack, before the snipers had even felt the need to execute their first targets. The count of remaining enemy combatants was dropping rapidly, and Warden lurched into a crouching run again, using his HUD to find the next target and relying on the snipers and spotters to keep the information current.

He took a running jump over one of the concentric rings that formed the mine and dropped ten feet onto a smoke-filled ledge. He rolled to absorb the impact and come up in a crouch. He emptied the rest of his magazine, taking down two more Deathless while their colleagues ran for cover from the attack of the cliff-leaping madman. Warden swapped in his last magazine, shooting two more of the fleeing enemy as soon as it clicked into place, then he turned left, searching the smoke for the last of the group.

He found the helmeted soldier waiting right where he was least welcome. Even as Warden turned, he knew he'd never make it; he could only watch as the enemy rifle swung round to point directly at him.

Warden was close enough to see the soldier's muscles tighten as it began to pull the trigger and smoke billowed around its legs. Then a glowing shape cut through its right arm and into its chest. The severed limb dropped and the rifle went with it, falling harmlessly to the ground in a spray of blood. The glow appeared again, springing forth from the throat to splash blood all over the ground.

"I say, Lieutenant, we really should stop meeting like this," Ten said, appearing from behind the falling corpse to grin like a madman before vanishing back into the smoke, a glowing Deathless knife in his hand.

Warden took a couple of deep breaths and made a mental note to have a chat with Marine X later. Then he slung his carbine on his back and picked up the Deathless rifle, checking the round counter from force of habit before remembering that he had no idea how to read their strange language. He picked up the enemy soldier's ammunition satchel and slapped in a fresh magazine, just in case, then moved out.

That leap had been a big gamble, taken in the heat of the moment. Now he took more control of himself, advancing methodically, paying attention to the information in his HUD and giving orders like a real officer should. He held himself in cover and concentrated on suppressing any enemy troopers so they could be flanked. It was bloody work that day – carnage, if truth be told. They'd ripped through the enemy like a chainsaw through rotten wood.

Warden watched as the body count increased and the number of remaining targets finally dropped to zero. They swept the mine for survivors and soldiers that might have escaped the survey then dealt with their own casualties. It turned out that he and Ten had been the only ones to rush quite so far forward; the rest had been more circumspect and their worst injuries were flesh wounds.

"They weren't civilians, sir," said Milton, catching up with Warden as he poked at a couple of enemy bodies, "none of them. They're all wearing military clones, and they're all armed, even the machine operators. It looks like they weren't taking quite as many risks as we thought."

"Good," said Warden, somewhat relieved that he wouldn't have a load of civilian deaths on his conscience, even if death amounted to no more than a temporary disembodiment.

Once he had checked the status of A Troop and satisfied himself that everything was secure, he moved to the target that had brought them here. The truck was intact, nothing but cosmetic damage from the firefight that had erupted around it. The tyres were in good order; the plan could proceed.

Then there was their unexpected find, the manufactory in the shed. Ten had swept through the building, checking for any Deathless they might have missed, and the area was clear. Within the shed, a manufactory unit rested on a large powered sled. Warden levered open a crate and found it full of weapon parts.

Milton whistled when she drew level with him. "Nice. That should make the captain and the governor a little happier."

"I'm sure it will. Let's get this sled moving and get it back to Fort Widley," he said.

"Sir?"

"Yes, Sergeant?"

"Shouldn't we crack on with the plan and let the captain know this is here?" Milton asked.

Warden shook his head. "No, this manufactory could be the difference between winning and losing. It's set up for military equipment and better than anything we have in Ashton or the Fort. We need to get moving because we can't stick around to guard it against the enemy. We have two missions now. But once this thing is on the move, we'll ask the captain if he can send backup. Otherwise, we'll move it just far enough to hide it, then pick it up once we've finished our primary mission."

Milton frowned but didn't say anything more. Warden was relieved; he valued Milton's judgement, of course, but she tended to focus on the immediate problems rather than take the longer view, which was exactly what made her a great NCO. No plan survived contact with the enemy and this was a stroke of luck they couldn't afford to ignore.

He left her to organise moving the huge piece of equipment and arrange for the enemy dead to be stripped of anything of value while he went to sort out the truck. The techs seemed to have everything well under control, retrofitting it to suit Warden's mad plan.

Satisfied the techs had the truck in hand, he turned back to the manufactory to get an update. Milton's team had manoeuvred it out of the shed, and the sled was moving slowly towards the ramps that would take it up the side of the mine and out into the rocky terrain between them and their new base of operations, Fort Widley.

Half a dozen Marines from Section 3 were surrounding the sled, walking with it as it neared the ramp. Milton was checking in with the Marines who had been looting the enemy dead for serviceable items. Warden made a note that they should take even broken kit, if they could carry it. Anything that couldn't be repaired would just be fed back into the manufactories in Fort Widley.

He was about to walk over to Milton when he noticed something going on with the sled. Corporal Green and Lance Corporal Long were having a somewhat animated discussion, gesturing at the side of the manufactory. One of the panels had lit up like a birthday party, lights twinkling and an image rotating on the large display. That was odd. It meant that whatever was displayed was being made, right now, and he hadn't certainly ordered anyone to turn it on.

Then Green and Long began to run, waving their arms and shouting. Warden felt the hairs on the back of his neck stand up. He was moving before he processed what was wrong. He couldn't hear it, they were too far away, but he could see Green and Long were screaming at their section to scatter. Milton turned to face Warden, puzzled that he was sprinting towards her. The sled with its heavy cargo was maybe three hundred metres behind her, down the ramp.

Warden could feel the burn as his lungs sucked down the thin Bristolian air, trying to support his furious sprint. He saw the realisation on Milton's face, the sudden awareness that something was wrong, terribly wrong. He tried to issue an order through the HUD but he didn't have the breath or the time.

He didn't see the flash, not really – it was too bright to register and the HUD blocked most of the glare. He felt the shockwave like a slap in the chest from the hand of a petulant giant, lifting him off his feet and throwing him out of consciousness. Warden's world went black.

19

"Move up," said Idol, waving to the team and aiming his rifle down the street to cover them. They headed for the next firing position in the odd crouching run that now seemed to be the only way they moved. They were making for a cluster of drop pods that had been flagged for investigation by the drone teams after the orbital bombardment.

Idol had decided that his team would take an active part in clearing the city rather than hang back in one place, waiting for the next Deathless attack. He'd put the plan to his team, asking for dissenting opinions, and if anyone had expressed serious concerns, he would have reconsidered. There were some suggestions, and they tweaked the plan to accommodate them, but it seemed his team were a lot more confident after the firefight at the brewery.

And so, with his team's backing, Idol had led them out into Ashton to hunt the enemy.

Now they were only a hundred metres from their target building. It was a substantial structure with steel-reinforced foamcrete pillars throughout and vehicle parking bays on the ground floor. Above, the building had floors for warehouse and distribution, a factory and an office, with solar units on the roof. The sturdiness of the building supported the weight of the machinery it held, although Idol couldn't imagine why it was necessary to have such equipment anywhere higher than the ground floor. Whatever the reason, it meant the building had not fallen victim to the violence that had flattened so many others in Ashton.

"We should get a good view of the square from the upper floors," Idol had said when they'd thrashed through the plan. The square had once been as nice a place as any on New Bristol to have a sandwich at lunchtime or to wile away an hour's spare time. Now, it was a burnt and shattered remnant, a dessert surrounded by the corpses of the city's buildings and populated only with the withered stumps of trees lost in the early stages of the invasion.

He knew he wasn't going to be best pleased when he saw what the arrival of a series of Deathless drop pods had done to his favourite outdoor space. On the plus side, if they found the occupants, they could shoot them for it. Garden vandals were usually treated far more leniently.

The loss of the square hurt, but the damage to the bio-domes that he and Adams had created was far worse. Built as simulacra of the outside world, they had been too fragile to withstand bullets and explosions and their contents were now dead and scattered. It would be years before they could be replaced and their plants regrown.

Idol shook his head, clearing it of distracting musings and bringing himself back to the present. He ran forward, working with the fireteams as they advanced. He wanted to be at the front, where he felt he belonged, for some reason.

Perhaps, he thought, *because leaders are supposed to be at the front.*

The target building seemed to be empty when they arrived, so he led the first fireteam straight in, taking the door himself and bounding up the stairs past the parking level, heading for the roof. His team were more cautious, checking the first level before they realised he'd dashed ahead. He could hear them cursing softly as he took the stairs three at a time.

He burst onto the roof and crouched down, hugging the low wall that formed the perimeter. It was topped with a short railing as a nod to health and safety, but this wasn't the sort of place you were supposed to be wandering around. Shuffling on hands and knees, he made his way to the far side of the building, trying to get a view of the square.

By the time his team reached him, he'd seen enough. The place was wrecked and there was no sign of the Deathless.

"Looks like they've gone," said Adams, echoing Idol's thoughts.

"Looks that way," agreed Idol, "but we should probably take a closer look, make sure they're not just hiding."

There were drop pods scattered across the square, some on the roads and some in the park. They were all open and empty, their former occupants nowhere to be seen. One had been neatly skewered by the foamcrete obelisk that commemorated the founding of Ashton. From the mess oozing down the polished sides of the pointed composite stonework, the Deathless troopers riding in it had been turned into a paste that resembled strawberry jam.

Serves them right, thought Idol, without sympathy.

"What the hell is that?" someone breathed in a near whisper, pointing down the street.

Idol looked, but it took him a moment to work out what he was seeing.

They were drop pods spread across much of the city, and most of the company had seen them falling from the sky after the orbital bombardment. They were common enough that nobody really noticed them anymore.

But here, in the square, were two much larger pods that really drew the eye. They resembled the common drop pods in shape and style, but they were far larger than the four-person pods the Deathless had dropped all over Ashton. These two were broad enough across the base for perhaps ten or twelve seats and were at least three times as high.

"Perhaps they're triple-decker drop pods for large teams?"

suggested Adams half-heartedly, "Or maybe they deliver a couple of squads with heavy equipment or large drones?" It was clear he didn't believe either suggestion and whatever the truth, it probably wasn't good news. "At least they're not big enough for tanks!"

"Yeah, at least it isn't tanks," agreed Idol absently, frowning down at the pods.

They watched for a few minutes longer but nothing moved in the street except dust on the wind.

It took them another fifteen minutes to clear the immediate area, check the pods and confirm that the nearby buildings were empty. Nothing. The Deathless hadn't stuck around, but they had left tracks across the park and away to the south-west.

Idol looked down at the churned up ground and around the square. "That way," said Idol, waving towards the south-west. "We'll follow these bastards and see if we can't show them what Ashton does to vandals."

"What, you mean shoot them?" asked Adams. "Only, I don't know if you've read the local news recently, but we don't usually do that."

"Well, now we do. Serves 'em right for smashing up my bio-domes, right?" barked Idol.

"Okay, you heard the captain. Let's move out and teach these bastards some err... civic pride!" Adams shouted to general amusement as they walked in the direction the muddy tracks indicated.

They moved down the broad street and soon picked up the trail. The boot prints of the soldiers weren't visible, but something had cracked the surface of the road and left deep impressions every couple of metres.

"Something's wrong," muttered Idol, picking up the pace and forgoing cover in return for speed.

Perhaps they'd landed some kind of power armour suits? The ogre suits were pretty massive, but maybe the Deathless had a clone type that was even larger, or maybe they had a second form of power armour that shattered the road, for some reason. Whatever it was, Idol was determined that his company would catch it and destroy it before it could wade into a firefight and tip the scales.

"Come on, you lot. Last one to bag a Deathless buys the first round!" he shouted, as he broke into a run.

It wasn't long before they found what they were looking for. They turned west at a crossroads, following the damaged road, and came to a junction where the Deathless had gone south. Huffing and puffing, Idol stopped near the corner, and everyone pulled up nearby, gasping for breath. Clone bodies started out in perfect physical condition, but they still gained weight and lost muscle if they weren't exercised enough, and the day's activities had already taken a toll.

When his brain had stopped swimming, Idol risked sticking his head around the corner. They were right there, advancing cautiously down the street. There were at least two dozen Deathless troopers, but his eyes were drawn to the two enormous humanoid machines that towered over the enemy soldiers.

Robots? Or giants in powered armour? thought Idol, shouldering his rifle reflexively. The things were huge, over five metres tall, and Idol wasn't keen to attack.

Then half the team rounded the corner and opened fire on the closest Deathless troopers. Someone hurled a grenade, and a long burst of fire tore into the back of a group of enemy soldiers sheltering behind a low wall. At any other time, it would have been a good response to the threat. The attack had certainly surprised the Deathless and they scrabbled to clear the street and return fire.

But the huge robots weren't fazed and they didn't run for cover.

Even as Idol shouted the order to retreat, one of the robots turned, pivoting its body without moving its legs.

The upper torso span neatly around, bringing a huge weapon to face the militia. Idol boggled at the thing as it spewed rounds towards his troops, chewing up the road surface and then eating through bodies, blasting them apart.

"Back, back!" he shouted, although his troops needed no encouragement and were streaming around the corner, desperate to get away from the monstrous robots.

Idol watched them go, waving them on. Then he, too, was

running, and all he could think about was the terrible Deathless weapon blasting apart his comrades.

"What the fuck was that!" shouted Adams as they pounded down the road for all they were worth.

"Don't know," replied Idol, "don't care. Just keep running!"

20

"Lieutenant? You're okay, sir, just a bit of a bump. How many fingers am I holding up?"

Warden tried to focus, but everything was a blur and his ears were ringing.

"Sir, I'm going to flush your eyes out. Try and keep them open, you've probably got some dust in there from the explosion, but this ought to help," the voice said. A damp cloth was wiped gently across his face then water was splashed over his eyes. As it ran off, Warden found his focus returning and his eyes began to feel better as he blinked them clear. A water bottle was pressed into his hand, and he swilled some around his mouth then spat it out, repeating several times to clear the taste of dirt and the gritty sensation, then he took several deep gulps.

"Again, sir. Can you tell how many fingers I'm holding up?"

"Yes, I can, Goodwin, thanks," Warden said.

Goodwin leaned back. "Okay, you're shouting but there's no blood coming from your ears, so I think you'll be fine. Let's put your HUD back on. Set it to compensation mode and let it establish a baseline for audio and compensate for your hearing loss."

Warden nodded consent and Goodwin helped him fit his HUD

back on. Immediately the sound around him quietened and he selected an option to confirm exposure to an explosion. The HUD ran a diagnostic hearing test with him and then began to filter external noises to help him recover. Speech became clearer and a flood of data started to come in.

"What happened?" he asked, still a little confused about recent events.

"The manufactory exploded, sir. Do you remember?"

He shook his head and immediately regretted it, wincing as pain shot through his skull.

"Yeah, use the HUD if speaking is a problem. You almost certainly have a concussion. You were closer than most when the explosion went off," Goodwin explained.

He remembered something! "Milton," he croaked, "did she make it?"

"She actually did a bit better than you, sir. She was facing away and moving in the right direction. The blast threw her around, but she landed without cracking her head. You're both pretty banged up but still operational. Sir, I want to give you something for the pain, but first I need to know if you've got any broken bones. Don't scream or it'll make your head worse. I'm going to check, now. Slap the floor if it's bad," said Goodwin.

Being felt up by a hot sweaty Marine while they were both covered in a thick layer of dust and filth wasn't even slightly fun. It was painful too but, improbable as it seemed, he didn't have any broken bones. Lots of bruises, though, and he was sure that some of his bruises had bruises.

Once Goodwin had established there was nothing seriously wrong and had checked the HUD readout for heart rate, blood pressure and blood oxygenation, Warden got a shot of painkiller and a dose of combat stimulant. Nothing major, just enough to let him work through the pain. Then Goodwin hit him with a massive dose of anti-inflammatories and a cocktail of other drugs to support his recovery.

After a few moments, Warden's head stopped pounding so badly and his limbs felt less leaden. He stood up and checked for dizziness, performing a quick balance test as recommended by the warning symbol on his HUD. Goodwin cleared him for duty and he thanked her, then looked over to where the manufactory had been on the sled. There was nothing left but a crater, a big one. He remembered it had been extruding something, turned on and active when it should have been switched off and dormant.

Warden walked over to Milton, who was sat on a lawn chair by the remains of a temporary hut that had been flattened by the blast wave. She was filthy, covered head to toe in dust.

"How are you feeling?" he asked.

"Like I got slapped in the back with a cricket bat. You?"

"Feels like I've got a drunken Welsh choir in my head and I just visited an incompetent masseur who moonlights as a shot-putter," Warden replied.

"Most of the casualties only have minor shrapnel wounds and some hearing problems. We lost Green, Long, McGee, Headley and Scott though, half the section."

"Yeah, I saw the HUD report. It's fucking bad news all around. The only saving grace is that more of our people weren't closer when it went off," he said, then looked around, kicking at the dust for a moment. "I'm sorry. If I'd listened to your advice and not tried to have my cake and eat it, we might have got someone here who'd have checked the thing over before moving it. They must have set it to produce an explosive charge if it was moved without authorisation."

"Shit happens. No point crying about it now. The lads understand and they were backed-up; they're already queued for redeployment in the cloning bay." She paused to work a kink out of her neck. "Marine X is a bit grumpy."

Warden sighed. Marine X was one of those people for whom boredom and inactivity were always the biggest problems.

"What's got his knickers in a twist?" he asked, although he didn't really want to know.

"If I understand it, he's been hoping he'll get killed next so we can redeploy him in that last ogre. He wants to try it on for size."

"Hah. It's tempting to slot the bastard now, but we'd have to wait for him to catch up. Anyway, you saw what he did on our most recent video night. Does he even need a suit like that?"

"Not in the usual sense of the word, no. I can't help wondering what he'd be like in it, though. Certainly a damned sight more effective than those Deathless bastards."

Warden nodded but he wasn't going to worry about Marine X's weird body fantasies.

"How long was I out?"

"About fifteen minutes. Pull up a pew," Milton said, gesturing at the rock beside her. "It'll take another fifteen or so for the techs to finish rigging up that monster and filling the hopper," Milton said, pointing at the dumper truck. The Marines near the truck barely came up to its axles. The thing was an absolute beast.

Warden sat down and pulled a slightly battered ration bar from his webbing. It looked just as squashed as he felt and it had the taste and appeal of sun-dried cardboard. Humanity had been an interstellar species for centuries but still couldn't make energy bars that tasted or felt like something you would actually eat if you had a choice.

Warden shook his head as he contemplated the horrible bar. *They can squirt my brainwaves through an interstellar wormhole the width of a pin and deploy me in a cloned body within a few hours,* he thought, *but they can't make a protein bar that you could persuade a four-year-old to eat, not even a chocolate one.* A few more gulps of water didn't ease the chewing, but it did wash the taste away.

"Do you think it'll work?" he asked quietly, nodding at the dumper truck.

"Maybe. It's not a bad idea, just a bit unusual. I think it's worth a try and even if it doesn't work, it'll be a good show. If you hadn't dreamed it up, the Deathless might have caused all sorts of trouble with this site before we noticed they were here. Plus we took care of a load of them all at once and with very few casualties. Not a bad day's work, all things considered," Milton mused.

They sat in silence for a while, watching the activity around the dumper truck until, finally, it seemed like it was winding down. Warden looked at Milton, she nodded and they began walking, somewhat gingerly, over to their reason for coming to this god-forsaken hole in the ground.

It was hard to grasp the sheer scale of the thing. Was there any land vehicle he'd seen that matched it for sheer size and bulk? Warden couldn't think of one. The spec sheet said it could carry six hundred and fifty tons of rock and that it had a top speed of about seventy-five kph, over firm terrain.

He nodded at the techs. "Cooke, Richardson, Barlow. Who wants to give me an update?"

Barlow piped up first. "We've got everything ready, sir, as ordered." He held up a data slate and flashed some sort of dashboard at Warden. "We're good to go as soon as you want."

"Will your modifications work?"

Barlow sucked air through his teeth like an old-time mechanic looking over a dodgy repair job.

"Should do, sir, should do. I, er, wouldn't like to guarantee the plan will come off as you hope, but I think the truck will do her bit. Probably."

"Good. Sergeant, that'll do for now. Get your team to their assigned places and let's move out, on the double."

~

Marine Fletcher was sticking well back from the group, still trying to get used to her new body as the Marines yomped across the open terrain. In what Lieutenant Warden had described as an 'ironic' situation, she found herself redeployed in one of the Deathless Ogre clones just a few days after being killed by an identical body on the bridge of the ship during her last action. Ten had been wildly jealous but Fletcher wasn't seeing the funny side.

For the attack on the open-cast mine, she had worn standard fatigues and webbing. Standard Deathless fatigues, at least. They hadn't been expecting trouble so nobody had worn power armour.

For the next stage of the mission, the plan called for an entirely different approach. They had ditched the rovers several kilometres out at a secure location, or as secure as they could find, and now she was suited, jogging along with the rest of the troop.

The rovers were designed for moving people and small cargoes; they weren't good for carrying full troops of commandos in all their gear and they certainly couldn't handle an ogre in power armour. They'd had to fit her into the armour once they had reached the drop-off point. Armoured, she was truly enormous.

Warden suppressed a grin as he imagined Ten's reaction when he saw her all kitted up.

But his good humour faded as he remembered how little power armour they had been able to bring for this mission. Some Marines were equipped; most weren't. The mission required speed and power and they just didn't have enough reliable rovers to carry all the armour.

The Deathless suit that Fletcher wore was performing well. It was high-quality work and Warden wondered, not for the first time, why the quality of the Deathless kit seemed to be so much better than the discipline and training of the enemy troops who used it. Then again, he was relying on a Penal Marine as a core part of this plan, so maybe he shouldn't be too critical of the enemy. Never look a gift horse in the mouth.

"Goodwin, how's it looking?" he said, glancing at the Lance Corporal sitting nearby, back against a rock, watching a data slate.

"It's all good, sir. We're on target for final approach in four minutes."

"Excellent. Get me a feed, would you? I want to be able to see the approach stage so we can get the timing right. Milton, make sure everyone is ready to go. We'll keep Fletcher and the others back until the fireworks start, then they advance as swiftly as possible. Goodwin, you stay here with Bailey and Parker, and once you're done with that," he said, gesturing at the data slate controller, "get us some drone support, okay?"

"Yes, sir. Three minutes to final approach stage. The feed is available when you need it," Goodwin confirmed.

A new video feed icon appeared in Warden's HUD.

"Roger that." Warden flicked on the video feed.

"Marine X," he said, "how are you doing?"

"Peachy, thanks, sir. No sign of trouble. How long till things get exciting?"

"A couple of minutes. Goodwin, send him the feed so he can see what's going on."

"Okay. I can see the target now with the old Mark 1 eyeball. We're starting to turn. Ground doesn't look too rough."

"No, but are you strapped on? We have no idea how bumpy this will get."

"Feels like a massage chair at the moment, but I've got a couple of lines keeping me in place so I can't fall off completely. We're lined up now."

"I see it on the feed."

"I've got a pretty good view here too," Ten confirmed.

"I'm revving her up now, Ten," said Goodwin, pushing the truck's accelerator control.

"Yeah, thanks for the heads up. Doesn't seem any bumpier. No signs of life."

"She's at sixty per cent speed now. You should be okay on this ground," said Goodwin, "unless I hit a boulder," she murmured.

"Lieutenant, we're not using this thing again, are we?"

"No, we're not. Strictly a one-way transport."

"Okay then. Goodwin, why don't you redline this thing and see how far over the manufacturer's specs it'll go."

"It won't go over specs at all, Ten. We didn't do anything to the engine."

"Ah well, about that. You might not have done anything to the engine but it's just possible that I might have. Couldn't just sit here twiddling my thumbs, right? And this plan will work a lot better if the truck's going faster, yes?"

Goodwin looked at Warden who rolled his eyes and gestured for her to go ahead.

"Yes," confirmed Goodwin, "the faster it goes, the more effective it'll be, but you still have to get off. I don't fancy your chances of disembarking safely anyway, let alone if you're going faster."

"Lance Corporal, I have been doing this job since you were a twinkle in your daddy's eye. I wouldn't have volunteered if I thought it wouldn't work. You just set that accelerator to maximum and get ready with your little party favours. I'll take care of this end."

Goodwin looked at Warden sceptically.

"It's okay, Lance Goodwin. If he says he's got it handled, we can trust him. I wouldn't ask him to feed my goldfish, but this is what he lives for. Open her up."

Goodwin nodded. "Okay, Ten, Lieutenant Warden says I can go ahead. Let's see what she can do." She slid the control to maximum and left it there. The haptic feedback from her slate was working overtime as the quarry truck accelerated, bouncing a little on the uneven terrain.

Over a thousand metric tons of truck, ore and added extras barrelled towards the enemy base, faster and faster.

"It just hit seventy-five kph, Ten."

"Walk in the park. I bet you can get it over a hundred and twenty-five. I'm pretty much relying on it."

"Doubtful but she's giving it all she got. What did you do to my engines anyway?" Goodwin asked.

"I'll tell you later. You just keep it lined up and get ready."

"Roger that, Ten," Goodwin replied over the comms, and muttered under her breath, "you mad bastard."

"Couldn't agree more, Lance Corporal, but I'm not going to bet that he's wrong," Warden agreed.

"That's it, starting to feel like there's a real driver behind the wheel now," Ten said.

"I don't know what you did, Ten, but she just hit a hundred and twenty, and she's still accelerating."

"Keep it going, Goodwin. The more speed you can give me, the better. Lieutenant, I think someone just noticed us. You might want to get ready to move."

"Roger that, Ten. I see lights on their wall. Keep us updated. Milton, let's get the first teams moving."

Warden turned his attention back to the feed, blowing it up to full scale as if he were there. The cameras were attached to the front of the enormous vehicle and he could now see the base clearly. It was monstrous. The Deathless had built walls at least nine metres high and they were topped with long, thick, spikes which jutted out like tusks. It looked like the whole thing was extruded from foamcrete or something similar. Tough, durable and extremely bullet absorbent. They must have some impressive fab technology to have been able to construct this edifice so quickly.

Their target was the entrance of the base, a wide gap, easily big enough for three rovers side-by-side. The gigantic dump truck was another matter, though. The wheels alone were five metres high and the truck was far too wide to fit through the gate. The plan wasn't to drive it in; Warden had something much better in mind.

"It's maxed out at a hundred and forty-one kph, Ten!"

"What's that in Imperial? Eighty-eight miles an hour? They're going to see some serious shit, now!" said Ten. "Cue the music."

Warden looked at Goodwin. "Music?" he asked, frowning.

"I have no idea, sir. You'll have to try Ten's feed."

He switched over rapidly, audio and visual on his HUD switching to the feed from Ten's perspective. Opera music was playing from the truck in front of him as it sped towards the enemy base. It blared from announcement speakers at full and deafening volume.

The music launched straight into lyrics, "*O Fortuna, velut luna, statu variabilis, semper crescis...*" It was rousing, but Warden didn't recognise the tune.

"Hadn't pegged him as an opera fan," muttered Warden, unsure he would ever get used to the man's foibles.

"What the hell are you doing, Marine X?" he asked, somewhat redundantly he realised, given that he could see exactly what Ten saw. Straps to his left and right were attached to the sides of the truck, holding him on top of the huge pile of rock and ore.

"Sorry, sir? Could you repeat that? It's a bit noisy here!" Ten replied as he busied himself with a reel of cable.

Warden resisted the temptation to shout and set the HUD to transmit text at the same time. "What is that music?"

"Bloody hell, sir. Surprised you don't recognise it, it's a classic! It's Carl Orff, 'O Fortuna' from *Carmina Burana*."

"Very informative, Ten, but I don't really care what it is. I'm more concerned about why you're playing it."

"Ahh right. You did say you wanted the enemy focussed on me, sir. Pretty sure they won't be paying attention to anyone else right now and maybe these buggers could use a dose of culture. Is there anything else, sir? I'm a little busy," Ten asked politely.

"What is that cable for?" Warden asked, dreading the answer.

"That's how I'm getting off this thing."

"Aren't you jumping off it?"

"Jumping off it, sir? Are you all right? You did take a nasty bang on the head earlier."

"I'm fine, thanks, Ten," said Warden, manfully keeping his annoyance in check, "but I thought you were jumping off the truck as it approached and advancing on foot?"

"Bugger that for a game of soldiers, sir. If I jumped off far enough away that it was safe, it'd be a bloody long walk. And I can't jump off now, it's doing over a hundred and forty kilometres per hour. If I jumped off at this speed, I'd be blown into last week. Or is that next week? Either way, I'd be dead. Nah, when you've got a plan like yours to implement, you've got to work with what you have to available. For instance, I found this winch drum in Ashton, and then I looked for some more kit, and I had what I needed to add my own garnish to your cunning plan, sir. Can I explain later, sir? If I don't get a shift on, I'm going to be in a spot of bother."

"Okay, get on with it, whatever it is." Warden shook his head, horribly aware that things had slipped beyond his control without a single shot having been fired.

The track Ten was playing was short but it was on a loop and very loud. Judging by the flashes of gunfire from the base, the Deathless did not appreciate Ten's efforts at cultural enlightenment. Warden switched back to the camera feed from the front of the vehicle and could see the great, spiny wall of the base drawing closer, spotlights picking out the truck.

And now there were more bursts of automatic fire to light up the night and reveal the location of the enemy troops as they targeted the truck. Information streamed across Warden's vision as Ten's HUD collated the flashes and marked enemy locations for the whole troop to see. The Deathless must be rather optimistic if they hoped to cause any damage at this range, but he supposed even an inexpert marksman could hit the truck when it was driving straight at them.

Around here, on the other side of the huge base, Warden's view was much the same as Ten's except without the bulky gatehouse or the gunfire.

Everything seemed to be working fine but he had no idea how Ten planned to get off the vehicle. Whatever it was, it would have to happen soon.

Goodwin hummed as she watched the feed then she thumbed a control. Gunfire erupted from the front of the truck, showering the Deathless base. They had rigged looted weapons to the truck, set to fire on full automatic when Goodwin sent the command. There was no hope of aiming them, which meant that bullets would be flying all over the place. Sure enough, the enemy fire stopped as they sought cover, despite the fact that it couldn't possibly hit them.

Warden sympathised. It wasn't easy to return fire while someone was shooting at you, even if part of your brain accepted that it was vanishingly unlikely you'd be hit. The baser, animal parts of the brain held the strong opinion that you should get your head down until it all went away.

"Lieutenant, we're in position," Milton said. "Are you joining us?"

Shit, he had been distracted by Ten's antics and, honestly, by the childish impulse to watch his own plan come to fruition. He flipped up his HUD and stuck his head up to look over the boulder towards the wall. Milton and the majority of A Troop were at the base, ready to start the infiltration.

He swore again and flipped his HUD back into place.

"Yes, get cracking, I'm on my way. The distraction is working perfectly."

He glanced at Goodwin and Bailey, both intent on their tasks. Parker noticed him and turned to give him a thumbs up, before returning to his binoculars to scan the wall for targets to flag for Bailey. Nothing was happening, so it seemed the Deathless were all heading for the gate, which was unlikely to be a good idea.

Warden broke cover and ran for the base of the wall.

21

The first reports were unclear, difficult to understand. A 'walking tank' was the way one shocked militia soldier had described it. Then a shaky video, shot on a hand-held communicator, arrived to provide details of the new threat.

Barely twenty seconds long, the video showed a pair of armoured figures walking stiffly down the street toward a militia position. At first glance, they could have been mistaken for normal Deathless power armour.

It was their strange gait which gave them away, their legs moved stiffly, the movement of the hips not quite right. Then they moved past a street lamp, and their scale became clear. They were at least five metres tall, maybe six, with bulbous chest pieces that jutted oddly forward.

Light troops followed behind but the two at the front took the cameraman's attention. Each arm bore huge weapons; a flamethrower on one and a pair of heavy machine cannons on the other.

As they walked, so large that the ground rumbled with each step, they sprayed fire at the retreating militia. Yellow and blue flame shot across the street, incinerating everything it touched and chewing even at the concrete of the buildings and structures behind which the humans hid. Then the dreadful fire would swing away, and the area would be sprayed with high-velocity, large calibre shot from the twin-cannon.

"Too many casualties," said Atticus, watching the monitors that showed the militia falling back and dying in large numbers. The destructive power was awe-inspiring and Atticus, as he watched the video for the twelfth time, had to admit to being impressed.

Years before, he had seen a demonstration of a similar system while it was still in development. A defence contractor had produced prototypes of a new form of armour and they worked well; the weapons were capable, the pilot had good control, the thing was stable and the armour was tough. It was an impressive demonstration.

The problem was the mass of the loaded unit. The entire demonstration had been run at a specially constructed site where the 'ground' was actually steel reinforced foamcrete. On normal roads or any surface less solid than rock, the vehicle just sank under its own weight as soon as it stepped off its transport. In any real-world situation, it was useless, and the experiment was abandoned.

"Come back in twenty years," the contractor had said, "or maybe fifty, and we should have materials whose performance allows this system to work." Nobody had really believed them.

It seemed, however, that the Deathless had overcome the problem and produced a deployable combat unit.

"That's not something you see every day," said Denmead as she watched the video play again on the big screen. The video showed the militia returning fire, standing their ground for longer than anyone could reasonably have expected, then being mown down as they finally broke and ran.

Atticus got to his feet, "No, no, it's not. But it is something I've seen before." Denmead looked at him quizzically. He wasn't surprised, it had been a little-known project at the time, and its total failure had led to it being buried.

"Come on; we need to stop these things quickly," he said, grabbing his rifle and heading for the door, "and I think I've got an idea that might just work."

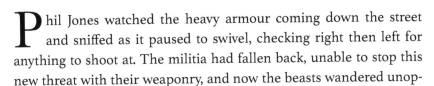

Phil Jones watched the heavy armour coming down the street and sniffed as it paused to swivel, checking right then left for anything to shoot at. The militia had fallen back, unable to stop this new threat with their weaponry, and now the beasts wandered unopposed through the city.

He had been watching this pair of Deathless robot walkers with his sniper, Pete Smith, for a few minutes from their hiding place in a patch of overgrown scrubland.

"Looks like a walking tin can. Short-range weapons only, by the look of it," said Phil, peering through his HUD, "but the grunts following have rifles and something that looks suspiciously like a mortar."

"One shot then relocate," said Pete, adjusting the scope of his railgun, "and bang!" He said it quietly as he pressed the trigger button. The gun hummed and, a hundred metres away, there was a flash and a bang as the round struck the huge Deathless machine in the centre of its mass.

"Definite hit," muttered Phil as the Deathless swung around, looking for the source of the attack, "no obvious damage. Bugger me, that thing's tough."

Behind the Can, the troopers had spread out and taken cover, spooked by the sound of the railgun. The two Cans kept coming, utterly undeterred, hunting the humans.

"Ninety metres," said Phil, shuffling backwards, "time to go unless we want to get really friendly with them."

"I hear you," said Pete, slinging his gun over his shoulder, "let's circle around and see if they like it from behind."

They crawled into the ditch at the back of the scrub and hurried away at a rapid crouch, looking for a new firing position.

~

"So what's this idea, then?" said Governor Denmead as she and Atticus hurried through the warehouse where they had established a temporary command post.

Atticus hadn't wanted her to be there. "Government has to continue, the caves of Fort Widley are the safest place we have, you should stay there rather than put yourself at risk in the city," he had said. He might as well have shouted at the wind for all the good it had done.

"No, time to explain, Governor. I briefed the men while you were dealing with your team. You'll just have to watch and for pity's sake, stay out of sight," he said irritably. He liked Denmead, and he hadn't meant to snap at her, but she was as stubborn as an ox. *Probably why you like her*, he thought grudgingly.

Mercifully she took it in good grace and let him get on with it. So now they were making their way through the abandoned buildings of the city, heading for a spot near the last known location of the armoured leviathans that the Marines had begun calling 'Cans'.

They were accompanied by a squad made up of Marines from B Troop, all of whom were now, like Atticus, wearing captured Deathless bodies. They carried the heavy weapons that had been captured from the enemy over the last few days.

The militia that each Marine had been leading had been left behind for this operation. Even though they couldn't order the governor to stay at Fort Widley, they could make sure that the militia was out of harm's way. This wasn't a plan for amateurs, however willing they had proved to be.

"They're coming this way," said Atticus eventually, stopping in the ruined shell of a fab plant. The roof was gone, blown away a few days before, but the foamcrete first floor was still in place and so were the walls of the ground floor.

"This will do nicely," said Atticus, looking around. "Find somewhere upstairs, towards the rear side of the building for the mortar, Corporal, and make sure your spotter has good lines of sight along the street. We'll have one sniper team down here, the other up on the roof if there's cover. Everyone else spread out."

"How will this idea of yours work, Captain?" Denmead was curious, but Atticus had been very coy about his plan.

"It's a bit risky, to be honest," he said finally, as the Marines found their positions and settled down to wait, "and I'm not sure it'll work. If it does, the next attack will be easier. It's all about making these Cans a liability rather than an advantage."

"But how do we do that?" Denmead persisted, irritated that Atticus wouldn't share.

"You're about to find out," he said, nodding at the window. "Looks like our friends have caught up with us."

Two Cans walked slowly along the street, their outsized bodies looking faintly ridiculous on their comparatively short, stubby legs.

"Three hundred metres, sir," came the report.

"Open fire at two hundred and fifty," said Atticus, "mortars and snipers."

Denmead frowned. "That didn't work before," she pointed out. "Why would it work now?"

"Because this time we have brought something special to the party," said Atticus, adjusting his HUD so that it showed him an enlarged image of the street. The enemy moved slowly, cautiously, checking each building they passed.

In his HUD, Atticus watched the range countdown. As it hit two hundred and fifty metres, there was a pop from the mortar, and both snipers fired. The rifles opened up as well and, in moments, the street was empty of all but the Cans, which continued their sedate stroll.

<Keep firing> sent Atticus. There was some sporadic return of fire from the enemy, but they obviously intended to let the Cans clear the way. They had learned the hard way that captured railguns were not impeded by the walls of Ashton's buildings, so now they kept well out of sight when the distinctive guns began to fire.

"Almost," muttered Atticus, letting his HUD return to normal vision when the Cans had reached the two hundred metre mark.

There were pops from upstairs as the mortars fired again, although as far as Denmead could tell, they hadn't hit anything yet.

She was just about to say as much when a figure dashed from cover on one side of the street. It was one of the Deathless Ruperts but dressed in the armour of a Marine, running fast, heedless of the danger.

Denmead watched, horrified by the risk the Marine was taking but unable to turn away. The Marine sprinted across the road, and, without stopping, reached out to slap something on the back of the leg of one of the Cans. The Can twisted at the waist, trying to bring guns to bear on the tiny figure, but a mortar round caught it in the chest, knocking it back a step and distracting the pilot.

The Marine darted past the second Can and then they were away, racing back to cover as quickly as they had emerged. Whoever they were, they dropped flashbangs and smoke grenades as they ran. Gunfire erupted from the buildings along the street, hosing the Deathless positions as the Marine dived over a wall and disappeared from sight.

Then there were two loud bangs from the street, accompanied by blinding white light. The first Can staggered, then toppled forwards as its leg snapped near the knee, right where the Marine had struck it. The twin-cannon fired repeatedly, throwing up huge sprays of dirt before the Can rolled onto its back and the pilot ejected from the front of the chest.

<Let him run> ordered Atticus, forestalling the snipers he knew would be targeting the fleeing figure. He raised his carbine, adjusted for wind and snapped off a burst that scythed the Rupert's legs out from under him. Moments later, a pair of Deathless troopers rushed forward and dragged the wounded officer into cover.

The second Can didn't fall but it did stop moving as viscous liquid gushed from the damaged leg and something burned brightly behind the knee joint sending up a plume of smoke. The Can pivoted, its upper torso turning until it could spray fire across the Marines' position.

Then a mortar round landed at its feet and the damaged leg

collapsed, spilling the Can to the ground. It fell forward, cannon digging into the ground.

The two railguns spat at almost the same time and the top of the Can crumpled in a spray of sparks. For a moment the street was quiet, then the Can exploded, sending gouts of flame and shards of torn metal into the air.

"Your secret weapon was a reckless Marine?" said Denmead, outraged at the hideous risk of the plan. "What if it hadn't worked or he'd been killed before he placed the bomb? What if he'd tripped and fallen flat on his face?"

Atticus shrugged as the Marines piled into the factory, clearly pleased with their day's work.

"Technically not a bomb – more of an improvised white phosphorous incendiary device. But in answer to your question, Governor, if we had failed we would have tried something else," Atticus said simply. "And now we know this works, we'll find a safer delivery method. Drones, for example."

She looked at him for a long moment, clearly unimpressed. "So why didn't you let the snipers kill the pilot?" she asked, curiosity eventually getting the better of her and driving away her anger, at least for a moment.

Atticus coughed, looking slightly embarrassed. "It wasn't a courtesy, I'm afraid. He's injured, so he's a burden. If they want to put him in another of those suits, they either have to wait for him to heal..."

"Or they have to kill him so they can redeploy him," she said, finishing his unspoken thought.

"Yeah. It's not very sporting, but these chaps aren't really playing cricket," said Atticus apologetically.

Another squad of Marines came into the factory, Lieutenant Hayes at their head.

"Good work, Lieutenant," said Atticus.

"Thank you, sir, although we lost Wilson when that bastard turned the flamethrower on us. We just weren't fast enough pulling back. Sorry, sir."

Atticus nodded. His HUD already showed Wilson's status as

'Awaiting Deployment', meaning that his backup was queued and ready to be loaded into a new body.

"I'll talk to Wilson once he's back on his feet," said Atticus, "remind him that we prefer our NCOs raw rather than barbecued. The rest of you," he said, turning around, "fall back, we're done here."

22

Ten checked the winch one last time. A couple of rounds pinged off the truck, and he spared a glance towards the base. The range was still extreme for small arms, and there was no sign of anything heavier, yet. He shook his head sadly. Honestly, if there weren't so many of these Deathless, they wouldn't be much sport at all. He returned to his checks, grunted in satisfaction and backed away from the winch, releasing the strapping that had held him on the cab and paying out the cable from his harness until he was right at the back of the truck.

Ten took a deep breath and blew it out slowly. Then he checked that his liberated parachute was in place, pulled the ripcord and waited as it unfurled behind him. He gave it one last look to make sure it wasn't tangled then pressed the button on the winch remote.

He was braced for the snap but at this speed, even in this atmosphere, the chute yanked him back and up with a vicious lurch, the straps of the harness punching into his chest. It was a sphincter-tightening moment and he took a second to catch his breath.

He was rising fast, over a hundred metres in mere seconds. Craning his neck, he checked the parachute again; it was still free and clear and fully inflated. Good stuff, time to get cracking.

The truck was five hundred metres from the base, now. The Deathless had got over their surprise at being fired upon and were shooting back, their bullets sounding like hail as they rattled from the thick alloy of the truck. *Have they spotted me up here?* Ten wondered, before concluding that they probably hadn't. Goodwin had put the headlights on full beam a couple of minutes before, and this thing was designed to be operated twenty-four hours a day; it was bright and obvious, with more lights than a shopping centre at holiday time.

With a bit of luck, the Deathless would focus on the unstoppable behemoth heading towards their gate. Ten wondered if they just hadn't realised how big the truck was. Maybe they were confused about the difference between very small and far away?

The remote strapped to his wrist showed him at three hundred metres, which was more than enough. He tapped the control and slowed the winch until it stopped paying out cable. Three hundred metres from the base – time to get the party started.

"Goodwin, can you start the light show and effects, please?"

"Do you mean you want me to fire the grenade launchers?" Goodwin asked, somewhat testily.

"Yes, fire the grenade launchers."

"Why didn't you just say that then? Firing now," she replied.

Bloody wet behind the ears, these kids, he thought. *No sense of style. Don't they realise how much fun this is?*

The pair of grenade launchers attached to the lip of the dump truck's hopper let forth a volley of grenades. Three each then a two-second pause and another three. Ten turned up the filtering on his HUD in anticipation; the auto-filter was good, but there was always a delay, and it was better to be prepared.

The flashbangs detonated across the front of the gateway, bright as the midday sun and as loud as any decent rock concert. Sure enough, the enemy firing paused again. The next set of grenades didn't land quite so nicely but they burst forth into plumes of multi-coloured smoke, lending an eerie feel to the battleground. More importantly, their smoke concealed everything from the enemy, himself being the most important part of that.

"Thank you, Goodwin, and now the percussion section if you don't mind."

"Firing."

The grenade launchers let loose with their distinctive popping noise again, this time emptying the remaining contents of their drums. Dozens of grenades flew toward the wall, striking all across it, some going through the gate, some over the wall, some falling before it. These weren't flashbangs or smoke-makers; they were high explosive fragmentation grenades. Even if the Deathless were all behind cover, they weren't going to like a shower of grenades.

"Now you're getting the hang of it, Goodwin. Good job. I'm getting off now; I'll let you know when I'm clear," Ten said. He reached out along the cable towards the linkage, pulled a plastic safety wedge free of the mechanism and then yanked the release. The cable dropped away, and suddenly he was pulling up, gliding higher on the updraft.

"Roger that, impact in five, four, three, two –" Goodwin replied.

The truck struck the gateway just before she hit one. The noise would have been deafening, even at this height, if it hadn't been for his HUD. The truck flipped forward as the edges of the cabin impacted the walls on either side of the base doors, the whole backend coming up in an achingly slow arc. For a moment, Ten thought it might flip over the wall. It didn't quite manage that, but the contents of the hopper were thrown forward like shrapnel from a bomb as the truck hit the huge spiky protrusions that festooned the top of the wall.

The arch over the gateway shattered, foamcrete falling in chunks the size of shipping containers. Moments before, there had been a lot of Deathless soldiers firing from above the gap in the wall. Maybe they'd all cleared the wall before the dumper struck, but they were having a bad day all the same.

For a few long seconds, it looked like the truck would come to rest in that position, upright on its cabin, wheels spinning in the air. Then it lost the fight with gravity and tipped far enough forward to come crashing down on the rubble and bodies, landing upside down on the remains of the gate.

Ten cursed; that might spoil the rest of the plan. Never mind, it was a good start. He flicked his HUD to standard night vision mode and the display changed to show a composite image of low light vision and infrared signatures, blended seamlessly to create a clear, detailed image. It wasn't quite daylight, but it was close.

Below him, there were clouds of smoke and dust billowing into the compound behind the wrecked gatehouse. There were dozens of buildings, large and small, of many different forms. One of the smaller ones was little more than a simple hut, standing near the wall but off to one side. That was all he'd have seen with simple night vision, but his HUD picked out infra-red signatures, highlighting any that were likely to be targets. Larger lifeforms, hot engines, or the flame from a rocket launch would be shown, but the HUD would filter out extraneous heat mapping information.

The hut showed hot; several Deathless waited inside. Ten brought his weapon to bear and neatly plopped a high explosive grenade through the thin roof. He searched for more targets; it was time to get loud.

Ten triggered a preprogrammed button in his HUD and music began to blare from the portable speakers strapped to his shoulders. He had been ordered to provide a distraction and he would do exactly that.

He began to sing along at the top of his voice. Ten was pretty sure he wasn't in tune but hopefully the Deathless wouldn't be too harsh in their reviews.

"A British tar is a soaring soul,
As free as a mountain bird,
His energetic fist should be ready to resist,
A dictatorial word!"

As he sang in a decidedly melodramatic manner, he accompanied the lyrics with well-placed rounds from the grenade launcher. Any Deathless foolish enough to cluster together or catch his attention received a small gift, along with any building that looked like it might house base control systems. There wasn't time to be dainty though; any unidentifiable buildings that came into view as he panned around received grenades as well. They must all contain something valuable, after all, even if they weren't storing anything as vital as personnel, armour or an operations centre.

The chute was carrying him over the base now, heading north-east so that, at some point, he would cross the far wall and be over open ground again. Ten refocussed, ignoring most of the base and looking for bigger, more important targets. One floated past, a hundred metres below or more, and he gave it three rounds. Sure enough, it detonated with a satisfying fireball far larger than his grenades would have caused. Score one for the good guys.

A long pull on the left toggle corrected his course and took him back towards the middle of the base. He craned his neck around to check the truck. Lights lanced through the smoke and dust around it, and he could see infrared signatures at their source. There were a maybe two dozen troops nearby but no more approaching it.

"Goodwin, standby for Phase 2."

"Roger that."

Ten turned to his front again, scanning left and right, then fired a volley of grenades towards a building that looked like a barracks. He ejected the drum, slammed another firmly into the receiver, took a deep breath and held the trigger down as he panned from left to right, spraying grenades indiscriminately across the base and paying no attention to where they fell.

Ten grinned as he imagined the Deathless trying to work out what was going on. Nobody fired grenade launchers on fully auto-matic mode; it wasn't even the slightest bit sensible. To the enemy, it would seem like dozens of troops had suddenly loosed a coordinated volley. It would feel like pure chaos down there, and they would have no idea which way to turn. They weren't finding anyone to fight, and confusion, ever present on a battlefield, would be rife amongst these ill-disciplined troops.

He ejected the spent drum and swapped in his last, then slung the launcher onto his back, pulling a magnetic strap tight to stop it bouncing around. He would save the last grenades for an emergency, just in case.

But now it was time to bring this thing down before he got too low and hit something tall, pointy and uncomfortable. In the dim and distant past, he had seen a Marine misjudge a group drop and land on an aerial that should have been removed before the manoeuvre. The comms tech had got a bollocking, but the other guy didn't need one; two weeks in the hospital and a nickname that still made Ten laugh had taken care of that.

Ten killed the music to float silently through the night. The huge ship at the centre of the base looked like a leviathan, set to burst forth from a sea of rock and sand and devour the planet. In a way, that's exactly what it was but, right now, it was his landing zone. There was a large raised section, smooth and flat, just right for not shattering your ankles after tripping on an unseen rock. There weren't any aerials either, and he sniggered at the memory. He had missed old Two-Arseholes since he'd retired. He'd have to send him an ecard, something like "I saw this aerial, and thought of you". That ought to get the proper reaction.

He grabbed both toggles, tweaking his approach with light touches and wondering what to do if he fucked it up. Knife to the throat? Grenade? What was the least painful way to avoid capture?

Then he hit the deck, at a shallow angle, running along the surface of the ship as he slowed, and unclipped the parachute. He ought to police his equipment, but he was hardly likely to need the thing again. He pulled a carbine from a strap on his hip. The lieutenant had said he wouldn't need everything he was carrying, but Ten had insisted. "A good scout is always prepared," he had said, to much rolling of eyes and sighing.

Ten checked the suppressor on his carbine and grinned. With a bit of luck, he would have time to get himself squared away before any clever bugger worked out he was there.

He'd shown the Deathless what a noisy commando was like; now he was going to show them what it meant to be discreet. This wasn't going to be a learning experience, except in the briefest possible sense, but maybe they would be more fearful, more hesitant when they were redeployed again. Fear was good; terror would be better, but Ten could live with an enemy that feared the Marines.

"You aren't going to need a suppressed pistol as well, Marine X," Warden had said in his exasperated tone.

"Weapon jams, sir. Got to have something quick to grab in an emergency," he'd replied.

"Fine, fine, just remember to bring it all back," had been the resigned response. "And remember, Ten, you're on your own."

"Well, thank you, sir. That's a great comfort," Ten had said as he had loaded magazines into his webbing.

He jogged forward to the side of the ship, looking for a way down. A building to his left, about thirty metres from the ship, caught his eye. There were a few Deathless in a well-lit room, with screens along one wall. They were wearing the office clones, Ruperts, like Captain Atticus.

"That'll be the command centre," muttered Ten, mildly satisfied that he had managed to land right in the middle of things. He crouched beside a protrusion on the hull and scanned the area. If he had spotted it from the air, he could have come down on the roof of the command room, but maybe that would have given the game away. Either way, he needed to find another way in.

The answer came to him a moment later. The roof of the building was at least ten metres above the ground but well below the top of the hull. There was a launcher turret nearby, and Ten jogged over, clambering onto it. The rangefinder in his HUD confirmed the distance to his target as he withdrew a slim, tubular package from a holster on his back. With a couple of firm twists and a few solid clicks, it took on the appearance of a short harpoon gun. He dialled in the range and charged it from an energy pack on his belt.

Ten attached a micro-filament line to the projectile, took aim and fired. There was a dull whine from the filament spool as the arrow shot across the open space and lodged in a sturdy structure on the roof of the target building. It buried itself in the wall, barbs gripping tightly. The line held firm when Ten gave it a tug.

It was a simple matter to tie the cable to the turret. The reel doubled as a tightening mechanism, drawing the line as taut as a guitar string, albeit a guitar string that could hold the weight of several men. He had to credit the designers of the device. A one-shot railgun purely for use as a grapnel. He'd had to bribe one of the colonists for fabricator time to construct it, but it had been worth the effort. Once the line was secure, parts of the barrel were repurposed to form a clamp to place over the line; then he only had to clip a short strap between the clamp to his harness, like so. And that was it, all from one neat little package that weighed less than a kilo.

Ten stowed the remainder of the device for later reuse then readied his pistol and clipped it to his chest for a quick draw. One last glance around showed no new enemies in the area and a check of the HUD showed lots of action elsewhere. Nobody noticed as he slipped off the ship and down the zip line.

It was a smooth ride, not like the death ride on the traditional Tarzan course. He landed lightly, moving quickly into cover and checking the area for new signs of enemy activity. Nothing. He weighed his options for a moment then dismantled the rest of the device and retrieved the arrow, digging it out of the foamcrete.

Within a couple of minutes, he stood on the edge of the building, leaning back with a length of thin rope ready to drop beside him. One quick tug to check the knots were holding, and then he jumped backwards off the building, dropping fast and swinging expertly back and to the left, towards one of the columns that supported the building. He bent his knees as his boots hit the foamcrete, then pushed off again, hard. This time as he swung back to the building, he was nicely aligned with the anchor point above him, his feet pointing at a window.

Three pistol rounds sent great cracks across the glass and by the time his feet struck the window, it was little more than a formality. He closed his mouth to avoid swallowing shards of glass, trusting the HUD to protect his eyes, and burst into the command centre.

His pistol found and executed two surprised Ruperts as his feet hit the floor. His momentum carried him forward into the room and he charged directly at their planning table, firing as he went.

Then he was over the table in a forward roll, and when he came up on the other side, he had a knife in his free hand.

He slashed the rope and dashed left towards three Ruperts who hadn't yet sought cover. The two on the right got the attention of his pistol and the one to his left lost his head to the swing of the vibro-knife.

Ten slid across the floor and into a crouch behind the end of the table. He slapped the pistol back onto his chest, sheathed the knife and unslung his carbine. The Ruperts were disappointingly slow and only a few light rounds thudded into the surface of the war room table before he had shouldered his rifle and returned fire.

He ducked again, listing for movement. Silence. Really?

Ten risked another glance, popping his head above the table to look around the room, but there really was no movement. He crept from cover, carbine ready, and checked the room, counting the bodies into his HUD to keep Lieutenant Warden happy. Nine dead Ruperts – no, wait, some movement in the corner. The carbine spat two more bursts and then there were twelve dead Ruperts, including the one who had been sheltering under a colleague as he tried to crawl away.

Ten sighed and looked around. He cocked his head in surprise. There was a metal tray in the middle of the table, with three intact glasses still on it. He leaned close, eyeing them suspiciously but no, there was no glass in the clear liquid. He drank each one in quick succession, just to be sure. Nope, no blood in his mouth, so no glass in the booze. Good to know. The bottle had been smashed onto the floor though. Pity. He would have expected the Deathless Ruperts to have had a bigger stash.

He sighed and crossed to the window nearest the gatehouse. Raising his carbine to his shoulder, he peered through the telescopic sight, his HUD automatically switching modes as he scanned the area. Deathless soldiers emerged from the prefabricated buildings, shining lights on the overturned dump truck, looking for an enemy. Eighteen at least, and maybe a couple of heat signatures nearby were light clones crouching behind cover. Either way, it looked like now was the time.

"Blow it, Goodwin," he requested, ducking down behind the wall.

"Roger that, fingers in your ears," Goodwin replied.

The truck detonated just as one of the unfortunate troopers drew close enough to touch the door of the cab, looking for the driver. An enormous explosion bloomed under the hopper, lifting it clear into the air before it ruptured. Huge chunks of metal flew outward as the fireball unfurled like a giant rose, sending lumps of shrapnel the size of desks tumbling through buildings and into the night. The safety glass in the windows above Ten, and in all the windows nearby, blew inward, covering the room in neat chunks. The enemy that had surrounded the vehicle were vapourised, as was every building for tens of metres, crumpled by the shockwave and scattered across the rest of the base.

Ten stood up to check the effects, nodding in satisfaction.

"Good job, Goodwin, that gave them a headache."

"Thanks, Ten. Happy hunting."

"Likewise."

Ten took one last look around the room then grinned as he spotted the liquor cabinet.

23

By the time Warden reached the base of the wall, Milton had already started on the breaching plan. Warden pulled his rebreather over his mouth and nostrils to filter out the cloud of dust that billowed out from the wall. He pinged Milton via the HUD as he unslung a cumbersome tool from his webbing; he didn't want to startle someone operating a mining laser.

Milton flicked off her laser and stepped back from the cutting face.

"Where do you want me?" Warden asked.

"Saved you a spot in the front rank, sir," she said, pointing at the spot she had just vacated. "Have you used one of these before?"

"No, this will be a first, Sergeant."

"It's easy enough, sir. That button is the dead man's handle, keep it pressed, and that one fires the laser. It's invisible but there's a red targeting lamp to help with the aiming."

"Okay, seems easy enough," muttered Warden, horribly aware that it was bound to be much more complicated than Milton had suggested.

The Marines were arranged in two ranks, one kneeling, one standing. They'd already excavated a sizeable hole through the rock, wide enough for two men abreast but not tall. They were cutting well below the wall because the rock was easier to get through than the foamcrete; there were scorch marks on the foamcrete above the tunnel, remnants of some aborted efforts to dig through the wall itself.

"Cease cutting," Milton ordered and the beams shut off. Warden took his place, crouching in the front line with Milton behind. The tunnel angled down and, as the dust cleared, Warden saw they were about halfway done. At Milton's order, the cutting resumed. Two minutes later, the first part of the work was complete, and everybody shuffled out of the tunnel.

Every metre or so, two Marines sprayed the floor, ceiling and walls of the tunnel with a layer of foam. It reacted quickly to the thin air and set hard in seconds, forming a skin that shored up the walls. The colony's engineers had assured them that this stuff was heat resistant and designed for exactly this purpose.

Now the teams reorganised so that a few Marines could get into the tunnel and begin cutting forward. A few metres of horizontal cutting, then they would swap teams again and begin cutting upward. Denmead's engineers had offered copious amounts of advice and the plan seemed sound, but Warden had his doubts.

Warden, no longer at the cutting face, put down his laser and checked the clock on his HUD. It was a bit tight but they were on schedule. In the hole, the teams swapped around again, Marines crowding into the tunnel to get as many lasers on the target as they could.

Then there was a long rumbling bang that shook the floor and caused everyone to stop cutting. When nothing further happened, Milton waved them on and the work resumed.

"That was our distraction coming home," said Warden as Milton joined him near the entrance of the tunnel, "but the scans are still showing no enemy troops anywhere near here. It looks like Marine X is drawing their attention."

Milton nodded, setting down her exhausted laser.

"Bailey, anything I need to know about?" asked Warden.

"All quiet on the western front, sir. You're good to go."

"Goodwin, I'm hearing a lot of gunfire but nothing bigger. What's the story?"

"Ten asked me to standby, sir."

"He got off it safely then?"

"Seems to have, though I've no idea how he did it."

"Roger that. As soon as you blow it, get a drone up and send us some updates."

"Yes, sir."

Warden glanced upward at the spikes again, then back at Fletcher, Campbell and the others.

"Corporal Campbell, we're all clear here, no sign of the enemy. Get over here as quick as you can."

"Roger. On our way, sir."

"Milton, how's it coming along?"

"We're almost up and under the wall, sir. Two minutes, at a guess."

Warden nodded. "Good. Everyone who is not manning a laser, stay sharp. I don't want them catching us with our pants down."

He crouched down at the end of the tunnel to see how it was coming along. The incline was going upward again and should emerge a metre or so the other side of the wall. They were fortunate that the huge wall had been set directly on the rock and was held in place only by its own huge weight. The production speed of the Deathless war machine was impressive, but nobody built foundations they didn't need.

Corporal Campbell arrived with the four from her section that had been redeployed in Deathless lizardmen clones. Fletcher was with them, seconded from Section 1 as she too was in a Deathless clone, an ogre with full power armour. The rest of Sections 1 and 2, who were still wearing standard Marine clones, would work together. Mixing power-armoured Marines with colleagues wearing basic bullet-resistant gear was not operationally efficient.

Likewise, the remainder of Section 2 who had survived without being redeployed in Deathless clone bodies had been seconded to

Section 1 under the command of Corporal Drummond. That left Campbell free for frontal assaults, where power armour really came into its own.

Warden was curious to see how they would handle the armour. He'd checked the personnel records, and none of the Marines had seen serious combat in power armour, though all were trained in its use. It just wasn't necessary for most situations, so it only came out when the environment itself was hostile. Only a handful of the Marines, mostly the NCOs and a few of the older officers, had any real experience in power armour. Warden himself had never used it in combat.

Very often, the combat power armour onboard ships of the line would be pristine, some even retaining the manufacturer's plastic film that protected the paint job. The suits that showed signs of wear and tear would invariably be the loading suits, similar to Fletcher's ogre model, and the repair suits used for spacewalks, both specialised models that weren't intended for use in combat. Not that being slapped around with a loader was going to be any fun for a boarding party, though.

"We're through, sir," Milton said, interrupting Warden's musing. The teams swapped places and more of the rapid setting epoxy was sprayed into the tunnel. Then they were ready to go.

"Campbell, head through and establish a beachhead," Warden ordered. "Fletcher, you might have to wait until we can get a line down to you from the top of the wall."

The ogre's massive bulk wasn't going to fit through the tunnel and the plan might go badly wrong if she got wedged between the narrow walls.

"I have some modes I haven't tried yet, sir. I think I might be able to scale the wall. Permission to test while I wait?"

Warden shrugged. "Granted. If you can find a way to get up there without making a racket, go right ahead. Not that I think anyone will be paying attention to us with Marine X still at large." As he spoke there was an enormous explosion, and every one of them took cover in alarm, some retaining more dignity than others. A rain of debris clattered from the sky, tiny fragments of metal and rock spattering the wall and the roofs of the buildings on the other side.

"Fuck me!" blurted Warden. "Goodwin, report!"

"Detonation successful, Lieutenant. Ten's data suggests at least sixteen enemy casualties. My drone is away and I'll have updates for you shortly," Goodwin replied.

"Beachhead secure, Lieutenant," came Corporal Campbell's voice over the HUD. "No sign of the enemy. The mothership is ready and waiting."

"Acknowledged," Warden said, looking at Milton and gesturing for her to get the rest of the troop through the tunnel.

Fletcher moved to the base of the well, just to the left of the tunnel. The ogre power armour was bright yellow, the sort of paint job you might expect to see on a racing flyer rather than a suit of armour. Warden preferred a spot of camouflage, even if it wasn't perfect and the enemy would likely have tools that saw beyond the visual spectrum, but not everyone was using a HUD all the time. The Mark I eyeball was still good for most occasions and in his book, that meant camouflage was a must.

"Switched-mode now, sir," said Fletcher, flexing her fingers. "Don't think I've set it to self-destruct."

"Very funny, Fletcher, I can't wait for your appearance at the next CSE show."

As he watched, huge spikey blades sprang forth from Fletcher's shoulders, and forearms and the gauntlets sprouted claws of shining metal. She flexed them, and they curled menacingly as she twisted her head and arms, looking up at the blades protruding from her shoulders and across the back of her forearms.

Warden walked over to her as she stepped up to the wall and brought her hand down against the foamcrete. The claws punctured it easily, and the spikes at the tips of her boots did likewise. Before Warden could get close enough for a better look, Fletcher had begun to make her way up the surface of the fortification as easily as if it were a beginners' climbing wall in a gymnasium. She paused halfway up, looking around.

"This is pretty neat, sir. It's some kind of melee combat mode, but it was also tagged for climbing assaults. These claws get into the wall like it's made of dough."

"Excellent. Get up there, hunker down, and keep an eye on things until we're ready for you to join us, okay?"

"Yes, sir."

Warden spared a glance back towards Bailey and the snipers, then followed his command through the tunnel, coming up on the other side, rifle at the ready. He crouched low, sidling quickly to the left until he was behind the cover of a storage crate.

His HUD led him to Milton and the rest of the team. Corporal Campbell and her team, Fletcher excepted, were clustered near the front, behind one of the many prefabricated units in the base compound. On this side of the base, the mothership was obscured by piles of storage containers that covered much of the ground inside the wall. An icon on Warden's HUD showed the drone Goodwin had launched was aloft and transmitting data, and he switched to an aerial view of the compound.

The icon marking Ten's position strobed slowly in a building on the other side of the mothership. A large sheet of cloth fluttered in the breeze; the lines snagged on a protrusion from the mothership. The whole area between the gate and the mothership looked like a year-old active war zone. But no, just one truck and one Marine were responsible. He shook his head in disbelief; he had asked for a distraction, but this was on another scale entirely.

Switching back to a low light view from his HUD, he made his way quickly to Milton's position, catching up with her as she advanced towards the hull of the mothership. They were at the rear of the ship, near the main engines.

"Right. You four, stow your weapons and pick up those crates, get them shifted," Milton ordered as Warden arrived. "I want a wall to give us cover while we work. With all the chaos out there, they might not even notice us."

Warden immediately understood her plan. She had identified an entry point and was using the crates like a set of giant children's building blocks, stacking them to shield the Marines while they worked. He checked the disposition of his team and sent Campbell and her command to help. Augmented by their power armour, they were able to move some of the larger, sturdier crates that littered the base. He mucked in too, and soon they had their own sturdy emplacement, part firing post, part fort.

Then they broke out the mining lasers and got to work on the hull, cutting into it on maximum settings while everyone else hunkered down to wait.

A few minutes later, another round of noise broke out from the other side of the base. Ten, probably, providing more distraction. Warden waited, checking the drone's view and making sure updates had been made to the HUD now that a live map of the base was available. Buildings that probably contained living troops were highlighted, identified by the drone or flagged by Marine X.

"Sir," Milton whispered urgently, trying to get his attention.

"Yes?" he asked, turning his head towards the breaching team and groaning inwardly as he took the scene in.

"The lasers are kaput," she said with an apologetic shrug.

There was a hole in the side of the ship but they hadn't breached the inner hull and it wasn't big enough for access. The ship was probably still spaceworthy.

Milton was looking at him hopefully, and Warden tried to keep his eyes from betraying his utter lack of a bright idea. How the fuck were they going to get in now?

24

"He is," Ten roared as the shotgun bucked in his arms and the lizardman rushing at him crumpled to the floor. His boot opened a door, and he dropped to one knee, throwing his arms wide as he exclaimed, "An Englishman!" in his best tenor.

The Deathless inside the room were clearly taken aback by the passion of his performance, rising to their feet to congratulate him. Ten favoured them with more of his best efforts.

"He is... an Englishman," he sang as the shotgun found his shoulder and he panned from right to left, firing as he went.

"For he himself has said it –" the gun boomed in the small room, "– and it's greatly to his credit," Ten roared over the noise as the Deathless screamed and the shotgun barked like a hellhound. "That he is an Englishman, that he is an Englishman!"

He rose up from his crouch and moved down the corridor, singing along at the top of his lungs as the music blared from his speakers.

"For he might have been a Roosian, a French or Turk or Proosian, or perhaps Italian! Or perhaps Italian!" he sang as he swapped in a fresh drum. He paused the music and the silence seemed strange.

"Lieutenant, how much time do I have? I thought I might try and arrange a little parting gift for our guests before I join you."

"Roger that. We need to choose a delivery window for our own present. Get to us within ten minutes and make sure you don't bring any more guests, we have plenty to entertain here already."

"Yes, sir," acknowledged Ten, walking towards the external door and noting the heat signatures arranged in a horseshoe on the other side. He let the strap take the weight of the automatic shotgun, strode towards the door and booted it open, tossing in a couple of grenades before stepping smartly to one side as the enemy opened fire.

The appearance of the grenades led to much movement amongst the Deathless troopers and a certain degree of shouting. The gunfire stopped as quickly as it had started and when the grenades went off, Ten made his move, dashing into the room and heading straight for a shattered window. He dived through, restarting the music as he flanked the enemy while they were disoriented from the flashbangs and fragmentation grenades.

He rounded the corner, covered in blood and dust and roaring along to the song like an amateur opera singer competing in a talent show, completely oblivious to utter lack of skill.

The shotgun boomed as he sang, "But in spite of all temptations." Two more Deathless fell before him and he dashed forward as the rest of the group turned.

"To belong to other nations," he sang as he jumped up onto a metal crate, "he remains an Englishman." He pulled the trigger and ended the Rupert cowering behind it. The remaining Deathless turned to flee.

Sorry, lads, not on the cards today, Ten thought as he aimed his weapon.

"He remains an Englishman!" he sang with as much volume as he could muster, and brought down all three of them as the song finished. He looked around and found no nearby enemies.

<Get moving, Marine X> came a terse message on his HUD. Ten sighed and killed the music again.

He dropped down from the crate and pulled a slightly battered jelly baby from his pocket.

"Heaven," he muttered, popping the sweet into his mouth. He

washed it down with half a canteen of water, one ear cocked for enemy movement.

Then he reloaded his weapons and looted the Deathless for ammunition and grenades. He found an access card in a zipped pocket on a Rupert's uniform, still intact despite the gaping shotgun wound in the middle of its chest. Bingo.

Then he spied a corner of plastic in another pocket and tugged it free. Weird, it looked like some kind of paper trapped between two films of plastic.

"A map," muttered Ten, "an actual physical map printed on actual paper."

Boggling at the idea that anyone might use physical maps, Ten scanned it into his HUD, then scanned the nearby buildings for context. The HUD hungrily slurped down the information and incorporated it into the troop's data store, updating the Marines' tactical displays.

Ten looked at the map symbols and although he couldn't read the legend, it seemed that the Deathless hadn't strayed too far from human norms; there was a lightning bolt over a building that looked like a generator, a red cross that had to be a medical bay, beds indicated a barracks and a weird gun-like thing that was probably an armoury. He had destroyed two armouries already but there were still two more. Excellent.

Ten stuffed the map inside his jacket to keep as a souvenir. It wouldn't be cheap to get it all the way home, or quick, but it would get to his storage unit eventually and be waiting for him if he ever retired.

He checked the HUD update, reviewing all the information submitted by the rest of the troop and letting them know his location, just in case they needed it. His HUD showed him the armoury furthest from the ship and plotted a route that would, hopefully, keep him away from the Deathless. If ever a job called for silent sneakiness, this was it. Then he swapped back to his suppressed carbine and grinned grimly into the darkness.

Music off, Ten ghosted into the night and disappeared.

25

Atticus sat in the makeshift command room watching the reports from the deployed troops. It was grim reading, made worse by the fact that Atticus could do literally nothing to help. He drummed his fingers on the console, fiddled with his HUD and eventually settled into a sullen silence broken only by occasional muttering of dissatisfaction.

"Tea, sir?" said Butler, walking in silence to appear, unexpected, at Atticus's side with a large mug of strong tea. Atticus grunted his thanks and Butler disappeared from view as quietly as he had arrived.

He sipped his tea gratefully. It had been a long week, and the end was not yet in sight. Fortunately, Command HQ was unusually quiet today. Colour Sergeant Jenkins was off in Ashton helping Lieutenant Hayes with the militia. Corporal Wilson was busy working on the new batch of clones.

Corporal Hughes wasn't particularly noisy, but she was off looking after the kids who were building and piloting drones to gather intelligence. The kids weren't the slightest bit fazed by the danger the Deathless invasion put them in. They had taken to their task of searching for the enemy and gathering intelligence with glee and enthusiasm.

The cocky little sods had even sabotaged a few enemy vehicles with weapons they had improvised and attached to the drones. Exactly how they had come up with the devices remained a question that Atticus decided he didn't need to answer.

He had suggested subtly that the footage of the attacks should be deleted before any of the parents stumbled across it; nobody was going to like the idea of children engaging the enemy, even indirectly.

But the kids were having too much fun to worry about the rules or getting into trouble. Atticus had raised an eyebrow at Hughes when she had cautiously broached the subject – *the captain certainly had no idea what was going on, ma'am, don't know what you're talking about.*

Plausible deniability, that was the ticket.

Yes, peace and quiet was a nice change. Then he became aware of a warning message on one the monitors. He set down his mug and leaned forward as it flashed on the screen. A proximity alert was firing for a spot a few kilometres from the caves, well behind their lines and far from any of their forces.

"Something's out there," he muttered, flicking through the Marine and militia monitors, checking for anyone unaccounted for or out of position.

"Shit," he said, "looks like an enemy squad."

"An enemy squad where?" said Governor Denmead as she came into the room. She had taken to wearing combat gear continuously so now she looked like a member of the militia, although she wasn't carrying weapons or webbing.

"About three kilometres from the cave system, right there," said Atticus, pointing at the map where a red pin hovered, flashing dimly.

"How can there be enemy activity that far behind the lines? How did they get past us?"

"I don't know," said Atticus uneasily, "but our forces are all accounted for and, with both troops deployed and the militia engaged, we have nothing left with which to investigate."

"What about the reserve? Did we not have a company of militia held back for just these occasions?"

"We did, but they're already in action on the other front." Atticus stood up and grabbed his webbing, which was fully stocked with ammunition and supplies, as always. Then he picked up his rifle and looked at Governor Denmead. "Desperate times call for desperate measures."

"Wait, what?" she said, eyebrows shooting up in surprise.

"They have to be stopped," Atticus said, checking the Deathless rifle he had collected, "because if they keep moving in the direction they're heading, they'll find the entrance to the caves and then this will all have been for nothing."

Denmead looked at him, face slightly grey. Atticus, still wearing the Deathless clone, towered over her.

"Butler," said Atticus, "suit up, it's time we earned our living."

Butler, Atticus's super-efficient valet, nodded and disappeared from the room, returning a few moments later with his webbing, weapons and armour.

"Ready when you are, sir," he said, adjusting his HUD.

"Just the two of you?" said Denmead, aghast. From the faces of the three other people in the room, it seemed that her thoughts were widely shared. "There could be dozens of them!"

"Hopefully not," said Atticus, "or this will be the most hopeless engagement since the Battle of Little Bighorn."

"I'm coming with you," said Denmead in a tone that brooked no discussion. She collected her things and rammed a magazine into her rifle. "Are you ready?"

Atticus looked at her thoughtfully.

"Are you sure? This is probably a one-way trip, a proper fight against superior numbers with little hope of victory."

"Don't exaggerate, Captain. Let's get moving." And she walked from the command room, slinging her rifle as she went.

Butler and Atticus shared a look.

"You heard the Governor, Butler. Time to make a difference."

Ten minutes later the three of them were ripping across the flat plains towards the enemy's location.

"They're still in the same spot," said Butler, who was watching the monitors while Atticus drove the speeder, "and the high-altitude drones are in position. Looks like a dozen light troops. They have a small vehicle but they're investigating a farm of some sort."

"There's a ridge to the east of the farm," said Denmead looking at her own version of the map, "we should be able to get within about eighty metres."

"Right," said Atticus as he angled the speeder and reduced the velocity, "there's the ridge, I'll stop well back from the edge, and we'll take the last couple of hundred metres on foot."

"What if they have drones out, sir?"

"That's a chance we'll have to take. We can't risk them moving on and spotting something they shouldn't."

They piled out of the speeder and finished the journey on foot, crawling the last few metres on hands and knees to keep below the line of the ridge. At the top, Atticus peered cautiously over, looking around for a few seconds before sliding back into cover.

"There's a steep drop, about ten metres, then it's flat to the farm buildings. One enemy wheeled vehicle between us and the farm. Eight troopers in view, two in the vehicle which leaves two unaccounted for if the surveillance was good." He sat for a moment, thinking. "Butler, did we bring any explosive ordnance?"

"Of course," said an aggrieved Butler, producing a clutch of grenades, "I always like to bring gifts to a party."

Atticus grinned. "Good, so here's the plan." He explained and it was clear that Denmead didn't like it any more than Butler, but neither of them had any better suggestions and time was short. "Right, get to it. See you on the other side."

Atticus strapped himself into the speeder as Denmead and Butler edged into position amongst the rocks at the top of the ridge. He checked through his plan, looking for flaws, counting the weak points and the things that could go wrong. Then he realised that this was a pointless exercise; sometimes you just had to act and trust the training and your colleagues.

He turned on the speeder, oriented himself as best he could and hit the accelerator. It shot forward, directly towards the ridge, and Atticus braced himself as the edge flashed in front of him and disappeared.

Then the speeder was airborne. It seemed to hover for a few seconds but the feeling in his guts told him that was an illusion.

The speeder fell quickly and landed heavily, bouncing hard on the rocky ground, its motors unable to maintain flight after the rapid drop. The bounce shook Atticus so that his teeth almost fell out and his head snapped back and forward, banging the headrest and the side of the speeder. Then it was done and he had barely enough time to glimpse the slab-like side of the enemy vehicle in front of him before the speeder slammed into it, pitching him against the restraints.

For a second, all was quiet and still. Then he tore the seatbelt off and jumped out, rifle in his hand.

The enemy troopers were moving now. The attack had caught them unawares but now they wanted to know what the hell was going on.

Atticus moved clear of the speeder, waving his arms and shouting incoherently, yelling randomly.

The enemy troopers, unsure what they were seeing, watched dumbfounded as one of their brother clones capered around like an idiot.

They shouted at him, maybe asking where he had come from or what was wrong. Atticus couldn't tell and didn't care, he just kept moving and shouting, counting steadily, diving to the ground when he reached five.

Then the grenades wedged under the seat of the speeder exploded and everything went white.

Atticus rolled to his feet and brought his rifle to bear, gunning down the two troopers who were struggling back to their feet.

Behind him, there was another explosion as the fuel in the much-damaged Deathless vehicle, its storage tank punctured by either the collision or the grenades, went up.

There was gunfire now as well, coming from the ridge and falling on the surviving Deathless troopers. Dazed by the shockwaves and the light, the Deathless were struggling to find their feet and return fire. Atticus blasted them to pieces as fire rained in from Denmead and Butler.

"Better check the other side," muttered Atticus as he dodged around the burning vehicles. There were two bodies on the ground; they must have been standing close to the vehicle when it exploded.

Two more were struggling to their feet. Atticus shot the first in its head as it staggered upright then drilled the second through the chest, knocking it straight back down again.

"And the pair makes eight," he muttered to himself.

<Two to your right, injured> sent Butler. Atticus turned to find two wounded troopers crawling away from the burning wreckage. He shot one as someone – Butler, he assumed – shot the other.

"Going well," murmured Atticus, moving towards the farm to check the buildings. A figure emerged, scouting carefully, looking for danger. Atticus emptied his magazine into the Deathless trooper, killing it before it had even seen him.

Then there was a rattle of fire from one of the buildings and he felt a series of stabbing pains through his chest.

"Bugger," muttered Atticus as he fell to one side, seeking the meagre cover of a stack of cement bags, "that wasn't what I had in mind."

∼

Butler saw Atticus go down and swore. The captain was in cover but getting to him would mean an eighty-metre dash across open ground in full view of at least one enemy soldier. Not good.

But Denmead was already moving, sliding down the steep side of the ridge before pounding across the plain.

"Oh shit," muttered Butler, seeing her move. Nothing to be gained by following, so he peered through his scope, checking the windows of the building for movement, hoping the Deathless trooper would show itself.

"Come on, you bugger, stick your head out," Butler murmured. Nothing. Denmead was halfway across the plain and the enemy was just playing with them, biding its time.

"Fuck it," said Butler. He took aim at the windows of the building and fired a few rounds through each, hoping to suppress any watching enemy long enough for Denmead to reach Atticus. He fired again and again, emptying his magazine then slamming in another.

Still no sign of the enemy and Denmead was almost at the captain's side.

Then he saw the glint of a muzzle and he smiled grimly. A quick adjustment, a pause for calm, then he fired, aiming for the other end of the barely visible gun.

The muzzle of the enemy rifle shook as Butler fired again and again. Then it vanished and Butler saw his chance.

He was off like a whippet, darting down the slope and zig-zagging across the plain. He ejected the spent magazine as he ran, sliding in a new one as he slid up beside Atticus and Denmead.

"Hold on, sir," he said, glancing at the captain's wounds, "we'll have you out of here in a jiffy and get you patched up." He pulled a morphine shot from a pouch and smashed it into Atticus's arm then peered around, looking for more enemy soldiers.

"I think I'm done, Butler," said Atticus, his breathing laboured. Blood dribbled down his chin as Denmead pressed her hands against his wounds. "A noble effort, Governor, and much appreciated, but this body has had it," he said, forcing a grin.

"Stay here, Governor," said Butler, hefting his rifle, "I'll check for movement." Denmead nodded, scrabbling in her pockets for bandages and tape while Butler disappeared towards the farm buildings.

"Stay with me, Captain Atticus," said the governor harshly, "we haven't enough clones that we can spare them on careless Marines who get themselves shot." She jumped as the sound of gunfire floated across the farm.

<Two more of the bastards> sent Butler, <looks like the intel was wrong>

"Typical," said Atticus quietly as Denmead tried to patch a large wound above his hip. Even with her limited medical knowledge, she could see that it was hopeless. There was just too much damage for her to deal with.

<Found a lifter> sent Butler, <on my way back to you>

A moment later it appeared, a big agricultural lifter with a low flatbed.

Butler jumped down and together he and Denmead manhandled Atticus onto the flatbed. His clone was heavy and even with two of them it was a struggle. Denmead climbed up and sat with Atticus as Butler gunned the engine and drove quickly back towards the cave system.

"Almost there," shouted Butler over the noise of the wind, "hang on."

They pulled into the cave that was serving as a garage and skidded to a halt. The area was suddenly alive as people rushed forward to help. A pair of medics appeared with a stretcher and one knelt beside Atticus, probing at his neck, feeling for a pulse, searching for any sign of life.

"I'm sorry, Governor," she said, her fingers covered in blood. "Captain Atticus is dead."

26

"Right, I confess, I'm buggered if I know what we're going to do now," Warden admitted. "We need to come up with a new strategy, some way to get into the ship now that the mining lasers are dead. Ideas?"

Warden had gathered his second-in-command, Sergeant Milton, and the two section leaders, Corporals Drummond and Campbell, into a small office in a pre-fabricated building. There were dozens of these buildings around, many completely unused, as if the Deathless were preparing to ramp up their occupation and had built a base capable of handling far more troops than they currently had available. Warden didn't want to think about that right now.

Predictably, there were blank looks all round until Drummond piped up, "We just want to disable the ship, right, sir?"

"More or less, yes. It's their main base of operations and the plan was to board it and destroy it from the inside because we don't have any weapons capable of guaranteeing the job from the outside."

"Can we attack the engines then? We've got railguns, grenades and some explosives from the mine. We should at least be able to stop them taking off without resupply. They surely won't have anyone who can repair that sort of damage?"

"Probably not, but keeping it from taking off doesn't stop them churning out more clones, and this base is tough enough to assault already. If they get numbers in here, we'll have a hard time winkling them out," Warden said.

"Yeah, especially now they know we've got the balls to bring the fight to them," Milton said, "it's not enough, Corporal. We need to get inside, but I can't think of a way to do it with the equipment we've got. We'll never blow a hole through the hull with the explosives we have; they're just not effective against impact-resistant spaceship hull-plating."

"I get it, Sarge. I don't know what to say, then. We can't blow or cut our way in, so we're screwed, right?" Drummond said.

"We could always trying walking in," said Campbell with some evidence of trepidation. She'd only been made up to corporal a few months before and was still slightly reticent about putting ideas forward.

Drummond laughed.

"Yeah, just knock on the door and then, 'I say, old chap, Customs and Excise, we need to inspect your cargo for contraband.' They'd probably let us waltz right in."

"Well, why wouldn't they?" said Campbell, a little flustered as she pressed on. "We look like them, after all." She took her helmet off to prove the point, showing her scaled skin and the weird alien features. "We haven't even repainted the armour, and they'll be expecting people like us to need to get into the ship."

"Told you it was time for her to be a corporal, sir," said Milton, beaming proudly. "Nice one, Campbell. With your permission, sir?" she said.

"It's better than anything I have," admitted Warden, "but there's a small problem. They use access cards, just like we do, and they're keyed to certain parts of the ships. We haven't found cards for this base or ship, so how do we open the ramp?"

"Like this one, sir?" Campbell said, producing a card and holding it up for them to see before snapping it in half. "Oh, clumsy me. My card doesn't seem to be working." She pantomimed waving the card in front of a security camera, and Milton grinned.

"That might work," said Warden sceptically, "but it's a hell of a risk. What if they talk to you or demand a password? There are lots of things that can go wrong, and we need none of them to happen for this to work."

"Stranger things have happened," muttered Milton, "but do we have any other options? And there's always a chance that it might work."

Warden sniffed, still doubtful, then nodded.

"Okay, let's go for it," he said, "and the best of luck to us all."

They filed out of the room, Campbell putting her helmet back on.

"Fletcher, unless there's any activity to worry about, get yourself down here, Campbell needs you," said Milton.

"Aside from Ten, it's pretty quiet, nothing close by," Fletcher said, silhouetted in the gap between two crenellations on the internal side of the wall. She hopped up onto the low wall between the two raised sections, paused for a moment then did a standing jump forward. She dropped to one knee as she absorbed the impact of the landing.

The noise was not subtle and Warden wondered if it was worth pointing out that there were perfectly good stairs only a few metres away. Probably not, he thought, and at least now they knew the armour could survive a leap like that. It might come in handy at some point.

Campbell and her team of Deathless-clone Marines moved out, walking beside the ship towards a clearly marked, but currently very closed, access ramp. The rest of the Marines crept forward, positioned well back and ready for an assault.

When they reached the yellow and black striped rectangle painted on the hull, Campbell pulled out her access card, looking at it as if she were amazed to find it broken. She tried it optimistically on the lock, and nothing happened. She tried it again, then she pressed a button and leaned towards a camera, gesturing with the card, one half flapping uselessly.

Surely this wouldn't work? They'd want to speak to her, to confirm who they were letting in and probably reprimand her for breaking her card. Warden was just starting to feel it was a waste of time when a warning buzzer sounded and the ramp began to open, showing blinking lights along its edge. Lasers projected an outline of its footprint as it lowered, lest some wet-behind-the-ears recruit got flattened on their first day. All very safe, very sensible.

Campbell stood back and waited, her impatience showing. A Rupert came down the ramp first, pistol drawn and held casually at his side, and for a moment it looked like Campbell was going to be questioned. Then the officer walked past, leading three short columns of lizardmen. They jogged away, heading for the gatehouse, off to deal with the intrusion, it seemed. Campbell stood to one side, waiting for them to clear the ramp.

Then the Rupert stopped, turned back and walked over to Campbell, clearly asking something as he went. Campbell held up the broken card in response and shrugged as if to ask what she could do about it. That didn't satisfy the officer, and it became agitated, yelling at the column of troops to stop and frowning hard at Campbell.

A whole platoon, standing to attention, eyes front, while they waited for their commander to rejoin them.

<I think he wants me to speak, sir. Orders?> Campbell asked.

<Zap him> Warden answered via silent HUD message.

<Engage on Campbell's signal. Quiet as possible, please> he broadcast to the whole troop.

Campbell tapped the side of her head, as if there was a problem with her communicator, leaning forward slightly and bringing up her hand as if she was going to remove her helmet. The officer leaned forward too.

Then Campbell's left hand reached out and clutched the back of the Rupert's head, his eyes going wide for as long as it took for her Fairbairn-Sykes to punch up under his jaw and into his brain.

"Fletcher. Take them," she ordered as she wiped the dagger on the front of Rupert's uniform, using her grip on his head to keep him upright until her knife had been sheathed.

Fletcher complied, walking straight up to the sergeant who stood to attention at the front of the platoon. It looked up at her, waiting for her to speak. Instead, she activated the blades and claws on her armour and grabbed his head with one massive glove, crushing it like an eggshell. Then she stepped forward and tore the throat out of a trooper in the next rank.

The Marines opened up at that point, silenced pistols spitting at the confused enemy troopers as they struggled to work out what was going on and how to respond.

Campbell moved forward throwing the corpse of the officer into the horrified ranks of his troops, her team in motion behind her, closing quickly. Their power armour put them in charge of the situation. She punched one trooper full in the face, not holding back on the suit's capabilities, and the front of his skull just crumpled around her fist.

Then her team fell on them, snapping necks and slitting throats. A Troop's suppressed weapons took care of any who were quick enough or far enough from the front line to aim a weapon. It was a brutal slaughter. Fletcher had sliced her way through the front ranks after killing the sergeant, the blades on her forearms parting more than one head from its shoulders.

Any that were quick enough to avoid her bladed arms felt instead the steely grasp of the claws and whatever limb they gripped was crushed in a heartbeat, crippling them. Fletcher killed them as quickly and efficiently as possible; there was no need for them to suffer, despite the fact they had attacked a peaceful colony that housed civilians and their children.

In seconds, they were all down and the area was suddenly quiet again.

"Strip weapons and ammunition," Warden ordered as Campbell's team moved back to the ship.

<Campbell, split your team and clear the corridors and main rooms. Bypass side rooms. We'll be right behind you to mop those up> he broadcast to the whole troop. He didn't want to be here any longer than was strictly necessary. Get in, cripple the ship, get out;

that was the plan. If it took too long, the enemy might reinforce from orbit, and Warden didn't want to be here when that happened.

Fletcher took the lead, charging up the ramp, and straight for the door opposite. The door lock went green as soon as she slapped the gauntlet of her suit on the pad, then the double doors slid open and she barrelled on.

From inside the ship, Warden could see it was built on a different scale to the dropships they'd stormed before. It was a pity they weren't capturing it but a ship this size, on the ground, was simply too vulnerable to orbital bombardment. There was probably a wealth of equipment in here that they could use in Fort Widley but, after the quarry, he was reluctant to try another unauthorised side mission.

"Lance Corporal Price, Richardson, Jenkins, Barber, I want you to hang back. Richardson, get your drones out – you too, Jenkins. I want visuals on this ship as soon as possible. Once that's done, Lance Corporal, you're to visit any location near this ramp we can loot for useful gear. Nothing we can't fit in a vehicle, if Ten hasn't already destroyed them all. We don't have much space in the rovers, but we lost half of Section 3 at the quarry, so see what you can find. Power armour is a priority and heavy weapons. You know what we need."

<That goes for the rest of you. Grab anything you think we really need or flag it for later collection. If you find something we can turn into a bomb, flag it> Warden broadcast. The micro-drones were already zipping through the ship, followed by their larger cousins, the combat drones.

A message from Milton popped up in his HUD, <Aft cabins cleared. No contact>

Updates began to populate the map, showing the layout of the ship and the disposition of the team.

Warden had almost finished clearing the starboard cargo bay when Fletcher got contact. She steamed into a shuttle bay on an upper deck and came under immediate fire from a dozen Deathless troopers. Campbell was already moving to provide support, but Fletcher would be on her own for the moment; Warden certainly couldn't get there himself. He checked the feed from her suit and saw her charge into the ambush, head on.

Fletcher fired her heavy machine gun on full auto as she closed the distance with the enemy squad that was sheltering behind a pile of crates. That forced their heads down – big mistake. She dropped the weapon as she leapt over the crates, crashing down amongst the middle group. A Rupert in scout armour fired his pistol ineffectually into her chest, the rounds pinging from it like stones skimming across an icy lake. Fletcher grabbed his head with both of her massive gauntlets and twisted viciously, snapping the neck as the synthetic muscle fibres in her power armour augmented the already considerable strength of her clone.

Bereft of a user, the Rupert's power armour went limp. There was a spray of gore as the neck tore and Fletcher wrenched the officer's head free, holding it in one clawed gauntlet and the body in the other.

She roared then hurled the body at the group on the left. They scattered like startled birds, and she turned to the other group. Using the helmeted head as an improvised club, she laid about them, gore spraying across the terrified Deathless soldiers. Each blow crushed another skull or caved in a chest.

Bloody hell, thought Warden, *Marine Fletcher might be in need of some serious anger management counselling.* Those poor buggers were going to wake up screaming if they redeployed, he was sure. He switched off the feed, not a little disturbed but confident that she had it all in hand. Maybe she was spending too much time with Marine X, listening to his theories on psychological warfare, and Warden made a mental note to discuss it with Milton.

Warden flicked away from Fletcher's video feed then spent a few minutes rummaging around the docking bay, flagging it as a hot zone for equipment to be pilfered before jogging off to help the others. Campbell and her team had done an excellent job leading the assault and most of the kills were down to them. Even where they weren't solely responsible, they had acted as bullet sponges to allow their colleagues to flank the Deathless and mop them up.

The Marines had moved with great speed and aggression and, in only a short time, they had taken a solid hold on the ship. They worked back, clearing any Deathless soldiers they had missed, then Warden set Campbell and her team to begin collecting anything of value. Their power armour meant carrying a crate of rifles was a one-person job rather than a team effort. The rest of the troop split up, making sure every room was cleared and setting charges in vital areas.

As each charge was set, they appeared on the tactical map in the HUD. They had identified the main power plant, engines and bridge, and they mined them all. It might not be enough to destroy the ship, but they would surely render it inoperable for an extended period. There were large fabrication plants concealed within the hull, and the configuration of the ship was almost entirely based around turning raw material into supplies and new fabrication plants. It was a factory, in other words, designed solely to act as a base on an alien world, churning out base-building kits and self-assembling forts.

Most of the troop had found something to take with them – small arms, ammunition, grenades and a lot of potential intelligence. They had so much loot, in fact, that Warden wasn't sure they'd be able to get it all out.

Ten joined them as they were piling their ill-gotten gains below the loading ramp.

"I've arranged the parting gift for our guests, sir, as ordered."

"Noted. Flagged on the tactical map?"

"Of course, sir. All ship-shape and Bristol fashion. Anything else I could be doing now?"

"Do you think there are stragglers out there?" Warden asked, gesturing at the ruined buildings near the gate and the relatively intact areas further away from it.

"Nah, I think they mostly stuck their heads up, like meerkats. Suicidal, meerkats. I'm pretty sure we got them all."

Warden glanced up at him, then back at the growing pile of loot.

"We need vehicles, Marine X. I'm loathe to leave behind anything we could use and even though we lost people at the mine, the rovers aren't big enough to let us take this lot."

Ten eyed the pile of gear. "There's some stuff in that building over there we should grab as well. There were a bunch of head sheds in there having a nice chat about their plans for New Bristol. I grabbed the obvious bits and pieces, but there might be more in there you'll want. I didn't bring the building down, either, just for you, sir."

"Well, that's very generous of you, Ten. Now, you've seen more of this place than we have. Any promising vehicles I might want to know about?"

Ten grinned. "I think I may have seen a couple worth pinching, sir. If I could borrow a couple of techs and a few drivers?"

Warden raised an eyebrow at that. "If you can get me proper vehicles, Ten, you can take all the techs and Marines you need." He ran that back in his mind and then amended it. "Within reason. All the Marines, within reason."

Ten winked at him as he walked off to pick a team. "Right you are, sir."

27

The Marines' assault on the Deathless base had played out on a feed from a high-altitude airship. Everyone had wanted to watch the attack, but Priscilla had put her foot down and refused all suggestions that a low-altitude drone should be deployed.

"Because I don't want to watch the Marines dying," she'd said in frustration when someone had pointed out, again, how easy it would be to get a micro-drone into position. "Don't ask again, or you're off the team. Clear?"

After that, nobody had mentioned it, but the whole team had still been glued to the low-res images coming off the high-altitude airship, watching until the Marines left the enemy base in their convoy of captured vehicles.

"That's enough for now," Priscilla had said, shutting off the feed. "Finish your sweeps, log your reports and then we'll call it a day."

A few days later, the Ashton Blues launched the first of a new type of unpowered drone, a glider dreamt up by Jenny to augment the slow-moving airships they'd been using for far-field observation. The ultra-light gliders were equipped with a cutting-edge camera system allowing them to see further than the other flyers.

"They're based on designs from Sol," explained Jenny as she

outlined her ideas. "The wings are photovoltaic membranes stiffened with carbon fibre rods, the camera uses next-gen metalenses to minimise weight and the processor can run the image recognition AI, so if the glider flies over something that isn't natural, it'll trigger an alert here at base."

Priscilla was impressed and she said so. She had wondered how Jenny had got bandwidth on the wormhole communicator to get new designs from Earth, but then she decided that she didn't really care, as long as they worked.

"The basic component designs are from Earth," Jenny had continued, "but we combined them here and used the AI to change the designs so that the parts fit our requirements." Jenny had shrugged, as if AI-designed ultra-gliders were a normal part of everyday life. "Then we sent the designs to the fabricators, churned out the parts and slotted them together."

Corporal Wilson had been impressed as well, especially after he'd watched the first ultra-glider being towed into the air by one of the larger long-range drones. The two drones had disappeared into the afternoon sky, climbing quickly until the glider detached and the powered drone returned to base.

Now the teams were reviewing the images that the ultra-gliders were producing, checking for errors or biases in the AI's programming and weeding out false positives. The images were excellent, far better than those produced by the cameras in the airships, but still not as good as the low-flying micro-drones.

"I don't like the look of that," muttered Priscilla as she looked over Luke's shoulder at a huge shape on the screen. "What is it?"

"No idea," replied Luke, fiddling with the image controls to try to resolve the details.

"Let's get a long-range drone out there to take a close look," said Priscilla.

"Already despatched. Should be there in," Luke paused to consult a timer on his data slate, "about twenty minutes."

"Bring it up on the Grid," said Priscilla, "and let's see what's going on."

Luke flicked at his controls, transferring the live feed from the ultra-glider to the main screens. The huge shape was looked too regular to be a simple hill but they couldn't make out the details. Priscilla could feel the hairs on the back of her neck rising as she waited for more information. In the corner of the screen, a map of the area showed the image in relation to Ashton. A red dot and a thin line marked the approach of the nearest long-range drone that Luke had re-tasked to investigate the target.

Twenty minutes dragged slowly past as the drone flew over the near featureless terrain. Priscilla peered at the main screen, her unease growing as the drone inched its way along the flightpath. As the timer ticked down, a shiver ran down her back and she shook her head.

"How high is the drone?"

"Er, about fifteen hundred metres, boss," said Luke, frowning at her tone. Priscilla was quiet for a moment.

"Take it higher," she said suddenly, "much higher, up to its operating ceiling."

"Why? Nobody'll see it at fifteen —" then saw Priscilla's face and gulped. "Taking it higher," he said, hands flicking at the controls.

The rest of the room had fallen quiet as the teams watched the drone's progress across the landscape.

"I'll need to divert course to reach altitude before we reach the target, so it'll take longer to get the new images," said Luke, pointing out an obvious downside.

"Just do it," snapped Priscilla, now thoroughly spooked but not sure what was worrying her. She felt a twinge of guilt. Luke wasn't being patronising, he was responsibly raising a potential problem with her. She'd have to apologise later, which would suck but would be the right thing to do.

Luke worked silently, altering the drone's flight path to give it time to reach its maximum altitude before it flew over the target. It soared higher and higher, the ground dropping away as Luke pushed the drone's motors to their limit. As it passed ninety per cent of its operational limit, progress slowed.

"That's it, four thousand metres, can't go any higher." He glanced at Priscilla. "Okay to fly over the target?"

Priscilla nodded and together they watched the drone level out and head towards the shape. It made just one pass, shooting hi-res video, and nobody said a word as the feed played on the main screen.

"I think we have a problem," said Priscilla.

28

"Let's come to order, ladies and gentlemen," said Denmead when the last of the councillors had arrived. The temporary space they had been using for meetings in Fort Widley had started to take on the appearance of a more permanent chamber. Most recently, a coffee machine had appeared in a nook that had been carved specifically for the purpose.

"This is an update meeting only," said Denmead, "so that we can apprise you all of the latest discoveries."

"What do you mean by an 'update meeting'?" asked Councillor Louise Dunbar, face schooled to the bland expression for which she was well known. "Are we not to discuss the situation as well?"

"Update and discuss, yes, but there's a briefing pack you'll want to absorb in full before we make any decisions."

"A briefing pack? I don't believe I've received anything," said Councillor Dunbar, poking at her tablet.

"The pack will be with you later this evening," said Johnson, Denmead's aide, "but this is sufficiently important that the issue can't wait."

"The micro drones have ranged far and wide," said Denmead, launching into the next part of her presentation before anyone could object further, "and the children have been prototyping a new type of ultra-lightweight glider with an enhanced camera lens system designed for high-altitude, long-range imaging. The first versions flew yesterday morning. They're solar powered, completely autonomous and very simple to make."

"We all know this, Governor," said Smith. "It's very impressive, but so what?"

"Since noon yesterday," Denmead continued, ignoring Smith's interruption, "when the first gliders passed beyond the areas covered by the previous generation of drones, our AIs have been scanning the images looking for anything of interest. Unfortunately, they found this," she said, flicking an image onto the big screen at the end of the room.

"As you can see, this image shows an object that is clearly not natural and the AI directing the drones sent two more to the area to build up a detailed picture."

The image changed, jumping from a blurry, low-resolution image to a hi-res version of the same thing.

"That looks like a habitat," said Grimes, leaning close to inspect the image, "and some sort of manufacturing or production plant."

"Are those chimneys?" asked Smith.

"That bit looks like a defensive wall with gun turrets," said Councillor Armstrong said, her brow furrowed as she squinted at the image.

"And this definitely isn't one of ours?" asked Grimes, leaning back in his seat, his face now set in a grim expression. "I mean, I don't remember building anything like this, but maybe one of you..." he fell silent as he looked around the table. It was an absurd suggestion and he knew it.

"It's about eight hundred kilometres to the south-west," said Johnson, "well beyond the area we've colonised and far outside even the outer limits where we've constructed solar farms, storage facilities or hydroponic farms. Our development plan won't have us putting anything out that far from Ashton for at least fifteen years, and that assumes a consistent level of success and continued population growth."

"And you'll note that the architecture is definitely not similar to our own designs. The domes, we think, are purely decorative, affectations maybe, or throwbacks to their collective history. Either way, this is clearly a Russian-influenced settlement built by the Deathless," added Denmead.

There was a moment of shocked silence as the councillors absorbed the news, then the questions began, all at once.

"What do we do?"

"How many people?"

"When was it built?"

"How big is it?"

"How do we destroy it?"

Denmead held up her hand and gradually the room fell silent.

"Let me put the scale up on the image to give you an idea," she said, tapping at her tablet. "At just over two thousand metres long and almost a thousand metres wide, this is by far the largest structure on the planet."

"It's the largest surface structure within several dozen light years," muttered Grimes, impressed despite the obvious scale of the threat.

"Quite," said Denmead, "and in some places, it is a hundred metres tall. We have no way to know how far it extends beneath the surface, but even if half of it is given over to manufacturing and food production, there's still enough volume within the walls to hold fifty to a hundred thousand people."

"How could they possibly have built this without us noticing?" asked Councillor Armstrong, her tone ratcheting steadily towards 'very angry'.

"Ah. I think perhaps you mean 'Whose incompetence allowed this to go unnoticed?', Councillor? As it happens, this city has been built in an area that wasn't routinely covered by our satellites. After all, there's no need to monitor areas that aren't populated," Denmead retorted.

"The last flyover was about eighteen months ago and, yes, we've checked. It wasn't there then, so the whole thing is less than eighteen months old. Whenever they started, to build so much so quickly speaks of an impressive amount of organisation and an astonishing quantity of material delivered right under our noses and through our orbital cordon without detection."

That shook them. Nobody wanted to consider the implications of a hostile nation slipping through their defences to build a city in secret.

"So this could have appeared any time in the last eighteen months, and they've just been sitting there all this time?" Councillor Stoat asked, incredulously.

"Yes, Councillor. With the information we have, that's all we can be certain of. It seems likely to me that they have only arrived much more recently, though. The problem is, how did they build such an installation so quickly? How could they do it at all? We have no sure way of knowing, at this point," Denmead said.

"Is it populated?" Grimes asked.

Denmead hesitated, then nodded. "We think so. Electromagnetic emissions suggest active communications from the inside. They're encrypted, obviously, so we can't know what they're saying, but it appears to be a near continuous stream of activity. There's some activity outside the structure – there's a road leading to the nearby mountains where it seems they've been mining or quarrying for something – but it's impossible to say how many people might be inside."

"So it could be empty?" Councillor Dunbar asked. "It could be a simple automated facility, one that's entirely devoid of life?"

"It's warm," said Johnson, "and these structures here look like cloning facilities, so even if it were empty a few months ago, it isn't now. The scale of these facilities suggests an output of maybe thirty clones a week, and our analysis suggests there may be more than a dozen of them, although there could be far more underground that we can't see. If they've been running for a month, then we could be looking at a population of one to three thousand. Unfortunately, since we don't know how long they've been there or how many cloning bays they have..." He trailed off without finishing the sentence, but the logical conclusion was obvious.

The councillors groaned.

"But they could just be banking blank clones," Smith pointed out, "setting them aside for a mass colonisation. They haven't necessarily deployed colonists to them."

That hope was thin, and they all knew it. Body banks were commonly used throughout the populated solar systems, but even a large city would hold only enough to cope with natural deaths which, given the advanced nature of the available medicine tended to be few and far between. No one, not the British, not the Chinese or the Japanese, stockpiled huge numbers of clones on the off chance they would want them later. After all, they required upkeep; you couldn't just stick them in a freezer and defrost them four years later after a natural disaster.

"So we're back to considering our response to the further invasion of our colony," said Councillor Stoat, "and I say we wipe the Deathless from the face of our planet." There was a chorus of nods from around the table, although not all the councillors were in favour. "We have the prior claim, we're longer established, and our colony is recognised by interstellar law," he went on, "and they attacked us. Nobody would object. It would be self-defence."

"And what would you propose?" Denmead asked, playing devil's advocate.

"A nuclear strike, obviously," said Stoat promptly to a round of varied agreement and horror. "As soon as Vice Admiral Staines arrives, this council should order him to bombard them from orbit. He'll have the arsenal to do it. One or two fusion warheads dropped into that valley would destroy the settlement entirely and preserve our safety."

There was immediate uproar from the council as calls and shouts erupted across the chamber. Denmead held up her hand for silence then banged it on the table when nobody took any notice of her.

"Thank you for your opinions," she said loudly. "Captain Atticus and I have already discussed these options, and discarded them on good grounds."

"You take a great deal on your shoulders, Governor," said Stoat sharply, "but this is something for the council to decide upon since it affects every person in this colony."

"We should at least hear the reasons," said Grimes in a conciliatory tone. Lots of nodding around the table.

"Of course," said Denmead, "and really it's very simple. While launching such a strike would, indeed, obliterate the contents of the valley, it would not resolve the larger war. We would have irradiated a large part of our own planet, but that would not prevent the Deathless from setting up a colony elsewhere or landing further settlers, including military expeditions. Which, we can assume, they would immediately protect with anti-ballistic missile systems.

"In addition, the settlers living in that city are people. Their soldiers might wage war on us, an unjust, unprovoked, illegal war, but that doesn't give us carte blanche to do as we please."

"It's a bit more than an unprovoked war," snapped Stoat. "They've bombed our city, murdered our civilians and destroyed our facilities."

"Do you think they would think twice before nuking us?" demanded Smith.

"They haven't nuked us," pointed out Johnson reasonably, "and the bombardments have focussed on our governmental and military structures, such as they are."

"I can't believe you're defending them," said Stoat, horrified and appalled. "They're alien scum who deserve to be eradicated!"

"Dammit," snapped Denmead, slapping her hand on the table again. "They're still people, and we share a common ancestry, regardless of how they might have diverged since their Ark left Sol."

Stoat looked like he was about to say something but Denmead, no longer in the mood for debate, powered on.

"Even if the nuclear option were morally defensible, which it isn't," she continued, "there are still two insurmountable problems. Firstly, any plan that involves the use of WMDs needs approval from the local military command, which is Captain Atticus. I have to tell you that he has already stated that he will be unable to approve any such action under his current rules of engagement unless or until there is a very considerable escalation in hostilities.

"Secondly, and more important from a strategic position, we have no information whatsoever about the enemy's other cities or their true capabilities. A nuclear attack would invite a nuclear response and our only opportunity for survival would be to destroy the Deathless utterly. As we neither know what other facilities they have on the planet nor what they might have in orbit or in transit, we cannot launch a pre-emptive strike, since to do so would be to guarantee our own destruction."

Denmead paused to allow this to sink in before continuing more calmly.

"For now, our only option is to continue the fight against the conventional forces. Captain Atticus is already altering his plans to allow for the impact of this city but, from a civilian perspective, we have to get used to sharing our planet."

There was a degree of angry muttering from around the table.

"Sooner or later, we'll need a diplomatic solution," Denmead went on, pausing as the councillors mumbled angrily again. "Every battle is a prelude to negotiation and peace."

Smith snorted. "But what sort of peace?" he muttered, shaking his head.

"And what sort of battle?" asked Grimes.

"Quite," said Denmead, looking around at her councillors. Then she nodded and stood. "The full briefing pack will be with you this evening, and we can discuss this situation again tomorrow."

Then she strode from the room, Johnson hurrying behind, leaving the councillors to discuss and squabble amongst themselves.

29

Warden had made them follow a roundabout path, purposefully guiding the convoy through a dust storm to conceal their route and prevent the Deathless from following them as they returned to Fort Widley. It had added hours to their journey, but Warden had thought it better to be cautious – they had already pushed their luck a long, long way.

Ten had found two Deathless APCs in a garage at the southern end of the Deathless base. They had, like the rest of the enemy's kit, turned out to be robust and well-suited to their purpose. They were also gigantic, with eight wheels and space for a whole platoon, support personnel, powered armour and heavy weapons.

Warden had crammed them full of kit pilfered from the enemy mothership then rifled through the rest of the garage and taken all the light patrol trucks they could find. They'd even found an ambulance, which Milton had insisted that they take.

When they finally reached Fort Widley and drove into the huge cavern that acted as the main garage, they found Captain Atticus and a company of the newly minted Militia of Bristol waiting for them.

"Just wanted to be sure, Lieutenant," said Atticus as he led Warden, Milton and Marine X to the command room.

"Er, have you changed, sir?" asked Warden, frowning at Captain Atticus as they walked. "You seem different, somehow."

"New clone, Lieutenant," said Atticus airily, as if being killed and redeployed were hardly worth mentioning. "You're not the only one who's seen a bit of action over the last twenty-four hours."

Warden nodded, eyebrows raised, but before he could ask more questions, the party reached the command room. Someone had rigged a load more monitors, and they were showing live images of the Deathless base, a direct feed from the small swarm of micro-drones the techs had left behind.

"There's incoming," said Johnson, Governor Denmead's aide, who had been watching the enemy ship as it entered orbit. "Two dropships, we think, heading for the base and due to land in a few minutes."

Ten grinned, playing with a remote control, almost bursting with excitement.

"You were successful, Lieutenant?" asked Governor Denmead, although the very presence of the Marines pretty much answered the question.

"Mostly, ma'am, although we took casualties at the quarry, I'm sorry to say."

Atticus nodded grimly as Warden ran through the pertinent events.

"We can talk about that later, Tom," said Atticus, "your casualties are already being redeployed. I'm not sure what more you could have done."

"Dropships approaching the base," said Johnson, leaning forward in his seat. The others peered at the monitors until, suddenly, three black shapes appeared as if by magic in the micro-drones' fields of view.

"Two dropships, Johnson?" asked Denmead, eyebrow raised.

"Or maybe three, Governor," conceded Johnson, "the resolution isn't all that good on the near-space sensors."

"You brought back two Deathless APCs, Lieutenant. Anything else?" asked Atticus as the dropships slowed as they neared the base.

"Small arms, munitions, armour, vehicles. No game changers, I'm afraid, but plenty of useful kit. We do have some potential intelligence finds that might be worth looking at if we can spare someone."

"And we left them a couple of surprises, sir," said Ten, still playing with his remote trigger.

"Hmm," said Atticus, eyeing him suspiciously. He turned to the techs. "Can we zoom in on the dropships? I want to see what happens when they land."

Robinson flicked at the controls, and the monitors switched to showing larger views of the three dropships as they closed in on the base.

"They'll be down in about thirty seconds," said Robinson, "they're well below the micro-drones now."

The room was silent as the dropships completed their descent, coming to rest inside the base, all neatly lined up. The ramps dropped, and scores of Deathless disembarked, dashing clear of their transports as if afraid they might be toxic.

"Looks like they've got the hang of rapid deployment," said Ten, grudging respect heavy in his voice, "but they're a few hours too late to do any good."

"Zoom in there," said Atticus, pointing at a clump of figures that were clearly inspecting the damage to the mothership. The view jumped down, not far enough to read facial expressions but far enough to show body language. "They don't look too happy, do they?" asked Atticus rhetorically as the clones, clearly officers, wandered around the base inside their protective cordon of troops. One, high-ranking maybe, kept pointing at things, sending his troops scurrying hither and thither.

Then he turned to face the mothership and gestured angrily. A squad of the rank and file lizardmen clones disappeared into the giant ship, and most of the officers followed a few seconds later. The ones left outside, maybe feeling a little exposed and unwilling to take more risks than were strictly necessary, hunkered down at the edge of the spaceship and pulled their cordon of troops a little more tightly around them.

"Like a child with a comfort blanket," muttered Warden.

"And about as dangerous," murmured Ten, so quiet that only Milton heard. She shot him a look, and he grinned expansively, all teeth.

"I think that's about as good as it's likely to get, Lieutenant," said Atticus.

"Very good, sir. Let's pull the view back a little so we can see the whole base again." He paused while the techs adjusted the view. "And Happy Christmas!" He activated an icon on his HUD. There was a pause, a few heartbeats only, but long enough that Warden wondered if it had worked.

Then the mothership was rocked by a series of explosions, in several locations near the engines and around the hull. Bright flashes could be seen through viewing ports around the ship. A huge gout of flame shot out from the open boarding ramp, hurling debris into the back of the troops waiting nearby. A lone figure stumbled out of the ship, raised its hand as if to signal for help then collapsed.

There was a muted murmur of appreciation from the people in the command centre.

"Well done, Lieutenant," said Atticus, nodding to Warden.

The troops who had set themselves up behind the convenient arc of cover in front of the boarding ramp began to stand and turn towards the ship.

"One second, sir," said Warden, activating another icon in his HUD. Explosives, concealed in the conveniently positioned crates that the Deathless had been using as cover, detonated, scything down the troops nearest the ship.

"Even better," said Denmead to general agreement.

"If I may, sir?" said Ten, waggling his own trigger.

"Very well, Marine X," said Warden, "but walk us through it, first, will you?"

"Of course, sir," said Ten, laying his hand on the tech's shoulder, "just zoom in there on that bit, the square building. That's an armoury, sunk about a metre into the rock. Nice little job, very tidy. They even put a good, solid roof on it so that you can't drop any nasty surprises in from above. As you can see, it's a beautiful location, with pleasant views across the landing zone and handily located near the front gate. A mid-sized property that clearly owes its design to the Brutalist movement of the mid-twentieth century."

Warden cleared his throat.

"Right, yes, sorry," said Ten, "turns out they store plastic explosive in big boxes, just like the ones we use. All you need is a handful of detonators and a remote control," he said, pressing the button on the trigger, "and it's bonfire night all over again."

"Are you sure, Marine X?" said Warden as the video feed repeatedly showed nothing of interest.

"Little warm-up first, sir," said Ten, "about now..."

Part of the southern wall of the armoury blew out, scattering foamcrete across the base.

"Now we build a little," muttered Ten, waving his hands like a conductor as more explosions tore at the wall of the armoury, "leaving the rear and side walls intact so that the finale is extra special."

More explosions rocked the building, and then there was a colossal blast that shattered much of the roof and blew out the southern wall completely. For a moment the feed was disrupted as the drone rode the blast wave, camera pointing erratically at the sky. Then everything settled, and the drone returned to station.

"Bloody hell," muttered Warden quietly, unconsciously leaning forward to get a better view.

The southern wall of the armoury had gone, blown to smithereens, and the roof had collapsed. The other three walls mostly stood intact but the area south of the armoury and two of the dropships had been less fortunate.

"It's all about shaping the blast," said Ten, enjoying his moment in the spotlight. "You just have to direct it to where it'll do the most good. A bit of plastic on the south wall to weaken it, then when the main charge goes off, attached to some other munitions for added 'oomph' of course, the blast heads south through the damaged wall, et voila! Maximum damage, minimum effort. A whole urban zone, ready for gentrification and completely cleared of infestation by unwanted parasites."

The command centre was quiet as everyone inspected the feed. A triangle of buildings extending from the armoury out across the base and past the dropships had been flattened. Most of the hastily erected buildings weren't all that resilient, with a few notable exceptions such as the wall and the armouries. One of the dropships had been flipped end over and was now resting upside down in a large pile of rubble, all that remained of a cluster of buildings.

A second dropship had been punched to one side and split almost in half by the blast. Useful for spare parts, maybe, but its flying days were over.

"Thank you, Marine X," said Warden weakly, still trying to understand the sheer quantity of damage done to the base. "I think that'll be all for now."

"Of course, sir, and thanks. I think this means I've won my bet with Sergeant Milton. She'll be chuffed." Ten saluted and left, sauntering out of the command room like he owned the place.

Nobody said anything for a few moments.

"Well," said Atticus brightly, "I would say that the enemy's operational capabilities with respect to this base had been severely, if not fatally, impaired." There was a murmured chorus of agreement. "The next step is to deny the enemy the ability to land fresh troops or to establish a new base. Or repair this one," said the captain, "although I think that's likely to be tricky."

"And how do we do that, Captain?" asked Governor Denmead, although she already had a pretty good idea of the answer.

"Vice Admiral Staines is only a few hours away. By this evening, we'll have as much strength as we're ever likely to get. The time for half-measures is over."

"Half-measures?" muttered Johnson, slightly surprised.

"Our next move is a direct assault on the three ships of the Deathless fleet," continued Atticus, ignoring Johnson completely. "Vice Admiral Staines doesn't have the ships to guarantee victory in a fair fight so we won't be offering one. Instead, the Marines of A and B

Troops will take the dropships and rendezvous with Staines aboard HMS *Iron Duke*. We'll bolster their numbers with volunteers from the militia. The ideal outcome is the capture of all three ships, rather than their outright destruction, but they'll be scuttled if necessary."

Governor Denmead frowned and looked distinctly disturbed.

"You want to include the militia in this? Isn't that a bit, well, risky? They don't have any training or experience in boarding ships. They're not well-trained professionals."

"True, but neither, it seems, are the Deathless," said Atticus, "so extra bodies might make a significant difference. We'll be using boarding pods, the Marines will lead, and we'll only take volunteers. This isn't an operation for the unwilling."

"It still sounds very risky," said Denmead doubtfully.

"And it is, Governor, it is," said Captain Atticus, "but I really don't think we have any alternatives."

30

The trip into orbit to dock with HMS *Iron Duke* was gruelling, to say the least. Goodwin punched the dropship through the atmosphere at the upper limit of the Marines' tolerance to acceleration. Several, all wearing the standard issue clones, blacked out and didn't come round until they were in free-fall.

The G-force was brutal because it was, in Goodwin's words, "Better to burn out than be blown to smithereens by a Deathless warship as we leave the atmosphere." Warden didn't think that had quite the rhythm she was going for, but he couldn't fault her logic.

Vice Admiral Staines was similarly cautious. After deploying scores of drones to monitor the enemy, Staines's fleet, if you could call it that, had stayed firmly on the opposite side of the planet, well away from the Deathless ships. The enemy had made no move to engage, yet, but best practice called for launches to be done in the fastest manner possible to minimise the chances of a vital ship being destroyed by the enemy.

And it was the ships that were important in this situation. Losing the Marines would be inconvenient, but they could be replaced in *Iron Duke*'s clone bays. Dropships, command shuttles and cargo landers were much harder to build and took a lot longer to make than a new clone. Losing a ship might be disastrous.

Warden and A Troop had no choice but to endure a punishing ascent into the heavens. At least the troop was back to a full complement of Marines, and with some upgrades to boot. Corporal Green, Lance Corporal Long and Marines McGee, Headley and Scott had all been redeployed in newly captured ogre clones and had been issued the hideously bright yellow power armour to go with them. Each carried a huge combat shotgun, courtesy of the raid on the Deathless mothership base.

The approach to Vice Admiral Staines's flagship had got a lot more comfortable once the dropships had reached orbit. In the deathly quiet of space, the dropships manoeuvred gently, closing slowly on the frigate. Then a series of interlocking doors opened to allow them access. Arms reached out from the deck to grab the dropships and pull them down, then the outer door closed and the bay repressurised, gouts of atmosphere filling the space.

Finally, the inner doors opened, and the deck slid into the operations bay beyond the airlock, which closed behind them. The elaborate procedure allowed the operations bay to function while the airlocks were cycling ships into, or out of, the frigate. Once the atmosphere pressurised, the engineering crews could move around the bay without wearing suits.

Fighter tubes worked the same way; each flyer sat on an electric sled during maintenance and rearming. The pilot would climb into the cockpit, the fighter would be driven into a launch tube then the airlock shut behind them and a low-energy railgun mechanism would accelerate them away from the parent ship.

The moment the dropship stopped moving, Warden unbuckled his harness and stood up, rolling his neck. He felt like he'd been hit by a stampede but this was no time for luxuries like a quiet moment to himself.

"Let's go," he said, clapping his hands. "I want everyone ready for action inside an hour, so make sure your gear is in order and resupply from *Iron Duke*'s quartermaster if you need to. Milton, you're with me, we're wanted in Vice Admiral Staines's war room."

"You've all seen the plan," said Staines, "so what's the consensus, ladies and gentlemen? Can it be done?"

"I can't comment on the orbital mechanics, sir, but the boarding action looks solid, so yes, I think we can make it work," said Warden.

Vice Admiral Staines looked at Lieutenant Hayes, who nodded. "I agree with Warden, sir. We can get it done."

"Midshipman Carruthers?" he asked the junior officer who would be running the boarding team from HMS *Iron Duke*.

"We're ready to go, sir. The schedule leaves no room for error, and it'll be uncomfortable for the crew but, mechanically, it's doable."

"And you, Sergeant Adams? Is your team ready?"

Adams held his hand up. "I'm not really a sergeant. I look after water filtration for the hydroponic systems; I'm not qualified for this. We've brought the best of our people, and we've all fought against the Deathless, but we're not soldiers. We'll go wherever you need us, but I'm not going to pretend I can contribute to this discussion."

"I've seen the reports from Lieutenant Hayes," said Staines, "and I think you've earned the rank. You've seen more real combat than many of the people under my command. You may not have the training, but you're battle-tested in a way that can't be accomplished in any simulation, and you've earned my respect. I'm sure you have the respect of everyone here."

Blushing profusely, Adams said, "Thank you, Vice Admiral Staines, you can rely on us, we won't let you down."

"Very good. Then I suggest you all get back to your teams and get kitted out. There's no time to train your people on power armour, Sergeant Adams, but we do have plenty of standard body armour you can use. As your role is to defend the breaches, it won't matter if your mobility is a little restricted."

"Thank you, sir. I'm sure we'll cope. We haven't had much body armour in Ashton, so that sounds bloody luxurious."

"Warden, Hayes, we do have power armour for your teams. We're primarily charged with exploration and survey duties, but the quartermaster keeps our supplies of armaments and armour at combat readiness. As such, we have plenty of spares in the event we need to deploy Marines. Unfortunately, the Nelson class doesn't have the fastest cloning pods, so there isn't time to deploy more of your colleagues for this action."

"Quite all right, sir. We're getting used to making do. Having power armour is a massive step up from our previous position."

"Good," said Staines, checking the time, "then let's get to work. I want you ready for boarding pod launch in no more than forty-five minutes. Dismissed."

31

"The basic problem," said Vice Admiral Staines as he sat in his command chair, "is that we're so damned short of resources." He drummed his fingers on the arm of his chair as he stared at a tactical plan of the planet and the enemy fleet.

HMS *Iron Duke* had a small contingent of combat drones, twelve all told in various configurations. *Albion* carried another six, making eighteen in total, all basically missile delivery platforms or anti-fighter craft fitted with short-range cannons. None of them were suitable for the type of ship-to-ship combat that Staines's plan anticipated.

"But we're not here to destroy the enemy," Staines said to the bridge in general, elaborating on his plan, "we just want to take their ships and kill their crews, so it's less about what we've got and more about how we use it."

He pulled up a live feed from the micro-drones that were shadowing the enemy fleet. They had named the three enemy vessels *Moscow*, *Omsk* and *Bratsk*. Staines had never heard of Bratsk but he had asked the bridge crew for names and those were the ones they had picked. Midshipmen Washman and Barnaby seemed to find the name Bratsk amusing, for some obscure reason. Well, if it improved morale then it was fine with him.

Staines stared at the feed. They were outnumbered and outgunned, but Warden's assessment of the Deathless ground troops was not complimentary. If the crews of their warships were similarly inexperienced, there was a chance this plan could work.

"This plan is risky and relies on our enemy's relative inexperience in space combat," continued Staines, "but we know very little about them and they might spot our trap."

It had been several years since Vice Admiral Staines had commanded ships in combat and that had been against a handful of small pirate vessels. Today's situation was far more serious with a lot more at stake.

"We're ready, Admiral," came a message from Warden.

"Understood. Happy hunting, Lieutenant." Staines signalled Midshipman Washman. "Let's get started. Get us in position, prepare to launch the pods in sixty seconds."

"Aye, sir," said Washman, sounding the manoeuvre klaxon and triggering the timer on the first engine burn, "three-second low-power burn, firing in fifteen seconds."

They watched the timer countdown to zero and then felt the acceleration as the ship adjusted its position relative to the planet.

"Burn successful, ready to launch pods," announced Washman. Staines looked at his monitors, checking that all was in order, then he nodded to his executive officer, Lieutenant-Commander Cohen.

"Launch pods," said Cohen, "standby for the second manoeuvre, ten-second mid-power burn followed by thirty-second high-power. Mark!"

Washman hit the control and the burn began again, much stronger and longer this time. After ten seconds there was a brief pause as the attitude thrusters reoriented the ship then the main engines fired. This time they all felt the pain, pushed into their seats by the acceleration.

"Burn successful, new orbit and direction achieved. We're at ninety-eight percent of the target velocity, two-second correction on low-power in fifteen seconds," announced Cohen. There was a pause and then another brief burst of acceleration. "Orbit achieved, engines at standby."

"Good, thank you, gentlemen," said Staines. "Let's put the forward view on the main monitors and see what might lie ahead."

The monitor switched to show a tactical view of the space ahead of *Iron Duke*. The boarding pods and the garbage pods that Staines had ordered to be jettisoned at the same time were picked out in bright blue, their trajectories shown in dotted blue lines. The current orbits of the three enemy vessels were shown in red with *Iron Duke*'s in green, a great looping swirl far outside the orbits of the other ships.

"That looks good," said Staines. Littering the orbit of inhabited planets with material that would normally be recycled was very bad practice but, from a distance, the garbage and boarding pods looked similar enough that an incautious enemy might ignore them completely.

Relying on your opponent's incompetence was a gamble, a big one. But it wasn't Staines's only move and now it was time for the next one.

"Ready weapons, Mr Cohen, everything we have. Target the lead ship," said Staines, "prepare to fire on my command."

This was the part of the plan about which Warden had expressed concern, since it presented a high risk to *Iron Duke* and her crew. Staines had pointed out that the men and women under his command were honour-bound to face danger in the performance of their duties and that, in this case, the Marines' safety was vital to the plan's success.

Warden wasn't at all happy and he had frowned deeply as Staines had outlined the plan. Warden had objected but didn't have a better suggestion, and as Staines was the vice admiral around here, he had concluded that it was his call and had politely, but firmly, made sure the junior officers understood that.

"The boarding action is our best bet," Staines had said, "so our concern is to maximise the likelihood of success." They had all agreed that the enemy would find a troop of irate Marines far more difficult to handle than any torpedo or railgun attack.

"Sir? Even when they come around the planet, they'll be too far away for our weapons to be effective. An attack would leave us horribly exposed," hissed Cohen.

"Yes, XO, but that's the idea. We'll fire early, expose ourselves, and make them focus on *Iron Duke*." He realised that he should probably have included the XO in the briefing and made a mental note not to exclude him again, however green he was. "If we were looking to defeat them with conventional torpedoes and railgun ablation, we would lurk out of sight and hope they didn't spot us. As it is, we don't want to destroy their ships."

"I'm sorry, sir, I don't understand."

Staines hid his frustration. The XO was young and hadn't seen combat yet. This was his first command position and he wasn't seeing the bigger picture.

"The Marines will capture the enemy ships, Cohen. We're only here to distract the enemy."

Cohen nodded, and it looked like he now understood.

Staines had discussed the options with Bonneville. They had done all they could to protect the colony, but after Captain Atticus and General Bonneville had explained their concerns about the potential population and economy of the Deathless, they had agreed that their priority was to gain intelligence. They needed to know more about the Deathless.

"And if you can capture a ship while you're at it, Will," Bonneville had said, "that would make life rather easier."

"We'll see what we can do," Staines had said, a little testily, but the general had been right. If they captured even one ship, especially a warship, it would be a significant coup. They could grow clones to crew it and have naval personnel deployed in little more than a week – far faster than conventional reinforcements might reach them.

Staines had requested reinforcements, as had General Bonneville, who was pressing the case for a significant commitment of warships with his counterparts at the admiralty right now. But Staines knew where the closest ships were and even those would take a long time to reach New Bristol, too long to make a difference to this encounter.

No, they had to take the fight to the enemy and capture their ships, not simply destroy them. If the boarding action failed and the Marines couldn't scuttle the vessels, Staines would switch tactics and engage in straight up ship-to-ship combat.

But Staines wasn't confident they could win that sort of action if all three Deathless vessels were still operational. His enemy had three ships, and they could only guess at their configuration. The sheer size of *Moscow* suggested it was an important capital ship, at least equivalent to a destroyer and very much more capable than his frigate.

The two smaller ships, *Omsk* and *Bratsk*, were harder to read. They were similar in size to his own support ships but that didn't tell them very much.

The biggest difference between their fleets was that the Deathless were following a long-established plan. They were in control, they had established a sizeable colony in a short timeframe and they had built an impressive military outpost.

Then the monitors flashed a warning; *Moscow* was coming around the planet, its support ships somewhere behind.

"Enemy in sight, sir," reported Cohen, somewhat redundantly.

"Very good, XO. Sound the combat alarm, prepare to fire the forward railguns."

The tactical map now showed the curved path of HMS *Iron Duke* as it looped around the planet and away from the boarding pods. The enemy was just over fifteen thousand kilometres away and closing fast.

"Seven hundred and fifty seconds to closest approach," said Washman.

"Begin firing, Lieutenant Ross," said Staines, eyes locked on the tactical display.

"Projectiles away," said Ross. There was a pause as the ships hurtled towards each other and a burst of railgun rounds shot across the intervening space.

"Enemy counter-measures deployed, sir," reported Ross, "it looks like they will be effective." Staines nodded as the tactical map updated to show the various projectiles and their trajectories.

"Keep it up, Lieutenant," said Staines, "let them know that we mean business." Ross and his team of ratings kept the fire coming, as per the plan.

They all watched the tactical screen as it updated to show the railgun projectiles and the enemy's counter-measures. They waited, watching to see if they had provoked any further action.

"Six hundred seconds to closest approach," said Washman.

"Five hundred seconds until boarding pod engine firing," reported Carruthers.

And now there was nothing to do but wait as the ships' positions closed at over twenty kilometres per second.

"Sixty seconds to pod engine firing," said Washman.

"Ready counter-measures," said Staines, "and prepare to fire again."

"Sound the high-G alarm," said Cohen, "begin attitude adjustment."

"Three-second low-power attitude burn beginning now," said Washman as the klaxon sounded.

"Target all three ships, fire railguns, fire missiles," said Staines.

"Firing now," said Ross, issuing orders.

"Incoming fire, reaction engine missiles," said Midshipman Kelly, her voice calm and measured, "launching counter-measures."

"Pod engines firing," said Carruthers, "ten seconds to impact."

"Five seconds to high-power main engines burn," said Washman

The alarm klaxon sounded again.

"Impact alert," said Cohen, "brace, brace."

There was a dull bang as something struck the outer hull. Then the main engines fired and *Iron Duke* began to move, heading out of orbit and following *Albion* and *Discovery*, who were already running for the darkness of deep space.

"Hull breach, sealing compartments, damage unknown," reported Cohen, reading off his monitors as they flashed red.

"Enemy firing again, high-velocity rounds and more reaction-engine missiles," said Kelly, "deploying counter-measures."

Staines watched as his crew's training came to the fore and they acted as a team, countering the enemy attacks and launching their own, smoothly working to negate or avoid the incoming threats.

And then they were through, and the ships' relative orbits carried the combatants away from each other.

Iron Duke's main engines shut down.

"Burn successful," said Washman, "velocity thirty kilometres per second relative to the enemy, firing window closing in three, two, one."

"Well done, people," said Staines, unclipping from his chair, "now let's get the damage under control and prepare for the next pass."

"Forty-five minutes till the new orbit presents our next firing window," reported Ross.

Staines nodded grimly. The pods were beyond his help for three-quarters of an hour. It was up to the boarding parties now.

32

"Prepare to launch," came the voice, "ten seconds."

Warden flexed his fingers as he sat in the boarding pod, re-familiarising himself to the feel of the power armour. It felt like years since he had last worn such a suit; it might have been only a few months but it had definitely been on a training exercise.

This one was a newer model, both in terms of design and date of manufacture. He'd had to pull the protective film from the HUD and tap his way through a pointless end-user license agreement before the suit would boot up and give him control. The power packs were fully charged, the weapons lubricated and loaded, the operating system patched and updated; he was good to go.

Warden looked around his troop. They were all suited, some running final checks on each other's rigs, their weapons stowed beside them. At the back of the pod, ten colonists sat in environment suits that would protect them against vacuum, overlaid with body armour. All the colonists, even the children, had to learn how to put on, maintain and work in an environment suit in case they had to deal with problems with local conditions or in the event they needed to be taken aboard ship. They weren't powered or suitable for long exposure to hard vacuum, but they were simple to use and well-suited to this sort of boarding action.

"Launching," said the voice, and the pod shot out of its tube, pressing the occupants against their restraints, "short burns to adjust attitude, ten seconds." The steering jets fired, orienting the pods in preparation for their final approach. "Manoeuvres complete, main burn in seven hundred seconds."

Warden took a deep breath and closed his eyes, running through his knowledge of the pod's systems. When they reached the ship, the pod would latch on, magnetically if possible but otherwise by mechanical means. A malleable ring, not dissimilar in feel to a latex glove, though the material wasn't remotely the same, would press forward from the outer rim of the pod and form a seal, into which expanding foam sealant would be sprayed. The boarding team would then choose when to activate the cutting lasers mounted on the pod to cut a large hole in the side of the ship.

"Three hundred seconds," said the voice.

Five *minutes*, thought Warden before his mind drifted back to the mechanics of the boarding action.

If the foam sealant failed or the area on the other side of the hull wasn't pressurized or the seal wasn't tight, everything would get a good deal more difficult. Breaking through internal doors was bad enough at the best of times, but if the enemy started sealing sections to close off atmosphere leaks, they could have real problems.

"Sixty seconds," said the voice, and Warden looked around again at his troop. They were completely dependent on their pilot identifying the correct portion of the target ship to latch on to. It would be educated guesswork, at best.

"And you'll have to do it without weapons, obviously," Staines had said when he had outlined the plan, "because it's a stealth-approach and we won't be anywhere near you when your engines fire."

So they were going in hot, possibly under fire but certainly in a zone where the enemy would be shooting.

Warden looked across the bay at Ten, who was snoring loudly despite having a cloned nose designed to be free from such defects.

Nobody else in the pod was relaxed enough to sleep as they made the long, slow approach to the enemy ship. He'd wake up once the pilot fired the engines to accelerate them into *Moscow*, though.

Milton sent him a message showing *Iron Duke*'s updated decoy route. He wasn't an expert on the matter, but it looked pretty hairy to him and the slightly wide-eyed expression on Milton's face suggested she was of the same mind.

Not that it made any difference. They were committed now, so either the plan would work or it wouldn't. If the enemy ships changed course or spotted the pods, they would be sitting ducks. Or, perhaps more appropriately, the Marines would be the sardines in a giant, defenceless can just waiting to be opened by a single well-placed shot.

Warden grimaced at the thought. He didn't like the lack of control but there was nothing he could do about it.

"Ten seconds to engine burn, get ready to rock and roll," said the pilot, "and the best of luck to you all."

Warden counted down under his breath, eyes closed as he waited.

"Brace for impact," said the pilot, a moment before a huge bang reverberated through the boarding pod and the passengers were slammed against their seats.

Warden let out a breath he hadn't realised he was holding. The pod had clamped itself to the hull of the Deathless ship, and now the malleable outer ring was being pressed against *Moscow*'s outer skin. His HUD told him that the sealant was being applied, then confirmed that the cutters had begun their work.

"Stand ready," he ordered, reading his HUD, "thirty seconds to breach."

The troop stood and readied their weapons, checking their gear one last time and making sure their power armour was configured to withstand a sudden loss of atmosphere, should everything go completely pear-shaped.

Warden sidled down the tight confines of the pod to check on the militia.

"Are you ready, Sergeant Adams? This could get sticky."

"Yes, Lieutenant, we're ready," Adams said. In his thin environment suit and light body armour, he looked small and flimsy next to Warden's power armour. The militia seemed nervous, as well they might, but they were impressively calm. The fighting on the surface had given them a great deal more confidence and the prospect of holding the breach against an enemy force didn't seem to disturb them.

"Good, you'll be fine. Just stick to cover and make sure no one can outflank us. We should hold most of their attention but let me know if you have more than you can handle, understood?"

"Understood, Lieutenant."

He checked the countdown on the boarding pod feed in his HUD.

"Ten seconds to go, folks."

The Marines collectively brought their weapons to bear. The front ranks were taken by Corporal Green and the other ogre clones in their hulking suits of power armour. They would take less damage from incoming fire than the rest of the troop, so they had been chosen to lead the breach. Warden had all the ogre clones on his team. Hayes and Carruthers had been keen to have ogres as well, but they had all agreed with the vice admiral's assessment that *Moscow* had to be their priority and the main focus of their efforts.

And so it was that Warden waited behind a team of ogres to board *Moscow* while Hayes attacked *Omsk* and Carruthers dealt with *Bratsk*.

"Cutters retracted, no pressure loss, inner door opening," said the pilot.

The two ogres at the front of the pod stepped forward as the door opened and shoved at the ship's outer hull. It was heavy, but it slid backwards, the lasers having sliced through wiring, insulation and inner hull. There was a loud clang as the whole section of hull fell into the room beyond, opening the way for the Marines to enter the vessel.

The room beyond was unlit, and the Marines activated their suit lights to reveal a warehouse-sized storeroom.

"Lieutenant, there's a drop to the floor of about two metres," Corporal Green said as he jumped down with a clang. The other ogres followed, rushing forward to secure the beachhead then fanning out into the huge space. Within seconds, the whole troop was inside, and the militia followed.

"Nobody here, sir," reported Green as the ogres completed their search of the room.

"Good," said Warden as Sergeant Adams began setting up to guard the breach.

There was a large pair of sliding doors on the opposite wall to allow transport sleds to move pallets around the ship. On a vessel this size, you couldn't hand carry the rations for lunch or you'd be at it all day.

Goodwin produced a security card they'd found on New Bristol. She had cracked it and, in theory, this one would be good for all low-security doors. The light went green as she flashed the card and the doors opened to reveal a wide T-junction.

Ogres flowed through the doors, taking up positions to the left and right and directly opposite the doors. Now that they had proved the cards would work, Goodwin handed one to each trooper as they passed her position.

"Section 1 go left, Section 2 straight ahead, Section 3 go right. Find Goodwin a console she can hack; we need to find the deck plan. We want the ship intact, no quarter to be given."

Each section moved swiftly to complete their assigned recce of the ship.

In minutes Section 2 had found a promising room. Warden ordered the other two sections to cautiously explore further, dealing with any resistance they met, while he and Goodwin moved quickly to catch up with Section 2. They found themselves in a repair bay full of racks of power armour and the tools and machines required for their maintenance. Three Deathless corpses, technicians maybe, were laid out on the floor.

Goodwin slid into one of the technicians' chairs, carefully wiping the blood from the console before calling up her notes.

"Still logged in," she muttered, shaking her head. Moments later, the tech specialist had access to the shipboard systems and was searching for the deck plans. The other sections were doing fine, according to the HUD updates, so Warden spent the time checking their feeds and getting a feel for what they were seeing.

"I've got the plans," said Goodwin quietly, "scanning them now." She pointed her HUD at the screen and flicked through the pages. Each image was captured, translated and incorporated into the Marine's tactical maps for display in their HUDs.

Warden and Milton reviewed the updated tactical map as soon as it was available.

"The bridge is a fairly straight shot and we're about midships," he said.

"Do you want to just steam down these corridors and see if we can get there before they know what's going on?" Milton asked.

"Yes, but I expect we'll get held up. Let's send the ogre team off on this route and the rest of us will use these other two corridors to get there as quickly as possible. If we meet resistance, the ogres should be able to flank it here, here or there," he said, flagging three junctions.

"Yes, sir," Milton said, moving off to assign responsibilities to the corporals in charge of the sections.

Warden paced the room as his sergeant organised the troop. Here there was a half-dismantled Deathless power glove, there a grenade launcher being stripped and cleaned. He found a rack of weapons and looked through them, as one might browse a bookshop. Halfway along, he found a wicked-looking item, all blackened alloy and vicious edges. He picked it up and swung it experimentally. The hilt had a familiar button where his thumb rested, and he flicked it idly, hearing a familiar telltale thrum.

"Lieutenant, everyone is briefed, we're ready to go," said Milton.

"Good, get to it, folks. Not you, Marine X, I have a job for you."

"Yes, sir?" said Ten.

"I saw this and thought of you," said Warden, passing him the weapon, "it seems to be in working order but remember we found it in a repair bay, so it may not be in top knick."

Ten nodded and smiled as he took the sword, like a gleeful child with a birthday present.

"We're off to the bridge. I thought you might like to have a look around and see if you can find any Deathless to mop up. Just keep an eye on your tactical map in case we get into trouble."

"Yes, sir," said Ten, a big grin on his face. Then he was off, loping away to cause mischief.

Warden shook his head.

"He's like a big kid, isn't he?"

"Yeah, a fucking dangerous kid with an unhealthy fondness for sharp, pointy things," agreed Milton. "Shall we crack on?"

"Yes, let's get going. Goodwin, you're with us."

33

Fletcher swiped the access card, and the doors slid open with a hiss.

Unusual, she thought. *Did they add a sound so you'd know the door had opened?*

She stepped over the threshold and found herself in a hangar. Goodwin had hoped to get the HUD to automatically translate Deathless signage, but it required more work than they had time available.

The hangar was enormous but completely empty. From the sheer size, it had to be the bay the Deathless had housed their huge base-building mothership. Right now, it was an empty cavern with support equipment, repair stations and storage around the sides. There were static and movable gangways to allow the technicians to effect repairs or modifications to the ship while it was docked. The scale of the room seemed too big, though it doubtless felt cramped when there was a ship docked within it.

They fanned out, ogres to the left of her, ogres to the right.

Damn, that leaves me in the middle, she thought, *right across from that massive airlock door used to deploy the ship.*

The airlock was clearly marked with yellow and black stripes all the way around the door. Above it, docking clamps hung from the ceiling. The design was familiar but she'd never seen it on this scale. The clamps would hold the ship in place, the four segments of the door would retreat to their corners, then the clamps would push the smaller ship down and out before releasing it entirely.

That meant the bay had to be cleared before launch or the technicians would have to be in environment suits, not to mention strapped down, along with all the equipment they were using. If the bay didn't reach hard vacuum before launch, even a small amount of atmosphere could drag objects or people towards the airlock.

The room was empty, though, and all she had to do was make it to the other side and then to the rest of the ship. Her HUD showed Lieutenant Warden making good progress towards the bridge but now they needed to make up for lost time, since their route had required a diversion to get further into the ship. Fletcher broke into a run, eating up the distance with long, power-assisted strides, her team coming on behind.

And then large swathes of cloth floated down from the upper catwalk, billowing out in silver-grey waves, and from beneath them came the enemy.

"Bollocks," she spat. "Contact!" she yelled over the local comm as six Deathless ogres, their EM-blocking camo-blankets discarded, leapt from the catwalk two storeys up, crashing to the deck. They charged immediately, spikes jutting from their shoulders and clawed gauntlets extended.

Fletcher's shotgun boomed. No time for finesse, she emptied the drum as she panned the weapon left to right. All along the line, the Marines fired, but the shotguns weren't effective against the Deathless power armour. Two of the ogres were knocked down, but they rolled with the impact and bounced back to their feet, hardly even slowed by the shotgun rounds.

Fletcher, no time to reload, dropped the shotgun and popped her own claws. This was going to get extremely physical and the Deathless had had plenty of time to train with their power armour.

The enemy crashed into her with an almighty wallop. Fletcher grappled at the ogre, gripping both wrists to prevent the Deathless bastard from slicing into her. Her muscles strained along with the fibres in the suit as the evenly matched pair tried to twist and turn to gain an advantage. She lashed out with a boot, aiming for a knee joint, but her opponent was quick enough to lift his leg, and her kick clanged uselessly against his shin, glancing off the armour.

He answered by trying to fall back and pull her off balance, but Fletcher countered that move by stepping into his left shoulder, lifting his right arm up as she let go. Then she powered a left cross into his face. She followed by grabbing his left pauldron and trying to wrench it down as she pulled the arm up, she almost had it, but he dropped to one knee and scythed his leg out, bringing them both crashing to the deck and separating them.

Fletcher rolled to her front and pushed upward, kicking her leg out hard to slam into his chest just before she brought herself upright. She spun around and in that moment saw that it was going badly for her team. Two Marines were down, she didn't have time to see who. That left four against six.

<Need backup. Fighting six ogres, losing>

<Negative, Fletcher. Section 1 is pinned down> Warden replied.

<Section 2 also pinned> sent Corporal Campbell.

<Roger that. We'll hold them as long as we can> sent Marine Fletcher, gritting her teeth for the next attack.

"Form up on me, let's back off and see if we can't get them to do something stupid," Fletcher suggested.

Lance Corporal Long was furthest back from his opponent, having executed an impressive sacrificial throw that had flung the Deathless trooper across the bay. Now, he drew one of the enormous pistols and fired repeatedly at the Deathless that had downed Marine Patricia Scott.

The high-calibre automatic boomed and rounds slammed into the helmet of the ogre. His magazine emptied, Long quickly swapped in another as the Deathless trooper fell backwards. Fletcher drew her own pistol and got off a couple of rounds before the Deathless responded.

Bringing up their left arms in front of them, the five standing Deathless looked crazy for a moment, like a bulked-up boyband. Fletcher didn't get it, couldn't see what they were doing, the mad fools.

Except they weren't crazy. With an audible clang, large metal shields sprang forth from their vambraces and rerebraces. Plates of metal shot up and down, and suddenly they had protection from incoming fire.

"Oh, for fuck's sake," Green roared and retorted with a flashbang. That only provoked the enemy – their group burst apart, and they came on, rushing forward with shields held high.

That was better than what Fletcher had expected, which was for them to pull their own pistols. She located the hitherto unidentified control for her own shield, activated it and lunged forward to meet her opponent.

She dropped to one knee as the Deathless ogre came on, right gauntlet and claws raised for an overhead blow. She slammed the shield up under its guard and into his chest and then she pressed the barrel of her pistol into the groin of the enemy and squeezed the trigger repeatedly, emptying the magazine.

At least one round must have broken through the joint as the barrel slide into just the right spot. The ogre jerked back and crumpled to the floor, clearly injured and out of the fight.

Pulling back, Fletcher saw that Jack Long was down, and Corporal Green was hard-pressed by two of the ogres. She holstered the pistol and scooped up the shotgun, switching in a new drum then aiming at the face of one of the ogres attacking Green. One burst, two bursts, three bursts, and it tumbled back. Its fellow slammed into Green and they rolled across the deck, furiously hammering blows at each other, each trying to score a fatal hit.

Fletcher turned as a cacophony of heavy machine gun fire drew her attention, just in time to see Marine Ann McGee punched from her feet.

And now the barrel swung towards her, as if in slow motion. Fletcher's shotgun was moving to meet it but too slowly, far too slowly to save her. The other two ogres were aiming their pistols, rounds pinging from Fletcher's shield as she crouched and struggled with her shotgun.

Headley, the only other Marine still standing, was backing away, tilting as if wounded and in no shape to help. This was it, she thought, they'd bought as much time for the troop as they could. She didn't look at the tactical map, not wanting to know if the mission was failing before she died.

And then a figure appeared from the shadows behind the three ogres, a bright shining bar of light held high over its head in both hands. The bar came down with ferocious speed and struck the right shoulder of the ogre's power armour, near the neck, cutting all the way through to the left side of its ribcage before spraying blood across the deck.

Fletcher gaped as Ten lunged to his left, following the momentum of the glowing sword and closing behind another of the ogres. She could only watch as Ten brought the blade up in a vicious backstroke, slamming it into the midriff of the Deathless ogre. It cut through to the spine, and then the light went out, sparking as the sword died.

The final ogre turned to face Ten, but it was too slow. The Marine had abandoned his new toy the instant it had failed him and now he dived towards the final enemy. Fletcher was still trying to bring her shotgun back around to target the ogre but Ten was a blur. He grabbed something from the floor, went into a forward roll, came up into a crouch and pulled the trigger.

The machine gun spat a torrent of death into the chest and face of the last Deathless ogre. Fletcher wondered if his last expression had been of horror, amazement or stunned surprise at the sudden appearance of Marine X.

Ten stood up as the ogre toppled back. He dropped his gun and walked back to the second corpse, wrenching the blade free. He looked at it forlornly, pressing the power switch and slapping hopefully at the hilt.

"Bugger," he muttered crossly. "I think I broke my glowstick."

34

"Anyone got a shot?" shouted Warden but the only response was a sullen silence. Great. Pinned down by a bipod-mounted weapon that was a combination of multi-barrelled shotgun and heavy machine gun. It was heavily armoured and the gunner wore power armour in a design they hadn't seen before. The bulk suggested it was intended for holding exactly this sort of defensive position.

"It's no use, we'll have to send someone around to flank him," he said to Milton. "I don't know how much ammo he has, but we can't sit here all day." Milton nodded her agreement.

The annoying thing was that Goodwin had a micro-drone up that was giving them a wide-angle view of the corridor, but they just couldn't get at the gunner. Warden didn't want to risk grenades this close to the bridge, and a couple of flashbangs had done nothing to shift the gunner from his position.

Warden was watching the feed in his HUD while he tried to decide who to send and what route they'd take to get around Section 2, who were stuck in a tough firefight of their own.

Then, from the right-hand corridor of the T-junction the gunner was defending, a large object sailed end-over-end passing over the head of the Deathless guard and clanging into the left wall. The gunner watched it go, eyes irresistibly drawn to it. Big mistake. Once it stopped moving and hit the floor, Warden recognised the sword he'd given to Ten.

And then, sure enough, Ten barrelled into the gunner, covering the ground inhumanly fast and tackling the Deathless trooper while he was distracted, knocking him clear of his weapon.

Warden reacted immediately, breaking cover and sprinting up the corridor towards the struggling pair. The gunner rolled Ten onto his back and got in a couple of good punches as Warden brought his rifle to bear.

"Nice try, sonny!" Ten roared as a glowing knife appeared in his hand. Then he punched it up under the chin of the Deathless trooper, the vibro-knife cutting easily through the thin under-jaw armour and slamming home. The gunner jerked like a fish gasping for air then collapsed on top of Ten.

Warden helped the struggling Marine flop the enormous over-armoured corpse to one side then grabbed his hand to pull him to his feet.

"Nicely timed, Marine X," said Warden, "take a breather. You've earned it. Done? Great, let's crack on then, shall we?"

He looked down the corridor in the direction from which Ten had appeared and saw that he had brought the ogres with him. Half of them, at least. Corporal Green and Marines Fletcher and Headley were trotting up the corridor. Warden checked his HUD for the first time since the firefight had begun and saw that Lance Corporal Long and Marines McGee and Scott were dead; the fight with the enemy ogres had clearly taken its toll.

"On, on," he shouted and began jogging toward the bridge, his Marines behind him, trying to catch up. A few unarmoured and lightly armed crew members offered little more than token resistance and the Marines rolled over them with ease. Then they were at the doors to the bridge.

"Fletcher, Headley, Green, open these for me, would you please?" said Warden when his card failed to grant access.

He stood to one side as Fletcher, Headley and Green sprinted down the corridor opposite the central pair of doors, their ogre suits making a colossal din as they raced towards the bridge. They cannoned into the doors together and their combined effort buckled them inwards. The stepped back a few paces and charged again, this time knocking clear through the doors and barrelling onto *Moscow*'s bridge.

Gunfire erupted from the bridge and Warden rushed up to the side of the doorway, risking a glance inside. Some of the crew were firing at the ogres, trying to find weak spots, while others poured pistol rounds through the shattered doorway. There were a couple of dozen Deathless Ruperts in there but no clones of other types, which was an interesting socio-political observation he squirrelled away for later review.

The viewscreen grabbed Warden's attention and he frowned as *Omsk* floated across the screen, damage from weapon strikes clearly visible. Vice Admiral Staines hadn't planned to destroy the enemy ship. Had the boarding actions failed, perhaps?

Then a burst of fire streaked across the viewscreen towards *Omsk* and he realised what was happening. The Deathless had lost *Omsk* to Lieutenant Hayes and her boarding team. The captain of *Moscow* had realised that and was trying to destroy the ship before it could be captured.

Destroy it and the Marines on board.

Warden began firing immediately, shooting the Ruperts as quickly as he could aim and pull the trigger. He killed as fast as he could, but the ship's weapons continued to fire. *Omsk*, no more than a few kilometres away, was looking worse and worse.

Then his rifle found the Deathless captain and he went down, crumpling to the floor, riddled with bullet holes. Warden breathed a sigh of relief, lowering his rifle. Ten and the ogres had finished the rest of the crew; the bridge was secure.

He looked up at the viewscreen. *Omsk* should survive, but he needed to get in touch with Hayes as soon as possible and find out what their situation was. That would probably require the comms system on the boarding pod. Would it be quicker to run back and get in touch from there or for Goodwin to hack the bridge command interface?

He was still pondering the best course of action when a Rupert stood, pulling itself upright on the command console. The captain of the ship, less injured than Warden had believed. The Deathless officer turned to face him and saluted with a smile. Warden shouted a warning as he raised his weapon, but it came far too late.

The officer slammed his hand down on the console, and a barrage of missiles sprang forth, racing across through the cold vacuum of space even as Warden pulled the trigger. The captain's body shuddered and collapsed back to the deck but the missiles sped on.

Warden turned back to the viewscreen just as the missiles struck *Omsk*. All the Marines turned, watching as the warheads exploded and the great ship cracked into half a dozen sections.

The pieces drifted, tumbling slowly through space as their orbits decayed, gravity dragging them inevitably towards a hard landing on New Bristol.

Omsk was gone.

And of *Bratsk* there was no sign except debris. Warden didn't know what had happened to the third Deathless ship, but he knew that eighty-three women and men, Marines and militia, had been killed in this action.

He watched in silence until the first chunks of debris began to burn up in the atmosphere of New Bristol.

EPILOGUE

"A rough day," said Vice Admiral Staines wearily, "but a successful one."

He looked around the conference room of HMS *Iron Duke*. Lieutenant Commander Cohen and Lieutenant Warden sat across the table while Governor Denmead and Captain Atticus joined via video from the command centre in Fort Widley.

"*Omsk* and *Bratsk* were lost in the action," continued Staines, summarising the day's events, "as were all of B Troop, *Iron Duke*'s boarding party and a significant proportion of A Troop. *Moscow* is serviceable and will be recrewed as soon as new personnel arrive through the wormhole. She'll need a new name; I suggest HMS *Ascendant*."

There were murmurs of polite approval from around the room.

"The Militia are being redeployed in civilian clones at the moment," said Governor Denmead, "and the Marines will deploy immediately after."

Staines nodded his thanks.

"And so it falls to us, Governor, to decide what action we must now take to safeguard New Bristol. Lieutenant Commander Cohen has been reviewing the files recovered from *Ascendant* using the translation software provided by Captain Atticus's tech-specialists. Mr Cohen?"

"Thank you, sir," said Cohen, flicking at his data slate. "You should all be seeing images showing the route taken by the Deathless fleet on their way to New Bristol. As you can see, it's an almost straight line from a large star, marked in blue, and a planet they seem to have called 'New Petropavlovsk-Kamchatsky', or NewPet for short."

Governor Denmead shifted uneasily in her seat.

"Are you saying that's the homeworld of the Deathless?" she asked. "It looks disturbingly close."

"I don't think so, Governor," said Cohen, shaking his head. "It seems to be a staging world, a stopping point on the way to somewhere else. I think it's where the fleet originated, or at least *Ascendant*, but it's difficult to be sure from the files we've reviewed so far."

"A staging world sounds ominous," said Atticus. "Why would they come to New Bristol if they already had NewPet?"

"There's no way to know for sure, sir, at least, not from the data we have so far," said Cohen, "but Lieutenant Warden and I have been discussing the Deathless economy and population problem." He paused to look at Warden.

"The briefing documents from the Admiralty suggested that the original crew of the Ark ship *Koschei* had a keen interest in functional immortality and, after what you were saying about the Deathless economy, I wondered what might happen if they had pursued that goal with vigour."

"I'm not sure I follow, Lieutenant," said Staines.

"Well, sir, we can infer from their presence and their equipment that the Deathless have a large, technically advanced civilisation with manufacturing capabilities somewhat in excess of our own. If the Deathless are functionally immortal in reality as well as in name, then without strict limits on childbirth, they would have experienced rapid population growth."

"And...?" prompted Atticus, unsure where Warden was going with this.

"And so it may simply be that they've run out of space and they're looking for new worlds to colonise," said Warden, "but there's no way of knowing without taking a look at NewPet."

"You want to visit the enemy's staging world?" said Atticus, one eyebrow raised. "What's your reasoning, Lieutenant?"

"It seems the logical next step, sir. We have *Ascendant*, we'll soon have a crew, and we have captured plenty of Deathless clones as well as a large number of cloning bays, so we can easily increase the number of Marines available to defend New Bristol," Warden explained.

"The mission plan that Lieutenant Warden and I are proposing is that we take *Ascendant* into enemy territory, specifically NewPet. The primary objective would be reconnaissance, the secondary objective would be to disrupt their supply lines," said Cohen.

"We would need a significant Marine presence to repel boarders and carry out ground reconnaissance as well as assault targets of opportunity," Warden added.

Staines drummed his fingers and frowned, clearly unhappy that such a proposal had been aired in open council, rather than first being run past him or even Captain Atticus.

"We need to know what motivates the enemy, sir," said Cohen, neatly deflecting attention away from Warden. "If there are as many of them as our population growth projections suggest, this won't be their only fleet, and New Bristol won't be the only colony under threat. This could be a multi-world invasion scenario."

That made everyone sit up, and now Staines frowned even more deeply at both Cohen and Warden.

"I'm not keen to split my command, Vice Admiral, but I must agree with Warden and Cohen," said Atticus. "We need to know, one way or the other, what's going on. I support their plan in principle and, with your permission, and after we hash out some details, of course, I will put forward the mission to General Bonneville for his approval."

Staines nodded. General Bonneville outranked him and Atticus had just forced his hand by, as was proper, requesting his approval of the mission. The Marine officer would be submitting a report to headquarters and, if Staines was opposed, the general could still approach the admiralty with it.

Staines narrowed his eyes, wondering if the captain, whom he was meeting for the first time, wasn't a far shrewder political operator than his rank and bluff honesty suggested.

"I certainly agree that reconnaissance is going to be vital," said Staines cautiously, "and I too am not keen to split my command. Nor am I entirely sure we should reduce the fighting capacity of our fleet around New Bristol at this stage. Governor Denmead is responsible for the colony and its citizens so I would like to hear her thoughts before we proceed. Governor, do you support this proposal, given the danger that New Bristol might still face?"

Denmead had been looking down at her data slate, apparently distracted. Now she focussed her attention on the vice admiral, pausing to phrase her next sentence carefully.

"As I told my councillors, every battle is merely a prelude to nego-tiation. We must know to whom we are talking, and we must discover what they want. The Deathless launched an unprovoked attack on a peaceful colony. It's time to find out why."

AUTHOR NOTES - GUERRILLA

We published Guerrilla in May 2018, two months after the release of Commando. It came in at a little over fifty per cent longer than the first book, which we had deliberately written as a novella. At the time, it seemed to us that we had accomplished what we set out to do, and although Guerrilla had run a little longer than intended, it hung together well.

But there were a few ideas we'd brainstormed for Guerrilla that never reached the final manuscript. The primary story arc of the Royal Marine Space Commandos follows, naturally, the Marines rather than the civilians around them. We have timelines and all sorts of notes so that, we, the authors know what the the civilians are up to in the background, even though you, the reader, don't.

For Guerrilla, we had secondary story arcs that would have woven through the novel while the Marines carry out their ultimate mission to attack the fortress base that the Deathless have deployed on New Bristol. While the Marines go and play with massive mining trucks, which, by the way, are pretty much a real thing (though ours is slightly bigger) and Ten sings light opera classics, Captain Atticus and Governor Denmead are hard at work. They have civilians to protect at Fort Widley, the Deathless are attacking Ashton and the civilian militia are fighting a guerrilla war against them.

But we hadn't written the arcs that followed the drone program run by the Priscilla, or the valiant efforts of the militia, like Captain Idol and Sergeant Adams.

Then came July, and James visited Cardiff for another 'writing retreat' as we call them. Seriously, we actually plot and write things, we don't spend the whole weekend eating takeaway food and drinking. The day before James was due to arrive, Jon got a message from Podium Publishing, who wanted to talk about audiobooks. We had a conference call that Friday evening, and by the following week, we were signed up.

That left us with a decision to make. Once the audio is recorded, the text of your book pretty much needs to remain unchanged. You can still fix typos or maybe tweak punctuation, but you can't add new scenes without causing all sorts of problems. So we took recommendations from other authors in our genre and found an editor who could help us improve the manuscripts. She's done sterling work and, as I write these words, we're working on her edits of the third book, Ascendant.

Commando, it turns out, had some typos, some slightly dodgy phrasing, some very dodgy punctuation (there's always dodgy punctuation) and a number of areas that could benefit from a general-purpose polish. That was fine, and we cranked through the suggestions and re-published the manuscript.

Guerrilla was much the same, in many ways, but it also had a few issues. By and large, much like Commando, they were minor. But then our editor pointed out that we had not delivered on the drone or militia storylines and asked if that was deliberate.

It wasn't, and as you may already have guessed, we decided to make Guerrilla the best book it could possibly be by addressing those minor issues. That meant writing a few news scenes, which caused the text to jump from 54,000 words to a little over 71,000. We waited with baited breath, worried that our editor would come back and say the new scenes didn't work at all or that we'd committed some horrible new errors to paper.

But she loved them.

We're pleased with them too, and if you're re-reading Guerrilla after already reading the original text, we hope you enjoy the new scenes.

After that, we tweaked to the prologue to fix one of Jon's last-minute quibbles, before, finally, he volunteered to draft a nice author note, the fool! Yet another thing to read and edit until it's all nice and pretty.

After all is said and done, though, Guerrilla is a book much improved. It's even better value for money than it was before. You'll get a pay off on the militia and drone pilot story lines. We've got new characters that you'll meet again in other books, and it's not all about Warden and his team.

So with the edits to both Commando and Guerrilla completed, we're now off to finish work on revisions to Ascendant, which are mostly about how // REDACTED // deals with // REDACTED // without having to // REDACTED // and how no-one else // REDACTED // which may or may not be a spoiler or a hint at the action to follow in // REDACTED // and // REDACTED // as // REDACTED // finally engages in // REDACTED //.

Thanks for reading,
    Jon Evans & James Evans
    September 2018

THANK YOU FOR READING

Thank you for reading Volume One of the Royal Marine Space Commandos series, which contains Commando and Guerrilla, Books One and Two.

The series continues with Ascendant, Gunboat and Dreadnought, and we hope you'll enjoy those as well.

It would help us immensely if you would leave a review on Amazon or Goodreads, or even tell a friend about the books.

Or contact us on Facebook to let us know what you thought of the book. We look forward to hearing from you.

Jon & James Evans

SUBSCRIBE AND GET A FREE BOOK

Want to know about upcoming releases?

Would you like to hear about how we write our books?

Maybe you'd like a free book, Ten Tales: Journey to the West?

You can get all this and more at imaginarybrother.com where you can sign up to the newsletter for our publishing company, Imaginary Brother.

When you join, we'll send you a free copy of Journey to the West, direct to your inbox*.

There will be more short stories about Ten and his many and varied adventures, including more exclusive ones, just for our newsletter readers as a thank you for their support.

Happy reading,

Jon & James Evans

We hope you'll stay on our mailing list but if you choose not to, you can follow us on Facebook or visit our website instead.

imaginarybrother.com

* We use Bookfunnel to send out our free books. It's painless but if you need help, they'll guide you through so you can get reading.

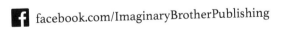 facebook.com/ImaginaryBrotherPublishing

ALSO BY JON & JAMES EVANS

The Royal Marine Space Commandos

Commando

Guerrilla

Ascendant

Gunboat

Dreadnought (out soon)

Free Stories

Ten Tales: Journey to the West

IMAGINARY BROTHER PUBLISHING

Jon & James began writing the RMSC books in 2017 and published the first, Commando in March 2018. Three more books follow later in the year.

We formed Imaginary Brother to handle the Royal Marine Space Commando intellectual property going forward.

If you'd like to keep up with the new releases, we suggest joining the mailing list at imaginarybrother.com/journeytothewest

As a thank you, you'll get a free copy of Ten Tales: Journey to the West* and access to desktop wallpaper based on the new cover art for the books by Christian Kallias.

The fifth book, Dreadnought, will be out in early 2019 along with the audiobooks from Podium Publishing.

* We use Bookfunnel to send out our free books. It's painless but if you need help, they'll guide you through so you can get reading.

ABOUT THE AUTHORS JAMES EVANS

James has published the first two books of his Vensille Saga and is working on the third, as well as a number of other projects. At the same time, he is working on continuing the RMSC series with his brother Jon.

You can join James's mailing list to keep track of the upcoming releases, visit his website or follow him on social media.

jamesevansbooks.co.uk

facebook.com/JamesEvansBooks

twitter.com/JamesEvansBooks

amazon.com/author/james-evans

goodreads.com/james-evans

bookbub.com/authors/jamesevans3

ABOUT THE AUTHORS JON EVANS

Jon is a new sci-fi author & fantasy author, whose first book, Thief-taker is awaiting its sequel. He lives and writes in Cardiff. He has some other projects waiting in the wings, once the RMSC series takes shape.

You can follow Jon's Facebook page where you'll be able to find out more about the RMSC universe. If you're a fan of Instagram, you can follow him there, and perhaps explain to him what it's for.

If you join the mailing list on the website, you'll get updates about how the new books are coming as well as information about new releases and the odd insight into the life of an author. Or insights into the life of an odd author.

jonevansbooks.com

facebook.com/jonevansauthor

amazon.com/author/jonevansbooks

goodreads.com/jonevans

bookbub.com/authors/jon-evans

instagram.com/jonevansauthor